Praise for the novels of Karen Marie Moning

BURNED

"Mac is back and badder than ever!"
—#1 *New York Times*
bestselling author J. R. WARD

"Dark, delicious suspense! Karen Marie Moning is my author of choice and Fever is my series of choice for action-packed suspense with a spine-tingling paranormal twist."
—#1 *New York Times*
bestselling author LISA GARDNER

"A masterwork by an incomparable writer. *Burned* is brilliant, sexy, and dangerous. I adore Moning! No one does it better."
—#1 *New York Times*
bestselling author SYLVIA DAY

"Prepare for a heart-stopping trip into the epic Fever world, filled with gasp-out-loud surprises and sweltering sensuality."
—#1 *New York Times*
bestselling author KRESLEY COLE

"A gripping story that combines excellent storytelling with believable characters that are rendered both superhuman and superbly human, with emotional fragility and psychological vulnerability in an unstable world fraught with danger . . . Fast-paced, with nonstop action set in a fascinating urban fantasy world of Dublin under siege, this is a smart, bold and textured success."
—*Kirkus Reviews*

"Moning is a master storyteller. I don't know how she does it, but she begs me to get on my knees and pay worship to the woman who has brought me the best, most labyrinthine stories and characters I've ever had the privilege to get to know. She weaves brilliantly, unapologetically, and without exception, and she has threaded the needle into me and I've been pulled, over and over, into her tapestry, and I don't think I'm ever getting out. *Iced* is no exception."
—*The Bawdy Book Blog*, five stars

"Moning has taken a beloved series and made it better. . . . [She] has a way of bringing the reader into the story with her imaginative writing style and characters that are colorful and entertaining. . . . Please give *Iced* a try, you will become a Dani fan just like I did."
—*Night Owl Paranormal*, Top Pick

"An exciting opening of a new Fever saga . . . Readers will enjoy that the prime Fever cast plays major roles and the introduction of two new unique dangerous Fae who widen the mythos."
—Genre Go Round Reviews

"[Moning] has always managed to give me everything I want in a book. . . . *Iced* will not disappoint."
—*Open Book Society*

"We get edge of your seat action and danger. We get the promise of so much more to come. All in all, this is an excellent start to Dani's trilogy."
—*Scandalicious Book Reviews*

"Of course, I ended up loving this book. Just like I love everything [Moning] writes."
—*Fiction Vixen Book Reviews*

SHADOWFEVER

The #1 *New York Times*, *Wall Street Journal*, and *Publishers Weekly* bestseller

"Moning has taken her heroine—and her readers—on a turbulent, emotionally devastating and truly unforgettable ride! Enormous kudos!"
—*RT Book Reviews*, Top Pick and Gold Medal

"Epic is the word that first came to my mind after I read the words 'The End' and closed the book on what was an amazing journey. I don't think I've ever read a more satisfying final book in a series. I can't even count how many times I was taken by surprise, shocked, blindsided and thrilled. I was left emotionally spent and completely happy with the many unexpected paths this story took."

—*Fiction Vixen Book Reviews*

"A simple review can never adequately describe *Shadowfever,* words on a page being spectacularly poor substitutes for the strength of feeling and broad emotional spectrum captured between its covers. Ms. Moning is more than a storyteller, her characters far more tangible than fictional beings could ever be thought to be, and she has created a world of infinite complexity that openly challenges us, dares us to experience it and remain only a passive observer, and then yanks us in with a shocking brute strength as it subjects us to the sharpest of pains sparsely interspersed with the warmest of joys. Enter into this final piece of the puzzle with a first-aid kit at the ready, as Ms. Moning is a master at inflicting wounds designed to injure but not kill, and she subjects both her characters and us to numerous events that leave indelible marks on the soft flesh of our hearts. Despite the pain, we revel in the emotional injuries, honored to be privy to a book capable of having such a remarkable effect."

—*Supernatural Snark*

"*Shadowfever* delivers an outstanding conclusion to a fabulous series."
—*Night Owl Paranormal,* Top Pick

"*Shadowfever* did not end the Fever series world with a whimper. It definitely was a bang. A big, wet and fulfilling bang. Take that however you feel is necessary."
—*Parajunkee's View*

"Ms. Moning, much like Mac, takes her story and runs with it, balls to the wall, 550 pages to its uncompromising and satisfying conclusion."
—*Fresh Fiction*

"*Shadowfever* is an explosion of mystery, action, passion, lust, love and magic. As I read this last book in the series I experienced surprise and wonder, shock and horror, sorrow and grief, hope and joy, and, in the end, satisfaction; I couldn't have hoped for more."
—Beyond Her Book

"I cried, I laughed, I screamed, I cursed, I dropped my Kindle due to astonishment, and I'm sure that I repeated that cycle several times throughout the book. I had this perfect way of how things would come together, and none of it happened the way I had it planned in my head. What KMM did was so beyond anything I could have divined, it made the book that much more awesome in my eyes. So, I'm sure as you may have guessed, I give this five stars. I would give it five hundred if I could. It was just that perfect for me."
—*The Romance Reviews*

"This series is exactly what an epic fantasy should be. An adventure. In every way."
—Penelope's Romance Reviews

"*Shadowfever* surpassed every expectation I had. For as many theories as I have discussed, I was completely shocked at most of the outcomes. There was not a single aspect I was disappointed in. My favorite part is that Barrons and Mac stay so true to their characters. Barrons doesn't change or yield to Mac. And I think KMM does an excellent job with keeping him so consistent. He stays broody, and possessive, and mysterious. An excellent end to my favorite series. This book gets an A++++++ from me. Thank you, Karen Marie Moning, for this extraordinary series."
—*Smexy Books*

"I was in shock at how perfectly Karen was able to write this. She is an absolute genius."
—*Yummy Men and Kick Ass Chicks*

"This book was everything I expected, wanted, needed, craved . . . and so much more."
—*Candace's Book Blog*

"I can't remember the last time I'd had so much fun watching a story unwind."
—*My Vamp Fiction*

DARKFEVER

"A wonderful dark fantasy . . . give yourself a treat and read outside the box."
—CHARLAINE HARRIS

"Moning's newest foray contains suspense and plenty of setup. It's a compelling world filled with mystery and vivid characters, and this, combined with the hint of sparks between Jericho and Mac, will stoke readers' fervor for *Bloodfever,* the next installment."
—*Publishers Weekly*

"*Darkfever* is masterfully rendered, a dark and sexy fantasy featuring a Buffy of the Fae, with a sly sense of humor and maturity of handling that's a delight to read."
—*BookPage*

FAEFEVER

"Erotic shocks await Mac in Dublin's vast Dark Zone, setting up Feverish . . . expectations for the next installment."
—Publishers Weekly

"Ending in what can only be described as a monumental cliffhanger, the newest installment of this supernatural saga will have you panting for the next. Breathtaking!"
—RT Book Reviews

"A gift of epic proportions to paranormal romance fans."
—Penelope's Romance Reviews

"An exciting read, with wonderfully described fight scenes and sizzling scenes with the Fae princes."
—Night Owl Romance

DREAMFEVER

"Freaking fabulous! So utterly wonderful that you really must read this series, if you're not already."
—*Literary Escapism*

"This book is absolutely riveting. By far, the most fascinating book I have read this year."
—Penelope's Romance Reviews

"Mac's evolution from typical twenty-something to unrelenting warrior has been shocking, graphic and painful. Moning pulls no punches as she sets Mac on this ghastly path!"
—*RT Book Reviews*

"This series should come with a warning on it. Because it's about as addictive as any illegal drug and will take over your life until the next book is finished!"
—*Book Chick City*

"Brutal, deep and leaving us with heaps and heaps of questions, *Dreamfever* is an undeniably great urban fantasy."
—*Vampire Book Club*

BY KAREN MARIE MONING

THE FEVER SERIES
Darkfever
Bloodfever
Faefever
Dreamfever
Shadowfever
Iced
Burned

GRAPHIC NOVEL
Fever Moon

NOVELLA
Into the Dreaming

THE HIGHLANDER SERIES
Beyond the Highland Mist
To Tame a Highland Warrior
The Highlander's Touch
Kiss of the Highlander
The Dark Highlander
The Immortal Highlander
Spell of the Highlander

BURNED

BURNED

A Fever Novel

KAREN MARIE MONING

DELL
NEW YORK

Burned is a work of fiction. Names, characters, places, and incidents are the products of the author's imagination or are used fictitiously. Any resemblance to actual events, locales, or persons, living or dead, is entirely coincidental.

2015 Dell Mass Market Edition

Copyright © 2015 by Karen Marie Moning

Published in the United States by Dell, an imprint of Random House, a division of Penguin Random House LLC, New York.

DELL and the HOUSE colophon are registered trademarks of Penguin Random House LLC.

Originally published in hardcover in the United States by Delacorte Press, an imprint of Random House, a division of Penguin Random House LLC, in 2015.

ISBN 978-0-440-24642-8
eBook ISBN 978-0-440-33981-6

Cover design: Eileen Carey
Cover photograph: © jessicaphoto/iStock (woman),
© Masson/Shutterstock (background)

Printed in the United States of America

randomhousebooks.com

9 8 7 6 5 4 3 2 1

Dell mass market edition: December 2015

In memory of Moonshadow, best cat who ever lived.
Rest in peace, baby.

You never know what people are made of until you see them under fire.
This one's for you, Dad—inspiration, warrior, hero.

Dear Reader,

If this is the first book you've picked up in the Fever series, at the end of *Burned*, I've included a guide of *People, Places, and Things* to illuminate the backstory.

If you're a seasoned reader of the series, the guide will reacquaint you with notable events and characters, when they were introduced, what they did, if they survived and, if not, how they died.

You can either read the guide first, getting acquainted with the world, or reference it as you go along to refresh your memory. You'll find a few nuggets not mentioned in the books. The guide features characters by type, followed by places and then things.

To the new reader, welcome to the Fever world.

To the devoted readers who make it possible for me to do what I love every day, welcome back.

Karen

BURNED

Eleven months ago, the Clarin House Hotel
Dublin, Ireland
August 6, BWC

JERICHO BARRONS

"Who is it?"

Two A.M. Humans sleep. Her voice through the door is drowsy, sweet, southern, and young. So fucking young. Innocent. In my zoo, MacKayla Lane is an exotic.

"Jericho Barrons."

"What do *you* want?" All trace of slumber is gone from her voice. She couldn't sound more awake if she'd rolled over on a rattlesnake in her bed.

I laugh silently, mirthlessly. More than she can handle. "We have information to exchange. You want to know what it is. I want to know what you know about it."

"Bright guy, aren't you? I figured that out back at the store. What took you so long?"

Sarcasm fails to mask the fear in her voice. I choose my next words carefully. I want her to open the door of her own accord, invite me in. It means something, that courtesy. "I am unaccustomed to asking for what I want. Nor am I accustomed to bartering with a woman."

She is silent a moment, liking my reply, that I placed her in a class of women with whom I am willing to barter. It makes her feel she has a modicum of control over the situation—as if I am a "situation." What stands on her doorstep is a fucking cataclysm. Words. Why do they always ask for words? Why do they ever believe them?

"Well, get used to it with me, bud, because I don't take orders from anyone. And I don't give up anything for free."

She called me "bud."

I might kill her for that alone before I'm done questioning her.

"Do you intend to open this door, Ms. Lane, or shall we converse where anyone might attend our business?" Formality makes her perceive me as older than I am, less dangerous. I will wear any skin to get in.

"Do you really intend to exchange information?"

"I do."

"And you'll go first?"

"I will." So fucking gullible.

"We can trade through the door."

In her dreams. My dick isn't that long. I came here for two things. I'm not leaving without them. "No."

"Why not?"

"I am a private person, Ms. Lane. This is not negotiable."

"But I—"

"No."

"How did you find me?"

Bedsprings squeak. The sound of jeans being pulled on.

"You procured a hired conveyance at my establishment."

"We call them taxis where I come from. And bookstores."

Is that a little spine? Does she have a backbone under all that fluff? "We call them manners where I come from, Ms. Lane."

"You should talk," she grumbles. "It's not my fault. Being threatened brings out the worst in me."

She opens the door. Peers out. Puny-ass chain across it. I could break it with a blink.

Fuck, I think. Just that. A multitude of various fucks all in one great big clusterfuck. As in: I am fucked if I want this . . . this . . . newborn imbecile. And she is so fucked if I take her. And fuck if I'm going to walk away. Letting her leave my store was bad enough. Should have killed the cabbie. Taken what I wanted then. Innocent. Soft. Smells good. Sleep-swollen. Hair a blond tangle of invitation for a fist. I see it spilling down her back, grazing the curves of her ass. Me under her, behind her. Driving up into her. What will she do? Say? How does she sound when she comes? Does she, like most women, lose a part of her soul in sex? Leave it lying there for the taking? Fuck. "May I come in?" I don't smile. My smiles don't make people relax.

"*I* wouldn't have let you up this far."

Her eyes are green, angry. Her nipples are hard. Lust is absurd. It strikes in the strangest places at the oddest times. She doesn't even realize she's feeling it. She's erected a barricade of propriety and lies between us. I despise the type of woman she is. I loathe her soft pink innocence. My body doesn't concur. I wonder why *her*? Why not, say, a streetlamp, for all we have in common? She's chiffon and satin ribbons. I'm raw meat and razor blades. I have never been drawn to my opposite. I *like* what I am. "Your nipples are hard," I murmur, allowing her the choice to hear it, or pretend she didn't.

She blinks, shakes her head. "How did you get up here?"

Ah, the human ear has splendid filters. "I told them I was your brother."

"Right. Because we look so much alike."

The lace of her sleep-shirt flutters with each breath.

She's trembling, trying to conceal it. I glance beyond her, at the tiny room. It's little better than a let-by-the-hour. It won't take that long to get what I came for. Business first. "Well, Ms. Lane?"

"I'm thinking."

"Don't hurt yourself."

"Don't be a jackass."

"You have till the count of three, then I leave. Two."

"Oh, fine, come *in,*" she snaps.

I do smile then but permit it only because she has closed the door to unhook the chain and can't see me. She opens it and steps back. I have found there to be little distance between the unlatching of a chain and the spreading of a woman's legs. As if they can never unbar only a single entrance. It's a disease called hope.

She pushes the door flat to the wall. She thinks it makes her safe. I enter. Don't bother to close it. That will come later. She toes a rug and a lacy bra beneath the bed. I will see much more than that before I leave.

"So, what is it? No, wait—how do you spell it?"

I pace a circle around her. She spins as I stalk her, unwilling to give me her back. I'm going to have it anyway. Every way. "S-i-n-s-a-r."

"Sinsar?"

"*Shi-sa. Shi-sa-du.*" I continue pacing. I like the way her body moves. If she glances down, she'll see my coat is open and my suit fails to conceal how hard I am. She never takes her gaze from my face. Few keep it there.

"Oh, that makes great sense. And the *du*?"

I stop circling, facing the door. She stops, her back to it. Three feet separate us. I can feel her. Smell her.

"D-u-b-h."

"*Dubh* is 'do'? Should I be calling pubs 'poos'?"

"*Dubh* is Gaelic, Ms. Lane. Pub is not."

"Don't bust a gut laughing."

"Nothing about the *Sinsar Dubh* is a laughing matter."

"I stand corrected. So what is this gravest of graves?"

Flippant. She has no business being here. Fio was right.

It would be merciful, Jericho. Kill her quickly before one of the others tortures her for days then rips out her throat.

Does mercy look like my middle fucking name?

Do it for me, Jericho. I can't bear the thought of what one of the others will do to her.

One of them? Or me, Fiona? Which thought can't you bear?

I saw the look in your eyes. Jericho, how could you want that . . . that . . . that foolish, empty-headed child! What could she possibly offer you?

"Too long," I say. Fiona has been with me too long.

"What?" she says blankly.

I'm suddenly furious that MacKayla Lane came to my city, thinks to play on the same field with me and mine, made herself my problem in any capacity. "Go home, Ms. Lane. Be young. Be pretty. Get married. Have pretty babies. Grow old with your pretty husband."

"Oh, screw you, Jericho Barrons! Tell me what it is. You said you would."

"If you insist. Don't be a fool. Don't insist."

"I'm insisting. What is it?"

"Last chance." For many things.

"Too bad. I don't want a last chance. Tell me."

I was lying anyway. Her last chance was her first one. She walked through my door. "The *Sinsar Dubh* is a book."

"A book? That's all? Just a book?"

"On the contrary, Ms. Lane, never make that mistake. Never think it just a book. It is an exceedingly rare and exceedingly ancient manuscript countless people would kill to possess."

"Including you? Would you kill to possess it?"

"Absolutely. Anyone and anything that gets in my way. Always have. Always will. Reconsidering your stay, Ms. Lane?"

"Absolutely not."

"You'll be going home in a box, then."

"Is that another of your threats?"

"It is not me who will put you there."

"Who will?"

"I answered your question, now it's your turn to answer mine. What do you know of the *Sinsar Dubh,* Ms. Lane? Tell me. And don't lie. I'll know." I could Voice her, force her to tell me everything. Little fun there.

"My sister was studying here. She was killed a month ago. She left me a voice mail message right before she died, telling me I had to find the *Sinsar Dubh.*"

"Why?"

"She didn't say. She just said everything depended on it."

"Where is this message? I must hear it myself."

"I accidentally deleted it." Her gaze darts to the side.

"Liar. You would make no such mistake with a sister you care enough about to die for. Where is it? If you are not with me, Ms. Lane, you are against me. I have no mercy for my enemies."

"I already gave a copy of this recording to the Dublin Gardai. They're working to track down the man she was involved with." There goes her gaze again.

"Give me your phone."

"Not a chance. But I'll put it on speakerphone."

She plays the message. Never takes her gaze from my face. The things I could teach her . . . if she could survive them.

"Did you know my sister?"

I slice my head once to the left in silent negation.

"You were both after this 'exceedingly rare book' yet never ran into each other?"

"Dublin is a city of a million-odd people inundated daily by countless commuters and besieged by a never-ending wave of tourists, Ms. Lane. The oddity would be if we had encountered each other. What did she mean by 'you don't even know what you are'?"

"I wondered that myself. I have no idea."

"None?"

"None."

"Hmm. This was all she left you? A message?"

She nods.

"Nothing more? No note or package or anything of the sort?"

She slices her head once to the left in silent negation. I scan her eyes. Deep but there, a hidden mirth. She just mocked me. My dick gets harder.

"And you had no idea what she meant by the *Sinsar Dubh*? Your sister didn't confide in you?"

"I used to think she did. Apparently I was wrong."

"Who did she mean by 'them'?"

"I thought you might be able to tell me that."

"I am not one of these 'them,' if that is what you're inferring. Many seek the *Sinsar Dubh,* both individuals and factions. I want it as well, but I work alone."

"Why do you want it?"

"It is priceless. I am a book collector."

"And that makes you willing to kill for it? What do you plan to do with it? Sell it to the highest bidder?"

"If you don't approve of my methods, stay out of my way."

"Fine."

"Fine. What else have you to tell me, Ms. Lane?"

"Not a thing." She jerks a frosty look from me to the door.

I laugh. "I do believe I'm being dismissed. I can't recall the last time I was dismissed." Let her think I'm leaving. It's time to close the door.

I'm nearly past her, nearly at the door, when I grab her and slam her back against my body. The back of her skull thuds into my chest. Her teeth clack together. She makes a wordless sound, protest, and another more guttural sound that is not protest at all. I band an arm beneath her breasts.

I can smell when a woman wants to fuck. I smelled it in my store. I smell it now. She can't see herself yet, she certainly can't see me, can't admit what she wants. But her body knows. Lust is a thing of the blood. Doesn't need head or heart. Her flesh is soft and pink. Her blood is red hot.

"What are you *doing*?"

"Need a fucking manual?" I press hard against her ass.

"You've *got* to be kidding! You're totally not my type and you're . . . you're . . . how *old* are you anyway? Eeew!"

"Your scent says otherwise." I inhale. So much sweeter this close.

"My scent? Like you think you can smell—you think I— Oh! Let me go! Now! Get off me! I'm going to scream."

"You will most certainly scream. I promise you that." Beneath my arm, her heart hammers, she breathes quick and shallow. Sexual excitement alters the lines of her body, fuses it into new lines against mine. A woman's spine changes when she wants to fuck, a subtle, supple shifting at the base, a sharper curve at that hollow where back meets ass. Breasts tighten and lift, the slant of jaw changes as the mouth prepares and muscles draw tight. I have studied humans for a small eternity. Intent infuses their every movement. Road maps to their inner navigation, plastered all over their skin. Born to be slaves.

"You're delusional. I don't want you. Get out of my room."

"So you can crawl back into bed, weep for the sister you lost and brood about your own ineptitude? Scribble down your silly plans and plot vengeance? You don't even know what the word means." But she could learn. "Are you in such a hurry to be alone with your grief? Is it such a grand bedmate? When's the last time you lost yourself in a good, hard fuck, Ms. Lane? Have you ever? I think it's always been gentle, nice and sanitary, and when it was over you lay there wondering what all the fuss was about."

"You're crazy! You know that, right? You're abso-frigging-lutely crazy. How dare you come in here and threaten and bully and be shitty to me then try to sleep with me? Then make fun of perfectly good sex!"

"I have no desire to sleep with you. I want to fuck you. And there is no such thing as perfectly good sex. If it's 'perfectly good,'" I mock in falsetto, "he should be shot in the head and put out of everyone's misery. Sex either blows your fucking mind or it's not good enough. You want me to blow your fucking mind, Ms. Lane? Come on. Do it. Be a big girl."

Her whole body jerks in my arms. "I don't even like you."

"I don't like you either. But my dick is hard and you're wet—"

"You can't know that!"

My hand slides to the top button of her fly. "Want me to prove it? If you persist in lying, you leave me no choice." I pop the first button, then the second. Her spine changes against my back, yet more curve, more pliancy. The human body is remarkable.

"Are you wet, Ms. Lane? Yes or no?" When she

makes no reply, I pop the third button. "Let's make a deal. I'll check, and if you're dry I'll leave."

She hisses.

"Answer the question."

"It's none of your business."

"Tell me to stop." I pop the fourth button. There's only one left.

"I hate you."

"I can live with that. Have you fucked since your sister was murdered? Let go, Ms. Lane. For once in your circumscribed little life, let the fuck go."

She is suddenly steel in my arms. She pushes back with her hips, twists and turns in my arms, slams her hands into my chest and knees me in the balls. Or tries. I block it with a knee at the last second.

"You don't know anything about me!" Her chest heaves, a pulse beats wildly at her throat.

"I know you better than those you call your best friends. I see you."

"Yeah?" Her jaw juts. Something flashes deep in her eyes. I go still. What was that? Something very different from what she shows on the surface. I didn't expect it. Interesting. "Just what the fuck do you see?" she practically snarls.

"A woman who's lived in a cage all her life. And hates it. Bored in there, aren't you? Waiting for life to happen. And when it finally does, it steals from you what you loved most. So take back. Explode. Lash out. Blow up."

She stares up at me, wets her lip.

"Scream. Curse. Rage. Take it out on me." I step forward, cup her hard between her legs, rub with my palm. The heat she's throwing off is amazing. "Tell me to stop."

She is motionless a long moment. Finally she slices her head once to the left.

I laugh.

I shove my hand down her pants, the fifth button pops off and clatters across the floor, I push my finger inside her and her knees go out from under her as she clamps down on me, hard. She's so fucking wet. We go down to the floor together.

"I'm *sick* of feeling like this," she hisses. "I hate my life. I hate everything about it!" She strangles me with my tie, clumsy in her haste to get it off. Still living in the world where boys undress completely and girls lie back and wait. Only two things need to be naked.

"Fuck the tie. Unzip my pants."

She yanks it open so hard she breaks the zipper of my ten-thousand-dollar suit. I pick her up by the waist of her jeans and dump her out of them. She pushes up from the floor to turn but I'm behind her. I shove her back to the floor. "Stay there. I want you this way."

"But you said I could—"

"Your turn next."

"This is about me, remember? That's what you said. I want what I want *now*."

"Try, Ms. Lane, just try."

To her credit, she does. But I'm stronger. I get my way first, not that she's complaining from the noise she's making. Fist in her hair, I spread her legs wide as they'll go, crush her flat to the floor. Later I'll take her on her hands and knees. Now I need her still as I can keep her. I grind between her legs and she makes a choking noise. Slick with all that wet she supposedly wasn't, I drive into her. Air explodes from us both. She arches her neck and howls. I don't move for a moment. Movement will fuck me royally right now.

She bucks beneath me. "Move, you bastard!"

"When I'm ready."

I close my hands on her ribs. She fights. She'll be bruised in the morning. I dredge up a few hated memories. My blood goes cold. I get harder. I begin to move, lose track of time. Four hours feel like four minutes. For something so soft, she takes her fucking hard, with a twist. I taste her. I could eat her alive. She closes her mouth on my dick. I close my hands on her head. I might not let her go. Slick with sweat, I defile her with reverence. Or revere her with defilement. Every. Inch. Of. Her. Motherfuckingfinebody. She likes it. No holds barred with this woman. I wouldn't have believed it of her. And she *does* scream . . .

Later I roll over on my back and let her rock her world all over me. Fuck if she doesn't.

She straddles me, ass to my face, reverse cowgirl, tangled hair swinging. And son of a bitch, the woman can ride. "Slow down." I close my hands on her ass to keep her from jacking me off in seconds.

She pushes up, drops her head down into a wet dream of a naked crouch that doesn't have one fucking ounce of inhibition, and shoots me a feral look between her legs, around my dick. "Stop holding me," she snaps. "You're a control freak. This turn is mine. Do what I tell you. If that means you come and get hard again, deal with it." She arches a brow. "Unless I'm wearing you out."

I smirk and say nothing. She knows by now that's impossible.

"Don't think this means I want to see you tomorrow." She's back at it and I'm about to explode.

"I suffer no such delusion. And ditto," I say savagely. She knows exactly how to work me, sliding up to the point where I'm almost out of her, teasing the head of my cock with short, fast pops of her hips before slamming down and easing back out slow. Pretty, pink Barbie fucks hard and raw like an animal.

Her head is thrown back, spine arched, she's oblivious to rules, to moral order, to all but inner imperatives.

And I wonder: could she live like she fucks?

My dick gets even harder.

I leave just before dawn.

At the door I turn back and look at her. And shake my head. Her back is to me. She's wrapped a sheet around herself.

"Mac."

She turns slowly and I say *Fuck* beneath my breath. Already she's changing. It began when I started putting my clothes on. Now it's nearly complete. Her eyes are different. Wary, guarded, tinged with that human emotion I despise the most: regret. I was wrong. She wasn't ready. Not yet.

By noon she'll hate me. By tonight she'll have convinced herself I raped her. By tomorrow she'll hate herself.

I cross the room, clamp a hand over her mouth and crush my arm across her chest, compressing her lungs so she can't draw a breath. She lives at my discretion. I can take her breath. I can give it back.

I wonder, pushed to the wall, stripped of all defenses, tested beyond endurance, just who might MacKayla Lane become?

I press my mouth to her ear. My words are soft. "Go home, Ms. Lane. You don't belong here. Drop it with the Gardai. Stop asking questions. Do not seek the *Sinsar Dubh* or you will die in Dublin. I haven't been hunting it this long and gotten this close to let anyone get in my way and fuck things up. There are two kinds of people in this world: those who survive no matter the cost, and those who are walking victims." I lick the vein fluttering in the side of her neck. Her heart is beating like a frightened rabbit. Fear doesn't arouse me. Yet my dick is so hard again that it hurts. I should end it here. Rip out her throat, leave her dead in her dingy, small flat. Perhaps I'll kill her tomorrow. Perhaps I'll chain her in my bookstore for a time. I'll give her a single chance to run. If she stays, I am absolved of responsibility for anything that befalls her. "You, Ms. Lane, are a victim, a lamb in a city of wolves. I'll give you until nine P.M. tomorrow to get the bloody hell out of this country and out of my way."

I let her go, and she crumples to the floor.

Then I bend over her, touch her face, whisper the ancient words of a druid spell, and when I am done the only memories she retains of this night are of conversation and threat. She will never know that tonight she was mine.

Don't hide your mistakes,
'Cause they'll find you, burn you

—"Get Out Alive" by Three Days Grace

Part 1

Some of us are born more than once.

Some of us re-create ourselves many times.

Ryodan says adaptability is survivability.

Ryodan says a lot of stuff.

Sometimes I listen.

All I know is every time I open my eyes,

My brain kicks on, something wakes up deep in my belly

And I know I'll do anything it takes.

To. Just. Keep. Breathing.

—From the journals of Danielle O'Malley

PROLOGUE

Fire to his ice, frost to her flame.

The Unseelie King stared down at the unconscious woman in his wings. She was his soul mate. He knew it the moment he found her. He'd been tortured by it every moment since he'd lost her.

In the brief time they'd shared together, he'd experienced the only true joy of his existence. Before that, darkness had ebbed and flowed in him as incessant as a stormy sea. He'd thought perhaps it was because he was young and in a quarter of a million years, give or take a few, the disquiet might ease.

To pass the restless eons, he'd made things, scraping together matter and reshaping it into mountains and trees, oceans and deserts, planets and stars, galaxies and black holes. All but one power was his: the Song of Making, which legend said had begun it all and could call forth the very fundamentals of existence. That magic belonged to the queen of his race alone.

The Seelie Queen rarely used any portion of the cataclysmic melody. As with all great power, it demanded great price. Legend held their race had stolen the sacred song in times more ancient than any of them recalled, as humans had stolen fire from their gods. If this seemed to imply the Fae had gods, the king knew better. There was nothing out there but him. He'd been looking for a long time.

Epochs passed. Civilizations rose and fell. Bored, dissatisfied, the king built and wrecked worlds and built again. He made a halfhearted attempt to live for a time at court with the Seelie Queen and count the centuries by her petty intrigues. The ancient tapestries claimed she had been sung into existence just for him. But her views were cold and limited, her court too gaudy and bright for eyes that had stared for eons at black velvet and stars, and theirs was a discordant melody with no fire.

Again, he wandered. Edgy. Alone. Seeking something he couldn't name.

On a tiny world in a tiny corner of a tiny and utterly unimpressive universe he wasn't even certain why he'd visited, he found her. Unpredictable, high-tempered, happy on her own, and nearly untamable, she was a challenge to seduce. It hadn't helped that he was broody, arrogant, selfish, and a god.

She didn't want a soul mate, she told him. And she certainly didn't want one with wings and an attitude problem.

Yet she'd not run. She stood her ground and watched him circle around her looking for a way into her heart. They fought, tested each other, challenged and demanded.

She knew what she wanted: the best.

He knew what he was: the best.

They enhanced each other's finest qualities, as true love will. He opened her provincial mind to galaxies of opportunity. She reminded him what it was to feel wonder and brought freshness to creations gone dull and stagnant. Together they spun universes more beautiful and imaginative than anything he'd created before.

Yet his happiness was tainted by something he'd never felt. He loved. He could lose. Human, she possessed a mere fifty more years at best, and with the passage of time would wither and die.

Unable to bear her mortality, the king constructed an opulent cage beyond time where death could never touch her.

Wild at heart, she'd despised his cage, but loved him more and agreed to dwell within it until that day came she could no longer bear it. They met in a shared boudoir of shadows and light and their love knew no bounds.

Still the king could not rest. He knew his woman's high temper, her need for freedom, and wanted her to have no limits. He sought the Seelie Queen's aid, but jealously she refused to use her magic to make his lover immortal.

On that day, he vowed to re-create the Song of Making himself, if it took him half of forever and cost him all that he held dear.

Vows, like wishes, are dangerous things.

Precision matters.

In time, the king came to understand part of the song's essence, glimpsed the fundamental building blocks. The fragments he melded into the partial song that birthed his dark, imperfect Unseelie were composed of exacting frequencies that interlocked seamlessly and made of their parts a far richer melody than their individual notes, chords, and vibrations.

Eons passed while he worked, until the day came he rushed to his lover's chamber with the results of his latest experiment, so certain of his success that he'd brought a vial of the new elixir to her himself—only to find her dead by her own hand.

Or so a treacherous enemy had made him believe.

They are replaceable, one and all, the Fear Dorcha,

dark traveling companion through the king's subsequent madness, had insisted. *You will forget her.*

But he never had.

Grief will pass, lisped the Crimson Hag, one of his more exquisitely terrible creations.

But it never did.

Even the grotesque Sweeper, who fancied himself a god, collector of broken, powerful things with which he liked to tinker, had lumbered beside him for a time, offering solace or perhaps merely studying him to see if he, too, could be collected, fixed.

He, who had once been whole, was halved, without hope of ever being complete again. And when you've known that kind of love, to endure the creeping passage of time without it is to live a half-life where nothing ever feels real.

He fabricated their reunion in countless illusions, slipping in and out of insanity, talking to her as if she were beside him, answering.

He'd lived lie after lie to escape the unbearable truth: she'd left him by choice, killed herself to escape him.

She'd left him a poisoned barb of a note that to this day infected him still: *You have become a monster. There is nothing left of the man I love.*

He carried it still, a small scroll tied with a lock of her hair. Despite Cruce's confession, he would carry it until the day she told him she was not its author.

The king stirred from his reverie and stared down at the unconscious female in his wings. It had been half a million years since he'd found her lying, lifeless, in their chamber. Since he'd dumped all the forbidden, arcane magic he'd used for his experiments into an ensorcelled tome, thinking to be free of that which she'd so despised.

Since he'd last held her. Touched her.

It was no illusion. She was here. She was real. Joy, that elusive, priceless commodity, was once again his.

He inhaled. She smelled the same as she had on the day he'd met her, of sunshine on bare skin, moonlight on silver oceans and enormous, sky-no-limit dreams. He closed his eyes and opened them.

She was still there.

After an eternity of grief and regret, he held the only thing he'd ever wanted as much as he wanted to be God.

A second chance.

Gazing down at her now, he found it simple to pardon Cruce for stealing her, forcing her to drink from the cauldron and erasing all memory of their time together, because somehow his soul mate was at long last the very thing he'd struggled to make her: Fae, immortal unless killed in one of a very small number of ways. He would eradicate those ways in short order.

He was whole again.

The Unseelie King bent his head and brushed his lips to hers. Lightly. Reverently. He'd sliced open his being and bled it out over memories of the woman he would never kiss again.

If there was anything divine in the Cosmos besides him, it was this moment, occupying space with her, the frequency of the vibration of her fundamental essence and his combined. Deep in his chest thunder rolled.

Lashes fluttered. She opened her eyes.

He drew back and stared down at her, unable to speak. Creator of worlds, God, Devil, he who toyed with the very matter of galaxies, words failed him now. His black wings shuddered with the intensity of his emotion. He shifted and resettled them.

There was wonder in her gaze as she stared up at him: a moment of precious, preconscious dawn where all is dew and promise and anything at all might bloom.

Beginnings are fragile things.

Was it as he hoped? Was the power of true love greater than the power of the Cauldron of Forgetting? Did the body recall, despite the damage done to the mind—memory, carved into gray matter, never obliterated? What would she say? What would her first words to him be?

Time ground to a halt and, as a human might hold his breath, the Unseelie King held his existence in silence, occupying the frozen moment with the study of tiny miracles: the silver-blond waterfall of her hair, the blush of her lips, the elegance of her bones.

Was that a flicker of confusion? Of duality preceding recognition? He knew her face intimately, had never forsaken a nuance, yet these were expressions he'd had no cause to learn.

After all she'd been through—eternities about which he knew nothing and might have contained any number of atrocities spent as they were at the Seelie Court with Cruce but more recently kidnapped, interred in a tomb of ice, and nearly killed by the power-hungry prince—he sought to reassure her by simplifying himself, reducing his essence again and again until it was small enough to string word to word and form sentences: alien to the stuff of which he was made but so necessary for finite beings.

"My love, you are safe. I have you now." He paused, to lend emphasis to his next words, a pledge he would keep until the end of time, which he was fairly certain he was in some fashion or another. "And I will never let you go again."

Envisioning their joyous future together as immortals, he waited for the first sound of her voice in half a million years.

She screamed.

*"It's easier to run.
Replacing this pain with something numb"*

DANI

So I'm blowing through the streets of Dublin—after ditching Ryodan's Humvee, giving him one less excuse to come looking for me, not that he seems to need any, other than because he likes to piss all over my day— trying to prioritize my plans for the future.

At the top of my list is figuring out how to save Christian from the Crimson Hag, publishing a much-needed *Dani Daily* to let folks know the latest scoop, rescuing folks stranded by the killer ice storm, while simultaneously devising stellar new ways to irritate the owner of Chester's.

After that are a few dozen subgoals I'm having a hard time putting in the right order, like getting in the know with the new Haven at the abbey, testing Dancer's Papa Roach weapon, figuring out who's stockpiling supplies and where so I can raid them, setting up new hidey-holes no one can find, and putting the big kibosh on Jo and Ryodan.

Problem is, I want to make breaking up Jo and Ryodan number one on my list, which is stupid because there's nothing but personal satisfaction I'd gain from it, and while I'm all about personal satisfaction, I'm beginning to see a pattern: jumping on the short-term-gratification train always seems to wreck me off the rails somehow. But criminy, he doesn't deserve her! And they're not even in the same league, and seeing them do that campfire-cuddle thing tonight about made the top of my head pop off!

Second problem is I keep bumping into snowdrifts, which knocks me out of fast-mo and butchers my concentration. Since I'm getting nowhere fast with my sub-list and it's more important than me actually getting to any particular place fast, I drop out of freeze-frame and start trudging around ice-crusted snowdrifts.

Bugger it, I forgot how cold it was down here!

In hyperspeed I vibrate too fast to feel. Slow-mo, my breath frosts the air and my eyeballs chill like little shrimp cocktails on ice.

I scowl when I realize where I am—Temple Bar, not too far from Barrons Books & Baubles.

I don't walk these blocks often. I may have defeated one of the worst Unseelie of all time tonight at the abbey but the silence and desolation of what once was the heart of the boisterous, *craic*-filled Temple Bar District dampens my exuberance every time I encounter it.

I can't forget how this part of the city used to be, crammed with people laughing and partying, musicians playing on the streets for tips, lamps glowing, neon colors splashed everywhere, the smell of flowers and grass and oh, feck me, the glorious scent of bangers and mash and thick Irish stew and all kinds of food I haven't had in ages! I'd been quick enough to zip in and snatch anything I wanted from any plate. It was the most exciting, wondrous place I ever been, with adventures around every corner.

Knowing Mac was just a few blocks down and over,

and if I blew in the door we'd go kill things and hang, made life pretty much perfect. Barrons Books & Baubles was my mecca, Mac and Barrons epic fellow crusaders, and the city a thrill-a-second battlefield.

I want *my* Dublin back.

I want this bloody ice gone.

I want the pubs open and the streets shiny with gaslights smudging the cobblestones and people living and laughing everywhere I turn. I want to whiz around on my bike, investigating stuff, and be fourteen and crack up with Dancer and idolize the girl that treated me like a sister.

People in Hell want ice water.

As I stand there a sec, getting broody-like, I feel the tip of something sharp and pointy in my back.

"Drop your sword, Dani," Mac says behind me.

My stomach cramps and I'm instantly sick to it. What the feck, did I conjure her with the mere power of my thoughts? Do I have another *sidhe*-seer talent I didn't know about, latent until now? Cripes, I hope not! I'll never get away from Ryodan! I'm always pissed at him, which means I'm always thinking about him. As soon as I think that, I realize I got concrete proof I don't have a new superpower, because, hey, if I did, he'd be here with me right now. I decide I'm hallucinating from lack of sleep and being forced to listen to too much Jimi Hendrix and Black Sabbath tonight. Which is, like, half a song of either.

There's no way Mac's behind me. I'd have heard her. I have superhearing. I'd have seen the lights of her MacHalo, brightening the glow cast by mine.

"Yeah, right, like I'm actually falling for this," I mutter. Sometimes I have an overactive imagination.

The tip digs harder into my back. I go still and draw a slow inhale. I know Mac's scent and that's it. A dry chittering starts on the rooftops, swelling into thousands of rattlesnake tails shaking, making me even more nauseated. I don't need to look to know what's up there. Oh, yeah, Mac is really behind me, bizarre entourage in tow. The few times I've seen her lately, she's had a flock of Unseelie ZEWs—Zombie Eating Wraiths is what I christened the gaunt, black-robed caste that glides on air and likes roosting on top of the bookstore—following her around like enormous, carrion crow waiting for a juicy corpse to pick clean.

Ain't gonna be mine.

I dig out a protein bar, rip it open, and cram it in my mouth for an instant rush of energy. I never avoid battle. Tuck tail and run isn't in my blood. Problem is, I only know two ways to fight: kill clean or kill messy—both of which involve killing unless I'm up against that feck Ryodan who can pluck me from hyperspeed and kick my ass ten ways to Tuesday.

There's no way I'm killing Mac. I'll take Door Number Two, a thing I never do, and run. Only for her.

I slap up a hasty mental map of the street and get my grid locked down as perfect as I can with all this snow and ice. I slit my eyes half closed in intense concentration and freeze-frame.

Nothing happens. My feet are rooted in the exact same spot, and I'm still feeling the tip of Mac's spear in my back.

My superpowers just disappeared in a moment of need for the *third* time. Un-fecking-real! What's the commonality? Why does it keep happening?

"I said drop your fucking sword."

I exhale gustily. Not because I feel sorry for myself. Self-pity is wasted emotion. It merely prolongs whatever trauma you suffered by keeping it alive in your head. Dude, you survived it. Move on.

But there are some things I wish had been different like, say, Ro had never taken me to the abbey after

Mom died, made me her personal assassin and taught me to kill before I got around to figuring out what I thought was right and wrong, because when you *do* figure out what you think is right and wrong—if it's four-square against the things you been doing—you got some tricky minefields in your head to dodge. Guilt, regret—things I almost don't even know how to spell they're so alien to me—I about drown in them every time I look at Mac.

Fortunately she's behind me at the moment, so I don't have to think about how she looks so much like her sister, don't get smashed upside the head by visuals of the last night I saw Alina, on her hands and knees in an alley, begging me not to let her die.

"Seriously, kid, drop it. I won't say it again."

"Not a kid. *Dude*."

"*Danielle*."

Gah! She knows I hate that wussy girl name! I test my freeze-framing abilities. They're still absent. There's no telling how long it'll be until they come back. Five seconds. Five minutes. Maybe five hours. I got no clue why it's happening and it's beginning to worry the crap out of me. I turn to face her, coat back, hand on the hilt of my sword, steeling myself for a whole-body flinch, and still I jerk.

She's different from the Mac I met a year ago. Glam girl turned sleek warrior woman. She was pretty when she came to Dublin; now she's lean, strong, and beautiful. Once, she said I was pretty and that *I'd* grow up to be beautiful, too, one day. As if I give a rat's arse about that kind of thing.

What is she thinking, pulling her spear on me, ordering me around? There's no way she knows I'm stuck in slow-mo. No one knows it happens to me. Cripes, if word of that got out!

She stares at me, green eyes narrowed with fury. She

has every right to try to kill me. A better person might even cooperate a little out of guilt and remorse. I'm not a better person. I wake up every day with a single imperative: live. By any means necessary. The only way Death will ever get his slimy bastard hands on me is over my dead body.

I wonder if she has some new *sidhe*-seer skill I haven't heard about that makes her willing to hit me up like this, so cool and confident. My superspeed guarantees my victory in any battle against another *sidhe*-seer unless I make a mistake, and I don't. She isn't wearing a MacHalo, which perplexes the feck out of me. Nobody walks Dublin, dark. Not even me. Maybe the ZEWs on the rooftops are her private army now, defending her against the Shades and assorted nasties.

I frown when another thought occurs to me. Did she set me up for quid pro quo down to the dirty details?

Dark alley nearby—check.

Me—check.

Hungry Unseelie—check.

I get a mental snapshot of me dying just like Alina. It's practically glowing on Mac's pupils.

I want to tell her revenge is a devil you don't want to worship. In destroying your enemy you become it.

You will take the girl to an alley on the south side of the River Liffey. Unseelie will meet you there. Sometimes I still hear Ro's voice in my head even though we burned her body and dumped the ashes in the sea. Not like a true haunt, just ghosts of memories still swimming down deep in my subconscious where I keep most of what I did for her when I lived at the abbey.

Why? I want to ask her, but she touches my forehead with something that's wet and smells bad, and mutters words I don't know, then I can't talk.

I know you're in there, I hear Ro saying, as if from a

great distance. *Remember the hell you endured. You're the one I want.*

I don't know what she's talking about. I'm right there. Looking at her. Even though it feels like from a million miles away.

Och, child, she says, *I couldn't have raised you better myself to fragment you into usable pieces. When I found you when you were five I knew God had forged the beginning of a very special weapon. Just for me.*

Old bat couldn't even keep track of my age. I was eight when she found me almost dead in a cage. Only time in my life I ever waited to die. Counting my breaths. Wondering which would be the last. There was a whole week back there I couldn't remember, just gone. From the day Ro took me in, I began losing hours and then I'd be somewhere else and wouldn't know how I'd gotten there. And there was usually something I didn't like seeing. Other times I was seeing it all happen except not in control, stuck in the sidecar of the motorcycle, where I couldn't steer or hit the gas. There was never a brake when things got weird like that. I was always just along for the ride, glued to the seat. Like the night I killed Mac's sister. Second worst thing I ever did and I relive it in nightmares, down to the last excruciating detail. Sometimes I wondered if the crazy old bat had been able to choose to let me see the things she sent me to do, or shield me from them.

If I dwelled on that thought I'd go nuts. Hate eats the hater. Ro messed with me enough while she was alive. She's dead now, and if I let her keep fecking with me, it'll be my own fault and she'll win. Even from her watery grave, she could steal hours, days, weeks of my life. Sometimes when really bad things happen, you put them in a box and never look at them again because they'll cost you the rest of your life. Some wounds never heal. You excise the savaged flesh and become the next thing.

"Drop your sword and I'll put down my spear," Mac says.

"Yeah, right. Then what? You order your creepy little army of Unseelie to drag me down that alley and eat me? No, let me guess: We head back to BB&B, make hot chocolate, hang out and talk?"

"That's the general idea. Minus the bookstore and hot chocolate. And they're not my creepy little army."

"Like, talk about what? Me killing your sister? And they sure look like your creepy little army to me. Go everywhere you do." Feck, it's good to see her. I missed seeing her. I was always scanning every room, every street, hoping to see her. Dreading it.

She flinches. "Maybe you could try not to say it that way. And I said they're not."

"Why shouldn't I? It's what happened," I say defiantly. Fecking pointless. She's never going to see it any other way. My fingers tighten on my sword. "I killed your sister. There it is. Fact. Dude. Never gonna change. I. Killed. Alina. You came to Dublin hunting her murderer. Here I am." I raise a hand and wave it around just in case she's missing the point, overlooking me somehow.

"Dani, I know you're—"

"You don't know *nothing* about me!" I cut her off hard and fast. I hate sentences that begin with my name followed by the claim—indubitably erroneous—that the speaker knows something about me. Those kinds of sentences rank right up there with the ones that begin with *You know what your problem is?* That's always a doozy. Talk about a trick question. Nothing worth hearing ever follows that preface. I snarl, "You hear me? I said you don't know *nothing*! Now get the feck out of my way and take your creepy little groupies with you!"

"No. This ends. Here. Tonight. And I said. They're. Not. Mine." She cuts a look up and mutters, "They stalk me. I haven't figured out how to get rid of them. Yet."

Instantly I want to be on the Dublin News-Channel-X investigative team, ask probing questions, get immersed in solving a thrilling mystery with Mac, but those days are gone and about as likely to come back as dinosaurs. I look at her, and she's giving me this totally fake I'm-not-going-to-kill-you look that's supposed to lure me close enough to get killed. But her fingers sure are tight on the hilt of her spear. And she's balanced real light on the balls of her feet like I am. I know that stance. It's preattack. Face says one thing. Body says another. I listen to the body. Keeps me alive.

She's wearing boots with low heels, fashionable, stupid shoes for ice. It doesn't matter how new and improved MacKayla Lane is, part of her will always be as pink and girly as the nails on the hilt of her spear.

I'm wearing sneakers.

Even slow-mo I'm faster than she'll ever be in those boots. There's no way Mac'll throw her spear at me. No more than she would put it down in a show of good faith. She's like me with my sword. We don't let them out of our hands. Not willingly. Well, I did it tonight for a Highlander who's mostly Unseelie Prince but I got no fecking clue why. The only unknown are those ghastly Unseelie on the rooftops—are they or aren't they here to kill me?

One way to find out.

I try to freeze-frame but don't even get a chug-a-chug of the engine, my battery's deader than dead. Feels like it's not even in the car anymore. Got cables leading nowhere.

I lunge for her and shove her off balance.

She grabs at me but I duck under her arm and push past her. When she snatches a handful of my coat from behind, I turn my head and bite her hand. Not swing my sword or blow something up. Bite. Like a child that doesn't have any other weapons.

"Ow! You *bit* me!"

"Wow, gee. See Mac's brilliant skills of observation," I say irritably. What am I going to do next—pull her hair? Then she might slap me and break a nail and we'll call each other names. The sheer humiliating wussiness of this might goad me into drawing my sword and killing her. I can't fathom how normal folks stand this. Above us, the wraithlike ZEWs chitter louder but stay put. "Get off me, stupid," I hiss. I try to yank free, but she's stronger than I remember.

The second I tug my coat from her fingers she grabs a fistful of my hair and pulls.

"Ow! You pulled my hair!" It *hurt*. Give me swords and spears and guns any day of the week.

"Wow, gee. See Dani's brilliant skills—"

"Stow it! Think up your own insults, unless it's too much work for your—"

"—of observation. And I did *not* pull your hair. I'm just trying to hold you. You're trying to get away. *You're* the one pulling your hair."

"—puny little brain! And of course I'm trying to get away, you fecking twit! And I'm not biting you now so let go of my hair!" I reach up, grab my hair, and we do this idiotic tug of war, then she lets go so abruptly, I crash forward onto my hands and knees.

I surge up instantly but duck again and roll fast out of the way twice, three times, when I hear the whine of her spear behind me. The ZEWs explode upward, rustling and shrieking like a flock of startled buzzards. Guess the spear slicing air freaks them out, too.

For a stupid, vulnerable instant I crouch near the ground and can't even move, trying to process that Mac *really* just swung her spear at me, made an undeniable attempt to kill me, as in remove me from this planet, as in end me *forever*. Seems I was holding on to a crippling hope of absolution, secret even from me. The air feels colder behind me, as if a murderous rage looms there. If you think emotions don't throw off energy, you're wrong.

I shoot to my feet, scrubbing at my cheeks with the balls of my fists. Ice chips must've flown up into my eyes when I rolled, making them sting and tear.

I break into a run.

My backpack drops like a stone from my shoulders. Bugger, she missed *me* but she caught the straps of my bag as I ducked, and all my food is in my pack! I don't know a single store in a fifty-mile radius with stock on the shelves. My superspeed will come back, and when it does I'll need food ASAP. I skid to a slippery stop on ice and turn to grab it.

Mac is standing, one boot planted on my backpack, spear raised, shining alabaster. The edges are razor sharp. I can see my name written all over them.

Message is clear.

"You can't go anywhere without food, Dani. Stop running. I just want to talk to you."

"You're not tricking me!" I hate it that she keeps pretending. Full frontal attack I can deal with. This sneaky crap is lower than low.

"I'm not trying to."

She sure as feck is. She just tried to slice off my head, for cripes sake.

The ZEWs resettle on the rooftops and resume that nerve-wracking racket again.

"So, what? I'm supposed to believe you came looking

for me to tell me you, like, forgive me? Just how stupid do you think I am?"

Her eyes fill with shadows and she looks sad. "Life is complicated, Dani."

"What the feck does that *mean*?" I could just pop out of my skin like an overpressured grape from sheer frustration. I hate it when people throw big sweeping generalizations at you that you can't even begin to interpret. Life is complicated so I'm going to kill you quick? Life is complicated so I'm going to torture you to death slow and talk the whole time, driving you batshit crazy in the process? Life is complicated ergo I might forgive you if you perform Herculean tasks of redemption? The options are endless. Who doesn't know life is complicated? What I want to know is how to apply that to the nuts and bolts of my existence. Folks never tell you *that* part.

"Sometimes the things we think will set us free . . . only make more chains. You either wear them or break them, and I . . . well, I don't want to wear them."

"Dude, ain't no chains here. I don't see nothing but you and me and weapons and death, if you don't get off my pack and walk away. Besides, even if you did say you forgive me, I'd never believe you! I'll always be waiting for the second you decide to try to kill me. You want me dead. Admit it. Just say it. Be honest, for feck's sake! You know you want me dead! I see it in your eyes!"

She doesn't say anything for a couple seconds, like she's thinking hard about what she's going to say next, and I don't even know I'm holding my breath waiting until she begins talking and it kind of explodes from my lungs.

"I don't want you dead, Dani. That's not why I came looking for you."

"Well, why the fuck not?" I yell. "I *deserve* to die!"

My hand goes to my mouth like maybe I can cover up

what I just said or scrape the words back inside some-how. I'm horrified. I don't even know where those words came from. There aren't many sins in my bible. Giving up is the greatest one of all. I just broke my own cardinal rule. Life is a gift. You fight to keep it. You never quit. Never.

Nobody wants you. Your own mother locks you in a cage, leaves and forgets you. Just die. It'll end everyone's misery, including your own. Maybe then she can have a life. One of you should.

I can't believe I just said I deserve to die. Maybe I'm possessed. Maybe I got one of those sneaky, diaphanous Unseelie Grippers inside me but it's only fecking with me sometimes ('cause I'm so super it can't possess me all the time!), making me say things I don't really feel and shorting out my powers. And maybe that Gripper has some kind of bizarre obsession with Ryodan. Weirder things have been happening in Dublin lately.

Mac shakes her head, giving me a totally fake compassionate look. "Oh, Dani—"

"I'm not falling for this so just shut up! Leave me alone or I'll kill you like I killed your sister. I swear I will. I'll kill you and then I'll kill everybody you care about. That's what I do. I kill people. I kill and kill and kill. That's who I am. That's who she made me." I used to daydream Barrons found me in the cage that day, instead of Ro, and imagine what I'd have turned out to be then, but he didn't. She did. It is what it is.

I run.

She follows faster than I would have thought possible. I wonder if Barrons did something to her, maybe that thing Ryodan said he would do for me. Is she as unkillable as them now? Is that where her balls are coming from? If so, I'm seriously pissed and even more jealous.

I leap snowbanks, dash down alleys, double back around, leading her on a merry chase through Temple

Bar, and still she manages to stay hot on my arse. I keep testing every couple of seconds to see if I can freeze-frame but my superpowers have taken the same vacation my conscience went on years ago.

She's yelling stuff but I don't listen. I hum my favorite playlist to tune out her and the racket of her creepy army.

I don't realize my feet have taken me to Barrons Books & Baubles until it looms up in front of me, only holy place I've ever known: amber lights and polished wood and diamond-paned windows and endless possibilities. Deep in a limestone arch, fancy columns and sidelights and brass sconces and a stained-glass transom frame the door I used to go banging through a million miles a minute, and just above it on a shiny brass pole hangs that colorful hand-painted shingle that might as well have once said Welcome Home but never would again for me.

I love this place more than any other. Gas fireplaces and big comfy couches you can really stretch out on and magazines and books you can read and dream about all the places in the world you're gonna see one day, and wicked-cool antique weapons and kick-ass modern ones, and killer muscle cars and cakes and presents and friends you thought you had. The hours I spent there are filed away in my storage vaults in superhigh-gloss Technicolor, brighter than any other memories. Sometimes I pull one out and relive it real slow, savoring it down to the last morsel. I love Mac. I miss her so bad. I wish—

Wishes aren't horses and I don't get to ride. 'Scool. I got feet that are usually superhero grade.

The bell on the door tinkles.

A man steps out.

Strong. Brilliant. Controlled.

Predator.

Unbreakable. Feck, to be so unbreakable!

He's everything I admire plus things I can't even begin to put into words.

I crush on Jericho Barrons violently.

My brain almost shuts down every time I see him and that's a lot of gray matter to stupefy.

Used to be, if I couldn't fall asleep I'd fantasize all kinds of ways I'd impress Barrons by killing monsters or saying something really smart or saving the world, and he'd see me as a grown-up woman and I'd glow just from the expression on his face, like that time I killed the Unseelie Prince in Mac's cell and he looked at me like he really saw who I was. Most folks don't. They fence me in with teenage rules that don't hold me for shit, seeing how I grew up. *You can kill but don't cuss. Break any rule necessary to save the world but don't watch porn or even* think *about having sex.* How do they come up with this stuff—hold parental powwows for brainstorming diametrically opposed ethics? Then Ryodan began popping into my Barrons fantasies like he had some kind of business being there, and he'd look all, well . . . like . . . Ryodan, and he'd laugh and do that husky groan thing he did on level four, so I terminated that happy little exercise in somnolence.

Now, I count sheep.

Lately even *those* buggers look like Ryodan, with clear, cold eyes and some weird kind of hypnotic hold on me.

Fecker.

I'm beginning to think I'm going to have to figure a way to kill him, permanent-like, just to get him out of my head.

"Dani."

I shiver. He has that effect on folks, throws off some kind of charge, supersaturates the space in his vicinity.

All his dudes do, but Jericho Barrons has it in spades. I play it real cool. Shove a hand in my pocket, thumb out. Cock my hip at a jaunty angle. "Barrons."

Time was, I planned on growing up and giving him my virginity. Or V'lane. It's a big deal to me, the divesting of it. One of the few things I got left that's gonna be my choice: the who, the how, the when. It's gonna be Epic with a capital E!

But the Seelie Prince V'lane turned out to be the Unseelie Prince Cruce. And Barrons is Mac's as much as something like him is ever anyone's, a fact that's never going to change, and I don't want it to.

A piece of paper flaps on the column behind his head. I get a bad feeling and take a sec to scan it.

"Gah! Are you fecking *kidding* me?" How the heck did they get something printed already? Even in hyperspeed, I couldn't have gotten a rag out this fast! But there it is, waving in the air like a great big slap in my face.

The Dublin Daily

June 26, 1 AWC

YOUR ONLY SOURCE FOR CREDIBLE NEWS IN AND
AROUND NEW DUBLIN
BROUGHT TO YOU BY WeCARE

GOOD PEOPLE OF NEW DUBLIN, THE ICE MONSTER THAT WAS FREEZING OUR CITY IS DEAD!

WeCARE was at the scene, fighting the good fight!

WeCARE will always have your back

UNLIKE

I can't read any more. I know they're getting ready to dis me. But my traitorous eyeballs sneak another peek and sure enough there it is!

. . . a certain bragging teenager that JEOPARDIZED the mission and was single-handedly responsible for getting many good, innocent people KILLED and taken CAPTIVE!

"Buh! Who is *writing* this drivel?" I was the hero tonight! I saved the fecking day with my winning combination of brains and skills. They even made the font size bigger on the slander about me! I know the tricks of the trade. Talk about your biased press! I feel my face getting hot and red. It pisses me off so much I'd rupture a gonad if I had one. WeCare sure as feck has them out the wazoo!

"Stop her!" Mac shouts.

I don't stand a chance against both of them. Heck, I don't stand a chance against Barrons by himself. He's like Ryodan. I can't compete on my best day.

Yet.

I fist my hands and take rapid deep breaths, clearing my head of the Wemightcarebutsureasfeckdon'ttellthetruth bullcrap. It takes me a sec to analyze possibilities and figure out how I'm getting myself out of this one. The answer is so simple it takes my breath away. I'm wired to survive on a gut level. My subconscious brought me exactly where I needed to be.

I duck past him and totally catch him off guard—or more likely he decides not to chase me for some mysterious reason, because there's no way I can outrun Barrons, not even in freeze-frame—then can't help myself and dart back and snatch the slanted scrap o' crap from the column and wad it up 'cause I sure as heck ain't letting it hang there, then I'm back behind the bookstore, hurrying to the first building on the left side of the Dark Zone.

Last time I was here was the night me and Christian searched the Unseelie King's library, the night the words in the Boora Boora books crawled off the pages and stung me like fire ants, and I accidentally set the Crimson Hag free.

Christian. The Hag. Cripes, I got some cleanup work to do.

When he showed me the hidden portal in the wall that's really a secret passageway into the ancient mirrors the Fae once used to travel between worlds, I'd committed the precise, unremarkable spot of bricks to memory. All weapons and escape routes—good. Not even Ryodan with his stupid contract on me can track me Fae-side. I figured if the city ever got too hot for me, I could always ditch it for a while.

It's feeling way too hot right now.

"Dani, don't!" Mac cries.

I leap into the brick. It's weirdly spongelike, then so am I, then I'm standing in a large, windowless, doorless room with blank white walls and a white floor and ten enormous mirrors of varying shapes and sizes suspended in the air. They hang without visible means of support, some motionless, others twirling lazily. No surprise there. Fae stuff, animate and not, rarely give a wink and sure as heck no nod to human physics. It's why Dancer's so fascinated by them. Some of the mirrors have intricately carved frames, while others have thin edges of welded chain-link. A few of the looking glasses within the frames are as black as night, some milky white, and others crammed with shadows you don't want to look at hard.

It's a good thing I know which mirror to take—second Silver on the right plops you smack inside the infinite, a-fecking-mazing White Mansion. I been itching to explore it anyway. If they follow me through, I'll use the labyrinthine corridors to lose them or unstopper another distraction because Rule Number One in the Mega O'Malley Handbook is and will always be: survival first, damage control second. Which is only logical. You can't do damage control dead.

If they don't follow me in, all I have to do is wait long enough for my superpowers to return, then come back because it'll be a couple days, if not a couple weeks later in Dublin. When Christian and me went through last time, we lost almost a month! Time doesn't pass the same in Fae realms. No way they'll sit in the White Room 24/7 waiting for me. I hate losing Dublin-time that I could be using to help my city but I can't help my city at all if I'm not alive.

Mac explodes through the wall behind me like she was shot by a cannon, slams into my back and nearly pushes me into the wrong mirror, and all I can think is what a disaster that would have been. I got no clue where the other ones go. Might be a world without air, a direct path into the Unseelie prison, or a galaxy filled with Hunters, or Shades, or gray women! I got a special hate on for the gray-folk caste of Unseelie. One of them almost killed me and forced Mac to make a promise she shouldn't have made.

I shove her off me and she stumbles back, nearly crashing into Barrons, who just entered the room with his usual stalky animal grace.

Jericho Barrons is an unshakable, undestroyable constant. He's the cornerstone of my universe. Or maybe together they are. I don't know. I only know as long as the two of them and BB&B still stand, some part of me that never used to feel okay, does.

I can't help myself—I watch them a sec. I love watching them together. I slow-mo it to absorb every detail.

Mac draws up short to keep from slamming into

Barrons, and her blond hair swings back over her shoulder, brushing his face as it does, and my hearing is so good I catch the rasp of it chafing the shadow stubble on his jaw, then one of his hands grazes her breast and his eyes narrow when he looks at what he touched in a hungry way I want a man to look at me like one day and, as they continue to recover from the near-collision, their bodies move in a graceful dance of impeccable awareness of precisely where the other is at all times that is unity, symbiosis, partnership I only dream of, wolves that chose to pack up and hunt together, soldiers who will always have each other's backs no matter what, no sin, no transgression too great, 'cause don't we all transgress sometimes and it fecking slays me, because once I got a little taste of what that was like, and it was heaven and they're so beautiful standing there, the best of the best, the strongest of the strong, that they practically glow to me, on fire with all I ever wanted in my life—a place to belong and someone to belong there with.

Together they mean to kill me and go on living, all happy, like I didn't even mean anything. They'll eat and have sex and adventures and I'll be nothing but six feet under in dirt—assuming anyone even bothers to bury me. Gone. Over. Finis. Done. Quit. Before I ever even got the chance to live.

I'm not sure I've ever been hap—

I terminate that idiotic train of thought. As soon as my *sidhe*-seer gifts come back, I'll get over this wimpy little emotional meltdown I'm having. Losing the superpowers that make me special plus seeing Mac up close and personal for the first time since she found out what I did is temporarily messing with my head. Key word there, temporarily.

Fourteen blows.

Hormones suck.

I wish I'd just grow the hell up in a hurry and everything would even out and start to make sense and folks would stop seeing me as a kid and I could finally—

Bugger it all! What am I waiting for?

I close my hand on the hilt of my sword and dive headfirst into the mirror, laughing as I go. I always crack up when I leap into the unknown. It's cotton-candy fuel, there's a big-top tent full of carnival magic in a good belly laugh.

Next grand adventure here I come!

The last thing I hear is Mac shouting, "Oh, God, no, Dani, not *that* one! We moved them! That one goes to—"

2

_____

*"There's bullet holes
where my compassion used to be . . ."*

MAC

"—the Hall of All Days!"

If not infinite, the ancient Fae "airport" that serves as hub for a nexus of Silvers is so vast it isn't worth splitting hairs over.

Fashioned of gold from floor to ceiling, the endless corridor is lined with billions of mirrors that are portals to alternate universes and times and exudes a chilling spatial-temporal distortion that makes you feel utterly inconsequential—think dust mote in a galaxy-sized barn.

Time isn't linear in the hall, it's malleable and slippery and you can get permanently lost in memories that never were and dreams of futures that will never be.

One moment you feel terrifyingly alone, the next as if an endless chain of paper-doll versions of yourself is unfolding sideways, holding cutout construction-paper hands with thousands of different feet in thousands of different worlds, all at the same time.

Compounding the many dangers of the hall, when the Silvers were damaged by Cruce's curse (a thing he tried to blame on his Unseelie brothers, in typical Cruce fashion), the mirrors were corrupted and the image they now present is no guarantee of what's on the other side. A lush rain forest may lead to a parched, cracked desert, a tropical oasis to a world of ice, but you can't count on total opposites either. No handy *Hitchhiker's Guide to the Galaxy* is propped on a convenient foyer table, near a cool beverage and tasty snack inside those time-tortured walls.

Barrons steps between the mirror and me, folds his arms across his chest, and spreads his legs wide. He's a tall, dark mountain of man I can't push my way through or around. I meet his implacable gaze and we have one of our wordless discussions.

But we have to—
No we don't.
But we can't—
Yes we can.
But she doesn't—
She'll figure it out.
But it's—
Not your fault and not your problem.
But I'm the one—
Bloody hell, Ms. Lane, how many "buts" are you going to throw at me besides the only one I want? He rakes a hungry gaze over my ass and I shiver.

After all we've been through together, he still calls me Ms. Lane, with one exception: when I'm in his bed. Or on the floor, or some other place where I've temporarily lost my mind and become convinced I can't breathe without him inside me.

"Sometimes I don't know why I even bother talking to you."

He lifts a brow an infinitesimal amount in a silent *makes two of us.*

Barrons thinks words are pointless and dangerous. If

I played it his way, we'd rarely speak, ocular or otherwise. Funny thing is, the more time I spend around him, the more I understand why he feels that way.

"But she's in the *hall*. It's a terrible place. I've been there. People don't escape." During my brief time in those ancient corridors, the glossy, seductive floors had been littered with skeletons. I'd nearly become one of them. In those mind-bending halls, you could live any reality you chose, die on the floor believing you were living a genuine, happy life somewhere real. The place is a consummate mind-fuck.

"You did," he says aloud.

"That's different. I'm the exception. To a lot of things."

A corner of his mouth lifts. "Modest, too. So is she."

"I had the stones." Chiseled from the Unseelie King's realm, they'd reacted to each portal I went through, changing the way the environment behaved and working ultimately to expel me.

"If you follow her through, you will only force her to take the nearest escape route. Any door, any Silver. She's not going to stop running from you. What if she chooses a world that has no air or is too close to a sun? She needs time to use that powerful brain of hers. You made it out. She will, too. Drop it. There are other things you need to be focused on. Besides," his gaze locks on mine, then I feel like he's sweeping my eyeballs aside and sifting through my mind, analyzing, discarding, hunting, "ah, yes, I thought as much. You're not ready yet. You will leave her alone until you are."

Autocratic has a picture of Barrons next to it in the dictionary. Unfortunately so does *addictive*. I poke Unseelie on both sides with my elbows and change the subject. "Haven't you found a way to get rid of them yet? It's been months."

One after another black-cloaked, chittering wraiths

continue to pop through the portal behind me. I have no idea why they've chosen me to stalk. I'm swiftly becoming the only human in an Unseelie sardine can, and just as smelly. It's bad enough they stalk me, but where they brush against me they leave a greasy, pungent yellow dust on my clothes. That's the least of the reasons I want them gone.

With rare exceptions—like tonight, when they inexplicably decided to roost up high—they make it impossible to fight. I can't get to my enemy without first slaughtering a few dozen of the ones smothering me. By the time I slice and stab my way clear, whatever I *really* wanted to kill has disappeared. My *sidhe*-seer talent, nulling, or freezing them in place for a few seconds, doesn't work on them.

As if that's not bad enough, every time Ryodan sees me he grills me about why an Unseelie caste is following me around, and when that man gets a bone he strips the gristle with his teeth and gnaws until the marrow is gone, so I've stopped going to Chester's or anywhere in public that I might run into him or his men, which is pretty much everywhere given the close watch they keep on Dublin and the surrounding districts. I'm bookstore-bound most days and nights, and me, cooped up, bored, gets riskier with each passing hour—idle hands make the devil's work and all.

Not the devil, beautiful girl. Angel. Your *angel.*

Yet another voice I pretend not to hear.

You wish to be rid of them? Your wish. My command.

Oh, yeah, fully deaf now.

I killed the first fifty or so Unseelie when they began stalking me, but it didn't matter how many I slayed, more appeared. Compounding my disgust, they release a huge cloud of that stinking yellow dust as they die, coating me and making me sneeze my head off. I haven't seen them feed on any humans, and as their only offense seems to be stalking me and ruining my clothes, I no longer kill them. It's pointless and disturbing.

I shoot Barrons a look. He has a full five feet of personal space around him in all directions. I, on the other hand, am a human dog with Unseelie fleas. "So, can you get rid of them or not?"

"I'm working on it."

"Can't you tattoo me or something?"

"Now she wants me to tattoo her. Will wonders never cease."

"It'd be better than walking around with these . . . these . . . these bloody flipping odiferous gnats!"

"Have yet to find one that works."

"Well, whatever's keeping them out of the bookstore should keep them away from me, right? Can't you just do to me what you did to it?" Inside those walls and beneath his garage are the only places I have any privacy.

"I've not isolated the precise element responsible. And no, I can't do all of that to you. You're animate. You might not be when I was done. I prefer you animate. Most of the time."

Most? I bristle but refuse to be distracted. "Just how many elements are involved in protecting a bookstore? Five? Ten? A hundred?" When he betrays nothing of his secret protection spell—not that I expected him to, Butt-the-fuck-out-of-my-business is his middle name—I press, "Have you considered asking the Keltar if they can help? They've been druids to the Fae for thousands of years and maybe—"

This time the look he cuts me holds a glitter of crimson and I shut up. I've seen that flash when he's on top of me, hands bracketing my head, eyes dark with lust. I've seen it when he's killing. I know what it promises: primal passion or primal destruction. Hard as it is to believe, I'm in the mood for neither at the moment. My problems have bred entire subsets of problems, which are no doubt having birth pains to spawn yet more problems, even as I pause to brood about them. Mentioning the clan of sexy Highlanders to Barrons is never a good idea, which I would have remembered if I'd not been distracted by the sudden realization that I'm wearing the last clean outfit I own and will have to do laundry tonight. Again.

I'm sick of hiding. Tired of washing clothes. Fed up with sitting back and doing nothing to help my city, my people, myself. Arguably the most powerful person in Dublin, possibly on the planet—with the exception of one currently frozen prince—I lay low so no one discovers the psychopathic, homicidal embryo I carry inside me—a complete copy of the *Sinsar Dubh*, the most dangerous, twisted, evil book of black magic ever created.

I know where to find the spell to be rid of the Unseelie that stalk me. I even know where to find the magic to hunt and destroy whatever has been freezing people and icing our city. In the pages of a book I don't dare ever open, not even for one tiny peek inside. The dark book possesses anyone that reads it, takes them over and corrupts them completely. I'm carrying a lethal bomb around inside me. As long as I don't touch it, I won't blow up into the greatest evil mankind has ever known.

For the first week after I refused to take the spell to lay Barrons's son to rest, the *Sinsar Dubh* was silent. For eight and a half blissful days I believed I'd gotten my happily-ever-after, and could settle down to a peaceful life of killing Unseelie, rebuilding Dublin, gardening with Mom, driving supercars with my dad, fortifying the abbey, bonding with my sister *sidhe*-seers, and having phenomenal fights and even better sex with Barrons. All I had to do was ignore the *Sinsar Dubh*. Never open it. Never use the limitless power at my disposal. Easy, right?

Not.

Temptation isn't a vice you triumph over once, completely, and then you're free. Temptation slips into bed with you each night and helps you say prayers. It wakes you in the morning with a friendly cup of coffee, and knows just the way you take it, heavy on the sin.

Every blasted day it's that afternoon outside the bookstore all over again, only instead of refusing the spell to save one man's son, I'm refusing to save an entire city.

It took me all of five minutes suffering the *Sinsar Dubh*'s goading to devise a plan of action.

Get rid of it.

Before someone finds out or I lose control and rain down death and destruction on everyone I care about. I'm not living this battle every day for the rest of my Fae-elixir-enhanced life. And hopefully the stalkers that impede my ability to move at every turn will vanish along with it.

While our city has been fighting the ice monster, Barrons and I, trailed by my ghouls, have been wasting weeks at a time making trips into the ever-changing White Mansion, sorting through endless libraries, scouring old manuscripts and scrolls, hunting for a ghost of a whisper of a legend: an infamous spell to summon the Unseelie King back to Dublin, so he can strip his damned book out of me.

Barrons thinks it's wasted effort and is getting impatient. He spent countless millennia searching ancient books for spells—and now I have him searching ancient books for a spell again. He says even if we manage to get his attention, the half-mad king will simply laugh, vanish as quickly as summoned.

I refuse to believe that. The king is my only hope.

Besides, he has a soft spot for me. Sort of. I think. That's about as conclusive as one can be with the entity that calls himself Unseelie King.

"You will obey me, Ms. Lane. You will not follow her. That is all."

Jericho Barrons turns in a ripple of muscle and beautifully tailored Armani and stalks through the portal, leaving me alone with too many questions, too few choices, and a hundred-odd Unseelie.

That is all, my ass. I'm my own woman. I'm Death walking. I'm the possibility for Complete and Total World Destruction. I can sure as hell make my own decisions.

I ponder the Silver, eyes narrowed.

I know Barrons.

If I follow Dani, he'll follow me, as will my confederacy of Unseelie. I imagine the parade we make: pretty blonde with the scary eyes followed by big, dark, tattooed man with the *really* scary eyes, trailed by a hundred eerily gliding, cobweb-dusted, black-cloaked, stinking wraiths. Hell, *I'd* take one look at us and run, even if I didn't know we had good reason to be pissed at me.

Barrons is right. Dani will only keep fleeing, anywhere, any way, possible.

And it's not our bizarre cavalcade causing it.

It's me.

You're not ready yet, he said.

It's my fault she went through the Silver. I'm getting better at recognizing pivotal moments, and there was one back in the alley where I might have been able to reach her, stop her from running. Or at least not drive her into Faery.

It didn't escape my notice that Dani hadn't attempted to use one ounce of superstrength in our absurdly normal mean-girl scuffle, nor had she freeze-framed out, which made it clear how desperately she hoped I would forgive her.

I'd pulled my punches, too, wishing desperately to forgive her. Turn back time to half-past innocence. But that clock's lying on its side, hour hand spinning wildly, in a dirty Dublin alley near a gold makeup pouch half concealed by trash, and an address carved in stone by a dying woman.

Broken.

You can't count on Dani remaining in normal-speed for long—there's no telling what might startle her up—so when she stumbled and the opportunity presented itself, I'd swung my spear to slice the straps on her pack, take her food, and eliminate the possibility.

I swear that was all I was after. Her food. Nothing more.

But the moment I raised my spear, I flashed back over all the evil I've been fighting and I saw my sister dead in that alley, and Mallucé torturing me to death, and the Unseelie Princes raping me, and Rowena slitting my throat in the cell beneath the abbey, and the *Sinsar Dubh*'s endless games, and for a moment I despised the world because I used to know who I was, and I used to be good, with no bad in me, or at least that's what I thought and there really is a degree of bliss and charmed innocence in ignorance. But when you fight evil every day, stare it in the face, engage it, learn to think like it, you face a choice: Be defeated by the limits of your own morality, or summon a beast in yourself that obeys none.

That I have such a beast, plus my psychotic hitch-hiker, keeps me as frozen as my compatriot prince, but while Cruce was imprisoned against his will, I've chosen my useless stasis.

Either way, we're both iced.

I do nothing. And my self-contempt grows.

Lines are thin. So easy to cross.

Impossible to uncross.

It had taken every ounce of willpower I possessed to pull my swing just enough to slice only nylon not flesh and bone, and if I had to do it all over again, I'm not sure I could.

I love my sister. I loved Dani.

Some things the gut distills to their essence no matter how hard you try to factor in compassion and mercy and understanding.

One of them killed the other.

And there is violence in my heart.

I couldn't blame this one on the *Sinsar Dubh*'s seductive whispering. This one was all me. I'd failed to convince Dani that I didn't want revenge.

I hadn't convinced myself.

3

*"Got an angel on my shoulder
and Mephistopheles"*

The Dublin Daily

July 17, 1 AWC

YOUR ONLY SOURCE FOR CREDIBLE NEWS IN AND
AROUND NEW DUBLIN
BROUGHT TO YOU BY WeCARE

Summer is here!
 There's no better time than now to take the WHITE!
 Step up to help rebuild a stronger greener New Dublin!
 YOU can make A DIFFERENCE!
 Now is the time to show YouCARE
 Join
 WeCARE

Today!

MAC

I crumple the paper without bothering to read past the propaganda for more of their slanted journalism. I despise that this flyer is where I get my news about the city. Once I *was* the news about the city because I was out there, fighting and making a difference, calling the shots . . . or at least having a clue what the shots were.

I want to see a *Dani Daily* flapping on a pole in the breeze. I want to read her bragging about her most recent kill. I want to know what the latest Unseelie threat is, in all the entertaining, flamboyant detail she liked to tell it. I'm still in no frame of mind to actually see *her,* but I sure would like to know she's okay.

That it was from WeCare's button-pushing rag I discovered what happened at the abbey the night the Hoar Frost King was destroyed offends me endlessly. I toss the wadded paper into a battered trash can.

I should have been at the abbey but we'd been in the Silvers again, had gotten back that very night, about an hour after the big showdown took place. We hadn't even known it was happening. If I'd gone, maybe no one would have died. I might have been able to save Christian from the Crimson Hag. I miss the sexy young Scotsman with the killer smile that I met during my early days in Dublin. I refuse to believe he's lost to us now. They say he's turned full Unseelie Prince. I hear his uncles have been hunting him but no luck so far.

They say.

I hear.

The voice of my news is as passive as I've become.

Hunting for Christian is yet another mission I should be on. He holds me responsible for the fix he's in from feeding him Unseelie to save his life. That, combined with whatever went wrong with the Keltar ritual Barrons attended at the circle of stones in the Highlands on

Samhain, seemed to have sealed his fate. He blames Barrons and me equally for his transformation. Which is total bullshit. I stood in the Hall of All Days and *chose* to go through to the desert world with four radioactive suns on which he was stranded, risking my own life to save his. Little thanks I've gotten for it.

I shove my hair back with both hands, prelude to tearing it out in frustration.

It's been twenty-one days since Dani dove through the Silver into the Hall of All Days, and I have no idea if she's dead or alive. I've been searching the city, entourage in tow, risking exposure, seeking any sign of her return. Standing in the alley, eyeing that damn spot of brick with increasing frequency, questioning everything I believe about myself.

I've discovered that, like the Fae, Ryodan and his men aren't as active on the streets between the afternoon hours of one and five, which gives me another hour to continue searching for a flamboyant new *D* carved into the cobblestone at the site of one of her more impressive kills, a note in the General Post Office that she's answered, or maybe I'll run into her friend Dancer. It's not as if she's going to let me know when she gets back.

I step up my pace. Behind me, beside me, my chittering troop doesn't miss a beat. I nudge them away with my elbows. It works for a few seconds, then I'm smothered in dusty, smelly Unseelie again. I brush cobwebs off my sleeves. Dani was right, they are gruesome.

They shall be your priests, MacKayla. Command them.

I had no desire to know that.

I do something Barrons taught me, mentally envision a shining gold and obsidian book, slam it shut and lock it, adding cartoonish touches for levity: dust exploding from its cover, an eye on the gilded face of the book closing as if euthanized. I finish by flushing it down a giant toilet.

It's right. I could conduct my search far more efficiently if I dispatched a hundred Unseelie to look for her. I could send them into the hall.

Not.

Despite the fruitlessness of my endeavor, it's been good to get out of the bookstore. Dublin is coming back to life, thanks to my mom and her New Dublin Green-Up group. Once the Hoar Frost King was destroyed, the ice melted dangerously quickly, the city flooded, and most people holed up indoors to wait it out.

But not Rainey Lane. She attacked on multiple fronts, organizing teams to sandbag and protect while dispatching others to truck fertilizer, agriculture, and rare livestock from outlying areas not decimated by the vampiric Shades. The moment it was dry enough, she mobilized yet more teams to remove abandoned cars that have blocked the streets since last Halloween, when the walls fell and riots ripped through Dublin.

When the streets were cleared of the largest debris, Mom got down to work in earnest, overseeing the fertilizing and sowing of grass, bushes, and trees. The new bloom on Dublin restored hope, motivating others to join up and begin repairs. The famed flags on the Oliver St. John Gogarty were rehung, the boxes above Quay's are overflowing with flowers, and it looks as if someone's planning to reopen Temple Bar.

My daddy, Jack Lane, settles what civil disputes don't end in brutality first (which doesn't leave him many cases to hear) and supervises one of the teams restoring power and getting street sweepers out again. The streetlamps now wink on at dusk and blink out at dawn, the civic centers are offering shelter to the homeless. What few doctors remain have set up a makeshift hospital at Dublin Castle, with Inspector Jayne and the ex-Garda that are now the NDG: New Dublin Guardians. Dad says soon we'll be fully up and running and generators will no longer be necessary. Seems Ireland had its fair share of engineers and hackers and they weathered the fall of our city better than most.

Food and medicine are the hottest commodities. Dublin's grocery and convenience stores are empty, the hospital and pharmacies ransacked, and we've lost so much farm-rich land to the Shades that rebuilding is going to take time. One of the few positive things about having half the human race erased from the planet is that many supplies are out there, if you can survive the long, dangerous trek, filled with Fae and human predators alike, to find them. WeCare was trying to get a corner on the supply market but failed, squeezed out by ruthless competitors.

There are currently three places to obtain food in Dublin, where the prices vary according to whim: Chester's, the Fae, and the black market. If you ask me, they're all black. Of course nobody *does* ask me because nobody sees me because I lay low all the time and I've got a boyfriend who isn't much for talking.

I snort. I just thought of Jericho Barrons as my "boyfriend." I doubt that cataclysm was ever a boy and he certainly can't be called friendly.

It's official. I'm losing it.

Solitude and inaction are unraveling me right down to the core.

Forty-five minutes later I'm on my way back to the bookstore, another wasted day beneath my belt, headed for another thrilling evening reading dusty, crumbling manuscripts. I used to love to read. But I used to read hot romances and great murder mysteries and autobiographies. Now I read one thing: dry, archaic Fae history and legend.

I decide to cut through the Dark Zone adjacent to BB&B, see what's happening, and make sure it's still empty. That'll make me feel better. I may not be able to actively fight, but at least I can keep tabs on one of my enemy's favorite campsites, ascertain they haven't come back.

My Unseelie swarm turns with me as I head down a narrow cobbled lane.

Nearly a year ago, my second day in this city, I'd gotten lost in these forgotten, trash-strewn blocks filled with dilapidated industrial warehouses and docks, crumbling smokestacks, abandoned cars, and thick, porous husks scattered all over the place, oblivious to the amorphous danger lurking in the shadows.

When I'd finally stumbled out of danger, or rather into danger of another sort in Barrons Books & Baubles that afternoon, it had been love at first sight—with the bookstore. The owner was another matter. That was war at first sight. I'm not sure much has changed, except that we both really enjoy the war.

Later that night Barrons had come to my rented room at the Clarin Hotel and tried to bully me into leaving. It hadn't worked. I might have been pink and pretty and terrified, but I'd stood my ground.

I frown and rub my forehead then pinch the bridge of my nose. Something's itchy in my skull. Something weird just happened while I was thinking about that night. As if there's a neatly wrapped bundle tucked away in my head and something disturbed it, kicking up dust, drawing my attention somewhere I might never have looked. Thanks to the *Sinsar Dubh* eternally infiltrating and attempting to usurp my thoughts, I've become a pro at navigating the dimly lit corridors inside my skull, sidestepping certain things, packing others deep into the shadows, picking up still more and carrying them into the light.

But this . . . I'm not even sure what it is.

It doesn't feel like part of the Book and it doesn't feel like me. As if someone else tucked a parcel away, taped it up in thick packing blankets, and left it in a small cave where I might never—

"You made oath, pledged détente," a voice hisses. "This is *my* territory now."

My gaze snaps outward and I'm surprised to find myself seven or eight blocks into the Dark Zone. My body is instantly battle ready, my hand on my spear. My wraiths chitter and flock upward to the roofs above, apparently liking the leprous, beauty-stealing Gray Woman no more than I. I really wish I could figure out what makes them decide to vacate my space at odd moments.

I savor the lack of constriction and expand my shoulders from the drawn-forward hunch I assume when they press close. With the exception of the night I saw Dani, it's been months since I've been able to stand in the street alone.

Now I'm face-to-face with an Unseelie enemy—one-on-one, with nothing in my way. It's exhilarating, like old times.

A good nine to ten feet tall, covered with open, oozing sores, the Gray Woman is hideous. I get briefly fixated on the long thin hands covered with suckers that nearly killed Dani that night, remember how I'd forced the vile Unseelie to give the teen back her life in exchange for a dirty bargain I should never have made, and would make all over again to keep Dani alive.

I stare up into her rotting face and think about the lisping Fae that killed my sister and the many times this bitch has fed, the countless lives ruined and lost.

I've seen none of Ryodan's men on the streets.

My flock isn't hemming me in.

The moment is perfection. I'm a *sidhe*-seer and a powerful Null. I have a weapon that kills the Fae. I don't need anything from my inner psychopath. My spear is enough. There's no taint of the *Sinsar Dubh* in this. I've sometimes wondered if the Book is responsible for the wraiths that stalk me, if it summoned them to torment me, believing if it prevents me from fighting the good fight long enough, I'll flip and succumb to its endless goading.

Not a chance.

I'm going to walk home today with a bounce in my step and a good feeling in my heart, knowing I got rid of one of our many enemies. I'm going to feel like the old me again, out there batting for the team, saving who knows how many thousands of lives by ending this foul, malevolent one.

"You will leave this place. It is mine. You swore free passage and a favor owed," the Gray Woman hisses.

This is what I've needed for months: a golden opportunity to kick self-doubt squarely in the teeth, remind myself that although the Book might needle me, I'm in control. I make the decisions, not the *Sinsar Dubh*. It can talk all it wants, it can intrude into my thoughts and tempt me endlessly, but at the end of the day it's me that's walking my body around and calling the shots.

The Unseelie are vermin; they've killed billions of people and would happily gorge on our world until there was nothing left. I despise them and I despise myself for not killing more of them.

My spear glows white when I battle. I'm the good guy.

"Guess what, bitch." I lunge for the Gray Woman. "I lied."

Yes, the *Sinsar Dubh* whispers.

And everything goes dark.

* * *

I claw my way back to consciousness, gasping for breath. I'm on my knees, in a gutter—no real surprise there—I'm intimately acquainted with Dublin's gutters, having puked in more than a few of them.

I hurt everywhere. I've wrenched my lower back, my arms burn, my knees are bruised, and I'm drenched.

I peer up, wondering if it's raining again. It does that a lot here.

Nope, sun is still out, well, sort of. It's kissing the horizon beyond the—I frown. What just happened? Where am I? Not in the Dark Zone anymore, I'm half-way across the city.

A soft chuckle rolls in my head. *Land of the Free, MacKayla. Home of the Brave, Beautiful, and Homicidal. You can't tell me you didn't enjoy that,* the *Sinsar Dubh* says silkily.

Something splatters on my head, drips down my face.

I touch my cheek and pull my hand away to look at it. It's covered with green goo.

And red blood.

My fingernails are stained. There's stuff beneath them I refuse to examine.

Not looking up, not looking up.

Keep acting like this, Princess, and I'll kill you myself. Don't think I can't.

I squeeze my eyes shut.

Nowhere to run, nowhere to hide, the Book says in a singsong voice and pastes an image of me, holding a gun to my own head, kneeling on the floor in Barrons Books & Baubles, on the inside of my lids. *Just kidding. Never let you do it. I got you, babe,* it twangs in a cheesy, over-the-top Sonny and Cher impersonation.

Grimacing, I open my eyes and peer warily up.

Fuck, fuck, fuck.

Impaled on the streetlamp beneath which I crouch, the Gray Woman has been tortured, flayed, and dismembered.

And left alive.

Bits of her wriggle in agony. Suckers open and close convulsively and she's somehow still making noise: moans and whimpers of horrendous pain.

I drop my head, and nearly vomit into the gutter.

Onto a human hand. Torn off at the wrist.

He got in the way.

"No," I whisper. I recognize the tatter of uniform attached to the wrist. It's one of Inspector Jayne's Guardians. I would never kill a human. Never harm an innocent. I may not like Jayne's methods—he took Dani's sword from her and would cheerfully relieve me of my spear if he thought he could—but he and his men perform a dangerous and much needed job for this city.

You did. And loved every minute of it. You are every bit as much a beast as you accuse me of being.

I shake my head violently, as if I might manage to expel the Book from my skull.

I'm in control, the *Sinsar Dubh* mocks in falsetto. *I make the decisions. Lovely MacKayla, when will you learn? You're the car. I'm the driver. But I can only drive you because deep down you want to be driven.*

I shiver, chilled to my soul. *I do not.*

I watched the Book "drive" other cars. I count myself lucky there are only two dismembered human hands in the street with me. I crouch on my hands and knees, head hanging down, eyes closed, trembling from the exertion of the awful things I just did and from self-loathing. Part of me wants to lie down right here and quit. I was so sure of myself, so certain I was in control.

And so unforgivably wrong.

There are only two ways an enemy can defeat you, Ms. Lane, Barrons said to me the other night, more lessons at the bookstore like old times. *You die. Or you quit trying. Then you die. Is that what you want? To die?*

I want to live. I have so much to live for.

I'm sure the man I killed did, too. My chest is hot and tight, my muscles locked down. I can't get a breath. I crouch in the gutter, trying to suck air, heaving soundlessly.

Get up, Mac, I can almost hear him growl. *Get the fuck up.*

The man orders me around even when he's not present. I hang my head and try willing my rigid muscles to relax. It doesn't work. I'm growing dizzy from lack of oxygen. *Can't breathe can't breathe can't breathe!* I'm starting to panic.

Sometimes if you get too focused on a goal, Ms. Lane, you make an unwanted element of it sticky.

Not getting it, I'd said.

Fear of the power you believe someone or something has over you is nothing but a jail cell you choose to walk into. By obsessing over freeing yourself from the Book, you become more certainly its prisoner.

I force myself to do the counterintuitive, the opposite of what I want: exhale instead of inhale.

Air screeches back into my lungs so fast I choke. I crouch in the gutter, sputtering, panting.

After a few moments I push myself shakily to my feet.

How did this happen? How did the Book gain control of me without me even realizing it?

I look around slowly. Commit my crimes to memory.

Bits of Unseelie and human flesh are scattered everywhere.

There is no piece larger than a tea saucer.

I sort through them and, after a time, gather the hand of the man I murdered, cradle it to my chest, and weep.

4

"Pain without love, pain can't get enough"

CHRISTIAN

It's summer in the Highlands, white and purple heather has taken over the countryside, carpeting the meadows and bens. Lavender thistles explode from fat prickly pods and pale pink wild roses tumble over rocky out-croppings.

The devil is in the details.

So, sometimes, is salvation.

I focus on the soft crush of grass beneath my bare feet, the wind in my hair as I run.

We race down the hill, my sister Colleen and I, to swim in the icy early-summer slate water of the loch. It's one of those perfect days, the sky a cloudless blue above a scooped-out grassy bowl that sprawls for miles be-tween the majestic mountains of our home.

Nothing compares to my Highlands, nothing ever will. The land brings me peace and joy.

Although I hear truth in lies, although I'm sometimes feared and the villagers cede me a certain aloof respect, this is where I fit. The Keltar name is known and it's a proud one. We're integral to our village, our people, feeding the economy when it wanes with work on our land and castles. We understand that when those in our care prosper, we're ten times stronger than we are alone. It's the meaning of the word "clan"—so much more than family.

Scotland is the passion in my blood. She is where I was born and will die, my bones planted in the cemetery behind the ruined tower ivy claimed, past the slab etched with Pict runes, but not quite to the tomb of the Green Lady, where the roots from the tree at the head of her grave twisted themselves to form a lovely nude moss-covered body with a fine-featured face.

Family is everything. I'll wed and raise my bairn behind the strong walls of Castle Keltar near the circle of standing stones known as Ban Drochaid, or White Bridge, whose purpose is known only to us and where magic beats like a living heart in the soil. I'll teach my sons to be druids like their da and granda before him, and my daughters to be like the Valkyries of old. I feel a keen sense of belonging. I know exactly who I am: Christian MacKeltar, descended from thousands of years of an ancient, revered bloodline.

The first of my clan walked the Hill of Tara before Tara was named. Before names were, we tilled the soil of Skara Brae, gathering stones to build enclaves for our women and children. Before even that we stood on the shores of Ireland in the churning surf as the clouds exploded with light and watched the fiery descent of the Old Ones from the stars. Bidden by these new gods, we removed to the Highlands to uphold the Compact between our races.

My ancestors' ghosts walk the castle corridors on the blessed evenings of the feast days of Beltane and Samhain when time is thin and reality liminal—my ancestors who embody duty, loyalty, and honor.

We are the Keltar.

We fight for what's right.

We protect and honor.

We do not fall.

When the Crimson Hag rips out my guts again and pain burns through me until I am nothing but torment, my flesh on fire with agony, every nerve screaming as my entrails are torn *again* from my ragged abdomen, I struggle to remain alive though this body of mine keeps trying to die because every time I die and consciousness slips away—I lose my Highlands.

Staked to the side of a rocky cliff a thousand feet above a hellish grotto, I breathe deep to smell the heather of my homeland, I run faster to feel the dense spring of grass and moss beneath my feet. I gather roses as I pass between bushes, and bloody hell—there was a thistle in that bunch!

I plunge into the icy waters of the loch, break surface and shake water from my hair. I throw back my head and laugh as Colleen dives in beside me, missing me by inches, drenching me all over again.

Below me, inside me, there's a pit that's dark and comforting and quite completely insane. If I sink into it, I can be free of all torture.

But I am Keltar.

I will not fall.

5

"We're building it up to tear it all down"

MAC

"You told them *what*?" Incredulous, I pace the rug in front of the gas fireplace in the rear sitting area of Barrons Books & Baubles, which is really Mac's B&B, but my name on the hand-painted shingle doesn't carry the same cachet. I turn and pace the other way. After what happened this afternoon, my nerves are raw. I can't deal with this. Not now.

He gives me a look. I feel it stabbing between my shoulder blades; the stress of that man's regard is palpable, even with my back to him.

"Your heels are damaging my rug. It's an eighty-thousand-dollar rug."

I say, "You like me in heels. Money doesn't signify anymore. And at least I'm not burning holes in it."

Does he smell the blood on my hands? Barrons's sense of smell is atavistically acute. I showered for an hour after I got home. I cleaned beneath my nails with a scrub brush until they bled. Yet I feel dirty, stained.

Still, I see the Guardian's hand, the silver wedding

band on his third finger, etched with Celtic infinity knots; a pledge of forever.

I found his wallet. I know his name.

I'll scream it in nightmares, whisper it in prayers. Mick O'Leary had a wife, a young daughter, and a newborn son.

"A wiser woman wouldn't remind me of that time. I'm still pissed about it."

The night Fiona tried to kill me by letting Shades into the bookstore and turning off all the lights seems so long ago. I was reduced to lighting and dropping matches all over one of his sixteenth-century Persian rugs in my desperate bid to survive. The way I feel right now he's lucky I'm not burning holes in the entire bookstore. The news he just gave me is unacceptable, and I've got fifteen minutes to vacate the premises before the event begins. He pretty much just said, *I've decided to put you under a microscope in front of all the people who might be able to figure out what's wrong with you, plus two of the Unseelie princes that turned you Pri-ya. So buck up, little buckaroo.* "Well, I'm not staying here for it," I say. "You're on your own with this one, bud."

Bud. He looks at me and I remember calling him that the night he showed up at the Clarin House, dwarfing my tiny room with its tiny bed, communal, impossible-to-get-your-turn-in bathroom down the hall, and four crooked hangers in the closet. My suitcase, so carefully packed with pretty outfits and accessories, had found a home in neither closet nor city. I wonder where all those clothes went. I haven't seen them for a while.

He'd reacted much the same then to my scornful appellation. Few call Barrons anything but "master" and live to tell of it.

Mockery gleams in his dark eyes. *Tread lightly, Ms. Lane. The floor upon which you walk is only as solid as the respect you cede it.*

The floor. I get a sudden strange vision that has nothing to do with the *Sinsar Dubh*: me falling forward onto the hardwood planks of my room that night, catching myself with my hands, rolling over and striking the back of my head, hard, and not caring. I was doing something . . . something that was utterly consuming. I frown. What? Looking at a picture of Alina? Reading a book about Irish history? Folding my clothes? It's not like I had a lot of fascinating choices in that tiny, cramped room.

How did I fall? Why? And why do I keep thinking about that day?

I have a fragment of a feeling, emotions sprung from an occasion for which I can locate no originating event. Exhilaration. Freedom. Excitement. Shame. Regret.

Normally that would bother me so much I'd go rooting around in my memory, but at the moment I have more pressing issues to deal with.

I shake it off and drop down on the chesterfield, glowering across the room at him. "You seem to have forgotten the small problem I have, Barrons. I'm hiding from all the people you invited here. I have been for months." The princes I can't even address. That he's permitting them in my bookstore offends me beyond expressing. "Why do you want this blasted meeting anyway? And why here?"

He cuts me a hard look. *See Mac cower. See Mac die.*

"Are you trying to piss me off?" I growl.

He gives me the ocular equivalent of a yawn. Only Barrons can pull off such a thing and still look menacing. *It's not as if there are any repercussions to consider. You wouldn't kill a scorpion if it was stinging your ass.*

I study my nails. There's a speck of blood beneath one. I don't know if it's Mick O'Leary's or mine from scrubbing so hard. He's wrong about that. I look up at him. "You have no idea what I'm dealing with."

Ah, such as a beast within? he mocks.

"Your beast is different." I continue talking aloud, refusing to accept the intimacy of a wordless conversation. We've had this argument. We'll continue having it until the day the king frees me. Neither of us will capitulate. I'm not sure either of us can even spell that word.

Perhaps not so very.

"Yes, but mine is more powerful," I say irritably. Powerful enough to fool even me—someone intimately acquainted with its seductive, evil ways.

His dark eyes glitter with challenge. *Care to test that, woman?*

The look he gives me sends shivers down my spine, and I feel it slip it into a gentler curve that achieves down-and-dirty doggie-style with sure, supple grace. There is no battlefield I prefer to the one I've found in this man's bed. We fight. It's what we do. I feel so much more intensely alive around him than I've ever felt with anyone else.

I'm obsessed and addicted and ripped-down-raw in love with Jericho Barrons.

Of course, I don't tell him that. Barrons isn't a pillow talk man. Sleeping with him, acknowledging our feelings for each other, has changed everything.

And nothing.

In bed, we're one couple.

Out of bed, we're another.

In bed, I steal moments of tenderness when sex has finally exhausted me to the point where I'm too bone weary to fret anymore about the enormous capacity for evil that's taken up squatter's rights inside me. I touch him, put all those things I don't say into my hands as I trace the red and black tattoos on his skin, the sharp planes and hollows of his face, bury my hands in his dark hair. He watches me in silence when I do, eyes dark, unfathomable.

I sometimes wake up to find he's pulled me close to him and is holding me, spooned into my back with his face in my hair, and those hands that don't speak like mine don't speak move over my skin and tell me I'm cherished, honored, seen.

Out of bed we're islands.

Ms. Lane and Barrons.

The first time he retreated into distance, it hurt. I felt rejected.

Until I realized I'd done it, too. It wasn't just him. Our boundaries seem sewn to our clothes; we can no more put one on without the other than take them off separately.

I sometimes wonder if our passion is so obsessive and enormous that we need distance between the bonfires. I'm a moth to his flame and it frightens me how willingly I'd burn my wings off for him. Destroy the world. Follow him to Hell. It's scary to feel like you can't breathe without someone. That a man has so much power over you because you love him as much as, if not more than, you care for yourself.

So I fly away for a while—maybe just to know I can—and he vanishes to do whatever Barrons does for whatever reasons he does it.

I always come back. He does, too. Actions speak.

I shift restlessly and change the subject. "You invite my enemy here. That's bullshit."

A Day in the Life: You search manuscripts for a spell that may not exist. You paint your nails. You clip your nails. Ah, let us not forget you examine your nails.

I scowl. "I do more than that. And leave my nails out of this."

You don't visit your parents. You don't go to the abbey. You're barely eating, and your clothes—

I cut him off by pretending to examine my nails again. This week they alternate black diamond, white ice, black diamond, white ice. The color scheme comforts me, as nothing else in my life is so tidily delineated. I'm acutely aware of the sorry state of my recent outfits and have no desire to hear what he thinks of them. It's difficult to care when you're always covered with yellow dust. He's silent so long I finally glance warily up to find him regarding me with an expression women have been on the receiving end of since time immemorial, as if I'm a species he simply can't fathom.

Do you think I can't protect you should you persist with your idiotic passivity?

Idiotic passivity, my ass. As today proved, activity is far more idiotic, and deadly. Is that why he arranged this meeting? To force me to be involved? "Of course not." I change the subject.

It's time. He says his next words aloud and there's a gentleness to them that undoes me. "You're not living anymore, Rainbow Girl."

I melt when he calls me that. There's something in the way he says those two words that makes it seem he's said a thousand and they all make me glow. It says he sees the pretty-in-pink Mac I was when I first arrived, the black, kick-ass Mac I've become (unless covered with Unseelie fleas), plus every incarnation in between, and he wants them all.

I *know* I'm not living anymore. No one could be more excruciatingly aware of that fact. It's driving me bug-fuck. Passivity isn't my nature and I'm choking on it, drowning in it, my balls held firmly hostage by a Book.

I stare up at him and tell him the words I can't bring myself to say out loud.

I killed the Gray Woman today.

A corner of his sexy mouth lifts. "Banner fucking day. About time."

I also killed one of the Guardians.

"Ah, he got in the way."

I have no idea what happened. I blacked out.

A human would be shocked, horrified, demand to know what happened. Barrons's gaze doesn't change and he asks no questions. He tallies debits and credits. "You took two lives and saved thousands."

Bottom line it all you want, the end doesn't justify the means, I say silently, pissed that he elevated the conversation I don't want to be having to a verbal level.

"Debatable."

I lost control of myself. It took me over and made me kill. Said I'm the car and it's the driver. The unspoken words hang like knives in the air anyway, cutting me.

"We train harder."

I hate mys—

"Never say that."

"I didn't," I mutter. Not technically.

"You are what you are. Find a way to live with it."

"Easier said than done."

"Someone told you life was easy. You believed them," he mocks.

"I just don't see why they all have to come here. Why not hold this little powwow at Chester's?" I change the subject swiftly.

Like a verbal dancer, he follows my lead, and I know why: as far as he's concerned the discussion is over anyway. He has the blood of countless victims on his hands, while I'm having a hard time dealing with one. To him, this day is no different than any other: I'm possessed by a malevolent demon and I sinned. Tomorrow I'll try again. I might sin again. I might not. But tomorrow always comes. For me and the demon. Despite my screwup, my action will ultimately save countless lives.

Barrons has the thousand-yard stare and conscience of an immortal. I'm not there yet. I don't know if I'll ever be there. I ended a life before its time today. A family man. A *good* man. I must find a way to atone.

"I have wards in my bookstore that neutralize the princes' power while within my walls," he reminds me.

"You're inviting my rapists into my home." I toss the dual reminder that he wasn't there to save me the night the Unseelie Princes captured me in the church, and that it's *my* bookstore, without inflection, still it detonates in the room.

Abruptly the air is so charged with savagery that I feel squished into a corner on the chesterfield. Barrons saturates space when he's in a good mood—not that I would ever really call any mood Barrons exhibits "good"—but when he's furious, it's hard to breathe. He throws off energy, crams the air with intensity and mass, forcing everything else to retract into itself.

"Or have you forgotten that little fact?" I want them dead. I think he should want them dead. I fondle the spear in my thigh sheath lovingly. "We could kill them together." I snatch my hand away hastily and busy myself plucking imaginary lint from my black Disturbed concert tee-shirt, which I'm wearing not because I've been enjoying their music so much but because it's how I feel. The images the *Sinsar Dubh* threw at me the second I touched my spear were graphically detailed and from this afternoon.

"You will not kill them when they come here. Nor will I." The three words are guttural, accompanied by a thick rattle in his chest. It's the sound of his beast trying to claw its way out of his skin. I can barely understand his last word. "Yet."

"Why?"

His chest expands so enormously it threatens to pop buttons on his shirt. He says nothing for a moment, face impassive, his body frozen on an inhalation. Finally his ribs relax and he exhales carefully. I admire his self-control. I want it for my own. I may be more sparing with mention of my gang rape in the future. Although I enjoy baiting this bear, I don't enjoy his pain. Just his fire.

When he speaks again, his words are precisely enunciated. "They are a known quantity, capable of controlling the masses. I've watched countless civilizations rise and fall. I've isolated seven components necessary to achieve the future I seek. Destroy the princes at this particular moment and it won't happen. They are currently linchpins. They will not always be."

The future he seeks? I want to know what Jericho Barrons plans, to be privy to his goals. I don't ask. He shares when he's ready and his reply was already generous for him.

And fascinating. I know what linchpins are.

When I was child, Daddy used to ride me around on his lap when he cut grass. I loved those hot Georgia days, drenched with the smell of a fresh mowed lawn, magnolia blossoms bobbing heavy in the humid, sticky air, a glass jar of sweet tea steeping on the front porch, near two ice-filled glasses topped with a sprig of mint from the garden.

One day I "helped" Daddy change the tire on the lawn mower and he taught me about linchpins. I think I fell in love with all things with wheels that day, sprung of a golden summer hour with the man who can always make me feel like both princess and warrior.

A linchpin is a fastener that keeps the wheel from falling off the axle. It's inserted crosswise directly through the axle's end, where it stays securely in place until manually removed. The end of the pin usually has a loop of metal so it's easy to pull out.

In a broader sense, a linchpin is a key component that

holds the elements of a complicated structure together. Some theorize if you can isolate the linchpin of a social, economic, or political assemblage, you can destroy it in one fell swoop with a minute nudge or adjustment. Conversely, if you identify linchpins and protect them until you've achieved your desired result, you can shape the outcome. It doesn't surprise me Barrons lives and breathes *The Art of War.* "I can kill them when they're not?" I want to be perfectly clear about this.

"The instant they're not, I will."

We'll fight about who does the honors later. I'll just have to make sure there are no humans in the vicinity when it happens.

"You could let Ryodan host this summit. At Chester's."

"And have your ghoulish army in attendance?"

"You could ward the club against them."

He snorts. "Now I'm your personal warder. You have no idea how complicated such magic is."

Actually, I have a fairly good idea. He hasn't died in a while and his chest is covered, both arms are fully sleeved, and half his back is tattooed with black and crimson protection spells. The magic in which he dabbles is dangerous. Speaking of magic, "Barrons, it's been three weeks since Dani disappeared. Isn't there some kind of spell you can do?"

"Ward this. Spell that. How did you navigate life before you met me?"

I shrug. "It's kind of like realizing you married *Bewitched.* Except not in the married sense," I add hastily. "But you know what I mean. Why break your back vacuuming when a saucy twitch of the nose can clean the whole house?"

"My nose has never twitched, saucily or otherwise. And that was an utterly absurd premise. The only price for using magic was compounded human stupidity.

Humans consistently engender chaos without violating alchemical principles."

"Oh, my God, you watched—"

"I did not."

"Yes, you—"

"Did not."

"You just said—"

"Inescapable pop culture."

"Oh, you *so* watched it." I imagine this big, barbaric man stretched out on a tangle of silk sheets, naked, one arm behind his head, watching the comic antics of Darrin and Samantha Stephens on a large flat-screen TV. The idea tickles me, turns me on somehow. It's so anachronistic, it makes me want to hunt down old DVDs, stretch out beside him, and lose myself in a simple show from a simpler time when the only price for magic was compounded human stupidity. Laugh together, do something mindless and fun. Then of course do something else mind-blowing. I'd love a few long rainy carefree days in bed with this man.

"Repetition of an erroneous assertion fails to alter reality. And you know we can't track her in Faery. That's why she went."

Great, now I'm hearing the theme song from *Bewitched* in my head. It's always a hard one to get out. "When she gets back, I want somebody tattooing her. The *instant* she gets back."

"Bloody hell, after all the grief you gave me. Have you forgotten our tattoos haven't worked right since the walls fell? Give it time. We'll find her. At the moment the most pressing matter on our agenda is this meeting."

The meeting. I shift restlessly and my amusement vanishes just like that. "Are you sure we can't move it somewhere else?"

"It happens here. You will attend."

He asks little of me and gives much in return. I can't imagine the world without him and don't want to. Once, I almost destroyed it because I believed him gone forever.

"Aye aye, master," I mutter crossly.

He smiles faintly. "You're learning, Ms. Lane, you're learning."

Katarina McLaughlin, Rowena's replacement as head-mistress of the abbey, is the first to arrive.

The slim brunette's patient gray gaze searches mine the instant I open the door, reminding me why I've been avoiding her. Her talent is emotional telepathy and I have no idea how deep she can go. In nightmares, she peels me like a pearly onion and reveals the rotted inner bulb.

I hold my breath while she completes her inspection. Does she sense the malevolence of the *Sinsar Dubh*? The guilt of my afternoon murder?

"How are you, Mac? We've not been seeing much of you lately." *You weren't at the abbey, defending us,* is the message I think I read unspoken in her eyes and am shamed by it. But I've been a little paranoid lately so I'm probably wrong.

I breathe a little easier. "Good, Kat. You?"

"Why weren't you at the abbey the night we battled the Hoar Frost King? We could have used your support, and that's for sure," she says in her soft, Irish lilt.

There it is, the knife through my already perforated heart. Nice to know I wasn't being paranoid, after all. Leave it to Kat to be so direct.

"Barrons and I were in the Silvers. I didn't get word until it was over. I'm so sorry, Kat."

Her sharp gaze moves from my left eye to my right and back, and she slowly nods. "It's as well. We lost many of our sisters that night. We can't afford to lose you. Speaking of losing—have you seen Dani? She's not been by the abbey since we defeated the Hoar Frost King. I've had girls out searching but they've found no trace of her and I've not seen a single of her papers. It's as if she's simply vanished."

I don't bat a lash. "I thought she was staying with you."

"We were arguing that night about where she should live. I believed she was trying to make a point by staying away, but the longer she's gone the more I worry. These are dangerous times, even for her. Would you mind keeping an eye out? And if you see her, tell her she's sorely missed. I want her to come home."

"Of course." I want her to come home, too.

"I'm hoping you'll drop by the abbey sometime, Mac. Spend a night with us, or a week if you've the mind. I've been wanting to hear the tale of how you managed to bring the *Sinsar Dubh* to us." She pauses then adds, "There's another thing I'd like to be discussing with you, if you've the time. About Cruce. Seeing how you know more about Fae princes than any of us."

"His cage is holding, right?" That's another of my recurring nightmares. Cruce gets out, somehow turns me Pri-ya again, and I run off with him to another world where we get down to populating it with little book-babies. Seriously. Books with feet and arms that cry all the time and want some kind of milk I don't have. My dreams have been beyond warped lately.

"Of course." She pauses again. "But there are other concerns I'd prefer to discuss in private. If you'll just come to the abbey, you'll see what I mean. This thaw . . . I thought when the fire-world threatening our home was gone . . . och, but then it didn't and it turns out it wasn't . . ." She trails off and for an instant her composure slips.

I glimpse an unexpected uncertainty in her and think, Oh no, not her, too. Coming into sudden power can do funny things to you if you care deeply about the world around you, and we both do. It's like suddenly getting a Murcielago LP 640, V-12 with a testy clutch when you're used to a six-cylinder Mercedes. You drive badly at first, jerky on the gas and brake, don't trust your own feet, sometimes even rear-end the folks in front of you when you try to start from a stop, until you get a feel for it. Or, like me today, crash into a wall and decimate whatever's in the way.

"Kat, what's wrong at the abbey? What's going on?"

"You'll just have to—" She glances past me. "Barrons."

"Katarina."

I feel his energy behind me, sexual, electric. Every cell in my body comes alive when he's near. He moves past us, into the alcoved entry of the bookstore, and I shiver with desire. My need for sex seems directly proportionate to how much emotion I repress, and I'm repressing violently today. When I first came to Dublin, I talked and probed and poked into everything, splashed my feelings all over the place, like the rainbow colors of my wardrobe. Now I wear black and let almost nothing I feel show.

Until Barrons undresses me. Then I explode. I vent the fire and fury of everything I feel on him and he blows it right back at me, a hot, dangerous sirocco that levels and reshapes, and it binds us in a sacred place that needs no sun in the sky, no moon or stars. Just us.

The bell tinkles as he opens the door. I love that sound and imagine it chimes *Welcome to Mac's home* each time it rings.

"The Unseelie Princes will be coming back with him," I warn Kat as I watch him go.

"And one Seelie Prince who is fool enough to claim to be king," Barrons growls as the door closes behind him.

"Can he really control them?" Kat asks.

She's visibly nervous. I don't blame her. The Unseelie Princes are deadly. The two joining us today rode the Wild Hunt in ancient times with two others of their kind, and became renowned far and wide as the fabled Horsemen of the Apocalypse. Cruce is War. I suspect Christian is becoming Death, which means Pestilence and Famine are soon to be my houseguests. Lovely. "He says he can keep them neutralized inside the store."

Kat says flatly, "You do realize he's not there, right?"

"Excuse me?" The man is certainly "there" enough for me. All six feet three of him and two hundred forty-five pounds of dense, solid, rough-and-ready muscle.

"Barrons. He's like Ryodan. I feel nothing when I reach for either of them with my gift. It's more than a void of emotion, there is no existence there. The space they occupy is blank."

"Maybe they can block you. Erect a shield around themselves. Barrons knows wards like nobody's business." Okay, he seriously needs to teach me that trick. I'm blocking with everything I've got, yet I suspect if Kat decided to probe me, I'd be in a world of trouble.

"I can also discern the presence of wards, Mac. Nothing just walked out that door. A complete absence of anything recognizable as life."

"Perhaps their wards are beyond our perception." I want to get off this topic of assessing people with her gift. I don't want her to think about doing it to me. "Kat, I'd love to come to the abbey. How's next weekend?" I'll find some excuse or another to no-show. I take her arm and begin gently steering her back and up the stairs, to the tables Barrons arranged for the meeting. "Hey, would you like something to drink? I've got soda, sweet tea, and water. I even brought some milk back last time I went through the Silvers," I lie. Barrons brought it from Chester's and I feel a little guilty getting so many perks. But not too guilty to drink it.

"Milk? Does it taste like ours?"

"Sure does. A little creamier."

"I'd love a glass!" she says, and we both laugh because the things we used to take for granted are now luxuries. That's the way it goes when the world falls apart.

You never appreciate what you've got till it's gone.

Barrons Books & Baubles has spatial issues. I suspect the Silver connecting the store to hidden levels beneath the garage where Barrons has his lair is partially responsible, but I doubt it's the only thing affecting this particular point of longitude and latitude. I sometimes dream an ancient god or demon coils slumbering in the foundation.

BB&B is four stories most days but other days five, and on rare occasions lately, seven. On Tuesday the mural on the ceiling was roughly seventy feet above my head, today it seems a quarter mile, minuscule in the distance. The harder I try to focus on it, the more difficult it is to see. I don't understand why anyone would paint such a blurry scene on the ceiling. I used to ask Barrons about it but never got an answer. One day I'll hunt down construction scaffolds so I can lie on my back beneath it and figure out what the darn thing is.

During my first months in Dublin, I stayed in the residential half of the bookstore and grew accustomed to my borrowed bedroom shifting floors. It even got to the point where hunting for it was kind of fun.

I expect nothing to be easy in these walls. And here is where I've known the finest hours of my life.

I stand with Kat at the balustrade that overlooks the

bookstore, facing the front entrance. The main room is about a hundred feet long by sixty feet wide. The upper floors are half the depth of the store, accessed by an intricate, curving, red-carpeted double staircase that reminds me of the Lello bookstore in Portugal. On the upper levels are a fabulous array of antiquities and treasures in glass cases or mounted on a wall. Here a plaque of the Green Man sees all, there an ancient sword shines above a war-battered, tarnished shield. I sometimes wonder if all these "baubles" are really Barrons's possessions collected during various centuries of his life.

Gleaming bookshelves line the perimeter walls from base to cove molding. Behind elegant banisters, narrow passages permit access, and polished ladders slide on oiled rollers from one section to the next.

As I gaze down, to the right is the magazine rack, fully stocked with last October's editions near more freestanding bookcases. To the left, the old-fashioned cash register sits waiting to ring up a sale, silver bell tinkling, and there's my pink iPod on a Bose Sound-Dock ready to play "Bad Moon Rising" or "Tubthumping" or "It's a Wonderful World."

Or maybe "Good Girl Gone Bad."

When the Unseelie Princes enter, flanked by Barrons and Ryodan, I inhale sharply and go rigid.

CRUSH THEM DESTROY THEM IMPALE THEM ON POLES, my inner *Sinsar Dubh* trumpets.

I close my eyes and dredge up one of the tricks I've learned. Occupy my head so thoroughly with something else that the Book can't get through.

When I was young Daddy used to read poems to me. The more lyrical and musical, the more I'd enjoyed them, and I guess I always had a morbid bent, and he must have, too, because he'd indulged me, on soft summer evenings in the kitchen while Mom did dishes and listened, shaking her head at our choices. I'd understood little of the meaning, just liked the way the words flowed. "The Cremation of Sam McGee" had charmed me. I'd found "A Dream Within a Dream" hypnotic, "The Bells" mesmerizing, I'd obsessed over T. S. Eliot's "Ash Wednesday" and in seventh grade recited "The Raven" for a school project, briefly earning for myself the label of nerd until I'd taken extreme fashion measures to change that. Now, looking back, I can see it was a grim choice, but at the time, grief and brutality had possessed the cartoonish proportions of childhood. It had taken weeks to commit the many complex stanzas to my brain.

Remember what the princes did to you, sweet thing, how they ripped you apart and turned you into a mindless animal. As if I could ever forget, the *Sinsar Dubh* slams me with images so graphic they give me an instant headache.

I block them, focusing instead on how Daddy taught me to break down the poem to memorize it: eighteen stanzas of six lines each, most comprised of eight syllables with a hypnotic placement of stressed syllables followed by unstressed. Trochaic octameter was what he'd called it. I only knew it was fun to say and he was proud of me for learning it, and I'd have done pretty much anything to make Jack Lane proud.

Once upon a midnight dreary, while I pondered, weak and weary, over many a quaint and curious volume of forgotten lore—

Break them, the Book demands, *force them to their knees before you, make them call you Queen.*

While I nodded, nearly napping, suddenly there came a tapping, as of someone gently rapping, rapping at my chamber door.

The rhythm of the poem captivates me as it always did, and I feel like a child again, whole and good and loved.

"'Tis some visitor," I muttered, "tapping at my chamber door—only this and nothing more."

Unlike Poe, I don't have to open the door. I can slide the dead bolt.

I keep reciting until at last there's blessed silence. Only then do I open my eyes.

"What on earth?" Kat murmurs beside me, staring down.

Gone are the wild, naked, primitive princes, with kaleidoscope tattoos rushing beneath their skin and mad, iridescent eyes.

They've civilized themselves.

In their place stand two black-haired, dark-eyed males that exude power, lust, and otherworldly magic. Torques of the royal Unseelie House glitter like diamond-crusted obsidian at their necks. I know how icy those torques are to the touch, how they vibrate with a hypnotic guttural cacophony, while the torques of the Seelie House croon an irresistible, complex symphony.

No longer do their heads swivel in an eerie, inhuman fashion; they have adopted human mannerisms and movements right down to the smallest nuance. The black wings I felt closing around my naked body as I died a thousand deaths beneath them are gone, concealed by glamour.

"I thought they were at war with each other," I say.

Kat says, "I thought they were insane, terrifying and revolting. We were both wrong. They recently joined forces. I hear the Crimson Hag has them worried."

"Christian," I murmur, and try hard not to think of what he must be enduring.

"He saved us, you know. Possibly the world. Dani was hesitating, trying to decide between her *sidhe*-seer sisters and the Hoar Frost King. It would have destroyed her to carry the deaths of our entire abbey on her conscience. His sacrifice spared her that horror. We owe him a tremendous debt."

"Any word on Christian's whereabouts?"

"His uncles are searching. All of us at the abbey are eager to help mount a rescue, if they find him."

Although it horrified me that he'd given himself up to the Hag, it also relieved me because it meant the man I knew was still in there, despite the madness. Deep down, he still cared about the world around him. I made a mental note to ask Barrons to aid in the search. He could lean on Ryodan to enlist some of the Nine to go scouting. We couldn't just leave Christian out there, being tortured and killed over and over. We owed him rescue for the sacrifice he'd made. What he was suffering in the Hag's sadistic hands would only drive him deeper into Unseelie madness. We needed to save him before he lost all trace of his fundamental humanity.

The princes ascend the stairs, identical but for a few inches' height difference. I realize I'm looking directly at them without weeping blood. I glance at Kat to see if it's just me or if she, too, can regard them directly. She can. And is—with fascination.

"They've fed enough to gain control of themselves," I say softly. When they first arrived in Dublin they were like rabid animals from long confinement and starvation, and flat-out terrifying. "They're studying us, learning from us." I get it: pacify the sheep before the slaughter. A panicked kill makes for a soured stew. These two, the worst of the Unseelie, are now the ultimate bad boys. Women will flock to them, lemmings on a suicide march over a cliff.

These are my rapists, the ones that turned me inside

out, ripped my mind from my body and shredded it. They are also, unfortunately, hot as hell.

I want them dead.

Yes, yes, yes, KILL, the Book surges to life again.

Ah, distinctly I remember, it was in the bleak December; and each separate dying ember wrought its ghost upon the floor.

The rhythm takes over. I roll the many internal rhymes and dazzling alliteration over my tongue silently while I assess the princes, building the syllables, brick by brick, into a mental wall.

My rapists are dressed like Barrons. Sleek. Masculine. Sexy. It pisses me off.

"Son of a bitch," Kat says softly. Kat doesn't curse. "Do you know how my girls will react to them? Cruce is bad enough."

"Son of a bitch," I agree.

Behind the balustrade, four long cherry tables make a square.

The Unseelie Princes take one side.

Barrons, Kat, and I take the opposite.

It's all I can do to not lunge across the space separating us and attack them. Two things stay my hand: Barrons wants them alive, and I'm afraid I'll black out again. Kat is vulnerably human.

After a few moments, Ryodan drops into a chair beside us, sandwiching Kat and me between a gentle hum of power. He pushes a hand through thick, dark hair, cut close at the sides, and assesses me with that clear, analytical gaze of his. I meet it impassively. His chiseled features are untouched by lines, and I'd guess him frozen in time, however he stopped aging, at about thirty, plus however many thousands of years he's actually lived.

Like all of Barrons's men, he's powerfully muscled and sports multiple scars, the most prominent running from his jaw down his neck and over his chest. He appreciates the finer things in life and pursues them without scruple. I want to know the history these men will never tell me. Although an animal exists beneath each of their skins, Ryodan hides his the best. He's the businessman of the Nine of whatever-they-are, managing financial concerns, maintaining their vast empire.

Barrons is the taciturn, primal leader of their small immortal army, the one to whom they all answer. He usually lets Ryodan do his talking. Probably because Barrons knows he would lose patience the moment one of his orders isn't instantly obeyed and butcher everyone in sight. Ryodan excels at chess, crushes his opposition in five or fewer moves. Barrons eats the board, with blood for ketchup.

"Got a lot of Unseelie outside the bookstore, Mac," Ryodan says.

"Got a lot inside Chester's," I rejoin coolly.

"He understands our needs," one of the Unseelie Princes says.

"They don't trail me everywhere I go," Ryodan says.

"Then again you understand them, too, from personal experience," the prince reminds me silkily.

I ignore it. "Guess you don't smell as sweet," I tell Ryodan.

"Or as rotten," he returns.

"I've been testing wards on them." Barrons puts the issue to swift rest.

Ryodan laughs but lets it go.

The six of us sit eyeing one another in silence. There is no air in the room, only hostility and rage. I breathe shallowly of it and slide my hand to the comforting hilt of my spear. And snatch it away, assaulted by horrific images again.

"You will remove the ward that prohibits our sifting, or you will take away her spear." The taller of the princes speaks to Barrons, but his gaze is moving, hot, sexual, devouring, over my body.

Barrons goes so motionless next to me that for a moment I'm not sure he didn't just vanish in that stealthy way of his. I inhale shallowly, wondering if this meeting is going to end before it even begins.

Then Barrons says softly, carefully, "Ms. Lane." I feel the tension in his body, mirroring the same tightly coiled rage in mine.

"I'm not giving you my spear," I say just as softly. "*It* can deal with it." Time was, they could weave the illusion that they'd taken it from me, but I got wise to their trick and it doesn't work on me anymore.

"I am not an 'it.' I am Prince Rath of the second royal Unseelie House created," the tall Unseelie says coldly. "My brother is Kiall, from the third. Once, you whimpered our names. As you begged us for more. Without the spear you are nothing. Human. Weak."

Neither Barrons nor I speak for a moment. Then he says, tonelessly, "I'm not removing the wards."

"Fine, they can leave," I say just as tonelessly. I am nothing, my ass. They don't know about my inner psycho.

Barrons shoots me a look. I feel it on my ear, needling me to turn my head.

"Look at me," he commands.

I scowl but look.

You said you trusted me to protect you. If I drop the ward, others can sift in. Unacceptable risk. Do not push me. My beast wants them dead.

Well, at least our beasts are in agreement, I retort saccharine-sweet. Seething, I slip the spear from my

sheath and slap it into his palm before I get any more
reminders of this afternoon.

Rath and Kiall rustle and chime in the bone-chilling,
inhuman fashion that had been their only mode of communication when they first arrived in Dublin, crazed
with hunger. I'd felt that chiming deep in my bones, as
my mind slipped away. When Barrons hands the spear
to Ryodan, who tucks it beneath his jacket, they resume
their polished facade.

"Right, *he* can have it but I can't," I grouse.

"*He* does not consider past *minor* insult bar to future
gain. Women are weak that way. Valuing things that
mean nothing at all. Lamenting events they clearly enjoyed," Kiall says, raking me with a knowing, intimate
sneer. "What was lost that night? Nothing. What was
gained? An experience beyond compare. Your human
women kill each other for our amusement, to eliminate
the competition for the privilege of such a night with
us."

I don't know who goes more rigid beside me, Kat or
Barrons. The room is a volcano waiting to blow.

I inhale, count to ten, exhale. At some point, when
I've mastered my inner demon, I'll pay a visit to the
gothic monstrous mess of a mansion on the outskirts of
Dublin where the princes have surrounded themselves
with worshippers. With my spear. And those women
that chirp bright, vapid nonsense like "See you in
Faery" will stop killing each other to lose their sanity in
a monster's bed.

When R'jan, the Seelie Prince who claims to be the
new king, enters, the Unseelie snarl like feral beasts.

R'jan reminds me of V'lane, before he dropped the
mask, revealing his true Unseelie self, Prince Cruce.
Gold-dusted skin pours like velvet over a powerful
body; he has the face of a stunning, imperious Arch-
angel. Long blond hair falls past his waist, unbound.

He, too, has modified himself into something elegantly human, with fawn leather pants and dark boots, a creamy cashmere sweater, a gold torque at his throat. R'jan laughs and dismisses his dark brothers with a regal, condescending wave as if shooing a bothersome fly from a banquet surely called in honor of him.

The Unseelie leap from their chairs, Barrons rises, Ryodan joins him, and for a moment all the males in the room posture, assessing, debating the pleasure to be gained from turning this room into a slaughterhouse against whatever it is they're after that made them agree to this meeting. Just when I'm certain they're going to succumb to savagery, Kat and I are going to be sprayed with blood and bone fragments, and I'm going to end up taking back my spear and using it after all, Barrons growls, "You will all sit. Now."

No one moves. I laugh softly. That's a mistake.

Ryodan is abruptly gone.

When he reappears, he's holding R'jan from behind, a scarred forearm around the Fae's throat. He presses his mouth to the prince's ear and says softly, "Need I remind you what I did to Velvet."

R'jan hisses.

"He said sit. He doesn't repeat himself. Nor do I."

When Ryodan shoves him away, R'jan drops down on the third side of our square, eyes blazing with challenge and hatred. Kiall and Rath slowly take their seats with elaborate indolence, as if they do so because they wish to and for no other reason.

I eye the fourth side, wondering who else we could possibly be waiting for. When our final guest walks up the stairs and sits at our table, it's my turn to bristle.

I know the face of an O'Bannion mobster when I see one. I helped kill two of them. Our final guest is black Irish with a light complexion, thick, dark hair and eyes, and the blood of a distant Saudi ancestor in his veins.

Broad-shouldered and handsome in a rugged, outdoors way, he moves with long-limbed grace.

Kat half rises, looking ashen. "Sean?" she says. "What on earth are you doing here?"

I glance between the two. I don't need a *sidhe*-seer gift to know there's deep emotion between them.

"Yes, what is an O'Bannion doing here?" I say.

"The name is Sean Fergus Jameson," the man says in a thick Irish brogue.

"First cousin to Rocky O," Ryodan says. "He tends to omit his surname in certain quarters."

"Why is he here?" Kat says again, resettling slowly.

Ryodan says, "You're looking at the three primary suppliers of goods in this city: myself, the princes, and the black market—like his fathers before him, also known as Sean O'Bannion. Seems your boy learned a trick or two working in my club, little cat. Bribed my suppliers. Got himself into the game."

"Only because you were charging half an arm and most of a leg for a simple meal," Sean says hotly. "We've women and children in our streets who've no way of paying such high prices. They were dying for want of milk and bread."

"You show your true colors, O'Bannion," Ryodan says.

"A good and honest heart?" Kat says sharply.

The look Sean gives her tells me everything: they're lovers, and I suspect they have been for a long time. How does he think to stand his ground against this kind of competition? He's a human among beasts.

Ryodan cuts Kat a hard, flat smile. "That's often how it starts. Just not usually how it ends. If the two of you had been talking about any of the things you should be talking about, you'd have known."

"You will stay out of my business," Kat warns softly.

Ryodan leans back in his chair and folds his arms

across his chest. "Start taking care of your business and I might. Business unattended is free trade."

"You had no right to force him to work at Chester's," Kat says. "The debt owed was mine, not his."

Sean gives her a quizzical glance. "Force? What debt? My working there had nothing to do with you."

Kat blinks and looks sharply at Ryodan. "You said the price was demanded of him, not me."

Ryodan lifts a brow and gives her a mocking smile.

"What price?" Sean says.

"I said, precisely, Katarina, that I'd had difficulty staffing lately, my servers kept dying, and your Sean was good enough to fill in. I also told you he was free to go. Both were true. From the first. When he decided to thieve on my turf, I fired him."

His tone makes it clear how lucky she is that he didn't kill him. I wonder why he didn't kill him. No one takes from Ryodan and survives . . . unless the cool-eyed manipulator has a long-term goal that makes him willing to suffer the poor fool's existence as Barrons does the princes.

"You pigs talk and talk and say nothing of interest to us. Too many of you here. Not enough of us. Or slaves," Rath says. "We demand more Unseelie at this table."

"Find another prince and we might take it under advisement," Ryodan says dryly. Cruce is locked down and the Crimson Hag has Christian. In other words, never going to happen.

R'jan says nothing. If any of the Seelie Princes remain, he wants no competition for the Fae throne.

Sean says, "Why is Katarina here?"

I say, "As headmistress of the *sidhe*-seers, she's the front line of human defense and protection." I don't add: and she sits on Cruce and keeps watch so he doesn't get out. I really hope she hasn't confided that to him. They say every person with whom you share a secret will inevitably share it with at least one more, that it grows in exponential leaps and bounds until the entire world knows what you wish it didn't.

Sean assesses me. "Why are *you* here?"

Ryodan replies, "She has her uses. Any more fucking questions, take them up with Barrons. You don't like who sits at this table, figure out how to get rid of them. But be careful, it's not hard to figure out how to get rid of you. Human."

Kat snaps, "You will leave him alone."

I glance at her but she's trying to send a silent message with her eyes to Sean. Unfortunately, he's now staring too fiercely at Ryodan to notice.

She exhales gustily and I echo it.

The males at this table are ruthless. The only way Sean can hope to compete in business with them is to be equally ruthless. As the princes adopted a degree of civility to optimize their survival, Sean will have to adopt a degree of barbarism to optimize his.

Leaving me to wonder the same thing I know Kat's thinking: how much of the man she loves will remain?

6

"I'm going be that n-n-nail in your coffin"

JADA

The woman moves through dark streets, thick with fog blown off the sea. Dusk cloaks her in mist and shadow as if she's a secret the night has sworn an oath to protect. Moonlight illuminates wet cobblestones and rain-streaked windows but glances off her as if deflected by an invisible cloak.

Like the Shades, she's a smudge in the darkness.

Born of long and unforgettable habit, she avoids the pale yellow pools of streetlamps.

Better to see than be seen.

Being heard is another thing. Sound skitters and reverberates, and unless one is a highly skilled hunter, it's difficult to secure the target in one's crosshairs by noise alone.

She can do it. She's as infamous as the legendary Queen's Huntsman. She's never missed her mark.

Her enemy isn't so skilled. The one she seeks tonight is sloppy, blinded by gluttonous appetite, but to lure it she's not enough. She needs an attractive, sexually viable man.

Stiletto heels that gleam silver kick gusts of fog into lacy, sharp-edged patterns as she strides through Temple Bar toward Chester's nightclub, where she will select her bait. She's dressed to kill, weapons concealed: gun strapped to her thigh, knives flush to her skin, a sexy chain of a belt that distracts the male eye as it swings at her hips, a lethal garrote. The ricochet of her shoes on pavement is loud, deliberate. She knows she's difficult to see and at the moment desires to be accessible.

Immediacy is efficiency.

Contempt for death is her way of life.

Nothing touches her.

To be touched is weakness.

As she turns down an alley, mist swirls back from long, bare, lightly oiled legs, the edgy hem and neckline of a black spandex dress, the supple body of a dancer, long hair pulled back in a high ponytail, the serene face of a stone-cold killer, before enveloping her again.

She's beautiful.

It's a weapon.

She has suffered the worst the world has to offer.

And thrived.

She's compiled a list of names.

And will hunt them one by one.

When at last the fog parts upon the face of her enemy, she will have no mercy.

This world had none for her.

7

"This night could almost kill you"

LOR

"Who am I?" the blonde kneeling between my legs demands.

I need to come so fucking bad my teeth hurt.

I know the answer she wants. She wants me to call her "mistress." Like she's the Dom. She's already tried to get me to say it twice, sneaking it in like she thinks I won't notice because of the mind-blowing stuff she's been doing with her lips and tongue and that flawlessly executed glide of teeth so few women ever master when giving head.

She's wasting her time. It's never going to happen. There isn't a submissive bone in my body. I'm alpha to the motherfucking core.

I pull her head from my groin and grin down at her. Hot, horny blondes are a dime a dozen at Chester's. Riots may have sacked Dublin last Halloween and a killer freeze might have shut the city down for a while, but it's rebounding fast. People have been flooding in, resettling both sides of the River Liffey, drawn by the thaw, restored power, and supplies, but most of all by the endless parade of sexually insatiable Fae that pack the bars and dance floors of 939 Rêvemal Street every night of the week, hunting human lovers. The hottest, most deadly nightclub in Dublin is bigger, better, and badder than ever: Chester's is Sin Central—if you want it, we got it.

"You're not *that* good, honey." I flash her a grin. My comment is guaranteed to spark one of two things: either she'll get up and walk out pissed or I'll get even better head.

I know by her confidence—and the hungry way she's been watching me all night—she's not walking.

She laughs and runs her tongue over her lips to make them even wetter, shiny with the spit of a pro and pre-ejac. I lean back against Ry's desk, since he's off at some meeting for a few hours, looking forward to her amped-up performance, watching her, watching the club through the glass floor beneath my boots, loving life. As long as women walk this earth, I'll be a happy man. If they ever get wiped out, I'm done. I'll go in search of K'Vruck.

She slaps the head of my dick then closes her mouth over it in one long perfect slide all the way to the base . . . does some kind of swirly thing, then an intense suck back out.

I nearly stagger.

Son of a bitch, she's good.

She has her hands on my ass, face grinding into my groin, my dick is down her throat, and I'm a frigging volcano about to blow. Problem is, I been ready for a good twenty minutes, but whenever I get close she mixes it up and shoves it out of reach. What was initially a turn-on has become a pain in the ass. Not to mention the balls. I'm beginning to think they might rupture. I'm dripping sweat and I'm not even the one doing the work, although I'm looking forward to getting down to it. The woman has one damn fine body.

I take her head in my hands and try to move her mouth on me the way I want.

She resists with a muffled laugh.

I pull her mouth off me and she looks up, smiling. Takes my breath away for a second. Her hair is a hot mess around her face, just the way I like it—bed-head always makes me want to fuck. Then again, pretty much everything does.

"Let me come, honey," I say. "There's plenty more after, if that's what you're worried about."

"Do I look worried? I know exactly what to expect from a man like you. Who am I?" She flicks her tongue over the swollen head of my dick.

I start to hit it, I'm so close, but then she does this twisting thing with her hands and mouth at the same time, and I get needles on my dick.

Pleasure killed by pain.

Velvet of her mouth.

Needles.

It's starting to chafe more than I like. And I've been known to play rough with the right woman. Or three.

"Mistress," she purrs. "Is it really so much to ask? For what I make you feel?"

I consider. She *is* blond with big, beautiful tits. Whole world knows I got a weakness for the combo. That's how I'd ended up in the boss's office, leaning back against his desk, leather pants around my ankles, buck-naked brick shithouse between my legs while the bass of Rob Zombie's *Pussy Liquor*—and when the hell is she ever gonna give *that* up? It's one of my finest skills and I haven't even gotten the chance to dazzle her—rumbles in the desk beneath my ass, pounding up from one of the subclubs below.

I love this place. One of our better investments.

"I'm giving you the best head you've ever had," she says. "Admit it."

Not a problem. I say so to every woman that sucks me. Women enjoy doing things they excel at, praise guarantees repeat performances, every repeat performance is more practice for the woman, which guarantees the next man even better head. Given how long I've been at this, and on how many continents, I'm pretty sure I've single-handedly improved the quality of head around the world.

"Sure, babe, you're the best. Head. Ever." Damn close anyway.

"Who am I?" she purrs.

I groan. "The bitch sucking my dick." We agreed on no names. She asked me to call her bitch downstairs when we were doing shots at the bar. Said it turned her on. Later, with a laugh, she switched it to princess. Now she wants mistress. High maintenance. Some women are worth it.

She cups my balls and squeezes, then begins sucking them with exquisite precision. All the muscles in my abdomen clench and I exhale explosively. I'm beginning to think this might be the best orgasm I've ever had. *If* I ever get around to the bloody fucking thing.

"You really don't get this, do you?" she says. Laughter tinkles and the hair on the back of my neck feels weird all the sudden. There's a darkness to the sound that might worry me if she wasn't so frigging hot.

Speaking of hot, I look down to see sweat running down my six-pack, dripping down my legs. I'm practically standing in a puddle of my own sweat. What the hell did Ry do? Crank up the heat in Chester's to a hundred? I'm burning up. Light-headed, like I have a fever. Which is impossible.

"Don't care. You're here. I'm here. Do that thing with your tongue again. The swirly thing."

"I'll give you a clue," she says, and somehow she's smiling while she's sucking and for a second I think I see rows of tiny needle-sharp shark teeth. Not what a man wants to hallucinate with a woman's hot wet mouth on his dick. I blink and wipe sweat from my eyes. Trick of the light. She has perfect teeth, movie-star white, framed to perfection by smears of crimson lipstick, most of which is all over my dick and stomach. Oh, yeah, I'll take a blonde with cherry red lipstick every day of the week that ends in *y*. Life is sweet. I laugh.

She cuts me a look then shoves me back on the desk and I'm cold where her mouth was burning, then she's on top of me, slamming down onto me, and I'm pushing up into her. I'm a grenade, pin out. Feels like my whole body is going to hit it, blow apart, come from head to toe. Bloody hell, sex has never been like this. I'm on fire, so frigging hot I'd swear the desk is burning.

Wait a second, it is.

Orange flames are licking up around us, like my sweat is some kind of gasoline sloshed across the lacquered ebony. We must have spilled some tequila. Must've been a candle on the desk. I'm sprawled on my back in fire and can't even feel it. She leans into me, joins me in the flames, fists her hands in my hair and we kiss.

It's unfucking real.

I half expect celestial trumpets to blare. I feel like my skin is melting and we're merging into each other. Strange shit. But my dick has never felt better.

"Who am I? Is it so difficult to give me such a tiny thing? A little respect. That's all I'm looking for, honey. I can give you so much in return."

Christ, she sounds just like me, right down to her inflection on the word "honey." I always get them to call me whatever I want. I'm always in control. Isn't much I like more than a beautiful woman tied to my bed while

I make her come till she passes out. So what's my problem? Like she says, it's a small thing. What can one word hurt? It isn't like letting a woman have the power for a change can bring about the end of my world as I know it, for fuck's sake.

I open my mouth and suck her tongue deep, grinding in, sliding out. I feel my dick inside her, and I also feel what she's feeling: me filling her, giving her all she wants except for this one tiny little thing that is so important to her for some reason. Maybe some man treated her like shit and now she needs to be called mistress to get back some of her own. Maybe I'm part of the healing. Maybe it'll make her come as violently as I know I'm going to. I like women. I *want* them to feel good. It's practically been my mission in life.

"Who am I?"

I try to shape the word twice and still fail. I'd honestly like to give her what she wants but submission just isn't the stuff I'm made of.

She clamps down on me and . . . aw, shit, she squeezes! She has muscles that could milk a herd of Holsteins dry. I buck and nearly get off but then she's soft again and I get the feeling she could do this all night if she wants. And this crazy babe might just want to.

"Mistress," I manage to growl. "Now make me come or get the fuck off me 'cause I'm jacking off."

"Tell me you want me more than life itself," she croons, all soft and sultry.

"Sure, honey." I've gone this far. If Ryodan ever finds out I called some babe mistress, I'll never hear the end of it.

"Would you die for me?" she asks breathlessly.

I'm beginning to see no matter how hot this woman is, despite her plentiful talents, she has serious-ass issues. Looking for some big strong man to play hero for her. Who the hell isn't? Every woman downstairs. I excel at the role. And I need to come. Simple enough exchange.

I grab her ass, grind up and drive deep. "Protect you. Rescue you. Guard your frigging honor if you have any left by the time I'm done with you, woman. Now *squeeze*."

"But would you die for me?"

I don't tell her I might kill her if I don't come soon. I might turn. She's kept me on the brink too long. I'm getting edgier than is safe with a woman. "Sure, honey. Whatever." She doesn't know I can't. She doesn't even know my name.

She pulls back and smiles down at me with rows of needle-sharp shark teeth.

Blond hair darkens to blood-black.

Red lips fade to white. Then ice-blue.

Flames leap up around us. Takes me a second to process—also blue.

Aw, fuck.

I stare up, a little slow to get it.

I'm too close to coming to think real fast. Hell, her tits are too far in my face for me to think real fast.

Unseelie. The bitch is Unseelie. I can't believe I didn't pick up on it. I'm not easy to fool. Well, sans blond hair and curves enough to happily smother a man.

She's dark Fae. Twisted buggers, one and all, some more than others.

And she wanted me to call her Princess . . .

Unseelie. Princess.

I narrow my eyes, staring up at her.

Nah.

The dark king never got around to making them. They're a myth. They don't exist. Damn good thing, too. The Unseelie Princes are problem enough.

Oh, honey, she purrs in my mind, *we certainly do. Trapped in a library for a small eternity. One of yours let us out. Good thing, too. Men have too much power on this world. We will fix that.*

"Get the fuck off me."

You called me mistress. You said you would die for me. I own you.

I laugh. "Yeah, right. Try pursuing that thought." I shove her off me but my hands go the wrong way, fly up over my head, and abruptly I'm slammed flat on my back, with both wrists manacled to one end of the desk.

Links snake around my throat.

My waist. My ankles.

Fuck me.

I'm chained.

I lunge up, testing the links, snarling. Magic doesn't work on me. Neither does glamour. Yet both seem to be. What the hell is going on?

We are a singular recipe. His final creation. Improved by the Sweeper. She smiles and there are those frigging shark teeth again.

I'm immobilized, pants at my ankles, dick sticking straight up, and this bitch has shark teeth. I'm beginning to think this might not be one of my finer nights.

"Say it again," she says, but now she's all icy, imperious princess. "Who am I?"

No way I'm saying it again.

Ever.

My mouth opens and it says, "Mistress," offending every goddamn fiber of my being. I think my balls actually shrivel.

She slaps me. Hard across the face.

"I'm going to kill you, you crazy motherfucking bitch," I say tenderly. My kind doesn't get loud when we're about to annihilate. We go soft and gentle. See us like that: worry. She doesn't know I'm one of the few in existence that can actually make good on that promise. She doesn't know who or what I am.

She'll be calling me master before she dies.

"Who am I?" she says.

I clamp my mouth shut and strain against the Fae compulsion, and still my vocal cords grit, "Mistress."

Oh, yeah, definitely killing her. Ten different ways, and slow.

"That's a good boy, Lor."

What the hell, she knows my name?

"Now we're *really* going to play," she purrs.

8

"This town ain't yours and this town ain't mine"

MAC

An hour into our meeting, we've got more problems on the table than I knew we had. Despite the bloom on New Dublin, our city has deeper shadows in which to die than ever before.

It's been an enormous test of self-restraint, negotiating concessions with the two Unseelie Princes that raped me; a Seelie Prince that's been shooting me looks like he wants to; Ryodan, whom I've never been able to get along with for more than a few sentences of conversation—oh, wait, I can't even do that; and the first cousin of the mobsters that put a price on my head. The *Sinsar Dubh* has been attempting to make its voice heard at every turn, but I pump up the volume on my seventh-grade recitation and drown it out.

A part of me wishes they'd all just stand up and battle to the death. Make it simple. Take control through bloodshed and war. I have no doubt Barrons would be the last one standing.

But humans would die, and in the Fae way of things, more princes would be born, or get transformed like

Christian, and we would end up slaughtering one another all over again, losing more humans every time.

I'm beginning to understand why Barrons wanted this meeting. Before the walls between worlds crashed, there was a system in place to run the city, the country, the world. But when that system collapsed, it was only a matter of time before someone or something stepped in and tried to become the new system. Though Barrons and his men prefer to wield power from the shadows, they'll step into the light long enough to reestablish the social order that best affords the existence they enjoy.

When Ryodan imparted the latest rough count of Fae and humans in Dublin, I was staggered. I had no idea how drastically our population was exploding. According to his sources, thousands more Seelie and Unseelie arrive in Dublin every day, intrigued by the news that the princes have settled here and the feeding ground is rich with humans willing to be enslaved.

The more Fae in Dublin, the more humans will follow, drawn by their power, sex, and ability to provide comfort and luxury—or at least the illusion of it—in a time of such hardship and food shortages. Our city is growing too quickly to be controlled by any one of the males at this table.

A shattered, rapidly growing world requires multiple fiefdoms to rebuild it into a unified territory before a single king or democracy can hope to take it over.

During the transition period, clever enemies work together, or there'll be no kingdom to govern. As each male in this room believes he's the one who will ultimately be in charge, they're willing to play nice until one of them decides the moment is ripe for a swift and bloody coup.

At which point everything will go straight to Hell again.

It seems a rather futile and endless cycle, either way.

Yet a truce offers the benefit of a period, however brief, of peace and—more importantly—the possibility that something might change during it, perhaps making it possible to tip the balance of things in human favor and get rid of *all* the Fae for good.

Even the one inside me.

For the moment, we concede that none of us can hold the population in check, so we've agreed to divide Dublin into territories and permit certain atrocities in exchange for a modicum of civility for the masses. Kat looks as miserable as I feel but there's no other way. Not yet. We justify our heartless calls by our commitment to one day defeat all our enemies so the people can live the remainder of their days in peace and prosperity.

We've become politicians.

Kat demanded the abbey be off limits to all Fae, and that Barrons and Ryodan immediately secure the perimeter with stronger wards, to which the majority agreed, five to three—then, of course, the Unseelie argued again for more Unseelie at the table so they could gain the upper hand, which, of course, the majority overruled, six to two, with R'jan on our side. The Unseelie seem unaware of what lies beneath the abbey walls. It appears the Seelie who were with us that night aren't talking. I pray it stays that way.

Rath and Kiall insisted their lairs be off limits to us, governed by their laws and none other. Any who enter belong to them. And all may enter if they choose.

R'jan demanded we recognize him as king of the Fae, but the Unseelie Princes instantly declared war against him and he recanted. For now. The three princes are a war waiting to happen. It's just a matter of time. Each will work tirelessly in coming weeks to pack the most Fae possible behind their claim for the throne.

The Song of Making could restore the walls between our worlds, shut them all out, and preclude possibility of war further ravaging our planet. I think I have a pretty good idea where it is. But my problem with doing anything to pursue it is twofold: the only one capable of using it is the concubine/Seelie Queen who's missing along with the king, and I don't dare go anywhere near the all-powerful song with the *Sinsar Dubh* inside me. I won't put that final, fantastical magic in its hands.

Deep down I feel the Book stir, sniffing around the edges of my brain, trying to skim my mind.

I swiftly bury all thought of the song in one of the many padlocked boxes in my brain and resume reciting silent poetry, vowing to never think about it again until the king has removed his parasite from my body.

> *And the silken, sad uncertain rustling of each purple curtain thrilled me, filled me with fantastic terrors never felt before . . .*

Ryodan lobbied successfully to restore the euro as the only acceptable currency, which baffled me at first. It couldn't be more worthless . . . unless every supplier of goods in the city agrees to provide for nothing but the euro. Then it becomes the only thing worth having all over again.

He argued that a unilaterally enforced currency was essential to achieving sustainable order, a point that wasn't easy to make with the three princes, as currency is an alien concept in their society. I agree it will restore a much-needed sense of normalcy to our city's inhabitants. I'm surprised the men are willing to give up the barter system with its immediate benefits for the chance to be king, but these are wild days and this summit attended by primal males that thrive in times of chaos.

Barrons says little. His presence says enough.

For the past twenty minutes we've been debating the finer nuances of how to get the money out there and reestablish it as the norm. I wasn't surprised to learn Ryodan cleared out the city's bank vaults in the early days right after the fall. He's always miles ahead of everyone in matters of business.

"What of the new *sidhe*-seers?" Kiall suddenly demands.

New? "Nothing about the *sidhe*-seers," I say instantly. "They are mine."

Beside me, Kat gently clears her throat.

"'Ours,'" I amend. "We already discussed that. You stay off their land."

He sneers. "It is not her group that concerns us. They are no threat compared to the other. I am surprised they have no representative at this table."

I glance at Kat, who looks as shocked as me. Chester's nightclub is the pulsing heartbeat of Dublin, and if there are new *sidhe*-seers in town, he knows about it. "Ryodan?"

Ryodan affirms it with a silent nod.

"There's another group of *sidhe*-seers in town?" Kat exclaims. "Why didn't they come to the abbey? We'd be happy to have them."

"They would not be so happy to have you," Rath mocks. "You are nothing alike. You are weak and pliable. They are steel."

Barrons says, "All *sidhe*-seers are off limits to you."

"Fuck you," Kiall says. "One of them infiltrated our compound and took out thirty of my finest before we were able to stop her. I keep her in a cage, happily mindless." He slants a look at me. "She sucks my dick at my command with the zeal of one I knew before."

Barrons's chest expands and I don't have to look at him to know his eyes are glittering bloodred. I see the change in the princes' faces across the table. Fury explodes in my blood so hot and hard, it hits my heart like a sledgehammer. Some days I'm made of nothing but triggers. Rape scars deep.

Destroy them now. You know you can, my dark companion purrs. *They humiliated and used you, made you feel powerless—you who possess more raw power than they could ever hope to achieve. Remind these pigs that the Fae have always been ruled by a woman.*

Sure, toss me a few crimson runes, I mutter at it. I'd kill to get my hands on those again, the strange binding runes it shared with me at critical moments, believing I would never figure out that I could also use them to seal the physical *Sinsar Dubh*'s cover closed. Until Cruce tricked me into removing them. I knew I shouldn't have pulled the damned things off down there in the cavern the night we sealed it on the stone slab. Or at least held onto a few for future use, rather than let Velvet sift them away.

I'd love to see if they'd also work on my inner copy somehow, but although the *Sinsar Dubh* goads endlessly, even saddled and rode me today, it offers me no runes or spells to use without price as it did before. A once-robbed John, it won't remove its wallet from its trousers again until it gets the action it paid for.

Nice try, sweet thing. NOT.

I pick up with my mental chant where I left off last time, muttering the fourth, fifth, and sixth stanzas of "The Raven." Beneath the table, I feel Barrons's hand move to my thigh, and in the strength of his fingers is his commitment to destroy them with me, the reminder to be patient. It cools my blood enough that I retain my impassive stare.

The Unseelie Princes hold a *sidhe*-seer Pri-ya. I wonder what her talent is, if they exploit it. I worry about her soul. She has no Barrons to rescue her. Inside me, the *Sinsar Dubh* falls silent. "Tell me about these *sidhe*-seers," I say to Ryodan.

"They're black-ops trained and militarily focused, led by a woman they seem willing to follow to death. Word is they connected after the walls fell. Some were soldiers, stationed in Iraq, others hail from Asia, skilled in martial arts."

"We want them *all* dead," Rath growls.

Before I can say it, Kat asks, "Have you met their leader?"

Ryodan says, "We've been tracking her but no luck so far. They speak her name like she's some bloody damned mystical warrior, protected by the elements. Their home was destroyed; they want a new one and intend to make it here."

I feel Kat's tension. I say, "You are in charge at the abbey. She won't take it from you. If we must enforce it, we will."

"I'm not so sure I'd be entirely sorry to see it go," she murmurs.

I look at her, startled, wondering if I heard her right. She's looking at Sean, her expression bleak. I ponder the irony that she denounced her mafia parents years ago to escape this very fate, yet now sits with us making barbarous laws in a barbarous time, enforcing them without mercy.

Black-ops trained. Mystical warrior. Lovely. Probably sporting egos the size of K'Vruck. Who knows what gifts they possess? It's possible that one of them, like me, can sense the *Sinsar Dubh* and she'll follow its siren song straight to my front door.

Distantly, I hear Ryodan and Barrons agreeing the princes may do whatever they want with any *sidhe*-seers who invade their walls, but those who steer clear are to be left alone.

I don't think this city is big enough for us all.

9

*"Oh, Death, you come to sting with your
poison and your misery"*

JADA

When she enters Chester's, both men and women pause
in conversation to turn and watch her pass. It might be
the body. It might be the walk.

It's definitely the attitude.

An enormous palace of chrome and glass, the underground club is a hot mess of humans and Fae, reeking of
sex, spices, and cigarette smoke, divided into countless
subclubs where anything can be obtained for the right
price.

Music breaks over her in waves as she transitions
from one club to the next.

She could find her own personal Jesus on the matte
black cement floors where hundreds of meaty, tusked
Unseelie that resemble rhinoceroses stamp the floor
with hooves and indulge their taste for voluptuous
women and Marilyn Manson; or do it her way, which is
all she does anyway, where Sinatra croons from speak-
ers mounted on the polished wood of a stately, old-
fashioned bar presided over by three enormously fat
Unseelie females with multiple breasts; or acknowledge

that she is, in fact, Titanium, as Sia belts out above a mirrored dance floor that pulses with flashing neon lights, crammed with young, mostly naked men and women, attended in air and on foot by golden, sparkling Seelie.

She scans bodies and faces, seeking the one she desires: the more beautiful, the better.

She would select one of the mysterious Nine that work behind the scenes of this club, but the monster she hunts may find them too barbaric or perhaps too dangerous to take the bait. Their formidable reputation precedes them into distant lands.

She has found mention of the Nine in millennia-old annals, tracked them into present times through paintings and photographs. She has identified six of them by name, knows a seventh only by his long silver hair and dark burning eyes. She found a very old portrait of him in Romania that astounds. She knows two of them are half brothers, with different fathers, although the world would never guess it by looking. She knows the sorrow the one she will permit to live may feel, but her ledgers must be balanced. She has been unable to cement either face or name for the remaining two into the meticulous compartments of her memory. The single time she saw all nine of them in one place, one was hooded, the other's face too heavily painted to see.

Knowledge is power.

Kasteo, Barrons, Fade, Ryodan, Lor, Daku.

She nearly smiles at the last name. He was once a gladiator for sheer love of the game, and in another century and land, an epic samurai. She anticipates their battle second most.

Their ways are as vile as the Fae, yet two of the six names she knows are not on her list. Two of them she will permit to live.

She hears and dismisses snatches of conversation as she passes.

"Who is she?"

"Never seen her before."

"Fuck, the bitch is hot!"

"You don't stand a chance, Bruegger. She'd tear you up."

"And I'd die a happy man."

"Think she's Fae?"

"Dunno. She sure as hell moves like one."

The Fae she has studied, as well, dissected and assimilated what she found useful. There are many of them on her list.

But she's not Fae. She's human.

She moves silently through the subclubs. In her wake, a man who was foolish enough to try to grab her ass as she passed clutches a broken and bloodied hand, and howls with drunken pain and fury.

This time she does smile.

No one touches her except in the clash of a battle she has chosen.

High above, behind the glass balustrade that shapes a perimeter walkway into an inner courtyard for the private upper levels, she spies the perfect worm for her hook and contemplates the anomaly: humans are not permitted up there. Only the Nine and their few chosen. Yet he is both human and up there. Unattended. Stripping and tossing his clothing over a chrome railing to a delighted crowd of women below.

He is nude then and she assesses him clinically. Yes, perfect.

As she approaches the glass staircase that provides access to the levels where the Nine are rumored to maintain their residences, in addition to the owner's office, the electronic heart of the enormous club, she processes the second anomaly: the stairs are not guarded at the bottom by two of the Nine, a minor challenge for which she was prepared. Inconceivable, were it not fact.

She would escalate to high alert, but she lives there.

Silently, without questioning her luck—luck always favors the arrow that knows its goal—she ascends the stairs.

10

---

*"There's a she-wolf in disguise
coming out, coming out"*

MAC

It's midnight, our meeting ended hours ago, and I'm alone in the bookstore. After Kat left with Sean, Ryodan said something to Barrons about cleaning up after the Hoar Frost King, which made no sense to me since the last of the ice melted weeks ago.

Barrons left to do whatever he does when he comes back with his heart beating, eyes brilliant, fury cooled. He won't have sex with me if he's hungry. I have my theories about why.

I once asked him what he ate and he said gently, *None of your fucking business*. In the grand scheme of things, it doesn't signify. He is what he is. You take it or leave it, and I'm not leaving. The man isn't vegan. He has a toothbrush. Life goes on.

After wasting hours poring over yet another tattered, disintegrating volume we brought out of the Silvers with a title that translates roughly as *The Fae Obscene*, I busy myself dusting and polishing shelves and counters, then check on the weapons I've hidden around the store. Anything to keep from thinking about this afternoon, and the terrible thing I've done. The terrible things I might continue to do unless I silence the Book forever. I consider going to see Inspector Jayne, learn the location of the O'Leary family, see what their needs are and fill them, but every time I begin to ponder it, I double over with guilt and grief, too sick to my stomach to move.

It's been a while since I tended my cache. I miss my weapons, but I'm not willing to carry them. After today, I'd rather not carry the spear, but I won't leave it lying around where someone else might find it, not even at the bookstore. Barrons despises the ancient Fae hallow because it could kill me. I like it for the same reason. A gun can kill you, too. You have to respect it.

I break down my Glocks, PPQs, my Sig and my Kimber, clean, reload, and rack. I save my Nighthawk Custom Falcon Commander .45 for last, because it's my current favorite, then move on to my rifles. I line them up on the counter, admiring them. I enjoy handling the metal and plastic, the cool iron of the bullets Dani and I made. I practice throwing my switchblades at a Bob I set up in a back room. I even polish my spear, holding it carefully, practice trying to block the horrific images the Book throws at me.

Eventually I run out of idle tasks and begin to pace restlessly, wondering why Ryodan didn't mention Dani tonight.

He must know she's missing. Surely he's looking for her. If she were here, she'd be arguing for a seat at our table. She's always battled for Dublin, made it her first priority, even when Ro was alive, threatening her, controlling her sword, directing it.

I used Voice on Rowena after I stabbed her, and know she used her gift of mental coercion to force Dani to kill my sister, but I don't know the details.

I thought I'd made peace with her part in my sister's

death. But it's one thing to sit in my bookstore, telling myself I can forgive her, entirely another to look her in the face, feel that forgiveness in my heart and communicate it to my arm—as the night we met for the first time since I learned the truth had proven.

I'd lashed out. Barely managed to pull back. I'm just grateful I didn't black out and lose complete control. I wonder why I didn't, what was different about the night I drew my spear on Dani and this afternoon when I drew on the Gray Woman.

"Alina, Alina, Alina," I whisper.

Sometimes I say her name in litany as if mere repetition might have the power to resurrect her from the dead. What no one tells you is that when someone you love dies, you lose them twice. Once to death, the second time to acceptance, and you don't walk that long, dark passage between the two alone. Grief takes every shuffling, unwilling step with you, offering a seductive bouquet of memories that can only blossom south of sanity. You can stay there, nose buried in the petals of the past. But you're never really alive again. Spend enough time with ghosts, you become one.

Still, I long for a summer day on the sand in Faery, a Corona in my hand with lime pulp dripping down the sides, near a volleyball net, even if only with the illusion of Alina.

Make it so, my hitchhiker purrs. *We can.*

"Been there, done that temptation," I mutter. "Get a fresh idea. The answer is still no."

The bell suddenly flies off the top of the front door in an explosion of hardware and screeching metal, shoots straight up in the air then crashes to the floor, where it gives a final, defiant tinkle.

I glance from it to the open door that used to be locked, startled and offended. I loved that bell. "You could have knocked," I say irritably to Ryodan, who's standing in the entrance. "I would have unlocked it."

"I assume you have the spear," he says.

"Of course I do." I hadn't breathed easy until Barrons handed it back to me when our meeting ended.

He jerks his head toward the door. "We've got problems. At Chester's. Now."

I'm not about to head off with the incessantly scrutinizing owner of Chester's only to have my dark parade fall into step behind us, and get slapped on a slide beneath a microscope again. The meeting tonight was bad enough. "You told me I could never enter your club armed, and I'm not responsible for your—"

"Cut the bullshit. The rules have changed. I don't care how many Unseelie follow you. I don't even care why. You get a free pass tonight. Move. Now."

I bristle. I don't take orders from anyone but Barrons, and I don't even do that well. I lean back against the counter and cross my arms. "Not until you tell me what's going on."

"We don't have time for this."

"I let you goad me into action once. We killed Barrons." Another thing I find hard to forgive.

"It was necessary to save your ass. What wasn't necessary was you waiting so long to obey me that you got me killed, too. Then you consorted with the enemy—"

And here we go. "Consorted? Really? What century do you and Barrons get stuck in sometimes? I did not have sex with Darroc. Furthermore, it's none of your business who I have sex with."

"As long as you're fucking Barrons it is."

Sarcastically, I retort, "I thought you killed each other's women, not took an interest in their fidelity or lack thereof. Speaking of fidelity and lack thereof, just exactly what are you doing with Jo, Ryodan? What kind of screwed-up wolf 'consorting' with the lamb situation is that?"

He makes a sound of impatience. "She wants. I give."

"I doubt it's that simple for her. Last time I was in Chester's—"

"Which was a month ago, and if you think that means I'm not aware you've become high priestess to the only caste of Unseelie that once attended the king in his private quarters, you're wrong."

That was what they were? How did he know that? Best way to stay out from under a microscope is to keep turning it around on the person trying to view you through it. "I watched the two of you together, and it's obvious she's in love with you—"

"She's a grown woman and understands what she can and can't have. I've never—"

"You just keep smashing through life, wrecking everyone else's to satisfy your own desires, don't you?"

"—misrepresented my intentions. You should talk. And there are reasons for what I do. Christ, woman, do you ever shut up."

"If you'd start talking about things I want to hear I might."

"You're pissing me off."

"You'd be surprised how easy it is for me to live with that."

He assesses me and I see him contemplating tossing me over his shoulder and loping away.

"I wouldn't if I were you. I'm a wild card, remember?"

He snorts. My threat rolls right off him. But I see in his eyes the moment he decides I'm on a bitching bent and not about to stop, that humoring me will take less time and ensure more efficient cooperation. "There's an Unseelie in my office. With Lor."

"So?"

"She's a *princess*."

I frown. "I thought the king didn't make any."

"You were wrong."

"Well, what's the problem? Throw her out."

"He's having sex with her. On my desk."

"Little confused here. What do you want me to do? Pop by with a fresh pack of Handi Wipes to tidy up your desk when they're through?"

"He's chained. Lor doesn't get chained. He chains." He pauses and I can see how much his next words offend him. "There was a time no threats to us existed on this world. The Fae changed that. It appears she may have turned Lor Pri-ya."

My jaw drops in disbelief. Lor is Pri-ya? The thought boggles the mind. "But Fae magic doesn't work on . . . whatever kind of things you are."

"He's calling her 'mistress.' Obeying commands."

"*Lor* is calling a *woman* mistress?" The ultimate caveman caved? Never. This could actually be a problem.

I lean back against the counter, study my cuticles, pretending to look bored, wondering what he wants from me and what he's willing to trade for it.

I want a favor owed from one of the Nine and have been trying to figure out how to get it for a while. Some things about me haven't changed in the least: all weapons—good.

There are numerous things I can imagine I might want at some point in the future that one of the Nine could easily accomplish. For now I'll take a blank check: one big, fat, juicy "I Owe Mac." Ryodan might be ruthless and drive me batshit crazy for so many reasons I could write a book about it, but he honors his debts.

"You don't want an Unseelie holding one of us Pri-ya. Besides, the bitch is in control of my office. Move. Now."

I still can't fathom what he wants from me. "Why don't you just kill her?" It's not like he can't. I know for a fact Barrons killed a Seelie Princess once. I was in his head, watching it happen. He shut me out before I figured out how he'd done it, what weapon he'd used.

He looks beyond me for a moment then cuts a hard look back to my face. "Until we know whether she can turn one of us Pri-ya, we're not getting close to her. None of my men saw through her glamour. Lor didn't know what she was until it was too late. There may be more of them walking around in my club right now. I need someone who can see what they are and has one of the weapons that kills them."

"Ask Dani. Doesn't she work for you?" I fish. I want to know if Barrons told him what I did, if he's hunting for her and how hard, if she's back and hiding from me.

His eyes change and I catch my breath. Crimson glitters. Not because of the Unseelie Princesses at his club, but at the mere mention of Dani's name. "I haven't seen her in twenty-one bloody fucking days. Not since the night we put the ice monster down. I've torn this city apart looking for her. Searched and interrogated and—fuck." A muscle works in his jaw. "If she's hiding from me, she's gone deep. She thinks she's invincible but she's just a kid. You."

I shake my head instantly, not about to confess my part in things with that glitter of crimson flashing. "We have to find her."

"I'm bloody well trying. At the moment we have a more pressing problem."

Time to negotiate. "What's in it for me?"

He flashes a mocking smile, and I don't know if he uses mystical powers of persuasion to pack his words with a little extra visual punch in my brain or if I'm just that visually motivated where certain things are concerned.

"Ah, Mac, consider what isn't: Barrons chained to a desk. Or maybe a bed. Getting fucked senseless." He pauses to lend his next words greater emphasis but I've already figured out where he's going and I don't like it one bit. "*Not* by you."

I'm out the door before he even finishes speaking.

11

---

*"Said he'd seen my enemy,
said he looked just like me"*

MAC

We step from the bookstore beneath a black velvet sky filled with stars and a three-quarter moon haloed in orchid. The Fae-kissed moonlight gilds the damp cobblestones an otherworldly silver and lavender.

New Dublin has skies so clear and pollution-free they compete with my rural hometown. Since the walls came down and Fae magic spilled into our world, things aren't the same colors they used to be. Now, new moon to full, the halo around it alters from pale gold to turquoise, orchid, and finally to crimson at the lunar peak.

In the distance I hear an unexpected noise: people talking, laughing, the rhythmic beat of music. I wonder if Temple Bar reopened tonight and inhale deeply of night-blooming jasmine drifting down from planters on top of the bookstore, reveling in the knowledge that Dublin is also blossoming, growing beautiful, *craic*-filled, and strong again.

"Last time you saw Dani," Ryodan says, as I climb into the passenger side of a black military Humvee. I have to shove two Unseelie that are blocking the opened door out of the way before I can close it. I hear thumps on the roof as they settle in.

Ryodan shoots a look of disgust upward then rakes it over me.

"Not my fault and I can't help it."

"You stink, Mac."

I grit my teeth a moment then say, "You said you wouldn't bring it up. *Any* facet of it." I used to be girly, pretty in pink, and smell good. I miss it sometimes. Especially the smelling good part.

"Dani. When."

"Thought you didn't repeat yourself," I say pissily.

He gives me a look.

"Not sure," I say.

"You really need to get over what happened with your sister." He drops it so flat and cold, it takes my breath away.

"What do you mean?" I say warily. How much does he know?

"Dani's involvement."

"How do you know about that? Did Barrons tell you? He shouldn't have. It wasn't his to tell. And if you ever tell anyone, I'll deny it," I say hotly.

I won't let the world persecute her for it. I've never told Mom and Dad, and I never will. In my more rational moments—like when I'm not looking at her—I understand Dani was the weapon and you can't blame the gun. Well, actually people can and do, which is why I'll take this secret to the grave. It was Rowena who loaded the bullets, aimed, and pulled the trigger. In my more rational moments I see Dani's pale face, eyes enormous, as she cries, "Well, why the feck not? I deserve to die!" And I want to take her in my arms and shake her, and tell her she doesn't, and to never say that again.

"I knew when it happened. We were watching her.

You tell anyone that, *I'll* deny it. If you tell Dani, I'll kill you myself."

Dark power surges to homicidal life inside me. A heavy, gilded book cover threatens to explode open. I drop down cross-legged on top of it, mentally muttering:

> *Open here I flung the shutter when, with many a*
> *flirt and flutter, in there stepped a Stately Raven*
> *of the saintly days of yore . . .*

Five stanzas later I'm composed enough to say, "You watched Dani kill Alina and didn't stop her?" Well, maybe I'm not so composed. I'm across the Humvee, half on his lap, and my hand is around Ryodan's throat, squeezing.

His fingers band my wrist hard enough to bruise. His other hand closes on my throat and there's about an inch between our noses.

Silver eyes stare coolly into mine. Being close to him is almost as disturbing as being near Barrons. He's every bit as sexual, though more contained. You don't feel like you're getting squished when Ryodan walks into the room. More like all your atoms are being caressed with a sensual electrical charge.

"Stop leaping to faulty conclusions, Mac. You'll fall. And I'll let you. I was watching Dani that night. She lost me. I didn't find her again until it was too late."

"Impossible. Dani can't outrun you." She was always bragging that one day, however, she would.

"She can give me a run for the money when she chooses."

"No, she can't. She used to complain about it all the time."

"Get your fucking hand off my throat."

"You first."

We drop our hands at the same time and I recoil to

my side of the Humvee. Belatedly, the full impact of what he just said sinks in. "Wait a minute, you knew since the day I got here who killed my sister and didn't *tell* me?" I say incredulously. "You let me waste all that time, hunting others?"

"Dani didn't kill Alina."

"She told me herself she did," I refute instantly.

"It's not what you think."

"What is it, then? Because the Unseelie that ate Alina sure thought so, too. They asked if Dani would bring them another 'blondie' like my sister." My hands fist at the memory, nails digging deep. I have Mick O'Leary's blood on my hands. I may as well have my own.

I search his profile. A muscle ticks beneath his left eye. Both hands are on the steering wheel, knuckles white. For an instant I see Barrons in him, a violently passionate man who controls it flawlessly, so the world thinks him ice.

"Answer me," I snap. "Did she or didn't she kill my sister?"

His only response is a rattle deep in his chest, the kind Barrons makes when he's deeply disturbed.

"Have I fallen down a rabbit hole into an alternative reality where you actually have feelings?"

He gives me a feral look and I glimpse fangs. He closes his mouth swiftly, is motionless a moment, then says carefully, "I protect the best and brightest."

IYCGM, Barrons's shorthand for If You Can't Get Me, is a number I can call on my cell phone that Ryodan always answers, but it's never proved useful. Eyes narrowed, I tell him that.

"Precisely."

"Do you sit around thinking up things to say to antagonize me?"

"Back at you, babe. When did you see her last."

Why doesn't he want her to know he was there that

night, following her? Why is he saying Dani didn't do it? What does he mean by "It's not what you think"?

Since he's already refused to answer those questions, I try another. "Why would you deny it if I told her?" When he says nothing, I say, "Quid pro quo, Ryodan. Take it or leave it."

"There are things Dani doesn't know about herself," he says finally. "It's a delicate situation."

I frown, not liking the sound of that. "What kind of things? What are you saying?"

"I answered your question. Answer mine."

I want to find Dani. Now doubly so. Is there something I don't know about the night Alina died? Something that might change everything? I should have enlisted his help from the beginning. The man has his ways. I sigh. "The night I chased her through a portal into Faery."

He grits, "Talk. Now."

By the time we get to Chester's, we're not speaking. Hostility is a wall between us. He blames me for chasing her through. He says if she dies, it's on my head. Like I don't know that. He insists I go looking for her. I tell him Barrons vetoed that for good reason.

He gets on his cell phone, which shouldn't work, and barks orders to his men. Says they're better off in Faery right now than at the club and orders them to start searching for Dani.

Then he's talking to Barrons and arranging for him to meet us at Chester's. I don't like that one bit. I have no doubt he's putting Barrons in the presence of at least one, perhaps multiple Unseelie Princesses, to encourage me to deal with the situation swiftly. It's one of his demands with which I intend to fully comply. I'm too starved for Barrons myself to tolerate the idea of another female touching him.

I stalk into Chester's, hand on my spear, a wave of

grim, ungainly, ghastly, gaunt, and ominous Unseelie trailing me like a morbid bridal train.

JADA

At the top of the chrome and glass stair, the woman pauses and looks down. The air inside Chester's just altered, charged by the presence of powerful newcomers.

She is highly attuned to subtle nuances from years of training and meditation. She has battled blind and deaf. And won.

These auras are far from subtle.

Three have entered from two different locations. She scans the dance floors, picking them out: there is the one called Ryodan, polished, bestial owner of this club; a second of the Nine known as Barrons, that keeps largely to the shadows, collector of antiquities and the most versed of them all in dark magic; and a young, blond woman that leads a small army of Unseelie as black as the shadowy nimbus that surrounds her.

All exude enormous power.

She glances at her bait, nude, perfect, and prime for the hook, then below.

There are possibilities. There are choices.

There is never emotion involved.

Two of the three who've entered are on her list but each will be a difficult kill, taxing her many skills, and to attempt it with both present would be suicide.

She plays to win at her choice of time, place, and method.

As they move through the subclubs, approaching her, one from the east, two from the west, she aborts her mission, slips down the stairs and exits Chester's.

She will reconvene with the others, dispatch tasks for the night, move to the next name on her list.

MAC

Once, 939 Rêvemal Street was an elegant aboveground nightclub frequented by Dublin's young, bored, and beautiful. It's now a fetish-filled underground orgiastic ball from a Daliesque painting.

The first time I came here was with Dani. It's gotten a lot worse since then. Or better, depending on who you are and what you want.

For the See-you-in-Faery girls, who call the Fae the new vamps, and will do virtually anything for the high of eating Unseelie flesh, the place is paradise. More Fae stake out their bizarre corner of the sex trade here every night.

As I push into the mass of people, laughing, drinking, eating things I try really hard not to look at, I toss coolly over my shoulder, "How do you justify the number of people who get enslaved and killed here every night in order to grow your damned empire?"

"Like prison camps, the darker side of Chester's could only be born in a vacuum of morality. I didn't create that vacuum," he murmurs behind me, close to my ear. His hand on the small of my back, he steers me around a raucous tangle of mostly naked people.

"But you exploit it. That's just as bad."

"We're all animals. Wolf or sheep. Shark or seal. And some are useless strutting peacocks."

I don't dignify his barb with a response. Let him think me a peacock. Better that than the *Sinsar Dubh* walking.

"I do nothing more than allow my patrons the right to choose which animal they aspire to be. If they say, 'Excuse me, Mr. Ryodan, may I be lamb to the slaughter?' I say, 'Good-the-fuck-riddance. Quit breathing oxygen someone else deserves more.'"

"You despise them."

"I don't despise them. I despise what any warrior would."

"Weakness? Not everyone can be as strong as you and me."

He laughs softly, near my ear, that I put myself in his category. "I despise their willingness to die. Humans come to Chester's of their own free will. I give them what they want. I'm not responsible for how fucking soulless their wants are." He closes a hand on my shoulder. "Slow down. You will first determine if there are other princesses in my club. Only when you've ascertained there are none will you ascend those stairs."

I bristle but he's right. I was hurrying, absorbing nothing. In my haste to eliminate anyone who could chain Barrons to a bed, I'd completely forgotten about searching for additional princesses.

I stop walking and go completely still—well, as still as I can with my train of Unseelie that never interpret my body language correctly slamming into me with soft puffs of yellow dust.

I push them away and permit the carnal madness of the place to wash over me, embrace it, open myself up and seek the lovely, cool *sidhe*-seer center in my mind.

Use me. I'm better, the *Sinsar Dubh* purrs.

I let Poe do my talking, refuse to engage. It pounces and runs with any answer I give, no matter how innocuous, like a psychotic ex-boyfriend craving emotional engagement. So long as I keep my mind occupied reciting the complex lines, I can't hear the Book as well, and it has the added boon of keeping me from replying absently, distracted by external events.

It used to be, when I first arrived in Dublin, that the presence of Fae made me nauseous, some more than others. I felt them in the pit of my stomach, a psychic acid. The afternoon I walked unwittingly into the Dark Zone adjacent to Barrons Books & Baubles, I'd nearly been on my knees puking for the final few blocks.

But repeated exposure to anything desensitizes—

repeated exposure to Barrons excluded, of course, which seems to have the opposite effect—and lately on the rare occasions I've removed my carefully constructed blockade against the incessant din and reached out to sense Fae, in the absence of crippling nausea, I've discovered each caste emits a different frequency.

In the acres of chrome and glass known as Chester's, beyond what the average human ear can hear, there's a secret symphony going on. It's the music of the Fae: the guttural, militant hum of the Rhino-boys; the piercing chime of the tiny, flying, puckish death-by-laughter fairies that look deceitfully like exuberant Tinker Bells; the ominous knell of the red and black uniformed guard that once served Darroc; the siren-song of Dree-lia and her new consort, who looks so much like the deceased Velvet he must be his brother.

I eliminate the diversity of each subclub until only one song remains: Seelie and Unseelie combined.

It's jarring, cacophonous. It gets on my last nerve. I wonder if they hear it, and if that's why the dark and light courts tried to eliminate each other all those eons ago—they literally couldn't stand each other's music. Humans kill for less.

If I could hear only the Seelie, it would be lovely. The Unseelie alone would be beautiful, too, in an eerie way. But together they chafe, antagonize, instilling and intensifying tension. I wonder how long we have until the light and dark courts war again, ripping apart our world in the process. For the moment, they're drugged on the endless availability of pleasure to be had. I know better than to think it will last.

I identify various castes and swiftly discard. There's at least one Unseelie Princess in here, and if I isolate her frequency, I can scan for more.

You'd think it would be so powerful, so unique, it would be easy to find.

It's not.

I stand there for five solid minutes grasping and coming up empty-handed. I begin to worry she can conceal herself even from me.

Behind me Ryodan and my Unseelie troop grow restless.

"Mac, time's wasting. What are you doing."

"I'm working on it. Shush." I just got a flicker of an anomalous frequency somewhere upstairs. The anomaly fades. Then it seems to be nearing.

"Do you feel something," Ryodan says suddenly.

Abruptly it vanishes.

"Mac, I feel—ah, fuck, where'd it go."

I think: What, Ryodan has *sidhe*-seer senses, too? Impossible. I sink deeper into my center, shed layers of muscle and skin, detach from everything and everyone, block out the world, block out myself. I become primal, ancient *sidhe*-seer without self, constraint, or definition.

Then there's something beyond the top of those stairs again, dark, chaotic and pounding, potently seductive, energizing, inflammatory: a version of Wagner's *March of the Valkyries*. From Hell. On steroids.

Once I've got it burned into my brain, ears attuned for only it, I let the physical world back in, become me again, resettling into flesh and bone.

And I realize why I had such a hard time pinpointing the princess.

I wasn't tuning myself out.

The same dark march is coming from me.

I open my eyes to find Ryodan watching me intently. "There is only one," I say, and begin pushing through the crowd.

There's a simple explanation, I decide as we ascend the stairs, then turn down a long glass corridor. A complete copy of the *Sinsar Dubh* is inside me. I possess all the Unseelie King's dark magic and spells from which he created his many castes. I probably sound like each and every one of them at varying times. I just never noticed it before because I had no reason to listen to myself.

Still, as I prepare to place my palm to the right of the door leading into Ryodan's office, I'm assaulted by a sudden image of whatever's inside swiveling her head and saying, "Hey, sis, what's up?" Since the day I arrived in Dublin, I've never been entirely certain who and what I am. I understand why Barrons rejects labels. You only know who you are in opposition to something, what you choose to fight for and against. The rest doesn't matter.

"Wait a minute." I turn back and am darkly amused to see that even my Unseelie "priests" have abandoned me. They huddle, facing one another, chittering with what almost seems nervous dissension ten feet behind Ryodan, who's standing half the length of the corridor away from me, allowing no opportunity for the princess to turn him into a mindless sexual slave. I forget what I'm saying, momentarily distracted by that thought. I'm a monogamous woman. I don't like to share. Yet the idea of this man as a mindless sexual slave is ... I shake my head. *This is Ryodan,* I remind myself.

Then Barrons joins him and eclipses the notion. His eyes are brilliant, his body emanating heat and power. If I pressed my ear to his chest, his heart would be thudding, slow and strong.

"How do you know what's happening in there if you can't see inside?" I ask Ryodan. The two-way glass is dark from the outside, transparent only from within.

Ryodan places his cell phone on the floor and slides it across the slick glass floor. It stops at my feet. "Tap the Skull and Crossbones app."

Of course, he has an app for everything. Figures he'd be able to watch the central hub of his universe from the phone that shouldn't work, via an otherworldly Wi-Fi network that doesn't exist.

I open the app, blink once then forget how to. "Oh, my gosh, he's . . . that can't be . . . holy cow." My face gets hot.

"Give me a break," Ryodan says irritably. "And give me my phone back."

I want to keep it. See what else is on there. I've heard rumors there's a level in this club reserved only for the Nine.

Barrons snorts. Barrons has reason to snort. I got the best one. I glance up and give him a charged look.

Yes, you did.

"Quit procrastinating," Ryodan says. "And get rid of the bitch. My phone." He extends his hand.

Not a chance. Not when I'm not sure how the princess will react to me.

I place my palm on the wall and the door whisks aside with a faint hydraulic hiss. Sex slams me in the face, scorching, drugging, volatile.

"I said, my phone."

I stand at the threshold and look in. The princess has her back to me, and Lor is beyond noticing anything. Ryodan and Barrons are another matter. They're too observant by far. There is also the small matter of the enormous possessiveness I feel where Barrons is concerned.

I step inside and place my palm on the interior panel.

Two males roar in unison.

"Ms. Lane, you will *not* close—"

"Mac, you will give me my fucking—"

The door hisses closed behind me.

12

"We are family, I got all my sisters with me"

MAC

Once I would have thought what was taking place in Ryodan's office was no more than what it appeared to be: an Unseelie of the royal caste subjugating a human, getting drunk on the pleasure they siphon from our souls. Immortal, jaded, void of anything that passes as passion, Fae royalty is incapable of emotion, but they can experience it through a human vessel. Especially during sex. Or torture. Preferably both at the same time. They either use the human up completely and kill it or leave a shell of a sex-starved slave. Death is the better option there.

But the Unseelie Princes just shocked the hell out of me, proved themselves to be ambitious and goal-oriented, willing to adopt a mien of civility to achieve their aims, and channel what used to be a maelstrom of uncontrolled hunger into deliberated action.

Considering the Fae have always been matriarchal, I have reason to assume the princesses are no less driven or capable of evolving than their dark counterparts. I wonder where they've been all this time. Feeding in private? Learning self-discipline and -control? Plotting to take over our world?

She's not throwing off the whirlwind of insanity and insatiability with which the princes first razed our world when freed from their prison, nor does she seem bent on the vicious, obsessive hunt of the Crimson Hag determined to complete her gut-gown. She appears composed, even dispassionate. I consider that perhaps like human women, she's not as governed by hormones, or whatever passes as Fae motivation, as the males. Perhaps the genders of any species share certain traits. As far as I know, it's the female Fae that bears what few young they manage, and may be biologically more pragmatic, to ensure their offspring's survival. I hope so because I don't want to kill her. Not now, not here with so many humans in the vicinity. As much as I want her dead, I have to find another way.

Then arrange a safer place to hunt her.

I take a deep, slow breath and release it. "We could cut to the chase," I say to her beautiful back. Iridescent, sparkling tattoos shimmer on each side of her spine, furling and unfurling as if caressed by a sultry Fae breeze only she can feel. They vaguely resemble wings.

Silver embellishments glitter along her backbone as if she's adorned her spine with metal piercings, with more of them on each side of her neck. Though immune to Fae thrall, watching Lor do what he's doing to her is getting me hot and bothered in a purely human way. No wonder the blondes keep lining up at his bed. He's a massive, lethal lion of muscle, sex, and power. He growls as he grinds up into her, and the sound is so rough and ready, so freaking hot and sexy, that my heart begins to hammer in the back of my throat and my mouth goes dry. I swallow hard and wet my lips before I continue, "What do you want?"

She glances over her shoulder with that telltale inhuman head swivel, assesses and disregards me.

She should take a deeper look.

"Mac, get her the fuck off me," Lor snarls. Then he groans again, in spite of himself.

"You will not speak," the princess commands Lor, and just like that he loses control of his vocal cords. Nice talent. I wouldn't mind having it myself.

"I said, What do you want?" I repeat coldly.

"Nor will *you* speak," she hisses over her shoulder at me.

My vocal cords don't feel any different. I test them by clearing my throat. It works.

Her head swivels again and she rakes an imperious, frosty glance from my boots to my hair. Her hips never stop moving. "What are you?"

"The one not killing you," I say, working hard to ignore the graphic sex happening right in front of me. "For the moment. What. Do. You. Want." I push my hair back, not surprised to realize it's damp, I'm actually sweating from watching them have sex. I'm overdue for some of my own.

"You are not human."

"I am, too," I say flatly. I may not be sure of much, but I was born. I was carried in a womb. And infected there.

"My power works on everything but Fae of the royal castes."

"You didn't come here to have sex," I evade. "You could do that anywhere. You came specifically to this club and chose specifically him. Why?" It's a ballsy move, stalking so openly into Chester's, alone, targeting one of the Nine and turning him Pri-ya in the owner's office. Why haven't we seen any of the princesses before? Cruce claimed all the Seelie were dead. He'd also claimed no Unseelie Princesses were made. Was anything he told me true? Where has she been? Is she newly arrived, jockeying for position by abducting one of the most powerful males in the city?

She wets blue lips and tilts her head to the side. Her eyes darken to inky pools that are suddenly neon cobalt. Beyond long, thick lashes, vertical slitted pupils dilate and shrink, dilate again as if she's taking my measure with vision humans don't possess. For a moment I think I glimpse stars in those pupils. She's different from the princes. There's a . . . vastness to her that exceeds theirs.

He made us last. We are his best. Enhanced.

Without thinking, I seek confirmation of that from the only place I could possibly get it.

Yes, open me, read me, it agrees instantly.

I sigh, resuming my chant, imagining Poe would enjoy that although his narrator was unable to silence the bird, his poem silences my book.

But the Raven still beguiling my sad fancy into smiling, straight I wheeled a cushioned seat in front of bird and bust and door . . .

The princess's eyes narrow, as if she hears my inner dialogue but can make no sense of it.

"Cruce said *he* was the king's last," I say. "And best."

"There are things Cruce does not know. Where is our brother?"

"Dead," I lie.

"Did you kill him?"

"Yes," I say.

There go the pupils again, dilating, narrowing. "It seems you would offer aid. I am unconvinced you possess anything that may interest us."

"Perhaps we share common desires." Where did this cold place inside me come from? Is it because I sat with my rapists tonight and made pacts? Or because I know how much I have to lose if I don't stay cold? "I have a great deal to offer. If the price is right. It's you who may not have enough to barter with."

She gathers a fall of blood-black hair from her face, twists it into a long tail then knots it at her nape before disengaging and sliding gracefully from the desk.

I can't help but stare at what she left behind. What hot-blooded woman wouldn't? Lor is chained naked to a desk, legs spread, affording me a gloriously intimate view. He's magnificent. A tall, massively muscled Viking with thick blond hair and not one spec of it on his body. Though his abdomen and thighs are crisscrossed with scars, the rest of his skin is sleek and velvety as the head of his—*Stop staring!*

I drag my gaze away, force it to the princess.

"I do not barter with humans. I command. But you have . . . Hmmm, you have something . . . What *is* it you have?"

I say nothing. Reveal nothing. I've learned from the best. I meet and hold her gaze, expressionless.

Time spins out. Finally she says, "The Unseelie Princes, fools that they are, think to rule this world." She spits on the floor. "We came to enslave this male and use it as our weapon because the dark princes are immune to our ways. Word reached us it can kill things that are difficult to kill, even our brothers. Fae magic is matriarchal. The light princesses are dead. This world is ours."

I realize if she came for Lor to eliminate her competition, rather than Dani or me, she must not know about the spear and sword. "This world belongs to us," I say. "If you try to take it from us, it will be war."

"A war you will lose."

"Try me."

Nude, she begins to pad a slow, predatory circle around me. I turn with her and she laughs.

"No, you most certainly do not wish one such as we unseen behind your back."

"Nor do you wish me unseen behind yours," I purr.

She laughs again and it's a caress to my ears. She's amped up her death-by-sex Fae heat. I feel it expanding around her, yet it doesn't touch me.

When I don't respond, her eyes widen, her mouth shapes a perfect, lush O of surprise. The sexual energy she's channeling pulses hotter. On the desk, Lor bucks and strains against the chains.

I wonder if I could somehow accept the energy she's so generously (foolishly?) throwing off, while rejecting the sexual component. As I consider it, she pads to a stop in front of me. We're the same height. She leans in as if to kiss me.

"Oh, what *are* you, you delicious *thing*," she says, and wets her lips. "Not like them, not like us yet like us. You smell of . . ." She trails off and stops in front of me, sniffing deeply, leaning into my neck. I don't move. I feel her snuffling at my throat. "Oh, yes, I like that smell very much but there is . . . something . . . it is most . . ."

She's definitely unaware I have the spear. I wonder if she even knows such weapons exist. She seems oddly out of the loop.

She recoils like a cobra, drawing up to her full height, back arched away, eyes narrowing, and hisses, "Oh! You smell of *them*. We will not go back. It finished with us. It said so. We will *never* go back."

She vanishes.

"About fucking time you got rid of her." Lor recovers his voice with a snarl. He sounds hoarse, from hours of yelling.

I stand, blinking at her sudden, unexpected disappearance.

She shouldn't have been able to sift out of the club. Then again, she shouldn't have been able to get inside in the first place. Either Ryodan's wards aren't working or she's beyond their compulsion.

I frown, trying to decide what she thinks I smell like that drove her away so completely. There are multiple possibilities. The stain of her brothers' rape lingering on my soul? The green goo of the Gray Woman I butchered? Perhaps she detects the sworn enemy of the Fae, my *sidhe*-seer sisters on my skin, in my blood. Or maybe the oily residue of the Unseelie that stalk me who—as if summoned by that last thought—swiftly begin popping, one after another, into the room with me, crushing close, giving Lor wide berth. Apparently it was the princess they were avoiding. I wish I knew why. I'd make Eau d'Unseelie Princess perfume of her flesh and spray myself with it if I thought it might work.

She said "them," so obviously it wasn't the singularity of the Book she sensed inside me, and that she would not go back. Go back where? And who'd put her there to begin with?

On the desk, Lor makes a sound of such raw sexual need that I shiver. "Mac," he growls. "I need. Get your ass over here."

Pri-ya is a hellish thing to be. It reduces you to a whimpering, broken, pathetic sex addict that will do anything for anyone at any time. I have memories I've interred deep. Places in my mind I'll never visit again.

Whimpering and *broken* are the key words there.

"What do you need, Lor?" I say dryly.

"What the fuck do you think I need? Sex. Constantly. I'll die if I don't have it all the time. I'm Pri-ya."

"Hm. Pri-ya."

"Sure as shit, the bitch made me Pri-ya. You saw her.

I had an Unseelie Princess on top of me. My dick hurts
so bad it's gonna explode. I need sex. I can't live without
it. This is torture. So either get on it, or find me a hot
blond babe that will. Which is any hot blond babe in
the club," he adds cheerfully.

I like Lor. He's aggressive, domineering, and part
caveman, but he doesn't have a cruel bone in his body,
and he flat-out adores women and children. I sometimes
think if the other eight weren't around, Lor would be a
very different man.

Leave it to him to try to capitalize on the princess's
visit, use it as an excuse to spend the next few months
in bed, receiving a steady stream of women whose sole
purpose is to have sex with him 24/7.

I know what Pri-ya looks like—and he's not it.
Though part of her magic somehow worked on him, the
Nine are apparently impossible to turn Pri-ya. I wonder
if they're too basely sexual to begin with. Perhaps the
charge they throw off cancels out her sexuality, or at
least dampens the full effect of it. I decide I'll stick close
to Barrons until I figure out how to get rid of her and if
there are others out there. She might not have turned
Lor into a permanent slave, but a temporary one is bad
enough. Deep in my *sidhe*-seer center, I activate an antenna of sorts to listen at all times for the gothic, dark
march of the princess.

I move toward the door. Ryodan can unchain Lor. I'm
not getting close to the man while he's naked. He told
me once he prefers a club over a woman's head because
charm wastes energy better spent fucking, and I believe
him. Although I see no club in the office, there are other
heavy objects.

"Aw, c'mon, Mac," he says, sounding aggrieved,
"would it really kill you to let them think I'm Pri-ya?
What have I ever done to you? Tonight was traumatic.
Bitch actually made me call her 'mistress.' I need some

good old-fashioned fucking to ease my pain. Maybe a sexy 'Yes, master' or two. Or two hundred. What's wrong with that?"

I raise my palm and prepare to press it to the wall.

"Seriously, honey, I promise I'll only take a few weeks to get better. I won't drag it out. I'm sitting on the jackpot right now. I'll do something for you. Anything. Name it. Well, not anything. But there's gotta be something you want."

I smile and retract my hand before it touches the panel.

Five minutes later I open the door and shake my head, tears welling in my eyes.

"We didn't get to him in time," I tell Ryodan. "She's gone but I was too late. She'd already turned him Pri-ya. Send all the blondes you can spare to take him somewhere private. Hurry. And I wouldn't go near him if I were you. It's not pretty. You won't want to remember him this way."

"She can turn us Pri-ya," Ryodan says.

"Afraid so."

There's a bounce in my step as I rejoin Barrons. I got what I wanted tonight, after all. A favor owed from one of the Nine is worth its weight in pure Faery dust. And now I finally get to go have sex with Barrons, and from the way he's looking at me, it's going to be one seriously long, hot night.

"You're going the wrong way," Ryodan says behind us.

I glance over my shoulder. "What do you mean? We're going back to the bookstore. I did what you asked. I got rid of her."

"You just told me she can turn us Pri-ya, and our wards don't prevent her from sifting while within the walls of my club. You will remain in residence, guarding against all princesses until we resolve the situation. You'll find ample quarters in that direction." He points the other way. "Perhaps you'll do what you should have done this time, and kill her next time."

My bounce vanishes. "You didn't *tell* me to kill her."

"It was self-evident."

"No, it wasn't," I say pissily. "I took a page from your negotiating-with-the-princes book. And you sent all the others into Faery. They're not even here to protect."

"I'm still here."

I look up at Barrons, who stopped walking and is regarding me intently, eyes narrowed. He looks as if he's about to speak, debates, folds his arms and says nothing.

"You could stand up for me," I grouse. "Tell him we're going back to the store, period."

He smiles faintly. "It would hardly be fair if you 'protected' only me."

His light emphasis on the word "protected" gives him away. No idea how, but he knows I lied. And he's amused. And he's going to sit back and watch it play out, see how stuck I get in the sticky spiderweb I've begun to spin.

Guess he really is sick of my "idiotic passivity."

So am I.

But as I learned today, it's way the hell better than idiotic activity.

Confined to Chester's with no escape from my carrion stalkers, forced to contend with Ryodan on a daily basis, surrounded by monsters, inhabited by a monster, I'm afraid there's more of it coming.

13

"I was ducking down to reload"

JADA

She needs to kill.

Purpose is strength and hers was impeded tonight.

No matter, when one avenue is blocked, another is revealed.

There are two on her list in the direction she's headed. They will be dispatched differently than her prior intended target, swiftly, with more mercy than they deserve. Though their crimes are many, unlike the Unseelie she seeks, they are human. She eliminates humans quickly.

She takes no pleasure in the kill. There is satisfaction in seeing debts collected, ledgers balanced. There are those she will protect at any cost.

As she turns a corner and enters a dimly lit street, her gaze lifts to the shattered streetlamp, then down to lightly misted cobblestones and back up again.

She pauses to absorb the scene: the Unseelie blood dripping from the jagged glass that housed the light; the many pieces of unmoving Fae flesh tossed in a heap; the small pile of human parts with wilted flowers placed carefully on top; the footsteps in the scattered debris, trails of blood and smears of green that map out movements.

She moves closer. Someone placed the human's picture ID on top of the flowers so he would be found and identified, bestowing the blessing of closure so those who cared might not wonder endlessly if their husband or father might one day walk in the door again.

If not for the blossoms, she would think it an act of vengeance, not compassion.

A killer followed by a merciful passerby?

She closes her eyes, analyzes, assesses, processes all she saw and factors in what she has come to understand about humans and monsters in her years of war. Working methodically, logically, she re-creates the events that transpired in this street.

She eliminates the possibility of two separate actors. This was the work of one.

Someone killed a Fae and butchered a human by accident in the process.

Someone killed *her* Fae.

If she felt, which she doesn't, her emotions would run the gamut from stunned to furious.

Neither disrupts her serene features.

Someone else adjusted her ledgers.

She wants to know who.

She steps closer to the pile of Unseelie flesh, notes the suckered fingers, the gray skin.

The individual spear wounds in each small piece by which the dismembered-yet-still-alive Unseelie was granted death.

From the shape of the wounds, she knows the killer.

Her name is also on her list.

She covets the weapon. Once she has acquired it, she will be unstoppable.

She lifts her head. A Fae is moving toward her, rapidly.

Powerful. Unseelie. She has been hunting this one but not to kill.

"You wish the Unseelie Princes dead," she says to the night. She knows the night is always listening. "I will do it for you. But you must do something for me."

She finds it necessary to repeat herself three times before the princess with ice-white skin and cobalt hair appears in the damp street before her.

"What makes you think I won't kill you where you stand?" Imperial ice drips from the princess's words.

"Perhaps you could. Perhaps you couldn't. Perhaps you could use an ally in this city whose strengths chink your weaknesses. Perhaps we both could. Not that either of us have many weaknesses. Still, there are those few. You and your brother princes are immune to one another, powerless to spell or destroy one another. I deem that a significant weakness."

Starry eyes narrow as the princess takes her measure.

Jada says, "There is the devil that can't get the job done and won't eat you, and the devil that *can* get the job done but might. We are both the latter. I agree not to eat you."

The princess's eyes narrow and she appears to be reconsidering her initial assessment. "Perhaps we can aid one another. If the price is acceptable."

"You will locate a certain Unseelie for me." She tells her the one she seeks.

"Even *I* do not approach that one," the princess hisses.

"Then I will not kill your brothers."

"It is impossible!"

"I said 'locate,' not kill. That is the price. It is non-negotiable."

"How do you think to kill the princes? You are *human*."

"I know where to obtain a weapon that kills Fae."

"There is no such thing."

"There is."

"All Fae?"

"Yes."

"And you can get this weapon?"

"Yes."

The princess is silent a time, then finally says, "Perhaps you have useful knowledge. I will not kill you tonight. You will show me this weapon and demonstrate its power."

"You will locate the one I seek first. Then you will take me there."

"Locate. That is all."

"Both. Or nothing."

"That would be *two* services rendered. The weapon becomes mine."

"Two princes for two services," she says flatly.

Ancient, cold eyes regard her. She is acutely aware of the precariousness of the moment. But one that fails to venture never gains.

Finally the princess says, "In times of war allies are useful."

"I will offer my services for your future needs. The weapon will be part of those services."

"I will consider it." The princess vanishes.

14

*"Fools, said I, you do not know
Silence like a cancer grows"*

KAT

My gift, if you can call it that, is an empathetic heart. I began crying the moment I was born and wept until I was five years, three months, and seventeen days old—the afternoon Rowena came to my parents' house and began teaching me to shield myself from the constant barrage of others' emotions.

I often think I've learned nothing, except how to stop crying, don a mask, and pretend the world isn't too much for me to bear.

I know how fragile we are, how biased the war that rages on this planet where the angels are made of glass and the demons of concrete. All you have to do is drop one of us and we shatter.

Last night I watched Sean across the dangerous expanse of a treaty table and realized our love is glass, too. I must become diamond dust to strengthen the mix.

In the days preceding the Hoar Frost King's defeat, Margery enlisted Ryodan's aid to tether a dangerous, drifting fragment of Faery that was about to demolish our abbey, and the price Ryodan called due from me the night I went to pay our debt was Sean filling in as a waiter at Chester's for a time.

So the dominos began to fall.

Sean can't bear to watch people suffering any more than I, and confronted by those in need, he became their provider. It's a strength I admire with all my heart.

Yet it's also the same treacherous foundation upon which both our families were built. Our fathers possessed an enormous sense of responsibility for their own. And their own came to them with problems and requests, each more difficult to address, to satisfy, than the last.

Over time, it corrupted them. The lime of murder, the viscosity of revenge, cemented the blood in their hearts until they, too, were poured of concrete.

I move through the dance floors of Chester's with purpose, my shields as high as I can raise them, yet I cannot block the immense loneliness of this densely crowded place, the hunger and despair, desperation and need. So many angels, so many cracks. They don't even require dropping, a fair jostle would do the trick.

I have the care of two hundred seventy-one women in Dublin. The eldest, Tanty Anna, my wise, gentle, ancient advisor whose eyes seemed to stare straight into heaven, is a month dead, murdered by the Crimson Hag. Christian paid the ultimate price for our freedom that night and I'm powerless to help save him. One of my younger charges, Dani, enormously gifted and enormously impulsive, has been missing for weeks now, and I fear the worst. Margery seethes and plots daily to take the reign I would gratefully relinquish, just not to her.

My soul mate has assumed charge of the black market and put himself in direct competition with two Unseelie Princes and a ruthless male that defies quantifying.

Now there are new *sidhe*-seers in Dublin, led by a

woman not even Ryodan has been able to track. I've never felt so inept in my life. I want to rebuild my abbey. I want to fill the walls a thousand strong again. I want the strength of concrete without the price of it.

When I came here months ago, seeking Ryodan to repay my debt, he said a thing I've been unable to stop thinking about: *Drop your blinders and raise the sewer to eye level; admit you're swimming in shit. If you don't acknowledge the turd hurtling down the drain toward you, you can't dodge it.*

I've come to get out of the toilet bowl and become the commode that flushes the shit.

The fragment of a Faery fire-world I prayed was responsible for the grass that grows tall and green beyond my bedroom window, directly above Cruce's icy prison, is gone now, yet the meadow is more verdant than before, exploding with poppies, red, fat, bobbing, opium-drenched blossoms that drug my senses on warm evenings when the projection of a great, black-winged prince circles my bed.

I have warded him out of my tangle of linens with blood-magic, an art I'd sworn never to practice, a line I wouldn't cross.

But it is no longer only myself I must protect.

Elaborate golden trellises have pushed up from the earth all over the abbey's grounds, draped with black roses that reek of exotic spices and far-off lands.

Dozens of standing stones have appeared in the gardens, etched with symbols I can't read. A pair of megaliths awaits a cover stone to become a dolmen. It makes me shiver when I pass.

Pearl benches frame a vast, brilliant, many-tiered fountain in which water sparkles as turquoise as a Caribbean sea.

Animals I've never seen before peek at me from trees fringed with lacy vines that grow strange beyond our walls, shedding brown bark for ivory threaded with silver, sprouting low-hanging canopies of sapphire leaves.

The floors in my section of the abbey are changing from stone to polished gold.

At night I hear male laughter echoing down our halls and corridors. The lights within our walls glow soft gold day and night, without electricity to source them. Our fires blaze, without wood to feed them. Our generators run only a small number of lamps. We removed the bulbs. Still they glow. Something unholy powers the rest.

Cruce is changing our home, taking it over, and I know it's only a matter of time before the jailer is evicted by the jailed, Paradise lost.

We talk of it amongst ourselves but so far have said nothing to outsiders. This is our home, for many of us the only good one we've known. If we do not find a way to stop the transformation, we will be forced to leave.

Soon.

We are not yet ready to admit defeat.

If we are driven forth, who will watch the abbey? Will we sit idly beyond its walls, praying the prisoner never breaks free?

I cradle my belly with one hand protectively. I've not yet begun to show. I devote most of my energy to shielding it. I must secure our future.

When I reach the bottom of the glass stairs in the glass house that the concrete demon Ryodan calls home, he is waiting for me.

But of course.

"Why did you lie about Sean?" I ask him.

"I didn't lie. You sewed my words into a cloth of your choosing. If you'll recall, I urged you to talk to him that night. Had you heeded my advice, you would have known, soul mates and all, confiding everything."

"Don't mock me."

"Don't make it so easy."

"You said you were collecting my debt from him."

"I said I was willing to accept the replacement of a missing server as full payment, and let you off the hook."

"And put me on another."

"You chose to become the worm. A little conversation goes a long way, Katarina. You've still not told Sean that Cruce fucks you in your dreams."

I say nothing and he laughs.

"Yet here you are. Seeking me again. Come for more answers to which you won't listen. I only waste my breath once. Leave."

I remain where I am.

He sweeps me with that cool silver gaze and arches a brow. "Be very certain you know what you're doing, Katarina," he warns softly. "If you ask something of me, I will not stop until I feel the request has been satisfied. As I deem fit."

I fix on two words he uttered. "You do not feel."

"It's you, my ever-serene cat, that fails to feel, denying at your own peril the hunger of your heart."

"Nor do you know anything of the heart, mine or any others."

"State your cause. I have pressing matters to attend."

I stare up into the face of the man that does not exist, that according to my empathic senses is not even standing there, and choose my words with care. I can proceed with nothing less than one hundred percent commitment to my course, and am fully aware this path will make or break me. I wish I could predict which one it will be, but I'm untested, unproven.

I resist the urge to cradle my abdomen. I must not telegraph in front of this man. I must become something else. He has a bold hand and a sharp chisel. The clay has chosen the sculptor. This male, whatever he is, possesses power beyond my humble skills. He and his men know what I do not: how to protect what is theirs. They are ruthless and hard. And successful.

If I think to care for my charges, for my child, I must learn to be similarly successful.

"I've come to acknowledge the turd."

He smiles. "It's about time, Katarina."

I suffered my father's disappointment mere days after I was born, although at the time I didn't know it for what it was, only that I was rejected and alone. As the years passed, his anger and disgust at the useless daughter he couldn't barter away to further cement his position grew so oppressive, I learned to avoid him whenever possible. My mother's greed and impatience, shallowness and fear, were my childhood companions.

Then there was Sean, with whom I grew, who loved me, uncomplicated from the first, even as I wept. Still, it's often difficult to bear the nuances of his every emotion. Filet mignon or rib eye, we're all imperfect cuts, marbled by fears and insecurities, even the best of men.

As we move deeper into Chester's, the barrage of chaotic emotions begins to subside, affording me a rare and blessed respite: the volume of the world's endless sensations has been reduced from a ten to a four. We navigate one glass corridor after the next, and I wonder that he leads me so deep into his club where others are not permitted. After a time, he glides his palm over a smooth glass wall and an elevator appears.

"Where are you taking me?" I ask as the elevator door closes, sealing me in a much too small compartment with a much too large man. I feel like Dante, descending into the inferno, but I have no Roman poet as my guide.

"From this moment on, any questions are mine. Assuming you wish to be concrete, without the price."

I stare up at him. How can he possibly know that? "You can read minds."

"Human thoughts are loud. We take what's offered. Humans offer too much. Of everything."

"What are you going to do? Teach me to fight?" I glance down at my slender arms. Though strong from gardening, milking, and working our land, I doubt I possess the ability to hurt another human being. I would feel their pain. I don't invite that.

"Not me."

He escorts me from the elevator into the most blissfully silent corridor I've ever walked. I turn in a slow circle, listening but hearing nothing. This level must be powerfully soundproofed. There's no faint beat of music, not even white noise, only the perfect absence of sound. "Who, then?"

He guides me down the hall with a hand at the small of my back, opens another door, and we step into a dimly lit, long room with faintly illuminated rectangles that lead to additional rooms beyond.

There are no furnishings here. No table, sofa, rug, or chair. The floors are polished ebony. The walls are ivory. A diffuse glow emanates from the perimeter of high, coffered ceilings with stamped leather insets above Romanesque cove moldings. There are large corbels on two of the walls, as if once treasures were displayed. The room is refined.

The occupant is not.

A man is stretched on the floor, staring up, arms crossed behind his head. Like the rest of Ryodan's men, he is tall, wide, powerfully muscled, scarred, and not there. He wears black camouflage pants low at his hips, feet bare. His arms are tattooed, his head nearly shaved, his face shadowed dark with stubble. He looks like a rogue military commander from a unit the world never hears about.

"Kasteo will be your instructor."

I stare at him in disbelief. Jo has told me tales of the Nine, though they've been of little use. Kasteo is the one that does not speak. According to Jo, something transpired a long time ago and he hasn't uttered a word since.

"Is this your idea of a joke? He doesn't talk!"

"You don't listen. Match made in heaven." Ryodan stalks over to Kasteo and looks down at him. "Kasteo will be your instructor," he says again, but this time it's an order and a warning to the man on the floor. "The woman feels the pain of the world. You'll teach her to stop feeling it. Then you will help her learn to control her environment. Finally, you will teach her to fight."

Kasteo, of course, says nothing. I'm not certain he even heard. He appears in a trance, elsewhere.

Ryodan walks to the door. "You'll remain with him until I decide you've gotten what you came for." The door closes behind him, and I stand there a moment, staring blankly at it, then at Kasteo.

I rush to the door and place my palm to the wall where Ryodan pressed it, but nothing happens.

I hammer on the door. "Ryodan! I must return to the abbey! Ryodan, let me out!"

The only response is the most enormous silence I've ever heard.

"This is not what I meant!"

I hammer until my fists are bruised.

"Ryodan, you can't do this! My charges need me! There are things you don't know! I came here to tell you!"

I feel as if I'm in the bowels of the earth, forgotten.

I shout until my throat burns.

The man on the floor never stirs.

I'm unable to count the passage of time in this silent, empty place.

After a length of it, I sink to the floor and lean back against the wall, one hand resting lightly on my belly.

Surely he'll feed me.

Surely there is a bathroom here somewhere.

Surely he'll come back so I can convey to him the urgent state of our abbey.

I sit and stare like the unmoving, unblinking man on the floor. After a time, I become aware of the simplicity of the moment. Not only is there no sound on this level, there seems to be a dearth of emotion.

Cautiously, I lower the shields I've held since I was five years old, barriers that have shut out the world, and walled me in.

Nothing.

Again, I lower, lower. When I continue to encounter nothing, I take a deep breath, brace myself, and drop them flat.

I gasp.

Still—nothing!

I feel no anger or greed, no lust or fear or pain or need. That's always the worst for me: the many crushing, painful needs that can never be satisfied. Here, deep below Chester's, there is absolutely no emotion charging the air, compressing me, forcing me into a defensive posture.

It's sublime. My heart can breathe.

For the first time in my life, I feel only me.

I didn't even know what I felt like.

For the first time in my life, I can hear myself think.

15

"I'm just a crack in this castle of glass"

MAC

I hear music in my dreams. I heard such exquisite melodies during my teens that one day I decided I was fated to be a brilliant composer, put songs to paper, and share them with the world. I joined the band that very day. I even signed up for extra classes and asked Mom and Dad to hire a tutor to help me learn to read and write sheet music. I plunged into the world of an aspiring musician with enormous enthusiasm, certain of my predestined success.

In less than a month my tutor stalked out of our house and refused to come back, and the high school band director asked me to please do the entire band a favor: quit.

I have no musical talent.

My clarinet sounded like an apoplectic yak. For the brief days I blew the trumpet, a hostile-sounding pig snorted along in jerky fits and starts with the rest of the irritated band. I never knew when a sound was actually going to come out of the horn and it always startled me when it did. My violin unleashed a trio of enraged, tone-deaf banshees, and I couldn't blow the flute well enough to make any more sound than with my lower lip on a soda bottle. Something about the pucker eluded me. The drums turned my arms into a pretzel-prison from which there was no escape. I would have given the tambourine a try—I really think I might have excelled at the hip-bump—but sadly the instrument wasn't offered at my school. I think that's why I love my iPod so much. I have music in my soul and can't get it out.

This morning, like the two before it, the melody of my subconscious has been different. Three mornings in a row I've awakened with the strains of a symphony fading from my mind that is beyond horrific. Last night was the worst yet, as if I'm becoming attuned to it, hearing it louder, feeling it more intensely.

My psyche is bruised, my spine hot, and my stomach cramped. The new song is unlike any of the others I've heard in my dreams. It doesn't leave me glowing, feeling uplifted and free, nor do I see dreamy, fantastic images while it plays.

I can use none of my usual vocabulary to describe it. I lie in bed with my head under the covers, trying to figure out what was so disturbing about the melody that I woke with pillows clenched to my ears, arms aching from the strain of having held them there half the night.

I search for words: scary? No. Worse.

Depressing? No. Worse.

Capable of making me insane if I had to listen to it too long?

Worse.

Is there worse than insane?

I roll over and poke my head from beneath the mound of pillows and blankets. I'm alone in bed, which I often am, at least while I'm sleeping, since Barrons doesn't require it.

However, I am not alone in the room.

Without the wards on the bookstore to keep them at bay—Barrons said it would take weeks to collect more of the necessary ingredients—my grim stalkers huddle close, pressed to three sides of the bed, on the fourth roosting atop the headboard, bony shoulders hunched upward, swallowing their heads and necks. Two crouch on the bed right next to me. My pajamas have cobwebs on them. I've been sleeping in pj's, not about to risk being unconscious, nude around any Unseelie.

Needless to say, sex hasn't been happening here. Although when Barrons is touching me, or even just next to me, I enjoy the same wide berth they grant him, I don't get off on being an exhibitionist, at least not to Unseelie.

Not only am I bitchy, bored, and too powerful for my own good, I don't get to vent on Barrons's big, hard body, and I'm massively overdue for it. I'm beginning to think it's all some part of the universe's conspiracy to see just what it takes to make MacKayla Lane snap.

Like a wake of vultures, every last one of them is facing me, peering down.

Well, in as much as they might face me, peering down, considering I've never seen beneath those voluminous hoods and can't even say whether they have faces or eyes. I used to think they were clothed. They're not. The dusty, cobwebbed, cowled cloaks they wear have the texture of black chicken skin and are part of them.

Ryodan said they were the caste that once attended the king in his private chambers. Do they stalk me—not because the Book within me deliberately summoned them—but because, like K'Vruck, they sense me as part of the king they once served? If so, when the king takes the Book out of me, they should vanish, too.

At the moment they're mute. Not a chitter, not a rustle.

I find their silence nearly as disturbing as the dark

symphony of my dreams. Had it gotten so loud they could hear it in my head? Did it button the lips of even my loquacious tormentors?

I wonder if, like the vultures they resemble, they, too, have highly corrosive stomach acid that makes them capable of digesting putrid carcasses infected with bacteria and parasites dangerous to their species.

At least they don't vomit like vultures when threatened or urinate straight down their legs to cool themselves and kill the bacteria they pick up wading through rotting corpses.

Good the fuck morning to me.

It's a broody one, as usual.

"Back up, you bastards," I mutter, swinging my legs over the edge of the bed.

They don't. They brush against my pajama bottoms, leaving it covered with cobwebs and yellow dust.

I can't get back to BB&B fast enough. At least there I slept in peace, got to have sex, and woke in a room free of vermin.

I perch on the edge of the mattress, staring up at my flock. The *Sinsar Dubh* said they were my "priests" and that I could command them. I know better than to trust the *Sinsar Dubh* and I worry that if I issue even one tiny command such as, "Get the hell away from me and that's an order," the Book will somehow own a piece of my soul.

Or maybe if you start ordering this caste around, it antagonizes them so much they eat you. Or perhaps they'll start vomiting and pissing, and then I'll be walking around all the time in upchuck and urine, stinking of three different things instead of a single bad smell.

One thing I do know is things can *always* get worse, most often at the precise moment you've decided they can't.

And so I remain, as Barrons would pithily say, idiotically passive.

I sigh and begin to dress, thinking I might kill for a Starbucks, heavy on the espresso.

I lose sense of time in Chester's. There are no windows, and if you stay there awhile it messes with your circadian rhythm. I think I've been here three nights now, listening for the music of an Unseelie Princess, and trying to figure out how to get past Ryodan's wards and explore the many secrets of Chester's.

Time and again I've turned around and walked away rather than call on something inside me to push past a particularly sticky spot, allowing the Book no opportunity to goad me.

I lost two and a half hours in the street that afternoon and have no idea what the Book did with me. I don't know if I spent all of it torturing and killing, or—I terminate that thought. No point in going there. It's done. I can't undo it. I can only never let it happen again. Brooding about it will only make me feel worse, and when I feel my worst is when the *Sinsar Dubh* talks the most.

As I round the perimeter balustrade and approach the top of the stairs, flanked by my gaunt ghouls, I realize it must be early morning, as the club is empty except for the many waiters and waitresses wiping things down. I hope they use antibacterial cleanser because virtually every horizontal surface gets used as a bed at some point. There are only a few hours when the dance floors are deserted. Ryodan closes the doors at dawn and doesn't reopen to the public until eleven A.M. I've heard that's when he gives his infamous nod to some woman and takes her upstairs. I've also heard that for an uncommonly long time it's been the *sidhe*-seer, Jo. Really, how much of a relationship can she think they're having when he's still "selecting" her every morning?

As if I've summoned the event merely by thinking of it, I turn the corner to see Ryodan standing at the top of the stairs, looking down.

Lucky me. I get to witness the nod. Woohoo. Could my morning get any better?

I stop abruptly and bony vultures pile into my back. They're still silent. It creeps me out.

I glance down to my right, past the railing. There's Jo, looking up, waiting. I wonder again what the hell he thinks he's doing with her. What she thinks she's doing with him. Anyone can see they're no match. Anyone can predict how this disaster will end. One morning Ryodan will walk to the stairs.

He'll look down and Jo will look up.

And Ryodan will look beyond her, to some other woman, and nod.

Jo will never share his bed again.

Barrons and his men are something else. I may not care for Ryodan, we have baggage between us, but I have to admit any woman takes one look at him and wonders. And wants. It's visceral. You know that when one of the Nine gets down to fucking, your world is about to get rocked like never before. And like it never will again. Unless you become a Nine groupie. Which I can honestly say might have its merits.

If I was Jo, and it was Barrons at the top of these stairs, what would I do? Like Jo, would I choose to take what I could get of the hottest, dirty, intense sex and passion I'd ever experience, and deem it worth a shattered heart?

There's no question it will break hers.

I see the hunger in her face. I see the light in her eyes as she gazes up at him. I see the tenderness and the desire and need in every line of her body.

It's not there in his.

He's untouched by her. She burns for him.

I want to grab him, shake him, demand he stop before he destroys her. I want to grab her, shake her, demand she stop before she's destroyed.

I hold my breath in silence. It's not my place to choose for Jo a path I'm not sure I'd be willing to walk myself.

Life is short. At the buffet of it, who doesn't want the best dessert?

Ryodan nods, Jo's cue to toss her cleaning rag and race up the stairs into his arms. They'll pass me and disappear into his office or a nearby bedroom, and I'll go downstairs and pilfer precious eggs from the Nine's private kitchen, whip up an omelet, and break into their espresso machine. Maybe even find some milk to add to my coffee. Oh, happy day.

Jo holds Ryodan's gaze for a long moment.

Her lashes drop to shield her eyes.

Slowly she turns her back on him and resumes wiping tables.

I gape, stunned.

Nothing against Jo, but I didn't think she had it in her. I want to leap up on the rail and cheer her choice to pull the plug before the bathwater drowns her.

Ryodan stands unmoving, looking down at Jo's back.

I begin to inch backward, feeling suddenly like the voyeur I am, in no mood to be caught at it.

Jo turns around and looks up at him. I know what she wants to see. She'll never find it on that implacable face. I want to shout at her to turn away again. Stop mining for gold where there is none. I tear my gaze from her and glance back at Ryodan.

Again, I gape. That's me, the flapping jaw this morning.

I didn't expect this. Not from him.

He drops his head forward in a gesture of sorrow and

lets it hang a moment. Then he inclines it slowly in acceptance and respect, and I see the tension in Jo's body ease a little when he acknowledges her as a valued loss.

I hold my breath, waiting for the bastard to nod to the next woman. The waitresses are all staring hungrily up, bristling with excitement that the boss's bed is once again open and their lives just got so much more thrilling. Some other lucky woman is about to get her world rocked and lord it over all the other waitresses until she, too, is rejected. She won't care. It's a status symbol. Like the disgusting Unseelie roaches they invite beneath their skin as fat burners.

Ryodan turns from the railing and is abruptly walking directly for me.

There goes my jaw again. I might need to muzzle myself to keep it in place this morning.

I search his face, trying to read it.

"Don't mine for gold where there is none, Mac."

"Stay out of my head."

"Wouldn't be so easy to get in there if it wasn't so empty."

"Jackass." I scowl at his back as he vanishes down the hall.

I'm heading up the stairs after breakfast when Barrons opens the door to Ryodan's office and inclines his head, motioning me in. I didn't know he was back. I suck in a breath. I wonder if we can evade Ryodan's radar and slip off to the bookstore. For heaven's sake, I'd take fifteen minutes. Anything would help. Part of his neck is now tattooed and I wonder what he's been up to while I was sleeping.

A good-looking kid stands inside. Tall, lean, and lanky, with thick dark hair that hasn't been cut in a while and beautiful aqua eyes behind glasses, I put him at about eighteen to twenty. He has a sort of brainy Canterbury scholar look, even in jeans and a blue tee-shirt. He gives me an appraising once-over as I step inside, then cocks his head as if processing some anomaly.

"Tell her what you told us," Ryodan says to the kid, closing the door on my ghoulish procession. I don't tell him it's pointless. He'll figure it out soon enough.

The kid says to me, "Who are you? And why do you smell so bad? Don't you have showers in this place? I can hook one up for you."

I have to unclench my jaw to answer. "I'm Mac. Who are you?"

The kid whistles soft and low. "Ah, so you're the one who broke her heart."

I don't ask her-who. I don't want to go there.

The kid goes there anyway. "Dani calls out your name when she sleeps. A lot. Sometimes Alina."

Ryodan seems to suddenly expand and saturate the air like Barrons does. "You won't be hearing it again. Dani sleeps at Chester's now."

I say nothing, keep my mask on.

"She doesn't sleep anywhere lately, old dude. Thought we established that last time you came calling. And the first time. And the twentieth time."

"Kid, you want to be careful around me."

"Ditto," the kid says mildly. "Old dude."

"You haven't seen her either?" I ask hastily, trying to stave off a completely unmatched battle.

"Nope," the kid replies. "But she's disappeared before, like I told the boss man here. And his lackeys. And his lackeys' lackeys. I hate it when she does this."

I almost smile. He calls Ryodan's men lackeys. I'd like him for that alone.

Unseelie begin sifting into the office since they can't use the door. The room doesn't hold many, considering how wide a berth they give all three males. Not just

Ryodan and Barrons, who they always steer clear of by ten feet or more, but also the boy that must be Dancer if he's heard Dani talk in her sleep. I grow more aggravated by the moment as they cozy up to my backside. Dancer? Really? They don't bother a teenage kid?

Barrons and Ryodan are eyeing him, too, no doubt wondering the same thing.

Dancer shrugs. "Guess they don't like my soap. They certainly like something about you. And dude, do they stink. So, what gives with this?" he asks me. "Why do they like you so much?"

"I find that fascinating myself," Ryodan says. "Answer the kid."

Barrons gives him a look. "Tell her what you just told us," he says to Dancer.

Dancer pushes his glasses up on his nose, managing to look adorably brainy and hot in a collegiate hunk way. I get what Dani sees in him. He's pretty much perfect for her. If only he had a few superhero parts. Dani is going to be hell on a man's self-esteem when she grows up, and while Dancer doesn't seem to suffer in that department, in this world caring about a mere human is a liability.

"After we defeated the Hoar Frost King, I couldn't let it rest. Something was bothering me. I get obsessive like that when facts don't gel, or do so in a way that seems to imply impending catastrophe. Then I have to—"

Ryodan says, "Not one fucking ounce of interest in your personal problems."

"Christ, you're a cranky bloke," he says to Ryodan. To me, he says, "Each of the Unseelie has a favorite food. The Unseelie that was icing Dublin and its inhabitants was devouring a specific frequency."

Okay, that's weird. "Why would an Unseelie feed off a sound?"

"Dani and I speculate it was trying to complete itself.

That it was aware it was derived from an imperfect Song of Making and was attempting to obtain the correct elements to evolve into something else."

"Go on."

"I was able to isolate the precise frequency: the flatted or diminished fifth."

I had less than a month of music theory. "What's the flatted fifth?"

Dancer says, *"Mi contra fa est diabolus in musica*— where the *mi* and *fa* don't refer to the third and fourth notes of the musical scale but to the medieval principle of overlapping hexachords."

I say impatiently, "Clarify."

"Also known as Satan's music, or the Devil's tritone, it's an interval spanning three whole tones, such as C up to F# or F# up to C, the inverted tritone. It's used in sirens, can be found in the hymn 'A Mighty Fortress Is Our God,' Metallica's 'For Whom the Bell Tolls,' 'Purple Haze' by Jimi Hendrix, 'Black Sabbath' by Black Sabbath, Wagner's *Götterdämmerung,* the *Dante Sonata* by Liszt, Beethoven's—"

"We get the picture. Get on with it," Barrons growls.

"Mathematically speaking, harmonies are created by notes sounding together in proportion to one another that can be expressed in numbers. The Devil's tritone is commonly assigned the ratio of 64/45 or 45/32, depending on the musical context . . . And your eyes are glazing and I haven't even gotten started," Dancer says. "Okay, then, it's jarring, disconcerting, some even consider it depressing. There's a lot of controversy about whether or not ecclesiastical sorts banned it in medieval times out of fear it could summon the devil, him—" He breaks off and grins at me. "—or herself. How's that for laymen speak? Personally I find it challenging, invigorating—"

"Again with the we-don't-give-a-fuck," Ryodan says. "Tell her what you told us."

The grin fades. "Like music, all matter is composed of frequencies. Where the Hoar Frost King took his 'bites' of melody from the world, it completely consumed that frequency."

"What are you saying? We have no flatted fifths left?"

He gives me a look like I have two heads. Math and physics have never been my strong suits.

I guess again. "It's quieter in the places he iced?"

Dancer says, "In a sense. Cosmically. And that's only part of the problem."

"What's the real world application?" I growl. Nobody likes feeling dumb.

"I'm getting there. I had a hunch. I've been going back to the scenes every day. I didn't find what I was looking for until a few days ago and have been observing it since, taking measurements, projecting and speculating on the potential ramifications of—" He breaks off and looks at Ryodan. "I think we better show her. Telling her doesn't seem to be working. I thought you said she was smart."

"I took Barrons's word for it."

"Apparently he was misinformed," Dancer says.

I have the beginnings of a headache. "Oh, shut up both of you, and just show me what you're talking about."

"I think the church is the closest spot where she can get a good look," Dancer says. "The one outside Chester's is still forming."

Ryodan looks pissed. "I've got one closer." Whatever it is, and wherever, he's not at all happy about it.

I follow the three of them to the door of one of the many sleekly concealed elevators in the club.

Because there isn't enough room for my volt of vultures to maintain their distance from the men when we step inside, I get a respite. I hear thumps as they settle on the roof of the compartment.

We ride down. And down. Through the walls of the elevator, I watch the levels of the club whiz by as we descend into the chrome and glass belly of the beast. Like the city hidden beneath the abbey, the private part of Chester's is enormous. There's no way they built it all recently. I wonder if it's been standing as long as or longer than the *sidhe*-seers' hallowed enclave, and if so, where they got the building materials back then.

We continue dropping for half a mile or more. I can feel tons and tons of earth around and above me and shiver. I've always hated being underground but my interment in Mallucé's lair beneath the Burren escalated dislike to near claustrophobia. I can barely breathe down here.

As we begin to slow, Ryodan says, "Do not exit until I do. Then follow me, remaining behind me at all times."

The compartment settles and the door swishes open.

I move into the dark, silent corridor behind his broad back.

The air is chillingly cold.

It's so dark that I instinctively open my *sidhe*-seer senses to scan for the unique Shade frequency—a trick I perfected last month when I discovered a ship down near the docks where several of the vampiric Unseelie had holed up—and instantly my head explodes with pain.

I fall to my knees, clutching my skull with both hands, crying out.

I haven't felt pain like this since the night I went to meet Christian at Trinity College. I made it only a few blocks before the *Sinsar Dubh* reduced me to a gibbering, drooling mess in a gutter in Temple Bar, crushed by the agony it was inflicting.

Spikes pound through my brain. My stomach cramps and my spine becomes a red-hot poker impaling my body.

Pain fills me until I'm nothing but a single, giant exposed nerve alternately being raked over coals, then diced and iced, before getting seared again.

Barrons has me then, his arms strong, sheltering. "What the fuck, Mac?" he growls. "What's happening?"

We are definitely not having sex so I must be dying. He called me Mac. "Music," I grit through clenched teeth. "That . . . damned . . . music!"

"You hear music down here?" Dancer sounds incredulous.

My only response is a whimper.

Distantly, through the pain, I'm aware Barrons is carrying me back onto the elevator.

"Get a picture of it," Ryodan says to Dancer.

"Already got a dozen, other places."

"When I tell you to do something, don't think. Don't talk. Don't breathe."

"Reality check, thinking and breathing, necessary to take pictures. Otherwise I might end up with shots of—"

"Fucking do it."

"—your nose hairs, or mine, or—"

"You won't have a fucking nose left, you keep talking."

I hear a cell phone camera snapping.

Whatever it is, I want to see it for myself. I didn't make the miserable trek belowground and suffer this pain to leave without getting a good look at whatever our latest problem is. I drag my pounding head from Barrons's chest and peer into the darkness beyond.

Ryodan shines the wide beam of a powerful flashlight out the door. My stalkers have begun popping into the corridor.

Halfway down the hall, I see a low-hanging round black globe. Not because Ryodan's flashlight has illuminated it, but because the beam has lit everything *but* the circular area suspended in the air.

One of the Unseelie sifts in close to it, and as more arrive, it glides back to make room, and inadvertently brushes the black globe.

The instant it touches it, the ghoul contorts, is stretched long and thin into a tatter of black-skinned robe and bones, and screams with such terror that the skin all over my body prickles in goose flesh. As its hood elongates impossibly, I catch a glimpse of something shiny, metallic, where I think its face should be.

The black globe swallows it whole. Which is impossible, given the globe doesn't have a twentieth the mass of the Unseelie.

My ghouls jostle and shove in panic. Each one that brushes the globe suffers the same fate. Stretched long and thin, then gone. The screaming is deafening, far worse than the hideous chittering. Some sift out. Others stand frozen.

The elevator doors close.

"Now do you get it?" Dancer says.

I'd shake my head but it would explode. I peer at him with pain-blurred eyes and whisper, "No."

"When the Hoar Frost King bit chunks of frequency from our world, it created a cosmic deficit. The fabric of our universe began to unravel. That alone was problematic enough, but compounding it, at each site where it fed it also deposited something, like an overfed scavenger, regurgitating unwanted bones. Whatever it expelled possesses astronomically compact mass and density." He pauses. When a lightbulb doesn't instantly brighten over my head, he says with elaborate patience, "It's. Deforming. Space-time."

"Are you saying what I just saw is a black hole?" I manage. The farther we get from the globe, the less pain I feel.

Dancer says, "I lack the ability to perform the tests I'd like to run. Speculation aside, I can only observe these facts: they share certain similar characteristics to black holes, they were no larger than pinpricks at first, they absorb everything they come in contact with, and they're growing. The one we just saw is the largest I've seen at any of the sites."

"It's the first place that got iced," Ryodan says.

"You didn't tell me any of this," I mutter crossly to Barrons.

Barrons shoots me a dry looks that says, *Far be it from me to disrupt your brood. You might be motivated to do something and then I wouldn't know who you were anymore.*

I wrinkle my nose at him and don't dignify it with a response.

"I didn't know you had one in the club," Dancer says. "I thought the one out front would get the honors. Dude, Chester's is going to be swallowed from the inside!"

"Dude me one more time and you're dead."

We ride the rest of the way up the shaft in silence.

16

The Unseelie King settles into what passes as an enormous red crushed-velvet chair in what might loosely be called a theater room before a stage so vast the edges furl out into night skies filled with stars. On the left, the Milky Way shimmers. To the right, a nebula stains the sky rainbow-bright.

He rests his head of sorts on a hand of sorts and broods.

His woman retains no memory of him at all.

She knows him only as the Seelie Queen's greatest enemy and believes that since the Unseelie Prince was unable to kill her, the king himself came to finish the job.

Though she conceals it with defiance, she is terrified of him.

To see his beloved gaze upon him with fear . . . there are no words. Neither split into dozens of humans, as he must be in order to walk among the tiny, strange, absurdly determined creatures who face such futile odds, nor as a god.

The joy that burned inside him upon seeing her again is ash.

He changes a channel of sorts with a remote of sorts and one of the more interesting cities on one of his more interesting worlds takes the limelight.

It is dying, as he suspected.

No matter, another will come.

But another of *her* will not come. In all this time, no one has touched him as she has. To have her back again and not have her at all is almost worse than believing her gone. It is as if a replication has risen from the dead, a perfect mirror image, nothing within. Should he take her into the White Mansion? Confront her with the residue of their love?

"Is that Dublin?"

Her voice is beautiful. She had names for him, endearments she called him. He would raze worlds to hear them again.

She stands behind him. Close enough that if she chose she could place a hand on his shoulder, were he not the size of a skyscraper and she the size of a pea. Once, she wore a glamour that met him size for girth, wing for wing, crown for crown. He does not bother to answer. Temple Bar is red, the River Liffey silver. She has eyes. She knows this world.

"Am I prisoner here?"

"You are." He was never letting her go. He would not turn and gaze fifty floors of wing and blackness down at her. He was uncertain what he might do if he did.

"What are you doing to Dublin? It ails. I feel it."

He doesn't want to see that beneath a cloak of ermine fur she's wearing a diaphanous gown of white that does nothing to conceal her exquisite body, her hair bound in a platinum braid. He would commit genocide on a dozen planets to see her in a gown of bloodred, pale hair spilling to her ankles, joy in her eyes, a smile of greeting.

"I do nothing. They do it themselves."

"Attend it," she says imperiously. "My druids are there."

"Give me an incentive."

"My druids are there."

"That is not one." He doesn't bother to conceal his bitterness. Should he take her beneath him? Discover if that makes her recall, if memory can be forced to return?

"You will not coerce intimacy where none is granted," she says sharply.

He goes very still. "I did not say that."

"You did."

She can still hear him. She may not remember him or the epic love they share but she hears his desires, as she always has.

"I would never."

"You would. You are the Unseelie King. You slew the one who ruled before me. You care for nothing and never have. You think you create but you destroy. That is all of which you are capable."

Anger and something deeper ruffles his wings. Her words are too similar to the note he still carries. "That is untrue."

"Show me. Help my druids."

"God does not step in and adjust minute details on a whim."

"You are not God. You are the Unseelie King, once the true queen's consort. You built an army of monstrosities and took them to war against my people. And destroy is precisely what you do."

Once, she helped shelter his monstrosities. Believed they deserved the light. That they could be perfected, freed. "For you, my love."

"I am not your love. I am Aoibheal, queen of the Fae. Return me to my court. I am needed there."

"Return you for what? You can do nothing to repair

the rift between your world and theirs, the many rifts in them both. Abandon it and abandon your foolish, petty court." Choose me, he doesn't say. Not that insignificant world. Not those tiny, inconsequential beings.

"To live with a foolish, petty king?"

She thinks him a fool and petty. He will not acknowledge the arrow shot as a question. She calls him a destroyer. She sees nothing of his glory, recalls no details of the worlds they once made together, so beautiful they often rested on a nearby star for time uncounted to watch them bloom.

"You say you love me," she says. "Show me. Restore Dublin. Heal their world and mine."

"Why have you always cared so much about these tiny worlds?"

"Why have you never?"

He had once. When she'd cared about him. He'd made himself small for her and walked in her manner, tending small things. But being small was so much more complicated than being God. "If I do this for you, will you share my bed of your own volition?"

He feels her anger, her instant denial.

On stage, he weaves for her a brutal, horrific glamour of what's to come. Dublin falling, the Earth dying, the lovely blue and white planet blinking out then gone. Attached to it by a planetary umbilical cord, the Fae realm also goes black and disappears.

Behind him, she gasps then says stiffly, "That is your price?"

"That is my price."

"And you will fix our worlds?"

"I will."

"And you can?"

"I can."

"One time only," she says tightly.

"I specify the duration."

"It is limited to a single human fortnight. Then you will never come to me again. You will not seek me. You will never cross my path."

"Before."

"When it is done. That is non-negotiable."

"Everything is negotiable if the correct pressure is applied."

The look she gives him is venom and ice.

He will concede for her. Always only for her.

"Say it," he demands.

"Yes," she hisses.

She said yes. Even spat with fury, the single word is an aria to once deafened ears. None has ever been sweeter on her lips. He will taste her assent before, like her memory, it too vanishes.

"Your tithe to this compact between us will be a kiss." He begins reducing himself to make it so. He will turn and touch her, take her in his arms.

He doesn't tell her that it's too late.

He will have, at the very least, a single kiss.

Without the Song of Making—which she has never known and he turned his back on long ago—none can save either world: Fae or human.

17

"I'd rather have a bottle in front of me"

MAC

I'm an aimless, trapped barfly, stalked by Unseelie ghouls who have once again replenished their numbers, confined to Chester's by Ryodan's insistence that I guard against a threat that isn't the threat he thinks it is, while driving myself crazy worrying about a genuine threat of cataclysmic proportions.

There's a black hole, or its close approximation, growing beneath my feet, and who knows how many more forming beyond the club's walls. There were numerous icings in Dublin, more outside the city, and according to Ryodan, hundreds in various countries around the world.

Are innocent people, like the Unseelie ghouls, accidently brushing up against them and dying? How large are the other globes? Was Ryodan's really the first or has the Hoar Frost King been in our realm longer than we know? Perhaps it started in China, or Australia, or even America. How solid is our information? How soon can we send scouts to learn more?

How close have I walked to one of those quantum

pinpricks, not realizing Death was right there in the street with me, a misstep away?

Tired of wandering from one dance floor to the next, growing increasingly aggravated by the patrons, I decide to stake out the Sinatra subclub. The old world elegance appeals to me and it's mostly empty—or at least it was before me and my dark, smelly army arrived. "Get off those stools!" I try to shoo them. They resettle with what I imagine are scornful looks beneath voluminous hoods. I recall the metallic flash I glimpsed as one of them was devoured by an impossibly dense globe of corrupted space-time and wonder what would happen if I tried to yank back one of their cowls to see a face.

I decide against it. I'd rather not know just how hideous my second skins are. I have enough nightmares.

I perch on a leather bar stool between them and begin watching an obviously inebriated bartender in a dirty, wrinkled tux that looks like he slept in it make the worst martinis I've ever seen.

Clubs call pretty much anything a martini now, and there's no question he got his credentials at the school of life. He should be ashamed. I rummage in my purse, pop an aspirin in my mouth, and crunch it to dispel headache residue.

Barrons went through the Silvers to join the rest of the Nine, hunting for Dani. I prefer him there than wandering around the city without me. Though I've not gotten the faintest tweak from my inner antenna, it won't be long before the princess resurfaces somewhere. And it's *not* going to be on top of Barrons.

Dancer says we need Dani now more than ever. She was the one who figured out what the Hoar Frost King was doing, and he hopes their brains combined hold the key to relocking the doors that are opening in great yawning black holes all over our world.

If it can even be done.

According to physics, what we seek is impossible but since the walls came down between Man and Faery, human laws of physics no longer apply. I wonder if the fragments of Faery worlds I call IFPs are contributing to the black-hole problem. The boundaries of our world are a mess and have been for a while, creating a highly unstable environment where pretty much anything could go wrong, as it did eons ago in the ancient Hall of All Days and the Silvers. I wonder that we didn't see something like this coming.

I munch an olive to get the taste of aspirin out of my mouth.

"Hey, you didn't order a drink! Stay the fuck outta my condiment tray!" the bartender barks, hostile, and a little slurry.

Whatever happened to pretty girls getting free drinks? Or at least one damn olive.

I peer up at my reflection in the mirror behind the bar. There I am, blond hair, blue eyes, terrific white teeth (thanks Mom, Dad, and braces!), a nice mouth with a generous lower lip, clear skin. I think I'm pretty.

"And you guys"—the bartender snaps at my ghouls, and I think, Good luck with that—"order drinks or get off my stools!"

"You've been grazing on candied cherries for the past ten minutes," I tell him. "You've eaten half a jar. Stow it." People are starving in Dublin but Chester's has condiments.

He flips me off with both hands and rotates the birds around each other.

I turn sideways on the stool so I don't have to see him and resume my brood. The city I love is finally coming back to life, and although I have personal problems, they are slightly more manageable—or at least a little less urgent at the moment—than our newfound global issues.

My dark companion attempts to seize the moment.

Read me, open me, I possess the answers you seek, it lies. *I will show you how to heal this world.*

Again with the been-there-done-that. I don't believe the Unseelie King dumped any knowledge about how to patch holes in worlds into his book of dark magic. It's another fake carrot at the end of the *Sinsar Dubh*'s endless profusion of sticks.

Besides, it wouldn't give a rat's ass about saving this world. It would leave and find another. And another. Ad infinitum. I've not forgotten it once said to me: *Can there be any act of creation that does not first destroy? Villages fall. Cities rise. Humans die. Life springs from the soil wherein they lie. Is not any act of destruction, should Time enough pass, an act of creation?*

Our worries about rebuilding, parceling out districts, and reinstating currency now seem insignificant, but Ryodan insists we carry on. Barrons agrees that not only must we pursue an illusion of normalcy, but conceal from the general populace the danger the world is in. They contend if people believe the world might be ending, it'll be the riots of Halloween all over again.

Oh, yeah. Politicians R Us.

I seriously doubt we're going to be able to hide it long. If they're still too small to spot, it's only a matter of time before they're not. People will start seeing them, messing with them, vanishing.

I half expected Barrons and Ryodan to say: screw it, pack up, we're leaving. They're immortal and there are countless worlds. There's nothing to stop them from circling their wagons and heading off for the universe's vast, untamed Wild West.

Yet, they stay and I'm glad they do because there's no way I'm giving up on my world. This is what we've been fighting about since the dawn of time when the Fae first arrived on our planet and began messing with it. Earth is ours. I'm not letting them have it. I'm not letting them destroy it.

Not on my watch.

Too bad I have no idea how I'm going to back up my ballsy position, but I've been in impossible situations before and got out of them.

My brain processes what I just watched happen. Apparently I couldn't keep my eyes off the pathetic excuse for a bartender and turned back toward him at some point without realizing it. "Oh, for heaven's sake, you just ruined that drink! Who taught you to pour?"

"Fuck you, bitch. Ain't your bar."

I stand and hurry around the counter. My flock rustles in behind me. "It is now. Get out. I'm taking over." I can't let him tarnish my profession anymore. He just served a smoked martini that had begun promisingly, with gin and a dash of single malt Scotch—then apparently forgot what he was doing and added vermouth, and insult to injury, an olive, pimento intact, instead of a lemon twist. Yellow was Alina's favorite color and I used to take my time making my lemon twists as complex and pretty as they could be, little origami fruit peels. My mouth puckers in sympathy for the silver-haired gentleman sipping the drink. It's no wonder the world no longer knows what martinis are.

"Who the fuck do you think you are?" the bleary-eyed bartender snarls drunkenly as I approach. "This is *my* bar. Get your ass back on that stool and buy a drink or leave, you stupid cunt. And get those smelly fucks out of here!"

I see red. Like I'd drink anything he poured. And I really hate the c-word. No clue why. It just doesn't work for me. Seems I have my own event horizon: inactivity, worry, and frustration have devoured my patience, sucked it away into a deep dark hole from which it may never return.

I walk straight for him and pop him in the face with my fist. Not too hard. Just hard enough to get him to go away.

His nose spurts blood—

YES BLOOD YES! the Book explodes. *Kill him, worthless piece of human trash! Take this bar and take the club and we will K'VRUCK THEM ALL!*

I rummage for my seventh-grade performance—where did I leave off? I remember being eleven. I was happy then, in a much simpler world. Or so I thought.

Bloodred like the blood of Mick O'Leary, the man you RIPPED to pieces with your bare hands then CHEWED—

For a second I can't find my place, the word "chewed" throws me off so badly, and instead of focusing I wonder if I had blood in my mouth that day and didn't notice. Panicked, I plunge into my recitation at the first place I can think of and shout, " 'Prophet!' said I, 'thing of evil, prophet still, if bird or devil! Whether tempter sent or whether tempest tossed thee here ashore—' "

The bartender clutches his nose and stares at me like I have three heads. I toss him the positively filthy bar towel he'd been using to dry clean glasses. Well, as clean as they could be considering the water in the sink behind the bar is disgustingly black with weak gray soapy suds. I realize I'm still spouting poetry and terminate mid-twelfth stanza.

"You're off your fucking rocker!"

"You have no idea. I don't have a rocker anymore. I don't even have a fucking porch to put it on. And there certainly aren't slow paddling fans or magnolia trees blossoming above aforementioned missing chair." God, I get homesick for the South sometimes. A sunny day. A polka-dot bikini and a swimming pool. One day I'm going back to Ashford. I'll walk around and pretend I'm a normal person. Just for a day or two. "I'll punch you again. So move." I crowd him with my body and force him to walk backward through my throng of Unseelie, out from behind the lovely bar I realize I'm really looking forward to tending.

It'll feel like old times, soothe me. Ground me to the real Mac Lane again.

"I'm telling the boss, you freaky bitch!"

"You do that. Tell him the name's Mac when you talk to him and see how well that goes over. Now get out. And stay out."

I turn to the gentleman who's completely unfazed by our bizarre altercation—this *is* Chester's—and is currently studying his awful martini as if trying to decide what went so wrong with it, and pluck the glass from his hand. It wasn't even the right glass.

"Smoked?"

He nods.

"Be right up."

I pull the drain on the filthy water, rummage beneath the bar for clean towels, wash my hands, grab a chilled glass, and stir a perfectly proportioned smoked martini. I'm so used to dealing with my wraiths, I slide smoothly through them.

When he tastes it, he smiles appreciatively and the ground beneath my feet solidifies just like that. Familiar routine is balm to a fragmented soul.

I begin rearranging the liquor on my shelves the proper way, humming beneath my breath.

Inside me a book *whumps* closed. For the time being. Looks like I've learned one more way to temporarily shut it up. Poems and bartending. Who'd have thought? But Band-Aids for my disease aren't what I'm after. I want a surgeon to perform an operation that leaves a deep incision where something nasty used to be, followed by a scar to remind me every day that it's over and I survived.

And for that I need a half-mad king. Not getting any closer to finding the spell stuck in this place.

"Hey, Mac," Jo says, dropping onto a stool. "What's with all the Unseelie behind your bar?"

"Don't ask. Just don't even go there."

She shrugs. "Have you seen Dani lately?"

That question has become a stake through my heart. One of these days I'm just going to snap, *Yes, and I'm the jackass that chased her into the Hall of All Days, so crucify me and put me out of my misery.*

I give my standard, noncommittal reply.

"How about Kat?"

"Not for a few days."

Beneath a cap of short dark hair, shimmering with blond and auburn highlights, Jo's delicate face is pale, her eyes red from crying. I shake my head and debate saying something about what I saw this morning.

My brain vetoes the idea. My mouth says, "I saw what you did this morning," proving my suspicion that the road between the two is as bad as the highways around Atlanta, under eternal, hazardous construction.

"What do you mean?" she says warily.

"Ryodan nodded and you turned away. You dumped him."

She inhales sharply and holds it a moment, then, "I suppose you think I'm crazy."

"No," I say. "I think you're beautiful and smart and talented and deserve a man that can feel with something besides his dick."

She blinks and looks surprised, and it pisses me off because she should know all of that.

"I understood from the beginning what he was, Mac," she says tiredly. "What *it* was between us. But he has such . . . and I never felt . . . and I started wanting to believe even though I knew better. Began telling myself all kinds of lies. So I moved on before he did. Pride was all I had left to salvage."

"Doesn't make it any easier though, does it?" I say sympathetically. I feel my bartending skills blossoming: the pouring, listening, steering away from complete anesthetization with alcohol toward something that might actually help, change the person's life, shake it up in a good way.

"I don't think I'm strong enough to stay away from him, Mac. I'm going to quit working here. I can't see him every day. You know what they're like. He may not have taken anyone else up those stairs this morning, but he will. I'm going to ask Kat if I can move back to the abbey."

"Know the best way to forget a man?"

"A frontal lobotomy?"

I snort, thinking of that song we used to play back home in the Brickyard that went, *I'd rather have a bottle in front of me than a frontal lobotomy.* "No. With two men."

She smiles but it fades swiftly. "I'm afraid I'd be needing ten to clear my head of that man."

"Or perhaps," I say, "a single incredible one." Stupendous sex is a drug, addictive, consuming. I know from personal experience.

"Sounds like you have someone in mind. I'm so not in the mood, Mac. He'd only pale in comparison."

"Maybe not." I lean across the counter and speak softly into her ear.

When she leaves, wearing a thoughtful expression, I ponder the seed I planted, hoping it yields healthy fruit. I think it will. I think it's exactly what she needs to buffer her heart, cleanse her body from craving the touch of a man we both know she can never hold.

Besides, there's a possibility it will piss Ryodan off, in

a territorial sort of way, which will still further ease the sting to Jo's wounded heart.

Heaven knows the man I pointed her at won't mind.

I smile and line a few choice bottles up on my counter, and try my hand at pouring high and flashy. Patrons love a good show.

When I glance up to greet a couple of new customers, I inhale sharply and stare right past them, staggered by the vision I see, unable to process my abrupt change in fortune. Talk about tall, dark, and utterly unexpected.

Time grinds to a halt and everything goes still around me, the thronging patrons receding beyond the edges of my periphery, leaving only one: the Dreamy-Eyed Guy, wearing an amused expression, is standing three clubs away, watching me toss my bottles flamboyantly, and I recall a night I watched him do the same.

He inclines his head, dark eyes starry. *Nice show.*

The Unseelie King is back in town, wearing his old skins again!

We've been scouring ancient books and scrolls for months, trying to find the spell to summon him, and the surgeon I need just arrived out of the blue! The one with butterfly fingers who creates and destroys worlds and can surely remove this great staining darkness inside me!

I didn't think he'd *ever* come back willingly, off with his concubine somewhere, rekindling her memory and reclaiming her love.

Elation floods me. I can get my life back, and while I'm at it, get rid of my smelly Unseelie, too. Approach the queen about the Song of—I swiftly terminate that thought and repadlock it.

I vault the counter, sending glasses flying and shoving startled patrons off their stools, but by the time my feet hit the floor, the Dreamy-Eyed Guy is gone.

18

"When life pushes me I push harder.
What doesn't kill me makes me stronger"

MAC

The next few days pass in the closest thing to hopeful peace I've known in months. Even surrounded by the debauchery of Chester's, my inner book remains silent. I don't know if seeing the king made it shut up for some reason, if familiar routine makes me that much stronger, or if it thinks it has me trapped in the cesspool of life here at Chester's and my capitulation is only a matter of time.

I tend bar amid my Unseelie coven, watch for the various forms of the king, keep an eye out for princesses, and await Barrons's return, hopefully with Dani in tow. I can't wait to tell him the king is back and we can quit losing time in the Silvers.

When the ruler of the dark Fae took an interest in Dublin before, his various incarnations often came to the club. The Unseelie King is too vast to walk among humans in a single human body. He has to divide himself into multiple skins, and when he does, not everyone sees him the same way. Where I saw a young, hot guy with gorgeous eyes, Barrons saw a frail old man, Christian saw a Morgan Freeman look-alike, Jo saw a pretty French woman. It's only a matter of time before we see one of them again, or I hear of a McCabe sighting or run into the old news vendor on the streets. I'll be faster next time because I won't be struck dumb and motionless by his unexpected return.

The thought of living divided like this, tempted every day by power I can't use, tortured by thoughts of what my inner monster might be able to make me do if I'm not vigilant one hundred percent of the time, is more than I can stand.

Can't eviscerate essential self, the king once said. But this copy of the Book *isn't* my essential self. It's his.

And I'll be damned if I'm keeping it.

At least now I can stop considering a risky plan B. The king came to Dublin once before because his book escaped. It seems logical if Cruce escaped, the king would return and re-ice him and I could demand he free me. Unfortunately I'm not entirely convinced the king would (a) return or (b) give a shit about any of it. His priorities spring of stars and infinity, not the tiny moments that span a human life. And there we'd be, with Cruce loose.

Dicey plan.

Humming beneath my breath, I finish polishing my bar. It's eleven in the morning and I've just opened my subclub for business. The glasses sparkle, so clean they squeak. Ice is stocked, glasses frosted, condiments fresh, liquor replenished.

I'm bent over, reaching in the fridge to pull out lemons and start making my twists, when I hear a deep baritone say, "Laphroaig. No ice."

The accent is Scottish, the voice one I've heard before. I glance up into eyes strikingly similar to Christian's, before he began turning Unseelie. They bore into mine, cheetah-gold, assessing. Same five o'clock shadow, chiseled features, and beautiful dark skin. Serious power rolls off the man.

It's Christian's uncle, the Keltar they call "the Inhabited." He once opened himself up to thirteen ancient, dark druids and has never been able to exorcise them.

I can sympathize with that problem.

The last time I saw him was the night we interred the *Sinsar Dubh* beneath the abbey. He was with his twin brother, Drustan, a druid who died in a fire but somehow came back to life and allegedly possesses an incorruptible heart; another of Christian's uncles, Cian, who spent a thousand years trapped in a Silver; and Christian's father, who was also druid to the Seelie. Talk about your messed-up family.

"Dageus, right?"

"Aye." He palms the glass I slide him and takes a sip. "What's with all the Unseelie behind the bar with you, lass?"

Another question I'm sick of. I get it a hundred times a day, at least once from every person that takes a stool and orders a drink, and as the day goes on, half a dozen times from the really drunk ones. I've heard every variation on every joke they could possibly slap lamely together in their inebriated, sex-obsessed minds.

"Ghosts," I say, "of all the Unseelie I killed. They haunt me." I've found it usually shuts people up. He doesn't look at all surprised, but then why would he? His ghosts haunt him from the inside.

"Where's the bastard that runs this club?"

"Around somewhere. Are you here because you've located Christian?" I ask hopefully.

"Nay. We've tried summoning the queen repeatedly to request her aid, but she's no' responding to any of our rituals."

I wonder if buried in their countless records and annals they have a summoning spell for the king. Although

I don't appear to currently need it, I file the thought away for future reference, aware that asking such a question might only open a new can of worms, and turn more pairs of intensely penetrating Keltar eyes my way than I'd like.

"Now that the Compact is broken, we've no influence over the Fae world. Christian's gone, without trace. The only thing of which we're certain is he's no' in Ireland anymore. We've fair torn the country apart searching."

"Can't you try tracking the Crimson Hag instead?"

"We've naught of her to use in such a spell. We'd need flesh, bone, a gut from her gown might serve."

"No recent sightings?"

"The Unseelie Princes claim she tried to capture them shortly after she took Christian, but they've since joined forces, and she's no' been seen again." He rubs a stubble-shadowed jaw. "It happened differently than I foresaw," he says heavily. "I was watching for the wrong signs."

I'm about to ask what he's talking about when Ryodan takes a stool beside him. "Keltar. Hear you're looking for me."

Translation: he was sitting upstairs in his office, watching his endless cameras, eavesdropping. I'm surprised he came down. Appears he has enough respect for the Highlander to do more than he does for most: acknowledge his presence and appear as requested. Interesting.

Dageus says just as coolly, "Hear you met with a Seelie Prince, had negotiations. You will be summoning him for us now."

Ryodan cuts him an amused look. "Will I."

"Aye."

"Think again."

"What do you want with R'jan?" I ask Dageus.

"He's a sifter and is currently in control of all Seelie.

I want him to dispatch other sifters to hunt the Hag for us."

"Couldn't you send some of your men as well?" I say to Ryodan quickly. "If Christian hadn't distracted the Hag and she'd kept killing that night, who knows what might have happened. We owe him, Ryodan. All of us. We can't just leave him out there, being killed over and over again."

"It's keeping her busy and out of my fucking hair," Ryodan says.

I should have known better than to try an emotional entreaty with him. I employ reason in my next attempt. "If we don't save him from the Hag, he'll be more problematic to you, to all of us, should he eventually escape. He was sane enough to sacrifice himself. That sanity won't last long in her hands."

Ryodan shrugs. "We put him down if he returns. No different than any other Unseelie Prince. If he's not useful, he's disposable."

"No other Unseelie Prince would have sacrificed himself," I snap.

"He is Keltar, and that is all the difference necessary," Dageus says. "In exchange for your aid, we'll help you reclaim the abbey from those who've taken over." He drops the bomb quietly.

"What?" I practically shout. "Someone has taken over the abbey?" I look at Ryodan and my hands curl into fists. He knew! And said nothing to me. "When did you find out about this?" I demand. "And why didn't you tell me? You *do* remember what's under there, right?"

"I'll handle it when the others return. And don't say that again in here."

I grit my jaw. I can't believe I just said it. Here of all places. No, I didn't spell out *what* was beneath the abbey but I said enough that a curious eavesdropper might decide to go looking.

Dageus says, "Three have already met their deaths. No doubt more will be finding graves the longer you delay."

Not if I have anything to say about it, and I could write a dissertation. I strip the apron from my waist and begin closing my bar down. I shiver, dreading the answer to my next question. All good coups begin with the deposing of the current leader. "Is Kat okay?"

"I'm sure she is. She's a survivor," Ryodan says.

I glare at him. He's never said anything that nice about me.

Dageus finishes his drink and slides it back for another. "I doona ken the names of the slain. During battle for possession of the grounds, a *sidhe*-seer escaped. We found her stumbling, badly injured, along the road toward Dublin. Drustan took her to the hospital at Dublin Castle. Your Inspector Jayne said he will commit the aid of his Guardians but only if the *sidhe*-seers turn over either the spear or sword to his troops. Permanently."

I slap lids on the condiments and shove them in the fridge. Not a chance in hell. "What happened, Ryodan? You were supposed to place more powerful wards around the grounds. That was part of our negotiations."

"My men have been busy, in case you've forgotten. Besides, you asked us to place more wards against Fae. Not humans."

"*Humans* took control?" This just keeps getting worse. "Who?"

"The new *sidhe*-seers say it's their home now."

I narrow my eyes and snarl. *Sidhe*-seers came into *our* town and took *our* home? I promised Kat we wouldn't let this happen. I promised her we would protect the abbey. We're the home team. Nobody takes our stadium. "How many are there? What weapons do they have? How did they take the abbey? Didn't Kat put up a fight?"

Dageus says, "If your Kat who was with us that night is in charge now, that may explain things. The woman we found said their headmistress has been missing for nigh a week, and someone inside their own group, Margery, invited the new *sidhe*-seers in."

Nearly a week? That means she disappeared the day after our meeting! "Have you seen her?" I ask Ryodan.

"What do you think, she comes to visit me," he says. "This is Katarina we're talking about."

"Bar's closed," I snap at a guy about to sit down.

He looks at Ryodan and Dageus. "They're sitting here."

"I said it's closed."

"Pour me a drink, bitch. It's a free fucking world." He drops a leg over the stool.

Ryodan smashes a fist out sideways, squarely into the guy's face without even looking, while saying, "Assuming I arrange this meeting, the Keltar will aid in regaining control of the abbey regardless of the outcome." The guy flies backward off the bar stool and crashes to the floor.

"Unlike you, we are men of our word. Unlike you," Dageus growls, "we are men. As in human."

"Humans break." Ryodan doesn't say it, doesn't have to, it hangs in the air: *We don't.*

The guy Ryodan punched picks himself up, gives us looks like we're all crazy, and backs away into the crowd.

I tell Dageus, "The meeting with R'jan happens after we free the abbey."

"It happens before or no' at all," Dageus says flatly.

"More *sidhe*-seers could die!" I say heatedly.

"Aye. *Once*. Christian is being butchered o'er and o'er again every day." The Highlander's brogue thickens. "Who kens it—perhaps he's died a hundred times so far. Have you any idea what that can do to a man?"

I shiver. Yes. It sounds too similar to the hell Barrons's son suffered. Regenerating only to be killed each time he was reborn. It turned the small boy into an animal, drove the child deep into madness from which there was no return. What is the same fate doing to Christian, even as we speak, who was highly unstable to begin with? He certainly hasn't had an easy time of it since I arrived in Dublin: catapulted unarmed into the Silvers for years by a botched ritual, fed Unseelie by myself, locked in a desperate battle for control over what he's becoming, and now held captive by a monster that rips out his guts every time he heals.

"His mind is fragile. His body is no'. 'Tis a dangerous and deadly imbalance that can go terribly wrong."

It certainly is.

To Ryodan, I say, "Summon the prince for Dageus or I'm moving back to the bookstore, and leaving you on your own with the Unseelie Princesses. With Barrons in Faery, you're the only one I'm protecting anyway."

To Dageus, I say, "Get your clan ready to fight."

"Och, MacKayla, 'tis no' a thing for which the Keltar need preparing. We were born ready."

19

"Hey, hey mama, like the way you move"

LOR

"Think you missed a spot," I tell the voluptuous blonde that's washing my dick.

I'm Pri-ya, I can't be expected to bathe myself. They've been giving me sponge baths 'cause I'm pretty much covered from head to toe in pussy juice. They feed me and fuck me and clean me. Reminds me of the good old days when a man protected women with his club and they took care of him in return.

This week has been one of the finest of my existence—well, at least in the past century anyway—a veritable fuck-party 24/7, with five to ten women in the room at any given time, their sole reason for existing to sate my many needs, all blond, all buxom, all horny as hell. Life rocks. It's better than Woodstock.

At first I pretended to be completely senseless, incapable of speech, but that gets old fast. Can't tell a woman what you want next if you're not talking, can't ask what they want, although I never have a problem figuring that out. You watch their faces, listen to the sounds they make. Do they whimper, or do that sudden inhale that turns into a killer, husky purr? Do they growl and turn a good fuck into a better fight? Most women in these times got a whole lot of frustration to take out in bed, when they know they got a man big and tough enough to handle it. Are they the kind that tries not to make any sound at all, like they're too tough to crack? That's just waving a big-ass red flag at this bull. Those are the ones that always end up making the most noise by the time I'm done with 'em. I especially like the ones that hiss like a cat when I fuck 'em hard from behind, rubbing back, horny and passionate and wild.

Damn, I love women.

One thing that seems universal is that after a good hard fucking, most of 'em love to lay back and have a man take his time with them, stroking 'em from head to toe, licking, petting, telling 'em how beautiful they are, making 'em come over and over, especially with their hands tied, not that I'm into your run-of-the-mill S&M. I like to know the woman in my bed *wants* to call me master. That being said, I do like chains. Something about the heavy links against soft, silken skin, telling me I can take my time doing whatever I want. Test their sexual limits.

"There's another sticky spot." I point to my groin where a smear of honey lingers. She licks it off with cat-like delicacy. Then starts sucking. Christ.

Once I realized the boss had fallen for my charade and wasn't checking on me, I quit being so disgustingly Pri-ya. According to the promise I made Mac, I got one more week of this, then it's back to the grind.

I mean to make the most of it. Then I'll hunt and kill the Unseelie bitch that has some kind of strange magic that actually worked on me.

Turn me Pri-ya? You can't amp up my sex drive. It's already over the top.

Aw, fuck me, this blonde's got a tongue that could

strip copper tubing clean! I grab her head and pull her up to kiss the honey from her mouth. As I roll her beneath me, crushed between a tangle of naked, horny women, and about to drive in deep, I hear a woman say sternly, "Get out of here. All of you."

What the fuck? I didn't even hear the door open. Has the boss figured me out? Did Mac rat on me?

I ignore it. They're gonna have to drag me out of this bed.

"You know I'm Ryodan's girlfriend. You know he listens to me. You want to keep your jobs?"

I freeze, halfway in. It's Jo. What the hell is she doing here?

Reluctantly, with a pissed off sound, the woman in my arms tries to disengage. I groan and hold on, won't let her go.

"In five seconds anyone that's still in bed with Lor is fired."

In two seconds my bed is empty. None of these women are willing to lose such a highly valued commodity as a place to work, food, and shelter, not in times like these. Not even for the glory of my dick.

I sigh then turn it into another weird-ass moan. I don't moan. I fucking roar. This Pri-ya business is taxing.

I roll onto my side and give Jo my ass, hoping she'll just say whatever she has to say and go away, send back my babes.

I try to summon a pathetic whimper but it comes out sounding too much like me: a pissed off, sexually frustrated grunt. My dick was ready, almost home sweet home, and now it's been relegated to a cardboard box beneath a bridge, cold and alone. It's swollen and painfully compressed between the bed and my thigh.

I'm supposed to be a sex slave, so I can hardly roll over and ask her what the fuck she's doing here.

I hear a rustling sound then feel her weight settle on the bed next to me.

Then there's the sound of a washcloth drizzling water as she wrings it out into the basin, and I think, what the hell, Jo's gonna finish the bath the blondes were giving me?

When she settles a hand on my back, I jerk. This is Jo. This is Ryodan's territory. I don't mess with the boss's stuff. Nobody does. It'd be nearly as stupid as pissing off Barrons.

"Mac told me you're Pri-ya," Jo says. "She says she doesn't remember anything from that time. That it's all just a blur of sex."

I'm instantly defensive: she looking to cheat on the boss? Women don't cheat on Ryodan. Fuck, they don't cheat on any of us. You don't give up the best.

She runs her hand over my back, down my ass. I tense but stay perfectly still, thinking.

"God, you're beautiful," she says softly.

Wait, I'm supposed to moan. I try but get another frustrated grunt. Shit.

"I need a blur of sex," she continues, talking and touching.

Who doesn't? My dick gets harder. She's not even my type. She's petite and brunette with huge eyes and a delicate face. She's exactly what I steer clear of.

But I'm supposedly Pri-ya.

I sigh. Looks like my game is ending sooner than I planned. I grunt with sheer frustration and roll over, look up at her to tell her to get her ass back to the boss and we'll just forget all about this. My dick snaps straight up pointing to heaven, expressing firm opposition.

I clamp my open mouth shut again, thinking, Aw, no, no, no, no, don't do that, honey, anything but that.

She's staring down at me with big, beautiful eyes filled with tears.

"You're not really there, right?" She searches my face and I instantly make my eyes go glassy. I been doing it for days, it's second nature now. She looks down at my dick and I try to will it limp but it doesn't work for shit. It's a simple beast. A woman is an occasion. My dick rises to it.

"I couldn't stand it if I thought you'd remember this. It's just that I broke up with Ryodan—"

Aw, shit.

"—not that you can really even call it a breakup because I knew from the beginning we weren't really together—"

Sometimes the boss really pisses me off. We never keep a woman more than a few weeks. Human women fall in love. It's just what they do, so you gotta be real clear from the get-go that things aren't permanent, and Ryodan did stupid things like sometimes putting his arm around her, and the fact is, I knew all along he was just doing it to keep better tabs on Dani, 'cause we'd pretty much all do anything to watch over that kid. We been watching her for years, keeping her alive, giving her the chance to grow up. It ain't been easy; the kid's a handful and we all kind of wonder what kind of woman she's gonna be one day. Can't help it. When you live as long as we do, you find yourself in bed with women you watched get born. It's weird and not at the same time. I know we gotta protect our own, by any means necessary, but when you're as addictive as we are, you gotta be careful who you let in the candy store and how far. And there's some candy you just don't put on the shelves. Not with humans.

"I knew all along he was just keeping an eye on Dani and the abbey," she surprises me by saying. "At first I was doing the same. Watching your back, trying to divine your secrets, decide if you were friend or foe. At least that's what I told myself. Kat wanted someone on the inside at Chester's and it made me feel special that she'd asked me. That *he* wanted me in his bed. I thought about it for all of one minute. There was no way I was going to pass up that kind of chance. Great sex on top of spying? I felt like a female James Bond."

She gives a soft, sad laugh that ends on a sob. "I didn't get a *sidhe*-seer talent like the others. I don't have a superpower. Just this damn sticky memory that doesn't even work because I imprint *everything* I see and end up with so much useless detritus in my head that I can never find anything useful. I have the meaning of every word stored up there but I don't know the filing system. Who am I? Jo, the busy researcher. Want a fact? I can't remember where to find it in my mind, but I can recall where I saw it well enough to know where to look."

She flicks herself lightly in the forehead with a finger. "I don't understand the point of my gift. It's useless. Everyone else is out saving the world while I hole up with books and hunt for answers. I wanted to feel extraordinary. Like I was *doing* something for a change. I didn't realize how hard it would be to go back to ordinary. Nothing changed at all. I just got hurt."

She starts crying harder and I'm fucking horrified. I can't stand tears. Not from a woman. I only know one thing to do. Kiss them away.

She's not my type.

She places her small hands on my face and bends over me, her mouth a few inches away. "Erase him for me, Lor. Make me forget him. Take the taste of him out of my mouth. Fill it up with you. You'll never remember that you helped me forget. Please, Lor, make love to me."

Ahhhh! I fucking hate that phrase. I don't make love. I fuck. That's it. Plain and simple. Fuck. Clearly defined.

No strings attached. As in rut and grunt and get my rocks off. I'm the caveman. I'm the sexual barbarian. I open my mouth to tell her that but all the sudden she pulls back from me and yanks her shirt off over her head and these positively fucking perfect small breasts pop out.

Don't know the last time I saw little tits. I forgot what they looked like. I stare and feel my eyes going glassy all on their own. Tiny waist, creamy skin flushed with embarrassment and desire, and pretty pink nipples that— Aw, shit, here I go.

Damn nipples. They get me every time.

"Lor, please," she says, hot tears falling like rain on my skin. "Make love to me, make me forget."

Slow and sweet, she bends over me and traces my lips with her tongue, breath warm, smelling faintly of peppermint.

I don't do this kind of woman.

Never this kind of woman.

And sure as fuck not the way she wants it.

Next thing I know I'm hiking that sweet, short skirt up over her sweet round ass, breaking my own rules, gonna screw a brunette, on the highway to Hell.

20

"Mama, I'm coming home"

MAC

Situated on one thousand acres of prime farmland about two hours from Dublin, Arlington Abbey is a self-sustaining fortress with multiple artesian wells, a dairy, beef cattle, orchard, and acres of vegetable gardens.

Whether Rowena performed powerful spells to protect it or the Shades simply chose to go in another direction when they decamped the city en masse a few months ago, about thirty minutes from the ancient mother house, the countryside was left untouched by their voracious appetites.

It's difficult to believe I haven't been out this way since mid-May, the night we sealed the *Sinsar Dubh* in the vast, heavily runed underground chamber beneath the fortress.

Time flies.

Especially when you keep losing it inside the Silvers.

After we defeated the *Sinsar Dubh*, Barrons and I retreated to his lair beneath the garage, leaving bed only when near-starvation forced us out.

A few days later we laid his son to rest, finally freeing the father from a small eternity of torment, and began discussing plans to return to the mother house and take further measures to protect the world from the great-winged prince beneath the abbey that has stood as a prison, in one form or another, in the middle of a grassy Irish field since the unlucky day the king selected our planet for that purpose.

I'd proposed pumping the chamber full of concrete the very night the king iced Cruce. Barrons later argued for removing the prince, intact in his prison of ice, and transporting the chamber into the Hall of All Days, to dump on some other unsuspecting world.

We did neither.

Obsessed with my quest to rid the world of the *other* book, the next thing I knew, we were stepping from the Silver behind the bookstore into a city so heavily iced it was nearly impassable. Our new enemy wasn't one that could be physically battled, not that I was currently effective in that department anyway. Getting involved would have turned too many eyes my way, raised questions about my stalkers, and put me in closer proximity to Dani than I was ready for. It was the hardest thing I've ever done to trust that others would handle the problem while I attempted to handle my own.

I stare out the window, watching the scenery whiz by. What the Shades didn't devour, the Hoar Frost King decimated. But spring has begun transforming the ice-ravaged landscape, pushing buds from skeletal limbs, and a thin carpet of grass shimmers in the moonlight. After the violent, killing frost, it may be years before the emerald isle regains its legendary green.

I sprawl in the passenger seat in the Humvee, one booted foot on the dash—Ryodan refused to let me drive, no surprise there, we're both control freaks—

bracing myself for the upcoming battle. My dark flock is hitching a ride on the roof.

I ponder the upcoming confrontation like a poker game I'm about to enter, and the various ways the cards might play out.

The metaphor is appropriate, given bluffing appears to be my strongest suit.

I love a good battle, especially on the right side, and we are. The abbey belongs to us. Assuming I go inside, what cards can I safely allow myself to play?

My spear is useless. I've been mulling over the two times my flock ascended to the rooftops and I drew my spear: the first against Dani, the second against the Gray Woman, trying to decide what pushed me over the edge the second time and gave the Book the leverage it needed. Until I can isolate the precise moment I lost control, the how and why, I'm not using my spear again.

I left my guns at the bookstore but have a switchblade in each boot. I won't use those either. Violence is the door the Book kicks through, sticks in a foot, and wedges open.

Barrons keeps the amulet locked in a vault beneath the garage. I wouldn't touch it anyway. We decided months ago that it was too risky to attempt to fool it twice the same way. Besides, I've thought of it so many times, I'm not certain it's not an idea the Book keeps planting. Nearly all my mental terrain is suspect to me. On days when it hasn't stirred much, I get worried.

You can't seek a weapon to use against it. You must become *that weapon*, Barrons has said over and over.

I know Voice. I'm good at it, too. There's a useful tool. If we get into a heated battle, I can keep a circle clear around me merely by barking orders. I get a mental picture of myself, standing, unarmed and passive in the middle of a raging battle, shouting: *Stay away from me! Don't touch me! Drop your weapon!*

I blow out a frustrated breath.

I can Null, but that's only effective on Fae. Present ghoulish company excluded.

I'm good in hand-to-hand combat. Assuming I don't black out.

My cards in this poker game suck. I need a redeal. Or at least a few wild cards.

I'm itching to meet the supposedly legendary *sidhe*-seer leader, stand in front of her and take her measure. I wonder about the women she commands, what their talents are, whether one of them might be like me, able to sense the *Sinsar Dubh*. I try to assure myself the likelihood is slim.

But if the Unseelie King really did make us to serve as prison guards for his dark disaster, it seems logical he'd also have made more like me, in case it ever got out.

I heave a conflicted sigh and decide I'm being paranoid. The *sidhe*-seers told me no one in their entire history at the abbey was ever able to sense the Book like Alina and me, none of them are Nulls, and considering we come from the mother house in the originating homeland where it was interred by the king himself, I sincerely doubt the "away teams" were likewise gifted. In fact, they're probably diluted from millennia of living in far-off lands, divorced from their heritage. Good military fighters but little more.

"Christ, stop sighing, you'll blow us off the fucking road. Something you want to talk about, Mac."

I look over at Ryodan, inscrutable as ever in the dim light from the dashboard.

I doubt my threat to quit "protecting" him was motivation. Ryodan pursues his own agenda. "Why did you agree to help free the abbey? You never do anything unless there's something in it for you."

"I want their new leader off the streets. She and her followers are killing Fae. Bad for business."

"What are you going to do with her? Kill her?" I don't like that thought. Though I, too, intend to see her deposed, I want her neutralized, not dead. There's been too much death in Dublin.

"Perhaps she can be recalibrated into a useful weapon. If not, then yes."

"What happened when you and Dageus met with R'jan?" Dageus had insisted on privacy for the meeting in Ryodan's office. I'd loitered outside, wishing I still had his cell phone with the handy eavesdropping Skull & Crossbones app. "Did he agree to send an army to hunt the Hag?"

"In exchange for an additional seat at our table."

"Who? There are no other princes." I wonder about that. Where are the replacements? Are they trapped somewhere, like Christian was in the Unseelie prison, becoming? Did eating Unseelie really hasten his transformation?

"An advisor whose vote will tie his with those of the Unseelie."

"And you allowed it?"

He says nothing, but I don't need him to. Of course he did. "The Unseelie and Seelie will always vote against each other out of sheer, stupid principle, canceling each other out, giving you the permanent upper hand."

When he still says nothing, I resume staring out at the scenery. And jerk. "What the *hell*?" I exclaim.

Ryodan looks over at me, then out the window beyond me. He slams the brakes so hard my ghouls catapult from the roof and explode in a tangle of chittering black robes on the road in front of us. "Fuck, I didn't even notice."

The scenery has changed. Drastically. Here, just ten minutes from the abbey, spring has been at work, not with gentle brushes, but wild splashes from the vats of a painter gone mad.

"Back up," I demand, but he's already doing it.

We find the line of demarcation, similar to the one the Shades left outside Dublin, an eighth of a mile back.

I leap from the Hummer and straddle the line, one booted foot on each side. My ghouls pack in beside me, behind me. I tune them out, a thing I'm getting better at the more smelly, dusty time we spend together.

To my left is a thin covering of grass and weeds. To my right is a carpet of grass too tall and dense to be cut by anything but perhaps a strong man with a scythe. Fat poppies bob, black and velvety in the moonlight, and atop willowy stands of tall reeds, shadowy lilies sway.

On my left are newly budded trees with young, tender leaves.

On my right enormous, ancient live oaks, massive branches stretching skyward, others reaching low to sweep the earth, explode with greenery, draped with lush vines.

Here, a weak cricket chirps, wakened from the unexpected and brutal winter to a paltry meal.

There, birds trill an exotic aria, tree frogs sing, and the heavily draped limbs rustle as small creatures leap from one vine-fringed branch to the next.

Foreboding fills me.

If you'll just come to the abbey, Kat had said, *you'll see what I mean. This thaw . . . I thought when the fire-world threatening our home was gone . . . och, but then it didn't and it turns out it wasn't . . .*

She was trying to tell me. She was asking for my help. Engrossed in my own problems, I'd heard none of it.

There's another thing I'd like to be discussing with you, if you've the time. About Cruce. Seeing how you know more about Fae princes than any of us . . .

She'd told me his cage was still holding.

Was it a lie? What else could explain this?

I shoot a dark look at Ryodan. "I thought you knew what was going on out here."

"It would seem there are a few things my sources neglected to mention."

"Why wouldn't your men tell you?" I fish.

"My men are not my sources."

That was half of what I wanted to know. "Who is?"

He slants me a silent, *Nice try. Not.*

I get back in the Hummer.

On the driver's side.

And lock the door.

He laughs. "Ah, Mac, I don't think so."

I lunge across the wide console, fling open the passenger door, slam it into gear, and start rolling forward.

Fast.

Ryodan curses and does exactly what I would have done, lopes alongside and explodes in, managing to dwarf the cavernous interior. "Strip my gears, woman, you're dead."

I shoot him a derisive look. "I haven't stripped gears since I was ten." I step on it and shift rapidly.

"Big Wheels don't count," Ryodan mocks.

"My daddy's sixty-four-and-a-half Mustang." After that debacle, Mom and Dad no longer left any keys hanging by the garage door. Sheriff Bowden brought me home. I'd made it a half a mile of screeching, jerking stops and starts that apparently the entire town of Ashford was witnessing out their nosy windows. The pillows I'd packed in to help me reach the pedals and steering wheel had worked as air bags when I hit the telephone pole.

It had been a while before Daddy got over that one.

Then he'd done what any wise parent would have: taught me to drive.

Give me raw, testy, ferocious power any day of the week.

I can find the sweet spot in my sleep.

I park outside the elaborate new gate on the enormous new stone wall that wasn't there two months ago.

Ryodan intuits my thoughts. It's not difficult, given my mouth is slightly ajar. Again. I don't know why I bother with preconceptions anymore. Even simple ones like expecting that when I close a door the room on the other side still exists, with drywall and carpet and ceiling lights, neatly intact. For all I know, it doesn't and never has. Perhaps it vanishes until I want it again, stored away on some cosmic zip drive to conserve quantum energy.

"It wasn't here last month either. Bloody hell, that wall wasn't here three weeks ago. And she said nothing of it. It seems our headmistress has been keeping secrets."

"Along with your inept sources." I'd really like to know who they are. I'd like them working for me. I'd insist on better info.

Right. If you'd wanted better info, my conscience pricks, *you could have come out here any time. Maybe listened when she asked for help. Did you really think it was over? Did you honestly delude yourself for even one minute that Cruce would lie dormant?*

Has Kat, like Rowena before her, been seduced by the evil that slumbers a thousand feet of stone beneath her pillow? I shiver. Not Kat. But where *is* she? And why did she tell us none of this?

"Perhaps a different caste of Seelie have settled nearby in large numbers and are affecting the environment," I propose as an alternative, which would still be problematic. I don't want *any* Fae anywhere near the abbey.

"Cruce seduced her," Ryodan says flatly.

"You don't know that," I defend.

"It began the night we laid the Book to rest. He came to her while she slept."

I look at him incredulously. "You know that for a fact? And you waited until now to say something? If not me, you could have at least told Barrons."

"I believed she had things under control."

"The great Ryodan, wrong?" I say in mock astonishment. "The world must be ending." Why didn't she tell me? Was that why she'd asked me to come out, so I could see firsthand the power he was using on her, on the abbey, and understand the battle she was fighting? Did she hold her silence because, like me, she feared condemnation and hoped to fix it before anyone else had to know?

Ryodan says irritably, "Bit busy hunting Dani and trying to patch a black hole beneath my club. While you and Barrons were MIA doing unknown things for unknown reasons with the Unseelie King's personal valets that stalk you for yet more unknown reasons, all of which you could explain anytime now. And yes, if we don't find a way to fix it, it is."

End-of-the-world talk doesn't make me as nervous as it once did. I often wake up in the morning surprised to find myself still here. I consider it icing on the cake if I'm still where I recall falling asleep.

A black SUV with dark-tinted windows pulls up. The Keltar have arrived. They get out, a small army of powerfully built, dark-haired, dark-skinned men. There's Dageus's twin, Drustan, a more thickly muscled version of his minutes-younger brother, with shorter hair—although it still falls halfway down his back—and a cool silver gaze, in contrast to Dageus's gold tiger-eyes. He's followed by Cian, an enormous Highlander with loads of tattoos and the thousand-yard stare of a man who's done hard time somewhere; then Christopher, the only one of the lot that looks remotely civilized, a forty-five-year-old version of Christian.

As we get out and join them, Dageus growls, "No' quite what it looked like last time. Place reeks of Fae."

Ryodan angles his head back and looks up at the barbed wire strung atop the walls. He breaks a twig off a nearby tree and tosses it high. The branch spits and crackles when it hits, then falls to the ground, scorched.

Beyond the gate the abbey is lit as if by a thousand interior lights. An acre of fountain that also didn't previously exist shoots water into the sky before spilling into a rippling pool of silver and gold. The gardens are surreal, vast bed after bed of spicy, jewel-toned blossoms I've seen only one other place. There's no longer any question in my mind what egotistical Picasso painted this voluptuous summer atop the canvas of Dublin's anorexic spring.

Beyond the gate a new *sidhe*-seer holds the prison that contains—or appears to be rather spectacularly failing to contain—the greatest evil the world has ever known (well, besides me) in the body of the most powerful prince the Unseelie King created. I should have known it wouldn't work. Cruce probably had a contingency plan all along; the equivalent of a paper clip tucked in his pocket to work his handcuffs loose, or a shoulder that conveniently pops out of its socket.

"Has it broken free, lass?" Dageus asks, looking at me.

Cautiously, I reach out for the Book entombed, hoping the one inside me doesn't explode into violent life.

KILL THE PRINCE CRUSH HIM DEVOUR HIM DESTROY HIM MAKE HIM BURN!!!!!

I grit my teeth to keep from clutching my head and groaning out loud. Yes, it's still beneath the abbey, and apparently, much as the king despises his book, my book despises the king's book. Whatever happened to the good old days when books just got along, cozied up together on bookshelves, hanging out, waiting to be read?

"It's still beneath the abbey where we left it."

"Has anything changed?" Christopher demands.

"I can't tell that from here. We'll have to see it." And I won't. I'll find a way to refuse. The last time I stood in that cavernous chamber, I didn't know I had a copy of the Book inside me. I'd still believed it was a lie the *Sinsar Dubh* had told me to make me doubt myself. Since that night, I've had far too many nightmares about getting imprisoned next to Cruce.

March willingly into the abbey, down into the prison, beside the very *sidhe*-seers and Keltar druids that possess enough power between them to imprison me?

Never.

I feel Barrons behind me before he speaks. My cloak of wraiths retreat, and like a supercar that's sat too long in the garage and is in desperate need of a hot, hard run to blow out its engine, my body fires on all pistons.

"Ah, fuck." He moves in, standing close without touching. He doesn't need to. I sometimes think our atoms are so glad to see each other that they send little messengers back and forth, ferrying desire, strength, and love between the islands we are. "I knew we should have moved it," he growls.

"At least pumped it full of concrete," I agree.

"The others," Ryodan says to him.

"Fade was the only one with me when I got your call."

While I'm trying to decide just how Ryodan managed to reach Barrons in Faery, Fade glides from the shadows, tall, packed with muscle and scarred like the rest. He's prowling in that half-invisible way Barrons moves only in private. If you've not seen it before, it's eerie and impossible to mistake for human.

The Highlanders close ranks on themselves.

Fade laughs, fangs gleaming white in the moonlight.

Two of the Highlanders move their hands to ancient, odd knives in sheaths at their waist. I wonder if they have mythic properties like my spear.

Ryodan shoots Fade a look he rebounds with a snarl, but he settles into moving like the rest of us.

Our army is small yet impressive. In two groups we stand, Barrons, Fade, Ryodan, and I, near Dageus, Drustan, Cian, and Christopher, preparing to meet our unknown foe.

And a known one that's somehow stirring, despite the ice and bars.

Provided war doesn't break out between us—which could easily happen with this much testosterone in such close quarters—I put our odds of reclaiming the abbey from at least one of our enemies tonight at reasonably good.

The new *sidhe*-seers didn't just take an abbey—they took a radioactive one.

I'm no longer certain what worries me more: the danger beneath Chester's, the one beneath the abbey, or the one inside me. I'd like them all to go away. Reverse order would be just swell. "Do you think things will ever get back to normal?"

Barrons gives me a look. "They were normal? Did I miss that century?"

Ryodan says, "Fuck normal. Give me a good war any day."

"No shit, boss," Fade agrees.

Drustan snorts. "You're daft, the lot of you. I'd give my left nut for a century of peace."

The rest of the Keltar heartily agree, adding various body parts to the mix.

Surrounded by alpha males that know more magic than all the teachers at Hogwarts, I'm about to ask who's going to do what to get us through the gate, when it becomes a moot point.

Powered by an unseen hand, it begins to move slowly open.

21

_____

"This house doesn't burn down slowly to ashes"

MAC

I used to know precisely where I was headed and how I'd handle things when I got there.

Before any event, I'd ponder the possible variables and decide what I'd say or do, if X or Y happened, or maybe Z. Although something as exotic as Z almost never happened in small-town Georgia. We closed schools and held parades when it did.

It's how I used to prepare for dates in high school: when Billy James asks me out will I say yes the first time or make him wait; will I wear the low-cut top or something flirty and sweet; when he tries to kiss me, will I let him; if he takes me to the less popular party at Amy Tanhauser's house instead of the party of the year at Heather Jackson's, will I dump him; if he wants to have sex, am I ready?

Ah, my long-lost shallow life.

Back then, things unfolded so predictably. I wore flirty and sweet, I dumped him when he took me to the wrong party, and I didn't have sex with Billy but I did have sex with his older brother later that summer.

My careful prep doesn't work so well anymore.

Each time I think I'm braced for any possible scenario, gravity changes, my trajectory shifts, rocket fuel gets dumped into my gas tank and I end up hurtling at inconceivable speeds at some entirely new crash site I'd never considered, a big, fat nasty planet I didn't even know existed that explodes on the horizon so suddenly no amount of frantic braking can save you from impact.

How do you brace yourself for a collision with the unimaginable?

The closer we get to the abbey, the more sultry the clime. On both sides of the drive, mist steams from the lush lawn. I feel like we're taking a bad trip down a yellow brick road, but what waits for us behind that curtain is no charlatan, rather an enormously powerful, staggeringly dangerous wizard of chaos.

Although it's two hours till dawn, in Ireland, for heaven's sake, I'm sweating and my hair is sticking damply to my face. It's hotter here than it was in Dublin. The fountain isn't the only new addition to the grounds. Golden trellises draped with black roses offer shelter above marble benches, and I suspect the scent of the blossoms would be drugging to anyone foolish enough to pause in the alcove beneath.

"They've stones now," Drustan says, eyeing a cluster rising from the mist, great bleached-bone fingers reaching for the sky.

"I care naught for the looks of them," Cian rumbles.

Dageus agrees, "Nor do I."

Cian grunts and points, a darker-haired version of Lor, at two enormous black megaliths. I think they might like each other. Grunts and all.

"A dolmen awaiting the cover stone," Ryodan murmurs.

Barrons says, "We bring jackhammers next time. I want those stones destroyed."

I agree. I watched Darroc usher an Unseelie horde into our city through a dolmen at 1247 LaRuhe, in the heart of the Dark Zone adjacent to BB&B. I later asked V'lane/Cruce to crush it. I want this one crushed, too, before it's completed and who knows what arrives on our planet next.

As we skirt the fountain, I say, "You do realize we're walking into a trap, right? Do we have a plan? Is someone going to tell me what it is?"

Seven male heads swivel my way.

"Would you shut her up," Ryodan says to Barrons.

Barrons slants him a cold look that shuts *Ryodan* up. I'd sacrifice my eyeteeth to perfect that look. Then again maybe that's precisely what's required: long, inhumanly sharp ones like theirs to pull it off.

"I doona ken why you permitted the woman to come. We doona risk ours in battle." Cian's brogue is so thick it's hard to follow.

"Tell that to Colleen," Christopher says grimly. "She's inside."

Drustan gives him an incredulous look. "You let her come tonight? And she's already inside? How?"

"We need all the information we can get if we hope to rescue Christian from the Hag. These women know the Seelie nearly as well as we do, the Unseelie even better. Colleen joined up with the new *sidhe*-seers a week ago, to infiltrate the abbey and search their archives."

"The new group? How?" I demand. "She's not a *sidhe*-seer."

"And you allowed this?" Cian explodes.

"Keep it down. They're going to hear us," I warn.

"Honey, they opened the front gate," Fade says. "They know we're here. Trap. Remember."

Christian's father snorts. "Try stopping her."

"Is she?" I press.

"What?" he snaps.

"A *sidhe*-seer."

"She has other . . . skills."

"Why the bloody hell are those Unseelie following you, lass?" Drustan demands. "At first I thought they were drawn to all of us for some reason, but the moment Barrons moves away from you, they're on you like midges. Is there something about you we should know?"

Seven male heads turn my way again.

"She said they're ghosts of the Unseelie she's killed," Dageus says.

"Not a ghost of truth in that one," Ryodan says dryly.

"Oh, just shut up, all of you," I say, exasperated, moving closer to Barrons again, reclaiming a little personal space.

We continue walking in silence toward the abbey.

"So, do we have a plan?" I say again after a few moments.

"Walk up to the front door and go inside," Barrons replies.

"That's not a plan. That's a suicide mission."

"We're a little hard to kill," Fade says.

"Some more than others," I say pointedly. "I'm not so sure the Keltar get back up quite as easily as—" I bite that one off myself when all four Keltar shoot me looks of death.

Clearly, I impugned their virility, when all I was trying to do is remind my team that the other team doesn't have the same Get Out of Death Free card.

"Why did you bring her again?" Dageus says.

"Because once she gets with the plan, she's as useful as the rest of us," Barrons says.

"It'd help if I knew what the bloody plan was," I grumble.

"Besides, we can use her Unseelie as body shields," he adds.

Well darn, that was one I hadn't thought of.

The front door, which was once slats of wood reinforced by steel, now looms black as polished obsidian, covered with ancient runes I've seen before.

Below the abbey, in the chamber that houses Cruce.

It swings silently open.

I move forward and pause on the threshold, looking in to get the lay of the land before I inadvertently plant a foot on a mine.

Seven men march past me, boots echoing on the stone floor.

I hurry to catch up. Well, I mostly hurry. I linger a moment, absorbing the raw fearlessness of their stride, the determination to never quit that squares their shoulders, and it fortifies my resolve. I will match the bar these men set so high. They all have their inner demons. And they manage them.

I will, too.

The entry hall is large and rectangular, with a ceiling that soars to open roof rafters. On three walls, fireplaces that could serve as small bedrooms blast more heat into the already warm room.

The sofas are faded and worn, dotted with handmade pillows and crocheted throws, the floors warmed by century-old rugs, the walls hung with antique tapestries. Chairs perch near tables that hold open books and perspiring glasses of iced drinks.

The room is empty.

"Where the bloody hell is everyone?" Dageus growls.

"Quiet. Someone's coming," Barrons says.

Several seconds pass before I hear the sound of people approaching. I envy his preternatural senses, rue that my monster has no such benefits.

I offer benefits with which you could retire from this

paltry planet and rule galaxies. You refuse them. Embrace your destiny and we will destroy the prince before we leave this world. It will be our parting gift.

Right. As if either *Sinsar Dubh* would leave my planet intact. Criminy, I can't even think about it without it stirring. I mutter Poe beneath my breath and watch as four women enter the room. I'm relieved to see they're ours. I sat at a table with these women not so long ago.

Leading the group is Josie, a skinny dark-eyed girl with platinum hair and goth makeup, followed by Shauna, a petite brunette with hazel eyes and a quick smile, and the twins, Clare and Sorcha MacSweeney. They are the women Kat brought to our clandestine meeting in a pub, after Rowena instructed a group of them to ambush me and try to take my spear. They failed. I accidentally killed a *sidhe*-seer in the process. Moira. I never forget the names of humans I've slain. I catch myself reaching protectively for my spear but stop, unwilling to invite more of the Book's unwanted commentary so near another copy of itself plus so many vulnerable humans.

"Why have you brought Unseelie inside our walls, Mac?" Shauna says grimly.

I sigh. "I didn't. They, I—" Shit, how do I explain this one? I blurt, "I was trying to do a spell and it backfired and they've been stuck to me like glue ever since." I practically roll my own eyes. It's the weakest lie I've ever heard myself tell.

Dageus gives me a look.

Ryodan laughs.

"They're harmless," I add. "They don't even kill anything. They just stalk me."

"The Unseelie doesn't exist that doesn't kill," Josie says coolly.

Sorcha moves past me, inspecting them from a

cautious distance. Then she surprises me by saying, "I'm not certain they're Unseelie, Mac."

I frown. "What else could they be?"

"I don't know but they're . . . different."

That would explain why I can't Null them, but not why my *sidhe*-seer senses seem to pick up on them as Unseelie. Or do they? Is that yet one more preconception I accepted without bothering to consider simply because they *looked* like Unseelie, and what else would they be? I realize I've never listened past their incessant chittering for their caste's dark melody. But I will, in the near future. At the moment I want no distractions.

Barrons says impatiently, "Who the fuck cares. They follow her. Where is the one that holds you hostage?"

Josie laughs, a brittle sound. "That's what you think? We're being held hostage? The woman saved us!"

"Saved?" I echo.

"Aye, saved. And we've no need of your army, Mac. We're just fine. The lot of you can be leaving now. *With* your Unseelie."

"I'm telling you," Sorcha says, "they're not Unseelie."

"We'd be finer if we knew Kat was all right," Clare says.

"And Dani," Shauna adds. "Two of our best have gone missing."

"Dani isn't one of our best," Josie says sharply. "She's a liability, a hotheaded child. And Kat, well . . . you see where *her* plans got us."

Josie doesn't look much older than Dani herself. And Kat's plans kept them alive this long.

Clare disagrees, "How can you say that when it was Dani and Ryodan that saved us from the Hoar Frost King?"

"They didn't save us from Cruce," Josie says hotly. "Jada did."

I narrow my eyes. "Who's Jada?" Was this the name

of the supposedly mystical fighter that was leading them now? "And what do you mean you're 'fine'? This place is a mess. It's obviously been taken over by—"

"No, it hasn't. Not anymore," Josie cuts me off. "Not since *she* came."

"Jada?" I guess dryly.

The skinny goth folds her arms over her chest and tosses her head, looking down her thin nose at me. "Aye, she freed us from our prison. When Kat went missing, the changes to our abbey escalated. The doors and windows closed, trapping us inside. But Jada understands his runes. She was able to open them. Since her arrival the changes have stopped. Completely."

I mock, "Gee, let's see, your lights glow without bulbs, your fireplaces burn with no wood or visible source of fuel, and there are Fae flowers and monuments scattered all over your land. Inside a stone wall that wasn't there three weeks ago."

"I said she *stopped* the changes. Not undid them. *Yet*," she adds with the fervent faith of a recent convert.

"Where's Colleen?" Christopher demands.

Clare says, "You must be her father. She's the look of you. She said you would be coming if she didn't send word soon. She's with a group of women in the Red Library, searching our oldest books. Unseelie Prince or not, your son sacrificed himself for us, and we will help you get Christian back. Jada has agreed to make it a priority."

Her last words rub me a thousand kinds of wrong. "One of your women escaped and told us the abbey was taken hostage and three of your women killed." They've accepted their conqueror, permitted her to choose their priorities. How quickly they've abandoned Kat.

Shauna says, "At first we didn't know what was going on, and aye, we battled, that's true. There were losses on both sides. But we swiftly realized the asset Jada is."

"She's a born leader," Josie says proudly. "She fears nothing and I've never seen anyone with such unobstructed vision. She makes plans and takes action and her plans yield immediate, concrete results. Have you any idea how long we've been floundering out here? Hammered by one threat after the next! I'll fall in behind her any day. You wouldn't believe what she's accomplished in the short time she's been here."

Sorcha nods agreement. "We aren't the first group of *sidhe*-seers to join her. The ones she arrived at the abbey with told us they lost their own leader a few weeks ago. Jada found them wandering Dublin, thinking of returning home. She talked them out of it."

"Do any of you even know where she came from?" I demand.

Josie slants me a scornful look. "Who cares? She's the most powerful *sidhe*-seer we've ever seen. Not even you possess such skills. In fact, *she* should have the spear, not you. They're training us. Teaching us to fight. Martial arts and weapons."

I refuse to reach for it. My spear is beneath my arm and there it will remain.

Deep inside me the Book sends out a dark, cold draft of brimstone and damnation, offering all kinds of power.

I don't need it. I am enough.

Shauna says, "Kat did a fine job keeping us together in the present. But Jada can lead us into the future."

I glance at Barrons. He's motionless, processing, assessing. We came here to roust a conqueror and received instead an unarmed welcome coupled with news that the abbey has embraced their conqueror.

Wants to keep her.

Likes her better than Kat.

Whoever this Jada is, I don't trust her one bit.

"You will bring her to us now," Barrons says.

Josie tips her head back and says down her nose to him, "We will inform Jada you've requested an audience. *After* Mac and her Unseelie leave our home."

Seven men blast past her so fast her short platinum hair flies straight up in the air, and one of them must have caught her with his elbow or fist—I'd bet blood it was Barrons—because she crashes back into a couch, goes tumbling over the side, and slams into the floor.

Grimly, me and my cavalcade of whatever they are follow the men.

By the time we reach the wing that houses Rowena's chambers—I have no doubt that's where "Jada" has decided to squat, like the Oval Office, mere occupancy confers power—our group has dwindled to Barrons, Ryodan, and me.

The Highlanders insisted on going underground to check on Cruce's prison after first making a detour to the Red Library to collect Colleen. Ryodan, who trusts no one, insisted Fade accompany them. Clare and Sorcha, who'd caught up with us by then, insisted we ask Jada before going beneath the abbey, and when the men stalked past them, looked impossibly torn before storming off after them. I remained silent the entire time, prepared to lie through my teeth about anything and everything if they tried to make me go down there where I might get caught in the sticky spiderweb of the powers that hold or are failing to hold Cruce.

As we approach Rowena's chambers, the stone floor changes from pale gray to stone that glitters faintly, as if sprinkled by silver dust, to solid gold etched with elaborate symbols, inlaid near the walls with glittering gems that wink with dark fire.

Ryodan stops abruptly.

"What is it?"

"Getting a read on anything, Mac."

I expand my *sidhe*-seer senses, reaching, searching. "Like what?"

"I feel the same thing I felt at the club the night you were supposed to kill the Unseelie Princess."

"You didn't expressly tell me to kill her," I remind crossly. "And you're not a *sidhe*-seer, so how could you possibly be feeling anything?" I glance up at Barrons. "Do you feel something?"

He slices his head once to the left and looks at Ryodan, who stands motionless a long moment then says, "It's nothing. Forget it."

But he doesn't look like he's forgotten it. He looks deeply disturbed by something. I expand my senses again, searching, but still get nothing. I cock my head thoughtfully and eye my stalkers, crowded close, left, right, and behind.

Absolutely nothing. In any direction, with the exception of what's beneath the abbey. So what the hell are they, then?

Rowena's chambers are composed of half a dozen rooms: a bedroom, an ornate, regal study, two libraries, an enormous, lovely bathroom with a huge old clawfoot tub, and a stark, uncomfortable waiting room similar to one at a doctor's office. I snooped through her suite once, but not as thoroughly as I'd like. I suspect there are more secrets tucked away in there, behind warded panels and floorboards, than grains of sand in an hourglass. More than once Dani and I burst through twin sets of French doors and forced our way into her chambers only to find the scowling headmistress had anticipated our arrival.

No such luck making an unannounced entrance today. As we turn the final corner, four armed women stand at the end of the hall, outside the closed doors.

They're impressive. I can see why our abbey embraced

them; it was that or die. Rowena didn't train her *sidhe*-seers. She suppressed them, deliberately kept them weak and needy. Jada's women are draped in ammo, clutch automatic weapons, and stare stonily at us as we approach, military training apparent in their strong bodies and stronger expressions.

I'd like them if I met them on the street. I'd like them a lot. I have enormous respect for our military men and women, the everyday heroes who provide the security the rest of us enjoy.

I don't like them in front of that door.

Kat belongs inside those chambers, not some outsider whose loyalty and objectives are uncertain.

They scan us, taking in the Unseelie at my back but making no comment. If they crossed continents to get here, they've seen stranger things. Criminy, if they served overseas, they've seen a small slice of hell.

They raise their rifles in sleek unison, targeting us.

"She's not taking visitors," clips a tall woman with short black hair tipped blond at the ends.

I fall back into my hive of Unseelie, a protected queen bee. The body shield idea works for me. I practically cuddle the smelly things. I may be tough to kill, even survived having my throat ripped out, but I don't need to experience a spray of automatic bullets to know it would hurt like a bitch.

Barrons and Ryodan are suddenly gone. I sometimes forget they can do that, become virtually invisible, melt into the current terrain, and reappear without warning.

Shots go off, guns fly and smash into walls, and ducking the whine of dangerous ricochets, I nestle into my worker bees. Between their hooded heads I watch a brief brawl that ends with four women unconscious on the floor and Barrons pushing the door open.

As I step over them, the black-haired woman uncoils cobra-fast, grabs my leg and yanks it out from under me.

Barrons is on her instantly but I go down backward, hard.

The strangest thing happens as I fall. I get a sudden weird flash of my room at the Clarin House, time slows to a snail's crawl and I'm suddenly living two different events superimposed.

I'm falling backward at the abbey.

Yet I'm also falling forward in my cramped room at the inn.

Barrons is looking down at me here, subduing my attacker and trying to catch me.

But at the same time we're at the inn, and he's the one who just dumped me on the floor.

I'm clothed here.

At the Clarin House I'm missing my jeans, the air is cool on my skin and I'm butt-ass naked.

I hit the abbey floor hard enough to make my teeth clack, and blink, shaking my head.

WTF?

Reality rearranges itself into a single vision.

I'm in the abbey, only the abbey.

Frowning, I push myself up and watch Barrons and Ryodan drag the women down the hall and dump them into a room.

"Time to meet *Jada*." Barrons growls her name the same way I feel it, irritably and accompanied by a death wish.

I stand up, eyeing him uneasily, trying to decide what just happened. The only time Barrons was ever in my room at the Clarin House was that night he came to bully me into going home. We'd argued, he grabbed me at one point and got physical, but then he left. The next day I'd hurt from head to toe.

My frown deepens.

I recall thinking the bruises were odd, more around the sides of my rib cage than across my front where he'd

actually had his arm banded beneath my breasts. I
didn't wear a bra for days. And I'd hurt all over, not just
my ribs. My thighs had ached, the muscles deep in my
butt had been sore. I'd just figured the interminable
flight over had taken a toll. I'd never flown that far before, or sat so long in between flights on hard airport
benches. I scratch my head, staring at him, feeling like
I'm trying to put together a puzzle minus half the pieces,
with no picture on the box to guide me.

He gives me a look. "Are you hurt? What is it?"

I search his face, searching my memory, trying to reconcile what I just saw with some version of reality I recall.

There is none.

"Get a fucking move on, Mac," Ryodan snaps.

At a complete loss to explain what just happened, for
a novel change, I silently obey him. "Don't get used to
it," I mutter.

We enter the spartan waiting room, move to the second
set of double doors, and I'm on the verge of proposing
we pause and listen a few seconds to get a feel for what's
on the other side when Barrons kicks the door open so
hard it flies back, slams into the wall, and splits down
the middle.

Women shout in alarm but I can't see past Barrons's
and Ryodan's backs.

I shut my mouth and step into the room, feeling un-
comfortably . . . obsolete. I may have unique *sidhe*-seer
gifts and there's no question that without my wraiths
hemming me in I'm a seriously badass street fighter, but
Barrons and his men are faster, stronger, and more
ruthless.

Before, one of my most valuable assets was that I
could sense the *Sinsar Dubh,* but that skill is no longer

in demand. Before, I could slay Unseelie better than the best, but now I'm afraid to draw my spear and give my inner demon the opportunity to manifest. Which begs the questions: what makes me any more special than the average *sidhe*-seer? Enforced passivity has me pondering that question too much of late.

Me. You could crush them in your sleep, said inner demon purrs.

I opt, instead, to crush the twinge of insecurity that invited the Book's commentary, resuming my silent recitation with a sigh.

Exasperated that I can't see, I push between them and am rewarded with a quick glimpse of a dozen armed women grouped around a central figure standing in front of Rowena's ornate desk, but Barrons pushes me back and growls, "Stay there."

His guttural words spark that freaky collision of dual realities again.

Stay there, he's growling, back in my room at the Clarin House, *I want you that way.*

But you said I could—

Your turn next.

This is about me, remember. That's what you said. I want what I want now.

I catch my breath and hold it. Something's trying to kick up from my subconscious through murky waters and it's having a hard time, weighted at the ankles by stones; a swimmer trapped in a dark cave where it was meant to remain forever.

Unless . . . somehow . . . the boulder blocking the entrance got jostled . . . nudged aside, freeing fragments of memory like tadpoles desperate to break the placid surface of my mind.

"She said she's not receiving visitors," a woman snaps.

"Put down that fucking gun or you'll be eating it," Barrons orders.

"Retreat and we'll let you live," she counters. "Don't move another inch."

"Try to stop me."

Try echoes in my mind. In my alternate reality, I hear him saying, *Try, Ms. Lane, just try.*

"Move away from her," Barrons growls. "Show yourself, Jada."

"*You* move," the woman counters. "What's behind you? Show us now!"

Move, you bastard, I'm snarling at the Clarin House.

"You will leave, immediately," a new voice says in a cool monotone.

Barrons laughs. "I'll leave when I'm bloody well ready."

When I'm ready echoes, and in my cramped, rented room, Barrons closes his hands on my ribs.

"Jada, it's here. They brought it with them!" one of the women cries.

"You aren't welcome here. I don't interfere with your world. Don't interfere with mine. You'll regret it," that same cool monotone says.

In both realities my ribs suddenly hurt. Between Barrons's and Ryodan's backs, I glimpse a beautiful woman, long hair pulled back in a high ponytail that falls to her waist.

She dwindles as a peculiar tunnel vision overtakes me, then I'm seeing only Barrons's back.

Then his face, as he stretches his big, hard body over me.

Images smash into me, one brick to my head after another, and I grimace, closing my eyes . . .

Barrons popping the buttons on my fly.

He makes me a deal: If I'm not wet, we won't have sex.

If I am, we will.

I'm wet. I'm so damn wet. I've never been wet like this before.

He was right. With Billy James's older brother, and all the boys before him, when it was over, I wondered what the fuss was about.

He was right: If it's perfectly good, it's not good enough.

And I knew that night, staring up at him, that touching this man would change my soul, alter me forever, that sex with him would blow my fucking mind.

My sister was dead.

My heart was in pieces.

I was useless and my life was meaningless.

I *wanted* my mind blown.

Then I'm on the floor, and his big, hard, beautiful body is on me and I'm in a rage of passion I didn't know I was capable of feeling, grabbing his waistband, busting the zipper, feeling him shove into me, throwing back my head and *roaring*.

Alive. So damned alive.

"Oh, my God," I breathe. "I had sex with you that night. All night. I didn't even know you. I didn't even *like* you."

Barrons mutters, "Ah, fuck. Not now."

"Jada, they set it free!"

"Are you certain?" the cool monotone says.

"Yes, wait . . . no it's—wait, yes . . . what the hell?"

Ryodan thunders, "I want to see Jada. Get out of my way."

Out of my way echoes. At the Clarin House, Barrons is saying, *I'll give you until nine P.M. tomorrow to get the bloody hell out of this country and out of my way.* Then he bends over me and begins to speak in a voice that sounds like a thousand voices, muttering ancient words.

Here, in the abbey, I freeze.

He didn't.

He wouldn't.

Some things are sacred. Until you act like they're not.

"You used Voice on me." My lips feel numb, my tongue thick. "You took my memory away."

"Now is not the time for it, Ms. Lane," Barrons says tersely.

"The time for it," I echo incredulously. "It was *never* the time for it."

"Yes, Jada, I'm certain," a woman says urgently. "They set it free!"

"Brigitte, collect the items and return with them immediately," the cool monotone orders. "Bring Sorcha and Clare."

"We bloody well did not," Barrons snaps. "And I said, Ms. Lane, we will discuss this later."

Barrons and Ryodan disappear then reappear in the middle of the group of armed *sidhe*-seers and guns go flying. Finally my line of vision is unobstructed! From within a blur of motion, I hear thuds of fists landing and savage female grunts. Then I see a dozen women sprawled on the floor, some holding bleeding noses, others squinting through rapidly swelling eyes, one clutching an arm to her chest that's obviously broken. Their guns are gone, in a broken pile near the far wall.

Ryodan is standing motionless in the middle of the fallen *sidhe*-seers, as if he's carved of stone, staring at the woman that must be Jada. He makes a sound like a soft implosion, a noise I've never heard before from any of the Nine, a ragged gasp of pure astonishment and . . . anguish?

Unable to fathom what could possibly elicit such a reaction from the cold, controlled man, I repress all I'm feeling—betrayal, shock, horror, bewilderment, and no small amount of fury—and move forward for a better look at the focus of his attention.

My age or slightly younger, tall, with a killer body that's long and lean and muscled and curvy in all the right places, it's the eyes that get me. They're emerald ice. They lock with mine for a long, frigid moment. Stone-cold eyes, they chill me, and I'm not easily chilled.

I look down, around me, and realize *all* the women in the room, including Jada, are staring at me.

Belatedly, I process the comments that were being made while my world was unraveling.

Guess the "away team" ain't so "diluted" after all. So much for my "rare" ability to sense the Book. One more way I'm no longer quite so special.

"Shit, shit, shit," I mutter.

"She has the *Sinsar Dubh*!" a brunette in green camo cries, pushing herself up. "Get her!"

"Bloody. Fucking. Hell," Ryodan says.

Women lunge up, straight for me.

Barrons moves in front of me like my personal shield. "Over my dead body."

"It happened before," Jada says tonelessly. "I'm certain it will again. And again. But that's how it works with your kind, isn't it."

"Bloody. Fucking. Hell," Ryodan says again.

"I can't believe you did that to me," I say numbly.

"Dani," Ryodan whispers.

"For fuck's sake, now isn't the time. Either of you. I said we'll discuss it later, Ms. Lane. And Ryodan, we'll find her." Barrons snarls, "Focus on the moment."

"I am," I clip stiffly. "Forgive the fuck out of me if this moment got tangled up with the one you stole from me."

"Easy to thieve that of which one was so eager to be quit," he barks, harsh and rapid as hostile fire.

Ryodan says carefully, "We just did."

"Did what?" I snap, not following him at all. Things are happening too fast. My brain is rubber cement, sticky and nonabsorptive.

I should run. I'm in the abbey. They know what I am. They're going to lock me up. Imprison me next to Cruce.

"Find Dani," Ryodan says.

"What the fuck are you nattering about?" Barrons practically shouts.

"Who even *says* words like 'natter'?" I know the answer. Men who steal people's memories.

"I don't natter."

"Spell it the fuck out," Barrons snarls.

"Jada," Ryodan says tightly, "is. Dani."

Part II

I go inside my head and become that other me,
    the one I don't tell anybody about.

The observer.

She can't feel hunger in her belly or cramped muscles
    from being in a cage for days on end.

She isn't Dani.

She can survive anything. Feel nothing.

See what's in front of her for exactly and only what
    it is.

Her heart doesn't break a little every time her mom
    leaves.

And she holds no price too high for survival.

I don't let go of myself and seek her often because once
    I got stuck there and she took over and the
    things she did . . .

I live in terror that one day I won't get to be Dani again.

—*From the journals of Danielle O'Malley*

22

"I have lived behind walls that have made me alone"

KAT

In the five days since Ryodan interred me beneath his nightclub, I have neither heard voice nor experienced another's emotion.

I should worry. I should care. I should be hammering on the door, demanding to be freed, but in these rooms I have experienced the first peace of my existence.

The entry room is unfurnished but the rest are not. There are four others: a bedroom with a soft pillow-top mattress so uniformly surfaced I know it was never used prior to my arrival; a bathroom with a large, gentle rain shower; and a kitchen stocked with food and beverages that tell me as surely as condemning words that Ryodan had been planning this for me, perhaps for quite some time.

The fourth and final room is the largest, walled with mirrors, housing a state-of-the-art gym.

Kasteo has not spoken a word.

Nor have I.

I've spent five days and nights simply feeling myself,

my unborn child, without the constant drone of inter-
ference I've endured my entire life.

Kasteo lies on the floor.

He gets up and works out.

Occasionally he showers.

He doesn't speak and I haven't seen him eat. Perhaps
he cooks while I'm asleep. I've seen no dirty dishes.

I, on the other hand, am voracious. Eating for two
with an appetite I've never known before.

I've become a hedonist, sleeping ten hours at a time,
taking long indulgent showers behind a locked bathroom door, making myself meals of meat and potatoes
and more meat, which I've not had in months.

Nothing, no one, disturbs me here. No emotion, no
voice, no seductive dark prince.

These five days and nights have been transformative.

I've realized, during this brief, unexpected, only vacation I've ever had from the world, what my problem is.

I've never been able to fully block the emotions of
others because I didn't know what silence felt like. I
found it impossible to strive for a goal I couldn't fathom,
to re-create a thing of which I'd no knowledge, like a
blind man trying to paint a picture of sky and clouds
and sun.

I now know a stillness in my center, that it exists and
where to find it, and I'm certain I can locate it again
amidst the boisterous din of Dublin, the abbey, even the
desperate and dangerous shark tank of Chester's.

The man who isn't there brought me to the blessedly
silent lair of another man who isn't there and gave me
the greatest gift I've ever received: the time and space to
take a deep breath and explore my inner terrain, com-
prehend the strengths I have to work with and the
weaknesses that have crippled me.

I can't begin to imagine why he did it. It seems a kindness from a man I would never have counted kind.

He has shown me that goal which always eluded me. That sacred inner place that is mine, and no one else's, the eye in the storm where I can stand unharmed by the chaos whirling around me with jagged sharp edges and bulk enough to knock me from my feet.

Rather than locking me away to torment me, he did it to show me a thing I was desperate to find.

It confounds me. I find myself questioning everything I thought I knew about Ryodan. Running prior conversations through my mind, realizing the man I believed moderately intelligent and highly manipulative of others—to their own detriment and destruction—is in fact highly intelligent and enormously manipulative of others, but I've begun to suspect it's because he's trying to fix what he perceives as the things they want fixed but don't know how. He sees the bird's-eye view and takes the hard, catalytic actions. Unsettling, disturbing to those of us that don't, makes it easy to call him bastard, heartless.

But why would he bother?

There are only two possibilities: either he wants whatever goal he will achieve by altering that person, or, unfathomable as it is, he cares about the world he pretends to scorn, and the people in it.

Then why run a den of such depravity as Chester's?

Unless . . . where better to sort the wheat from the chaff?

Even I know it's impossible in times of war to save everyone. For the love of Mary, it's impossible in times of peace. Is the nightclub his distillery where he sorts the vintages and tucks into his personal cellar the most complex, interesting wines, the most potent and impressive whiskeys?

And he considers me of value.

Easier to believe he wants something of me, although I cannot imagine what.

I'm eager to test myself, experience emotional commotion. See if I can maintain my newfound balance.

Yet I've developed a grudging respect for the man who brought me here.

You'll remain with him until I decide you've gotten what you came for, he said.

So I remain. I came for the strength of concrete without the price of it. If Ryodan is true to his word, I will leave with it.

I'd stay here a very long time to reach that goal.

Before I sought him out that night, I'd already admitted to myself I wasn't good for the abbey. I knew I wasn't the one to replace her, a mere week after Rowena died. But there was Margery and she was toxic, and the *Sinsar Dubh* was stirring and my women were in need, so I stayed and battled to the best of my ability, without weapon, without the strength of sometimes-necessary deceit and sleight of hand.

I was unfit to lead.

So I don't hammer the door, I don't shout for salvation.

My salvation is currently stretched on his back on the floor, staring up at the coffered ceiling, wearing black camouflage pants, tattooed and hard and silent.

Ryodan brought me here to give me silence.

I wonder, clever man that he is, if he brought me here also to somehow give this man words.

What could make someone stop speaking a thousand years ago? I can barely grasp, much less accept that anyone has lived so long.

How would it feel, if you cared for such a person, to watch his complete retreat? To see him day in and out, yet never converse again? To know that he *could* speak to you if he chose to, but won't? Day in, day out, your brother in arms, in your reach yet completely unreachable.

Ryodan has ordered this mute, dark man to be my teacher.

Will he obey?

I need instruction to cement my newfound center. I need training, discipline, and strength. I'm not leaving without it.

I lean back against the wall and study him, as I have for nearly a week now. He's not catatonically withdrawn. He simply doesn't interact with anyone around him at all.

"Kasteo," I say. "I've stopped feeling the pain of the world. Help me learn to control my environment. Teach me to fight." To one who stopped living a millennium ago, I say, "Show me how to live."

The man who has stared at little but the ceiling for nearly a week, who has not so much as once acknowledged my presence, slowly turns his head to the side and looks across the floor at me.

Then stares back at the ceiling.

23

*"The nights go on waiting for a
light that never comes"*

CHRISTIAN

I'm fourteen, finally old enough to enter the circle of standing stones for the first time. Ban Drochaid—the White Bridge, as these stones are called—was once a bridge through time, for the right Keltar for the right reasons. But my clan abused the gift, and the Fae queen who'd granted it took it away.

Still, the stones hold ancient power. Only one avenue was closed to us.

I stand with my da and uncles between the dual bonfires of our great May celebration, and prepare with solemn pride to help them usher in the season of rebirth with ritual and chant.

Our women, no less strong than our men, gather round, clad in the old ways, with brightly colored skirts, laced blouses, and bare feet, in honor of the coming feast, which will be attended by the entire village that thrives in the valley below our mountain.

The night sky is black and crystal clear, with thousands of glittering stars scattered like diamonds on a cloak of mink. Diamonds.

I want a girl with a mind like a diamond . . .

"Dani," I whisper through lips that are cracked from dehydration. I taste blood, it bubbles in my throat, choking me. Pain lances my ribs, my gut, my groin.

Focus.

The heather has not yet begun to bloom, and although the grass is still recovering from April's unexpectedly frosty kiss, yellow May flowers have blossomed and are strewn everywhere, on doors and windows, on the livestock, around the necks and in the hair of our women, scattered around the stones.

My da and uncles awe me, tease me, push me, teach me. I want to be like them when I am a man: wide-shouldered, with a ready laugh, a spine of steel, and courage beyond compare.

Was she worth this? Dying over and over? You gave yourself up so she could fight for those sheep. Fuck sheep. You're not a sheepdog anymore. You're a rabid wolf.

I gave myself up to watch her shine. Because I knew what the massacre of so many people that she loved would do to her. Steal the light from her eyes. I wanted to watch her save the world, and feel on top of it.

I inhale sharply. I just stumbled as I passed between my uncles, took an inadvertent elbow in my stomach, nothing more.

There's Tara, our housekeeper's daughter and Colleen's best friend. Later tonight a group of us will go for a midnight swim in the loch and shriek from the icy slap as we plunge deep. I'll try hard not to stare at Tara's wet blouse when she gets out, but och, the lass is growing in all the right places and I stare in spite of myself. She always spots me, tosses her head of fiery curls, catches the tip of her pretty pink tongue between her lips and smiles, eyes shining.

Near her stand Jamie, Quinn, and Jonah, the elderly,

impoverished MacBean's grandsons, orphaned when their parents died last year in a car crash. This is their first Beltane without them. They join us nearly every evening for supper, lonely but not alone, as food is more plentiful in our household than theirs. Old MacBean was injured a decade ago, walks with a cane and has only the food he can harvest from the land.

I look around, smiling, filled with plans. I will one day be laird, as my da before me. I'll live in a mighty old rambling wonderful stone castle filled with history and tradition, take a bonny lass to wife—

Dani is unprotected and that bastard Ryodan is—

Pain rips through my entrails and I scream.

I know why I'm obsessed with her. She's the innocence I've lost. As I was going dark, she was getting nothing but brighter. She's the ready smile of a fourteen-year-old that believes the world is one long, incredible adventure. Her dreams are still intact. She's everything I'm not anymore. She tackles life with abandon, lives in the moment, never gives up.

She reminds me of Tara, dead three years now, of a rare bone disease. I wept at the funeral for the girl who smiled all the way through her brief but brutal decline, to the twilight that came too soon.

I see the ghosts in Dani's eyes. You'd have to be blind not to.

I want to chase them, as nothing can chase mine.

I want to keep her from ever changing into something so terrible as I've become.

I want to shelter her from the hard truth that life takes from you, whittles away at your hope and scrapes the flesh from your bone and leaves you so changed you can't even recognize yourself in the mirror anymore.

I want her to always be Dani, as she is now, but the thing I was becoming got so fucked up about it. I hope the last action I chose to make as a free man cancels some of it out.

I thought turning Unseelie Prince was the most difficult battle I would ever face.

I was wrong. I thought I was in Hell. Then I found out what Hell *really* was. It's enough to wrench a laugh from my cracked lips at the sheer absurdity of it.

Pain stabs through my abdomen, sears and rips and gnaws with tiny razor teeth right down into my groin as I'm flayed alive. I scream again, flee back to the Highlands, and see the . . .

Bonfires.

The crisp air smells of roast pig and gently charring peppers and potatoes. We're about to walk the livestock between the twin fires, twins like Colleen and me, like my uncles Dageus and Drustan, before driving them out to the summer pastures. We'll relight the doused fires in our castles from the sacred, protective flames of Beltane. We'll feast and my family and friends will dance and life will seem like one perfect, long dream from which I plan to never awaken.

I have no idea how long I've been staked to the side of a cliff. I've recounted every day that I can recall, relived it in extraordinary detail.

It has kept me from falling.

It has kept me from going mad.

Unexpectedly, it has also silenced the monster I was becoming.

I no longer loathe and fear what was happening to me, because so much worse has happened to me. Perspective is a funny thing. You think your back is to the wall, then something worse corners you, and the first threat looks puny in comparison.

There is only me now, a Keltar who's been mutated with immense power and perhaps will always be, but each time I've died on this cliff and held my own, maintained my sanity, reminded myself of my heritage, who I was born to be, the madness of the Unseelie Prince faded a little more. Strengthened by my ordeal, staked to the side of this bloody godforsaken cliff, the prince overtaking me was overtaken.

I am not a man that was once a Highlander, who got swallowed alive by the depravity and homicidal mania of a death-by-sex Fae.

I am a Keltar druid who now happens to possess Unseelie power and a bloody enormous sex drive. Not sure that last part's much of a change.

My head sags forward, blood gushes from my cracked lips. She's at it again, needling away, yanking out my entrails and knitting feverishly on a gown that will never be complete.

The cruelty of it is intolerable. My entire body is on fire with pain.

Fires.

The Highlands.

Beltane.

I recall this particular night of my fourteenth year for three reasons.

It was the first night I was recognized as a Keltar druid. Heady stuff for a young lad.

It was also the night Uncle Dageus warned me, made me suspect my happy dream would end before I was ready.

Like Tara.

Like I won't let it for Dani.

When Da and the others place the sacred chalice and staff on the slab, Uncle Dageus moves close and puts a hand on my shoulder, pulls me aside and gazes down. Golden eyes so like my own stare into mine.

Fire purifies and distills, he says. *Fire transforms. You must remember that when the time comes it seems only to ravage and destroy.*

So, too, does pain.

One day you will walk through flames, lad.

Of the Beltane fires? I ask curiously. This was not a tradition with which I was familiar, but many of our more complex druid rituals were cloaked in secrecy until certain ages.

Flames of another kind. Hellfire. You will believe you canna possibly endure the agony.

At ten and four, I shiver, startled by the solemnness and sorrow in his eyes. There's gravity in his low voice that makes me more than uneasy; a young man that prides himself on his courage, I taste the sudden ash of fear.

I canna prevent it. The stones are closed to us now. I would spare you if I could.

Are you foretelling my future? I ask warily. *Do I lose my virginity this year?* I add quickly. I'd pose that question to none other of my uncles, but Dageus was different. The eyes of women follow him everywhere. I want to be like him one day, lady killer (but not a lady murderer) with the same slow, sexy smile that melts my (pretty darned hot, she's only ten years older than me) aunt Chloe every time.

I'm ready. I want Tara to be the one.

He smiles sadly.

It's whispered among my clan that Dageus has glimpsed moments in the years to come. That when he traveled through time—before the Seelie Queen took away our power to navigate the centuries in hours of need—he saw hours, even days, of our lives. He's never spoken of it, but we've always suspected. He has a canny sense of premonition that's proved invaluable on more than one occasion.

I doona ken the how and when it happens, so I doona ken how to prevent it, short of locking you away and that's no' a life. Time is tricky. It may or may not come to pass, but if it does it will test you beyond imagining. If that hour comes, you must hold on to one thing.

I shiver again. *What?*

Love. You can only be broken without it. So long as the smallest spark of love, pure, protective, and good, exists within you, that which is Keltar in you will survive. You will return.

Return.

I know a harsh truth.

So long as I stay in the magnificent Highlands of my mind I will *never* return.

You must face the fire. I doona ken how long you must endure. You must hold on, remain aware. You must be prepared when your opportunity arises, or it will fail. Uncle Dageus laughs softly. *Every man's time comes eventually. It will not, however, be yours. With luck, you'll live forever.*

I'd stare up at him, rejecting it, refusing to believe he had any powers of prophecy. Telling myself no one lives forever (not knowing I'd turn Unseelie Prince) and his rambling only made him half mad, likely from the constant chatter of the thirteen dead Draghar within him. Then I'd torn from his grip, raced off, and refused to speak to him for days.

Now I wish I'd asked him questions, now I wish I knew what he saw, what my opportunity is because I sure as hell don't see one.

Love?

Can I even feel it anymore?

I've hated everyone and everything around me since the moment I began to change. I ran from those who cared about me. I concede it's possible my hatred hastened the changes, fed the wrong things, starved the right ones. But love? To feel it here and now? I'm not sure it's even possible.

Och, but of course it is.

It's what I've been doing all along. Like my da and all my clan before us, the Highlands are our greatest love. I was shielding myself without understanding the nuts and bolts of it. I'm not a man that could wed a woman, follow her to another country and live there. I'm wedded to my motherland, to the very soil of Scotland.

I add to those mountains and valleys the faces of those I ache for and would protect, etch them in vivid detail on the backs of my eyelids, my mother and father, my siblings Colleen and Cara and Cory, and Tara, och, my sweet, sweet Tara—the third reason I recall that evening so clearly, she took my virginity that starry night on a mossy bed near the loch and bloody hell did I love her for it, and love doesn't die just because the person does, although it would be infinitely easier if it did—my friends and villagers and the lovely, brilliant, risk-taking, cocky Danielle O'Malley who conceals her broken heart behind a gamine grin, and I roll them all up into one ball of light and hold on.

I take a final look at my clan, inhale the scent of roast pig and potatoes, whisper a farewell to my long-dead Tara, shove away from my blessed retreat and force myself to embrace awareness.

I will be ready when my chance for escape comes.

I open my eyes and stare into the hideous face of the Crimson Hag as she slices my gut open.

Again.

24

"And I'm gone, I'm gone, you know it"

MAC

I have a small psychotic break, overwhelmed by too many shocks to process. My brain pulls the plug on my body.

I should run. I should figure out how to make my feet move. At the moment they are neither attached to my ankles nor controlled by conscious thought.

I flip channels, my remote stuck on three train-wreck movies I can't stop watching: *IhadsexwithBarronsandhetookmymemory/theyknowI'mthe*SinsarDubh/*JadaisDani/WTF?*

Barrons and I had sex the first night I met him. And he removed that memory like a thief in the night, as if he had every right to, when he had none. For months before I ended up in his bed (again!), he was walking around with a graphically detailed memory of every intimate carnal thing we'd done that night—and oh God was it graphic and intimate and carnal!—while I'd recalled none of it.

He knew what my ass looked like in every possible position. He knew what my face looked like when I came and that I swallow. That night, grieving and alone in a city I didn't know, a city that had been hostile and unwelcoming since the moment I stepped foot in it, I'd become a wild thing, scrapped all my inhibitions, had sex like I'd never had it before, tried everything I'd ever wanted to try with enormous enthusiasm and not one ounce of self-consciousness.

It was no wonder he was always looking at me like he wanted to have sex. We'd *had* sex and he wanted it again. And I couldn't blame him. It had been rock-your-Id-to-its-hedonistic-core phenomenal. Raw. Dirty. Mind-blowing. Addictive. I'd painted that dilapidated room with pain and passion, used sex like a bandage for the jagged wound Alina's death had sliced into my soul.

As if that little secret exploding out of my subconscious isn't enough to deal with, the new *sidhe*-seers have one among them that is my worst nightmare. The willowy brunette in army-green camo pants and tank is like me: she can sense the *Sinsar Dubh*. Not only am I not unique anymore, I've been outed.

Oh yeah, I need to run.

My feet are roots.

The third thing is perhaps the most stupefying.

I just saw Dani three weeks ago. She was fourteen. A cocky, swaggering kid.

And I'm supposed to believe this grown-up, controlled, beautiful woman is the rambunctious, sparkling-eyed teenager I chased into the Hall of All Days?

"Impossible," I whisper, peering at her, searching for some trace of the effusive, laughing, brilliant, funny girl I know. The one I love.

It's not there.

If it's her, I should be relieved that she's back and alive.

If it's her, I'm *so* not.

This woman is about twenty and absolutely frigid. She doesn't look as if she's laughed a single day in her life.

Besides, this "Jada" has supposedly been in Dublin for a few weeks. In black leather pants, a fitted top (with a plunging neckline, and if those are Dani's boobs life isn't fair), and black leather jacket, she looks composed and cold as a colonel. When she runs a hand over her perfect (straight, not one ounce of curl) red hair in its perfect high ponytail that swishes her waist as she moves, I catch a quick flash of silver and gold at her wrist, the only adornment she wears. It's not like she needs much. In addition to being stone-cold, she's that kind of beautiful, too, with startlingly high cheekbones and arched brows above glittering eyes. Is this really Dani's pixieish face grown up, matured from delicate with a sharply pronounced jaw to sophisticated, sculpted, and cool?

Is it possible Dani lost years in the Hall of All Days, and returned a mere week of our time later, this much older? And immediately began collecting *sidhe*-seers to form a small army?

Anything is possible in post-wall Dublin, and certainly in the fickle hall. Running the *sidhe*-seers is precisely what a grown-up Dani would try to do. Dublin and her *sidhe*-seer sisters always came first to her.

Still, I don't see a trace of the "Mega" in this icy woman.

Ryodan begins to pace a slow circle around her, reminding me of the way Barrons stalked me that night he decided I had no right to something that was indisputably mine.

She stands still, completely at ease with something like him behind her back.

That seals it. It's definitely not Dani. She would never

let Ryodan behind her. She would spin with him. Like I did with Barrons.

The women on the floor begin to push up, but Jada gestures to them and commands, "They'll only take you back down. Remain on the floor. I won't have any of you injured by them."

"We're better fighters than you're giving us credit for," Green Camo who outed me growls.

"These are two of the Nine I discussed with you earlier. Remain down."

Green Camo may be my enemy but I totally get the look of fury and frustration that flashes across her face. Accept that you're outgunned? Stay on the floor and don't even try to fight? What kind of life is that?

Ryodan suddenly kicks up into that way of moving that's a blur, then Jada is a blur and there's a small whirlwind of commotion in the middle of the study accompanied by a ferocious smudge of sound that could be raised voices or just plain snarling. I feel like I'm watching a cartoon featuring two Tasmanian devils, then suddenly Jada and Ryodan reappear, facing each other: he's spitting savagery, she's pure ice.

"Don't touch me again," she says with arctic frost. "Men have died for less. Even men who aren't men."

"You cut it off," Ryodan explodes. "That's why I couldn't get a lock on you last week at Chester's. You fucking cut my tattoo off. And you mutilated yourself in the process."

"I've never had a tattoo on the back of my neck."

"I didn't say it was on the back of your neck."

"That's where you touched me."

"I touched other places, too."

"And will pay for it. Sleight of hand. A diversionary tactic. Intent infuses action. You're easy to read."

"Redundant much, Dani. Should have left it at sleight of hand."

"I'm not Dani. Nor have I ever had a tattoo. But if someone thought to place a mark on me I neither wanted nor approved, I would certainly cut it out. I'm no cattle to be branded."

I rub the tattoo on the back of my skull and shoot Barrons a pissed look. "Moo," I say frostily.

"Don't even start," he says. "It saved your life repeatedly."

"It was for your protection," Ryodan says.

"Precisely," Barrons clips.

"I don't need protection nor have I ever," Jada says. "I protect. I hunt. I am the predator, not the prey. Leave now and I will permit you to go. We will, however, meet again."

I slant a look up. "Precisely."

" 'Permit,' " Ryodan mocks. "Explain your ability to move in hyperspeed. *Dani*."

"If this 'Dani' is to be identified on the basis of a single attribute, one might propose anyone—even you— are this person upon whom you seem so fixated, as you, too, share that talent."

Jada is suddenly gone and I feel her touching me, patting me down at light speed, looking for the Book, finding nothing. By the time Barrons blurs into motion to blast her away, she is standing near the desk again.

Ryodan told me Dani could move fast enough to give him a run for his money. When she chose. I frown. He also said there were things Dani didn't know. Exactly what kind of things?

The women on the floor stare up, watching, awaiting the next command from their leader.

"She's not carrying it," Jada informs Green Camo.

Green Camo says, "I feel two. One where it should be. The other coming from her."

"Of this you are certain."

"Unequivocally."

"You will leave now," Jada informs Ryodan and Barrons. "But she," Jada looks at me, "will remain."

Was that a flicker in those icy emerald eyes? I narrow my eyes, staring back, searching for some hint of Dani O'Malley. It isn't there.

"She," Barrons growls, "is not remaining anywhere but with me."

"Maybe I want to stay here with them," I say, not meaning a word of it. "At least the *sidhe*-seers only tried to kill me. Not steal pieces of my mind."

"I didn't steal anything. I merely kicked it beneath a rock until you could deal with it. It's not my bloody fault it took you so long. Had I wished to excise it completely I could have."

"It's not your right to excise anything. Temporarily or permanently."

"Take her below," Jada orders the women.

"Don't push me," I warn.

"You'll go willingly or you'll be dragged. I don't understand how you have become another *Sinsar Dubh* nor do I care. I've seen stranger things."

I shoot a glance at Ryodan and am surprised to see he appears completely unfazed to learn that I am the *Sinsar Dubh* walking, or rather, about to be running.

"It's unnecessary to understand how an animal became rabid to put it down," Jada continues. "You'll be dealt with accordingly."

"Good luck with that," I say coolly.

My inner copy is perversely silent. I know why. It's waiting to see what I'm willing to do. That's a big fat nothing. It's going to have to protect itself, offer me something I can use free of price.

Nice bluff, MacKayla, it purrs. *Try again. You will never let them lock you up and you know it.*

You *will never let them lock us up,* I retort silently. *I*

*will not kill these people. Give me crimson runes. I'll
only use them on the others, not you. I swear.*

*You will kill everyone and destroy everything around
you in order to survive. It's the way you're wired. I
know. I'm the wiring.*

I recite feverishly:

*And the Raven never flitting still is sitting, still is
sitting on the pallid bust of Pallas just above my
chamber door . . .*

"Look around you. You can't even control one Book.
How do you think to control two," Ryodan says.

Jada/possibly Dani says coolly, "In fishing for information, one might advocate the use of interrogatories."

Ryodan laughs. "Ah, Dani, there you are. You can
run. But you can't hide."

"If by that you mean this Dani person to whom you
so erroneously and tediously refer also remarked upon
your deliberate omission of proper punctuation as a
psychological tactic intended to subtly coerce, the logical conclusion is merely that multiple women find your
methods transparent," she delivers in a cool rush.

If Jada wasn't currently threatening me, I'd like her
for that one. I should run but I'm stuck on this train
wreck channel, trying to decide if Jada could possibly
be Dani, trying to silence my inner demon o'er whom
the lamplight isn't streaming so well. It's goading me,
scaring me, telling me they're going to imprison me and
no one will care. No one will save me.

Barrons won't let that happen.

Barrons took your memory, the *Sinsar Dubh* reminds. *He's mercenary to the big, badass core. You are
not the exception to his self-serving rules. There are no
exceptions.*

"You signed a contract I keep in my office," Ryodan says to Jada. "Drop by, I'll show it to you."

"I signed nothing. But if I had, a coerced oath endures only as long as the coercer holds greater power. There's no power greater than mine in this room."

Ryodan says softly, "Holy strawberries, Dani, we're in a jam."

I look at him like he's sprouted two heads. Holy strawberries? In a jam? Even Barrons looks stumped.

He continues, "But don't worry. Holy priceless collection of Etruscan snoods—you really butchered that one, by the way—I've got it in the bag. How about this one: holy borrowing bibliophile, let's book."

Jada's eyes narrow almost imperceptibly.

"Ah, but I couldn't possibly have heard that one, could I. Unless I was there when you didn't know it. As I've always been there. Dani. I know what's wrong. And we're going to fix it."

"My name is Jada and there's nothing wrong with me. I'm superior in every way."

Now she sounds like Dani.

"I tasted your blood. I know your fucking soul. I felt you in Chester's and I felt you tonight."

"Like you, I have no soul. Like you, there are ledgers to be balanced. You're in the red. Unlike you, I don't sit at a desk and endlessly shove papers around."

"You talk as if you know me."

"So I've heard. If you tasted someone's blood against their will, it is likely that person will kill you for it."

"Bring it on. Dani."

"Jada."

"You think this keeps you safe. You think you don't feel."

"There are ledgers. Those I kill. Those I reward."

"There are *legends*. You used to be one."

She says coolly, "I am legend."

"Dani's a legend," Ryodan says. "Not you."

"This Dani appears to matter to you."

"Always."

"Perhaps you had a funny way of showing it."

"How would you know."

"I've heard."

"You've heard, my ass. I know you. I saw you when Dani was ten. *Jada*. You looked right back at me. We fought that night. I won her back from you and I will again. I've seen you other times as well. You may wear a woman's body now but it belongs to Dani. You have no right to be here."

I gape at Ryodan. Is he saying what I think he's saying? Not only did Dani leave and come back older, but she came back as someone else? There's a word for it . . . I rummage for what remains scattered around my brain from the entry-level psychology course I took . . . aha! Dissociative disorder. Is he saying she's fragmented? And he *knew* this? No way. I would have seen it. Wouldn't I?

Jada trains her emerald gaze on me. "She is who doesn't belong here. Faulty logic imprisons one *Sinsar Dubh* while the other is permitted to roam Dublin. It is what it is regardless of the vessel."

"Oh, you should so talk," I snap. "Dani."

"I. Am. Jada."

"Whoever the fuck you are," Barrons growls, "you're not touching Mac."

"Well, you're not touching me either," I growl up at him.

"Deal with it, Ms. Lane."

"Deal with it?" I say incredulously. "Ms. Lane, my bloody ass. You called me Mac that very night, that first night we met and screwed our brains out, and what do I get ever since? I'll tell you what I—"

"During. You changed. You became the woman after.

A stiff blindered horse that spooked on new terrain. I expected better—"

"Oh, and because your *expectations* weren't met—"

"They were bloody well exceeded, which is why the after—"

"You think you have the right to just strip the entire experience from one party to the—"

"—was such a grand disappointment, and if—"

"—event as if they—"

"It wasn't an 'event.' It was a motherfucking revelation."

"—don't even have the right to remember whatever the hell mistake they—"

"Which is precisely why I did it. You thought it was a mistake, then you—"

"—chose to make, just like they might *choose* to keep the memory, because after all, they were there and it *was* theirs and possession *is* nine-tenths of—"

"—started getting all tight-lipped and pissy and I knew if—"

"—law."

"I *am* the law."

"Apparently. *Heil.*" I click my heels together and salute.

"Can't you two find a better fucking moment for this," Ryodan says tightly.

"Really," Green Camo agrees.

"Stay the hell out of my business," I snap at both of them.

"Don't decorate the goddamn room with it," Ryodan fires back.

"As if you're not doing some decorating of your own. You're just pissed that my argument with Barrons derailed your argument with Dani."

"Mac can decorate anything she bloody well pleases. With anything she pleases," Barrons says tightly. "Her business, your blood, half your fucking face, who gives a fuck."

"Nice defense, *Jericho*. Not. He can't push me around, but you can?" Frosted sugar coats my words.

"Merely trying to keep us on point," Ryodan clips.

I say, "I'm dead on point. The point is—"

"That I am not Dani," Jada interrupts coolly. "The point is the three of you are dysfunctional, volatile, inefficient, and in my way. Not to mention—" She pierces me with that emerald ice stare."—a grave threat to our world."

"Oh, *I'm* dysfunctional, Ms. Alter Ego? Really? Pot meet kettle." The second I say it, I wish I hadn't. If Jada really is Dani, her current state is my fault.

Someone enters the foyer behind me, boots tapping smartly on the floor, and Jada stares past me at the new arrival.

"I couldn't find Clare and Sorcha," the woman behind me says.

"No matter. You will place them as I instructed you. Quickly."

The look on Jada's face chills me. It tells me she believes she's won.

Place them? What "them"? I frenziedly sort and discard possibilities, racing to a terrifying conclusion: if Jada actually *is* Dani, she knows how to immobilize the *Sinsar Dubh*—with the four stones we placed on the slab in the cavern. The same stones Kat retrieved from the cavern and tucked away for safekeeping. Once the *Sinsar Dubh* was no longer on the slab, they were unnecessary and we worried about leaving coveted objects of power lying around the cavern since we couldn't close the doors. Jada's been in residence long enough to have found them.

I'm always blocking lately, with the exception of my

constant antenna for the Unseelie Princess. Now, I cautiously open my *sidhe*-seer senses.

And gasp.

I feel them! The pulsing blue-black binding presence of the stones is here in the room with me!

Lock you up, lock you down, make you sleep beneath the ground, the *Sinsar Dubh* coos.

Make you sleep, too, I retort silently.

"She brought the stones," I say to Barrons. "Stop her!"

He's on it before I finish speaking. There's a blur of motion as he lunges for the woman Jada called Brigitte, but Jada blocks him and they collide with such force that they both go flying backward to opposite sides of the room and crash against the walls.

Then Barrons and Ryodan are rushing Brigitte, who's already placed one of the stones in the far corner, but they slam into Jada, who manages to get there a split second before them. She grabs Brigitte and freeze-frames her to place the next stone but collides with Barrons and one of the stones goes flying, smashes into a painting on the wall and drops to the floor. The painting crashes down on top of it. I lunge for it, determined to get at least one of the damn things so they can't box me in, but the others beat me to it by a mile.

I leap for it again and get slammed into a wall by a blur. I pursue the stone obsessively for a good thirty seconds but all I get for my effort is a bloody nose and three broken fingers.

I finally back off and watch the three blurs whiz around the room as they fight a battle I can't even track, much less get in on, feeling bizarrely invisible.

Jada's women are doing the same thing, with the exception of Brigitte, who's being used as a hockey puck by three players who aim for and block goals at the speed of light. She's bloodier every time she surfaces for a split second before vanishing again.

I sidle toward the door. If I'm not in the room, they can't trap me.

Every *sidhe*-seer in the room moves to stop me. Their expressions are icy, easy to decipher.

I am the target.

I am the enemy.

Green Camo gives me a condemning look that makes me want to throttle the bitch. I've subdued the Book this long, and done a bang-up job with one small exception. I'd like to see how well she would handle being possessed by the Unseelie King's darkest demons.

Draw your spear, the *Sinsar Dubh* purrs. *Destroy them. You know you can.*

And let you take over and kill them all? Not a chance.

I quit moving, lean back against the wall and sigh, thinking it's funny how things change so quickly. Last season I was Dublin's MVP, the hunter, and everybody wanted me on their team. This season I'm the hunted, a liability that kills innocent people, and now the world wants to neutralize me.

The *sidhe*-seers know my secret. They're going to stalk me as relentlessly as I stalked the *Sinsar Dubh*.

End goal: put Mac down.

If Jada really *is* Dani, she'll publish a cool, accusatory *Jada Journal* and post it all over the city long before the sun is up, outing me to the world. There'll be no place I can hide unless I pack up and leave this planet for good with Barrons—

I'm not even talking to Barrons at the moment.

My mom and dad will know what I've been concealing from them for months. One daughter dead, the other damned.

The snarling blurs accelerate, darting this way and that. Brigitte goes slamming into a wall and I wince in sympathy. My bones have already begun to heal. She doesn't have the same gift.

Gift? Longevity could be used against me just like it was against Barrons's son. For Cruce to be influencing the environment, he must be cognizant in his icy prison in the cold stone chamber deep below the earth, aware his body is frozen, that he's trapped. Do the minutes creep like hours? Immortal, does he tally the seconds as they tick by, stretching to hellish infinity?

You will soon know, the *Sinsar Dubh* reminds silkily.

As will you.

Fight, you fucking fool.

You. I dig in my mental heels, determined to outwait it, wagering my humanity against its psychopathy, betting its survival instincts will kick before mine, if only by a split second.

Make me do it, sweet thing, you won't like it.

I'll like it better than I'll like killing all these people. They already think I'm the enemy. If I release the *Sinsar Dubh* and slaughter these women to free myself, I'll have proved myself the enemy to anyone left alive. Including me. The rest of the abbey will come after me in force, for good reason. But I won't even know that. I'll be a straitjacketed bookworm burrowed into the binding of an insane, homicidal book, staring helplessly out from the pages of my own life, as they're writ by someone else, and I'd commit atrocities that would damn a saint's soul.

Suddenly Brigitte appears and collapses in a battered heap. I study the blurs, concluding Jada now has the stones and is trying to place them.

As they whiz around the room like small tornadoes, furniture flies, lamps topple, and bulbs shatter. Rowena's stately study has become a shambles of trashed furniture and demolished decor.

A jolt of energy suddenly hits me and I flinch. The

sensation is familiar. The night we interred the *Sinsar Dubh,* I had to reach both of my hands into the field generated by the stones to remove the crimson runes from the cover and felt instantly lethargic, nauseated. I'd assumed it was just another facet of my *sidhe*-seer senses. Now I realize how lucky I was that we'd warded the Book on top of an altar. If I'd had to actually step *inside* the energy field that night, I would have ended up as trapped as the *Sinsar Dubh.*

On the east end of the study, flush to the wall, a line of blue-black flickers and solidifies. Two of the stones have connected. They flare and begin to emit a chilling chime.

Assuming Barrons and Ryodan defeat Jada and the next two stones don't get positioned, assuming I don't feel the third stone flare to life and suddenly develop psychopathic tendencies of my own—where do I go from here?

Do I leave with Barrons and trust him to protect me? I can't protect myself. I can't use the spear with any certainty that I won't kill again. I can't outrun Jada. My ineffectualness chafes. God, does it chafe.

Last season's MVP vanishing into obscurity.

Oh, yeah, I feel invisible.

I jerk again.

The third stone just connected with the other two, and I watch a second line form at the perimeter of the north wall of the study.

If the last stone is placed, two more blue-black lines will appear on the south and west ends, squaring me in, and I'll be trapped in Cruce's hellish, conscious stasis. They'll collect the stones, gather them close around me as we did with the Book, then carry me down, deep into the earth where I really hate being. No crimson runes are necessary to seal the cover of my Book; my body is lock enough. It's not like anyone can pry open my skin and read it. The brilliant wards and runes on the towering walls of the cavern will connect to the field of the stones, and intensify it.

I'll lie upon a slab, staring up at the ceiling far above (unless adding insult to injury, they put me facedown, God, that would suck), trapped in waking paralysis, a spelled Sleeping Beauty longing for the kiss of a prince (just not Cruce!).

Am I really going to stand here and let them imprison me? Become the Disney heroine that can't save herself?

Accept that you're outgunned? the *Sinsar Dubh* mocks. *Stay on the floor and don't even try to fight? What kind of life is that? It's now or never, sweet thing.*

For the first time since the moment I withstood the temptation to take the spell and free Barrons's son, I seriously consider opening the godforsaken book and doing whatever I must to walk out of here alive. This time, however, Barrons isn't in my head to offer counsel and strength.

This time it's only me facing the greatest test in my twenty-three years. What am I willing to do to survive? What price am I willing to pay?

Evil isn't a state of being, Barrons once said to me. It's a choice.

My life flashes before my eyes: who I was, who I am now, what I might become. Whether I can live with myself assuming I one day claw my way back to control. The casualties on my conscience, the ashes I might find myself standing in. I remember the Book killing in the streets of Dublin, remember the Beast it became as it exploded upward, terrifyingly powerful even in amorphous form.

My body would give it corporeality. Nearly immortal corporeality.

I know what the Book did the last time it walked

Dublin's streets. Killed with unadulterated psychotic glee.

The stakes are simple: me or the world.

Can Barrons save me if I let the *sidhe*-seers trap me? *Will* Barrons save me?

A strange calm settles over me as I realize it's irrelevant.

The bottom line is we choose our epitaphs.

Every moment of every day we decide upon the actions that define us—or so a wise man that wasn't wise enough not to steal my memory once told me—it's all about what we can live with and what we can't live without.

I can't live with being the woman who freed the *Sinsar Dubh* to save her own ass, butchering who knows how many people in the process, and who knows how many more before I'm stopped. That's not going to be chiseled on my Urn. No grave, I'm not getting stuck beneath the ground for freaking perpetuity. And if I have to have a bloody Urn, at least I'm going to choose the inscription.

Heroes fight, the Book derides my decision. *Victims give up. Barrons is right, you're a walking victim, a lamb in a city of wolves. You deserve to die.*

I don't reply. Sometimes the most heroic action you can take looks a lot like inaction to the rest of the world. Sometimes the hardest, longest walk is the one the white-hat takes offstage.

They'll think they outsmarted you, trapped you. They'll never believe you chose it. Your "noble" sacrifice will be for nothing because they won't see it that way, the Book goads.

Totally sucks. And is perfectly probable. Whether or not they understand what I did has no impact on the value of my action. Either I decimate this place and stalk out, probably to destroy the entire world—but hey, I'll be alive—or I let them put me on ice and trust that those who love me will find a way to rescue me.

While accepting that I may never be rescued.

It may not be the best way for me.

But it's the right way.

Sadness fills me. I don't want to be done yet.

I hope Mom and Dad figure it out. I want them to be proud of me. And I hope Barrons—God, I'm so pissed at him right now I can't even complete the thought! Tears press at the back of my eyes but I refuse to let them flow.

The fourth stone explodes from the blur of motion, skitters across the floor, sliding toward that fourth corner, sliding . . .

I brace myself for what's about to happen.

I accept that it's necessary.

I'm afraid. I hate being afraid.

I won't get paralyzed looking that way. I square my shoulders, straighten my spine, tuck in my stomach and angle my head, notch my chin slightly upward. What's that saying? Die young and leave a pretty corpse.

I wish I were as invisible as this battle raging around me makes me feel, fought by opponents with whom I can't hope to compete because at least then I'd be able to—

About fucking time, the *Sinsar Dubh* growls. *Your wish. My command.*

Then it roars, *RUN.*

Part III

If you know the enemy and know yourself, you need not fear the result of a hundred battles. If you know yourself but not the enemy, for every victory gained you will also suffer a defeat. If you know neither the enemy nor yourself, you will succumb in every battle.

–Sun Tzu, *The Art of War*

25

"No one sees my face, sees me coming"

MAC

After the walls fell last Halloween (and I was no longer Pri-ya), with most of Dublin's inhabitants dead or gone, I got to indulge one of my greatest teenage fantasies: I walked into Brown & Taylor and shoplifted everything I wanted.

An Alexander McQueen scarf of black skulls on pink leopard silk, a pair of totally come-fuck-me Christian Louboutin heels adorned with silver spikes that perfectly complemented the black dress I snatched off a Chanel rack, a classic Burberry raincoat lined with checked silk, a glamorous smoky faux-fur stole. A Louis Vuitton limited edition satchel, Prada wallet and purse, Dolce & Gabbana python boots, lingerie to die for!

Then I went next door and raided Estée Lauder's makeup counter, before moving on to Lancôme. I'd crammed my backpack with all those expensive moisturizers I'd never been able to afford and filled another with foundation and blush, eye shadow and mascara.

I'd commandeered two rooms on the fourth floor of Barrons Books & Baubles (last time I saw them they'd decamped to the fifth and switched sides) and set up my own private store stocked with feminine essentials: nail polish and remover, cotton balls and lotions, makeup and perfume and insanely expensive jewelry. (Over time, I added three diamond-crusted Rolexes I found lying in the streets to my hoard.)

I'd packed four enormous closets full of boxes of tampons and those invaluable skinny liner pads for heavy days when a tampon isn't enough. I'd lugged home crates of vitamin D, aspirin, cold medicine, and soap. Then I went back for more and piled mountains of toilet paper in the second room. I raided three pharmacies and stashed away antibiotics and various medicinal supplies and ten years of birth control and condoms. At that point I figured I'd be lucky if I lived that long.

But there's a second fantasy I never got to indulge that I'm fairly certain I won't outgrow: wanting to go places I'm not allowed to go so I can see things I'm not supposed to see.

I can now.

I'm invisible.

I'M FREAKING INVISIBLE!

It's incredibly difficult having something inside you that's sentient and pretty much brilliant, and not at all nice, that can skim your mind to an uncertain degree, observe everything you do, study and analyze you, and wait forever for the perfect moment to seize the upper hand.

It's worse than sleeping with the enemy, it's living with a parasite inside you that is pathologically obsessed with a single goal: take you over, annihilate your will, and do whatever it chooses with what used to be your body. We're conjoined twins, forced to share blood and oxygen, battling daily, sneakily to be the one who controls the supply.

Last night, when I stood in Rowena's study bluffing

the Book, outwaiting it, trying to force its hand to save us, that's all I was initially doing.

Bluffing.

But my bluff became conviction, and the moment it did, the Book stepped in and saved our asses by turning me invisible.

Not just invisible—undetectable!

I'm no longer stalked by suffocating, smelly wraiths. Last night, they vanished, and I haven't seen them in eighteen blissful hours.

I'm still corporeal—that was the first thing I tested after I dashed from the study, a split second before the fourth stone was placed. I didn't look back. I ran faster than a demon from Hell breaking out with Cerberus snapping at its heels. I ran until I burst through the front doors of the abbey, into the steamy, nearly tropical night beyond, where I'd stood in the driveway, gasping for breath. I'd looked down and seen nothing but two small indentations in the grass where I was fairly certain my feet were.

I'd headed straight for the fountain, scooped up a handful of water, and heaved a sigh of relief when it worked. Although the warm water had turned invisible the moment I cupped it, I'd felt its wetness, been able to dribble it from my hand and watch it become visible again. For a moment I was afraid I was a ghost. I'd hastened to one of the large standing stones and forced myself to place a hand against its eerie, obsidian coolness. It, however, had not vanished. Apparently only small things did.

As I'd made the long trek back to Dublin on foot, not willing to boost one of the SUVs and stir any suspicions, the *Sinsar Dubh* had insisted I leave this world because they would never stop hunting us.

I refused.

We argued all the way back to Dublin, which had

taken most of the night. It threatened, cajoled, bullied, even tried to charm.

I'd been unmoved.

So long as I don't draw my spear, which spurs a mind-less killing frenzy, I remain in control of my feet, and I'm staying on this world, period, the end.

I've drawn my line in the sand, and the Book had damn well better toe it. There's no question this is war. A lukewarm one at the moment but war nonetheless.

We've established a détente of sorts. The Book is now willing to toss me a bit of aid because—although it taught me the hard way that if I draw my spear to kill, it can make me kill others—last night I taught the *Sin-sar Dubh* a harder lesson: I'm willing to sacrifice myself to save the world from what I might do to it.

It's never going to let that happen.

So it's keeping me invisible. Any small items I pick up or put on also vanish from the realm of the seen.

When I arrived in the city early this morning, I further tested the extent of my corporeality by shouting at two See-You-in-Faery girls hanging outside Chester's while chucking a couple of rocks in their direction. They heard me, and were hit by my inexplicably materializing rocks. It was deliciously fun. Upon my return to the bookstore, I experimented more and realized if I wasn't careful I could give myself away by sitting on a soft chair or sofa, creating a petunia-shaped indent. It appears minor things become invisible when I touch them but major things don't. When I walk across the rug, my invisibility has no impact on it. When I press the handle to flush the toilet, it remains visible.

I suspect if I tried to turn myself over, the Book would take further measures to impede me. No worries there. I'll sacrifice myself if there's no other choice but I certainly won't go hunting for the opportunity.

In the meantime, the *Sinsar Dubh* has decided to keep me as cloaked as a Klingon Bird of Prey.

"Works for me," I say cheerfully as I bang out the front door of Barrons Books & Baubles. It's two in the afternoon, the time of day the erstwhile ex-owner of my shop and man who dominates the top of my lengthy shit-list never comes around. I just finished showering (carefully wiping down the tile before hiding the damp towels in the back of a closet) and changed clothes (into the first outfit I've liked in a long time, pity that no one can see it, including myself, topped off with a lovely skull-bedecked pink scarf that I no longer have to worry about getting stained and smelly), pulled on soft-soled boots, and grabbed a few protein bars from my stash. I was actually stupid enough to look in the mirror, prelude to putting makeup on. Ha. That's not going to happen. No need to style my hair either. Eating was a special challenge, since I can't see myself or the food and you don't realize how heavily you rely on a peripheral visual awareness of your body to eat until you no longer have it, but after stabbing myself in the nose and chin a few times (I decide against washing my face again, if I have chocolate smudges, no one can see them), I managed.

It's time to find out what's going on in the world, all those details I've been missing. Time to do some long overdue investigating.

MacKayla Lane: unstoppable supersleuth.

For the first time in months, it's fun to be me.

Unfortunately, being corporeal means I'm as subject to the elements as everyone else, and it's once again raining in Dublin; a torrential spring downpour, good for the newly planted flowers and trees but bad for me.

Once I grabbed it, my umbrella became invisible, too, but that just makes me a larger, unseen obstacle, and foliage isn't the only new addition to Dublin's streets, there are *people* out walking, just like old times, hurrying to and fro, chins chucked down beneath hats and umbrellas.

Twice passersby collided with me when I didn't sidestep fast enough, and both times I nearly lost my parasol and took a brief but thorough drenching. This being invisible is tricky stuff. It may take me a while to get the hang of it. I make a mental note that once I reach my destination, I'm going to have to dry off so I don't leak a trail of water everywhere I go.

I'm halfway to Chester's when I turn the corner and run smack into the Dreamy-Eyed Guy who's standing outside an old brownstone converted to condos, looking up.

I flail for balance, taking a third soaking which I hardly even notice.

My savior is here, standing before me in the flesh! He'll take back his Book and I'll be visible again and go saunter around in front of Green Camo girl and prove I'm no longer a threat!

"There you are," I exclaim excitedly.

"Not quite," the Dreamy-Eyed Guy says. "But then you aren't quite either. *Quite* the couple we make. You've chocolate on your face."

Freaking figures. I scrub irritably at my chin, my cheek. "We need to talk." I snatch the human form of the Unseelie King by his arm before he vanishes on me again. Like other large objects I touch, he remains visible.

He locks surreally beautiful eyes with mine, staring right through my invisibility cloak, but why wouldn't he? It's an illusion perpetrated by a part of him.

"What have you done now, Beautiful Girl?"

"Not me. You. It's your fault."

"Fault schmault. Lies in the stars."

Not about to get sucked into an existential debate, I get to the point. "Get your Book out of me."

"Talking to it?"

"No," I deny instantly. "It talks to me. I almost never answer."

"Cold fire. Jumbo shrimp."

"Huh?" I don't want the half-mad king. I want the sane one.

"Almost never: oxymoron. Risky couplings. Gray lies." He removes my hand from his arm. "Not my book."

"Bullshit. You made it." I latch onto his arm again. No way he's leaving without fixing me this time.

"So you say."

"It's a fact."

"Nasty little buggers. Sport Halloween masks. Trust none of them."

"Get. It. Out. Of. Me," I grit.

"How many times must your king say it? Can't eviscerate essential self."

"Oh! I *knew* you were going to say that! It's not *my* self. It's yours. And you're not my flipping king."

"Didn't say I was. Certainly not flipping. Although occasionally I do a cartwheel."

He's making little sense. But he rarely does. I suspect it's even more difficult for the virtually omnipotent being to communicate when he's functioning than it is for one of his multiple human parts. The only way the Unseelie King can walk among humans is by parceling out his vast sentience and power among a dozen or so human bodies. "I can't live with your monster inside me. I shouldn't have to."

"Ah," he clucks with mock sympathy, "because it's not fair. And life always is. There is that whole 'sins of the father' thing."

"You're not my father. And no, it's not fair."

"In a manner of speaking, you are unequivocally the king's and always will be. Caveat: what you fear most will destroy you."

"Exactly. So, get it out of me."

"Stop fearing it."

"*You* dumped it. Why shouldn't I?"

"And we're back to square one. BG wake the fuck up, can't eviscerate essential self."

I stare at him. "What are you saying? You never got rid of it? Are you trying to tell me you dumped all your evil into a book and it infected me and made me evil—and it didn't even work for you?"

"Try to behave with it."

Then the Dreamy-Eyed Guy was gone, just *gone*, leaving a final cryptic comment floating on air.

" 'Ware the Sweeper, BG. Don't talk to its minions either. It's not about eating the candy. It's about giving away words." Soft, enormous laughter rolls through the rainy streets like thunder. "Even that broody ass poet's."

Try to behave with it? *That* was his useless advice? Sweeper? Minions? Candy? What the hell is he talking about?

I stomp my foot on the sidewalk, slip and fall on my ass into the overflowing gutter. "Fucking fairies," I yell, shoving wet hair from my face. "I hate you. All of you. Fuck you, Dreamy-Eyed Guy!"

A sudden breeze snatches the umbrella from my hand, turning it visible again and sends it whirling down the street, chute over handle, before smashing it into a brick wall. Metal spokes snap and it collapses on itself. Lightning crashes and thunder rolls.

I'm not sure but I think the Unseelie King just said "Fuck you, tiny insignificant very wet human" back.

After a moment I drag myself up, collect my battered

umbrella, and begin slogging through the rain toward Chester's.

After drying myself off thoroughly in one of the restrooms, I make every effort to stride purposefully across the crowded dance floors of Chester's, but were I visible, someone watching would see an erratic zig followed by a stumbling zag that vaguely resembles a drunken bumblebee. It's impossible to avoid people who have no idea I'm there.

I take two pops to my rib cage from flailing elbows, a backhand to my jaw (they call this dancing?), and a fist to my thigh (really, who gyrates like that?) before I even clear the first subclub.

I pause in an unoccupied space between clubs, assessing my surroundings, seeking the clearest path.

It's easy to find. Behind a tall dark mountain of a man for whom the crowd parts with the same mystical obedience as the Red Sea opening for Moses.

"Barrons," I growl.

Thanks to the challenges of my recent transformation, coupled with the *Sinsar Dubh*'s endless harangue about why I should leave Earth this very second, quadrupled by how pissed I am the king didn't even seriously consider my request—perhaps the king's parts are all different, some more sane and logical than others, and I should start hunting McCabe—I've not had time to brood about what Barrons did to me.

Bristling with righteous indignation, I stalk off into his Red Sea wake. With only a few minor mishaps, I move in close behind him. I may be invisible but my body still responds to him and it makes me even madder. I'm tense at first, worried he'll sense or smell me, but whatever the Book is doing that keeps my stalkers from locating me seems to work on Barrons, too. I wonder why he's here. I wonder what he thinks happened to me. I'm itching to know what transpired after I left the abbey.

As we pass the guards (Fade and a massive white-haired man with burning eyes) and ascend the sleek chrome stairs to the upper level of the club, I breathe more easily and focus on watching his every move so if he suddenly stops I don't crash into his backside. Despite disliking him intensely at the moment, I have to admit it's a damn fine backside. He strides with the purpose I was aiming for, directly to Ryodan's office, slaps a palm to the wall and steps inside, oblivious to one Ms. Lane, superspy, hot on his heels.

I realize, as the door hisses closed behind us, that I'm about to eavesdrop on an unguarded conversation between Barrons and Ryodan. Fascinating. To say I'm all ears is the understatement of the century. I glance down to make sure I'm not dripping, grateful the floor is glass and I'm not leaving indents in carpet that might give me away.

Ryodan is sitting behind his desk toying with a black-handled, curved black blade that looks ancient. With the exception of the dark knife, the desk is empty. I imagine he had it cleaned more than a few times after Lor's unexpected tryst last week. The ebony blade is highly polished and reflects the low light as he rolls it between his hands.

He's dressed as impeccably as ever in tailored dark pants and a crisp pinstriped shirt rolled back at the cuffs, revealing thick, scarred forearms and a silver cuff that matches the one Barrons wears. It reminds me of the one I saw on Jada's wrist last night, and I wonder absently where she got it. I didn't get a clear look since it was half covered by her sleeve.

I move forward, taking care to not bump into anything, which is trickier than you think when you can't see yourself, and inspect him curiously. Though I'd never let him know I think it, Ryodan is hot as hell. If I were visible, I'd never stare this hard. Something about him discourages it. His chiseled features are stonier than usual, his jaw shadowed with stubble. Rather than his urbane businessman self, he seems more a savage mercenary forced to wear a suit. His thick short hair, nearly shaved at the sides, is standing up as if he's been running his hands through it. Repeatedly. From those small details, I know Ryodan is deeply disturbed.

"No longer pretending to do paperwork," Barrons mocks.

Ryodan doesn't bother to glance up. "She sent me a message this morning. Said if I don't give her Mac, she's going to demolish Chester's. You believe that shit. Threatening me. Few weeks ago she was a kid. Now she's a fucking woman. A grown-up, self-possessed woman with a mind like my blade, cold as ice and on fire at the same time. Dangerous as hell. She was dangerous when she was a kid."

"I sent a message to the abbey," Barrons says. "Said if they don't give me Mac, we're going to raze the fucking place."

Ah, so both sides think the other whisked me off somehow. The night must have ended in a hostile stand-off. I'm surprised Ryodan didn't head straight back to the abbey this morning with the Nine, abduct Jada, and lock her in his dungeon.

"You believe they have Mac," Ryodan says.

"Undecided. One moment I felt her, the next I didn't. Haven't felt her since."

"Worried about her." It's a question, though Ryodan's voice doesn't rise at the end. I wait expectantly for Barrons's answer.

"No."

I bristle. That's it? A lousy no? Doesn't he care? Is this

what our relationship is going to come down to: me finding out while invisible that I don't even matter to him?

"She'll be back," Barrons says.

"She's a vessel for the *Sinsar Dubh,* has virtually unlimited power at her disposal, there for the taking. I'm not certain you or I could resist such temptation."

He's not? Shit, shit, shit. That's it. I'm doomed.

"She managed it once. She'll do it again. Mac's got a light inside her that's inextinguishable."

I beam, feeling ten feet tall and bulletproof. If Barrons's faith in me is that unshakable, I can do anything. Then I scowl. If he had so much faith in me, he would have trusted me to handle what happened between us that first day. Eyes narrowed, I flip him the bird.

Ryodan says, "She looked eighteen, nineteen."

"Physically, I'd put her at twenty," Barrons says. "Mentally, closer to thirty, in hard war years."

If they're talking about Jada aka possibly Dani, I agree with Barrons.

"She's cold as ice."

"You used to worry she'd get herself killed before she managed to grow up," Barrons says. "Moot point now."

"She's fucking beautiful."

Barrons studies him a moment then says, "Old enough for you."

"That's not why I watched over her."

"Bullshit. We all saw the woman she could become. Just didn't think she'd do it so quickly."

"I wanted her to have— Ah, fuck, it doesn't matter."

"The childhood she missed. It's gone. Adapt."

Ryodan smiles faintly. "I loved watching her be young. Cocky. Swaggering around like she was invincible. She was supposed to have years of it."

"She's still swaggering. And feeling invincible."

"She was healing. Until she and Mac fell out. It fucked

with her head. I was going to be the concrete pillar that held up the roof while she redecorated her bunker. Give her time to choose who she wanted to be. Thought if I could keep her from having to make any brutal choices for a few years, she'd merge. Let her rebel against me rather than taking on the whole world. That opportunity is gone now." Ryodan doesn't say anything for a long moment. When he speaks again his voice is low, rough. "It's as if *my* Dani died."

I catch myself about to suck in an audible shocked breath. I may be unseeable but I'm not unhearable. The grief in his voice made me abruptly aware of my own. If Jada really is Dani, I'll never again see that gamine grin, those sparkling eyes, listen as she mutilates the English language as only Dani can. The night I chased her through the Silver was goodbye, my last look at the teen I'd grown to love as a sister. He's right, it *is* as if my Dani died. The fourteen-year-old is gone, just gone, never coming back.

"When do we abduct her?"

Ryodan carefully places the dark blade on the empty desk and looks up. "We don't. It won't work with 'Jada.' She'll only get more remote, harder. Lor's going to lose it when he sees her. He adored the kid." He rubs his jaw and for a moment the only sound in the office is the scratch of rough beard against hand. I hold my breath, suddenly acutely aware of every noise my body might make. "Speaking of Lor, how the fuck am I supposed to get him back from being Pri-ya."

Barrons says, "He's not Pri-ya."

"Mac said—"

"She lied," Barrons says flatly.

Gee, could you rat me out a little quicker, Barrons?

"And you didn't tell me."

"There are a few things you didn't tell me either. You knew Dani had an alter."

"Mac knows too much," Ryodan says, changing the subject.

"So does 'Jada.' It's a different world now. Women are different. We evolve. As does our code."

"Convenient for you. Tell that to Kasteo. Ah, sorry you stupid fuck, you chose the wrong millennium to try to keep the woman you wanted."

"That's not why we did what we did and you know it."

"What I know, brother, is you break every god-damned rule for Mac."

"Back at you, Ry. Difference is, I'll help you do it."

"Lor has never been Pri-ya." Ryodan shakes his head in disgust. "The princess can't turn us. Son of a bitch, Mac's ass is—"

"Mine," Barrons says flatly. "You will never go there. You have a problem with Mac, you work it out with me. I am her shield, I am her second fucking skin."

Whuh. I don't currently need one but it's kind of a turn-on.

Growling, Ryodan pushes up and is out the door so fast, I freeze, uncertain who to stick with. Then Barrons makes my decision for me by taking off after Ryodan, and I have to run to keep up with them. I scowl down at my shoes. Though my boots have rubber soles, they're still making noise. Fortunately, so are theirs.

I have no doubt where Ryodan's going and I'm not missing it.

If Lor thinks this means he doesn't still owe me a favor, he's wrong. He got nearly the full two weeks he bargained for.

Barrons ratted him out. Not me.

26

"Under my thumb, that Siamese cat of a girl"

LOR

"You are, hands down, the hottest fuck I've ever had," Jo tells me as she collapses back on the bed, laughing. Her short dark hair's a mess, her makeup's gone, she's slick with sweat and kinda glassy-eyed from lack of sleep.

And one damned hot fuck herself.

"God, where do you men come from? Are there more like the nine of you out there?"

I'm not going to say it. I don't say stupid things like, "Better than the boss?"

Her face tightens and she closes her eyes. I kick myself mentally. There's not a whole lot going on up there right now so kicking it doesn't take much. Like, one foot and two toes. Not even the big one.

Jo's been in my bed for twenty-four hours straight, leaving only to eat and piss, before climbing back in and going at it again, one second a tigress spitting fire, the next snuggling up to me, a tiny slip of a woman under one of my arms, cheek on my chest like I'm not the bloodthirsty monster ancient cities called the

Bonecrusher, who gorged on blood and death for break-fast and fueled their worst nightmares and lived by the motto "If you can't fuck it, eat it, or use it for a weapon, kill it."

I'm also not going to skim her mind for the answer she didn't offer. People think we can read thoughts. We can't. We just hear what they're thinking real loud, some of us better than others, on top of their brains. Humans give stuff away all the time, practically tattoo-ing their darkest secrets in neon on their skulls for any-one to see. Perverse fuckers. If they shouldn't think about it, they do. If they should think about it, they don't. "What the fuck do you mean 'not a chance'?" I bellow indignantly.

She props herself up on her side, elbow bent, cheek resting on a dainty fist, and stares at me with fascina-tion. Her short spiky hair is sticking straight up around her delicate face and she looks abso-frigging-lutely de-lectable. "What are you doing? Reading my mind? Can you *do* that?"

She's not as disturbed by the possibility as most hu-mans. I unclench my jaw and growl, "You could have taken out a goddamn billboard as loud as that last thought was."

Her eyes sparkle with delight. "Can you help me find things in there? Maybe create a filing system?"

"Are you fucking kidding me?"

She drops back on the pillow, smiling. "I'll make it worth your while. God, I can't tell you how glad I am that I took Mac's advice and came here! She was right. You *are* just what I needed."

"Mac *told* you to fuck me? As in sent you here?" I'm having a hard time deciding what I'm most pissed off about: that she thinks the boss is hotter or that Mac took advantage of my supposedly Pri-ya state by lining up her friends to score an epic fuck. Women.

"I'm so glad you won't remember any of this," she says cheerfully. "I can say anything. Do anything. Do you know how *freeing* this is? I may stay here for weeks!"

It's like the thousandth bloody time she's said the same bloody thing and I'm getting bloody sick of hearing it. *I'm so glad I came to see you! And even gladder that you won't remember any of it!* Fuck that noise. I'm remembering every goddamn detail.

"Exactly how is Ryodan hotter?" I don't believe he is. "What does he do that I didn't?" I can't believe I just said that. But I'm doing all kinds of shit I don't do lately, getting trapped in magic, making deals with Mac, screwing a brunette for the first time in forever.

See, I got this hierarchy, and if blondes knew about it, they'd probably stop lining up at my bed. The lighter the blonde, the more perfect the roots, the less tempting they are to keep around. No woman over twenty-five is still platinum to the roots. Just ain't happening if the babe ain't Fae. The kind of woman that dyes her hair platinum is on the prowl for exactly what—and all—I'm willing to give: a fuck.

The darker the hair, the more complicated the deal. If she's not obsessively maintaining her roots, her nails, her clothes, she expects things like discussions, dates, disclosures. Bloody hell, she wants respect. Which I'm all about giving. I respect them the entire time they're sharing my bed and I treat them great when they're not, flirting them up, telling them how beautiful they are, while pointing them at the next man to help them get over me. I even get food for their kids, medicine and shit, 'cause times are tough. But if one of them starts to get clingy, I suddenly got a whole lot of work to do. Like, in another country.

By the time you work your way down the hierarchy to a brunette, you got yourself a woman who knows who she is, likes it enough that she ain't gonna change, and is probably gonna try to change *you,* if push comes to shove.

Pushy, that's what brunettes are. Even the dainty, fragile-looking ones.

Big-boobed blondes are all about the fun, the sparkle, the bling, the heat, the moment. I love 'em. I'm bugfuck crazy about 'em. They keep my life simple and sweet. They don't inspire any of the feelings that made me the Bonecrusher.

"It's not what Ryodan does," Jo says slowly. "It's more what he *is.*" Her eyes take on a serious sheen. "He's like, unbelievably brilliant, ten steps ahead of everyone else all the time."

Bullshit. He's not that smart. I beat him at Triad. Once. About ten thousand years ago.

"I used to think he didn't care about anything or anyone, but he does. Just not me. His passion runs deep. That's why he's always so controlled."

Give me a motherfucking break. He's controlled because he's a control freak, plain and simple. Damn near every time he moves us, he ends up running the empire: king, dictator, or rutting pagan god.

"I think he's the glue that holds you guys together. You're his family and he'd do anything to preserve it."

Okay, so she's right about that. We had some dark times. Without the boss, I'm not sure where we'd all be. Scattered across the globe, if not galaxies. Living alone. Living hard. But he forced us to stay together. And we're glad he did. Well, most of us are.

"I see how he feels about his world and I want to be one of the parts he prizes. I want to be worth fighting for. Worth the same kind of effort he puts into the things that matter to him. Like Dani."

I don't tell her no human matters to the boss like Dani. "What the fuck does any of this have to do with sex? You aren't talking about hotness, babe. You're talking about wanting the man that doesn't want you as much as you want him, and probably only for that reason. Boss is no fucking prize." Chicks. Christ. They just don't get it sometimes.

"Ryodan's—" She breaks off and shakes her head sharply and I see the moment she decides to lighten it the fuck up—*thank you!*—but then she goes and screws things up by saying with a soft laugh, "Well, for one thing he's not blond."

I glare at her suspiciously and shove a hand through my blond hair. I refuse to believe a woman—*any* woman—practices my hierarchy in reverse. "What the hell does that have to do with anything?"

"Blond guys are hot and sexy and . . . well, *fun* and all that, but for some reason I usually avoid them. It's the dark-haired guys that get me. I don't know, I take them more seriously. They come off as more . . ." She sighs dreamily. ". . . dangerous. Ryodan is definitely more dangerous than you. I mean, really, what do you do? You screw blondes and act like a caveman. But back to what I really want to know: can you read minds and could you help me organize my thoughts? And if so, what do you want in exchange?"

"Ryodan," I manage to say without snarling. Well, okay, so maybe I snarl a little. "You think he's more dangerous." She not only just insulted my dick and what I do with it, she's now moved on to insulting my fucking existence.

"I don't want to talk about him. I came here to forget him. Can we just not talk about him?"

"You're the one who brought him up."

"I did not."

"Indirectly. Don't tell me I'm the hottest fuck if I'm not."

"I'm surprised you're still talking. I thought Pri-ya

meant pretty much brain-dead. Don't you have better things to do with your mouth?"

"Oh, honey, I got plenty of better things to do with it. Better than any fuck out there." And I'm gonna prove it. She likes danger? I'll show her danger. "And some of us got too many brains to kill."

She laughs. "You? Yeah, right."

I growl. A few chains would definitely help. We'll see just who she thinks is the hottest fuck by the time I'm done with her.

When she pushes herself up to climb on top of me again, I shove her back and snarl, "Arms over your head, woman."

With a husky laugh, she falls back and complies.

She's gonna stop laughing real soon.

Scowling all the while, wishing I *had* chains in this room—bloody hell, how can she look at this face of mine and not see danger?—I dig around in the sheets for the scarves my parade of blondes donated to the cause, knot them around her wrists, and tie her real tight to the posters at the top of the bed.

Then I do something I never let myself do, and tie her feet down, too, thinking, Man, she should not be letting me do this, followed by, Man, I know better than to do this.

I got Jo spread-eagled naked, legs wide, totally at my mercy, and I'm not gonna have one fucking ounce of it. She's not getting out of this bed until she's had the most explosive orgasm of her life, followed by a few hundred more. I'm keeping her for weeks.

I'm keeping her until she's telling me I'm the hottest fuck she's ever had and means it. Until she's Lor-Pri-ya. Until she sees there's a little more going on here than Mr. Fucking-Second-Rate-Nice-Guy who's *fun,* for fuck's sake, and wasn't one of the most vicious killers the old world knew. I can keep it under control. I've been soaked in sex for the past week and a half. The lethal edge is off my appetite. Mostly.

We're a competitive bunch at Chester's. We don't take kindly to being called second best. It's why we don't poach each other's pussy. We get territorial, even if we screwed 'em just once. Level 4's turnover is the highest in the club.

She's looking straight at me, catches her lower lip with her teeth. "I never let Ryodan do this to me," she says breathlessly.

Wise woman. Not so wise now.

Score one for Lor. I'm doing something the boss didn't do.

I'm about to do a few other things I guaran-damn-tee Ryodan didn't do, too.

27

*"Are you in the firing squad or
are you in the lineup"*

MAC

Being invisible in a closed elevator with Barrons and Ryodan is quite possibly one of the most stressful experiences of my life. It nearly ranks up there with being tortured by Mallucé.

You don't think about the many ways your body has of announcing your presence until it's absolutely essential you remain one hundred percent silent. I could sneeze. Hiccup. Pass gas. If I forget to walk with my feet slightly apart, my jean-clad legs will swish against each other. One of my joints might pop. I may be young but my bones keep getting broken and occasionally my knuckles remind me of it. A single belly growl would out me in an instant. These are men with dangerously acute senses.

I make a mental note to forgo eating when I decide to go sleuthing next time so I won't have to worry about my stomach gurgling as it digests. Then I realize if I don't eat, it might growl from hunger. I conclude I'll have to eat frequent, small, easily digested meals to minimize the likelihood of either from happening while I scout the restricted half of my world.

I press back in the far corner opposite them, trying to be as small as possible, holding my breath and praying it's a short ride.

Although it feels interminable, we stop after only two levels. Ryodan stalks off the elevator with Barrons behind him. Again I have to run to keep up.

A few doors from the end of the hall, Ryodan slams his palm against the wall and roars, "Get the fuck out here now, Lor!"

I catch up to them as the door whisks open and stand behind them, peering in.

Ryodan storms into the room. And stops. Mid-step.

I lean forward and—Oh. Wow. Oh. Looks like Jo took my advice. Plunged into it with alacrity and abandon.

I wonder irritably how many times I'm going to have to watch Lor have marathon sex this week. The universe seems to be taking some kind of perverse pleasure rubbing my face in his carnal abundance and my lack thereof.

The three of us stand, staring.

Jo and Lor are frozen, staring back. Then again, Jo's pretty darned well restrained so I'm not surprised by how immobile she is.

Barrons laughs softly. "Didn't see this one coming."

Jo is tied to the bed, spread-eagled, with Lor straddling her. They're not actually having sex at the moment, but by the tangled sheets, how sweaty Lor is (gotta love a hardworking man), and Jo's bed-head, it's obvious this isn't their first go-round.

I've seen way too much of Lor naked lately. I scowl at Barrons, wishing we'd had sex more recently. Like five minutes ago.

"Get the fuck out of here," Lor growls.

"You're a dead man," Ryodan says softly.

Straining futilely against the scarves—even from my limited perspective I can see Lor knows how to tie knots right—Jo says, "Ryodan, it's not his fault! It's mine. He didn't want to sleep with me, I forced him—"

"Where the fuck do chicks get that phrase?" Lor growls. "No man wants to *sleep* with a woman. He wants to fuck her. And nobody forces me to do shit."

"—to do it. I heard he was Pri-ya. I took advantage of him."

"He's a dead man because he lied to me, Jo. Not because he fucked you. Though I'd rather not have seen it."

I peer at Ryodan from the side. He's watching Jo through narrowed eyes and I realize it really does bother him seeing them together but it's not emotional. It's purely territorial. Still, that's something and I'm glad Jo got the satisfaction.

Jo meets his gaze and says quietly, "I didn't mean for you to see it."

"He's not Pri-ya. He's faking. That's what he lied about." Ryodan drops the bomb casually and watches it detonate.

Jo blanches and her gaze flies back to Lor's face. "Is that true? You're not Pri-ya?"

"What the fuck's the difference? You wanted to fuck me. You asked me to get the boss's taste out of your mouth. I did."

"Taste out of your—" Ryodan says. "Christ, Jo."

"It's not like I thought the idea up all by myself," Jo says defensively. "Mac's the one who—"

"Get off her, Lor," Ryodan orders.

Great, now Ryodan has one more reason to dislike me.

"—told me to do it because she thought it would be—"

"Don't go getting pissed about it now," Lor cuts her off. "I'm the one that should be pissed. This didn't have a damned thing to do with me. Just my dick. You know how many times you told me how glad you were I wouldn't remember this? Well guess what, Jo? I remember every goddamn detail. Etched into that puny-ass little brain you think I have."

"She thinks you have a puny-ass little brain. And she told you that," Barrons marvels.

"Apparently. She also thinks I'm not dangerous."

"Ah. I see why you tied her up."

"You're *faking*?" Jo says again, like she just can't wrap her brain around it. "The whole time I've been saying and doing anything I felt like because I thought you were—"

"Been right here with you, babe," Lor says with a savage smile. "Whole. Time. Every bloody word, every confidence, every howl of pleasure. Want to tell me some more how perfect my dick is and how hot I am?"

I study Lor, realizing I might be seeing a little more than a mere territory dispute on his face. Did Jo get under his skin?

Jo pales. A parade of expressions stampede across her fine-boned features: embarrassment, fear, self-consciousness, wariness. It takes mere seconds for her emotions to march to the beat of a different drum as she concludes the thought she began a few seconds earlier. "Wait a minute," she snaps. "Does Mac *know* you're not Pri-ya?"

Aw, shit. That was never supposed to come out because no one was ever going to learn about our little pact. Glad I'm invisible.

"Sure does," Lor says flatly.

Why does everyone rat me out so fast?

"Get the fuck off Jo. Now," Ryodan says.

"Jealous, boss?"

"Don't push me. In the corridor. Unless you prefer we air our business in front of Jo. In which case she dies."

Jo gasps.

Ryodan turns and stalks from the room so suddenly I almost don't get out of the way fast enough. I flatten myself back against the wall outside the door and hold my breath again, but not too long because that can result in a huge, noisy exhale. I ease it out slowly when Jo demands, "Untie me."

"Not a chance," Lor snaps. "I'm not done yet."

Then Lor joins us in the corridor. Naked. Still hard, too. He slaps a palm against the door, and as it slides closed, I hear Jo yell, "Hey! I said untie me! I never would have come here if I'd known you weren't Pri-ya!"

"Not scoring any points with me, honey," he says over his shoulder.

"You can't leave me like this!"

"Sure can," he says. "Don't worry, babe. I'll be back to finish what I started."

"That's not what I—" The door closes, cutting off the rest of Jo's words. The rooms around here are seriously soundproofed.

"The fuck you will," Ryodan says.

"Because she's yours?" Lor says. "She's done with you."

Ryodan glances at the door, making sure it's closed. "I was done with her months ago. Kept waiting for her to move on. Just not with you. It seems you've forgotten two of our critical rules: we don't fuck one another's women. We don't lie to one another."

"It wasn't as if I went looking for it. She came in and sent all my babes away and she was crying, for fuck's sake, and you know damn well I can't stand it when chicks—"

"Dani's back. She looks five years older. Possibly more. She's taken over the abbey."

Lor goes motionless. "How the hell did that happen?"

"We don't know," Barrons says. "She's not talking to any of us."

"So encourage her," Lor says.

"She's more difficult to encourage than she used to be," Ryodan says.

"How is she? What happened to her? Is she okay?"

"Get your fucking clothes on. In my office in five."

"What about Jo?"

"I'll take care of Jo," Ryodan says coolly.

"You're not killing her," Lor says sharply.

"Never said I was. But that's the third rule you seem to be forgetting: I run this place. I run you. If you don't like it, too fucking bad. You're not leaving, so I suggest you get back on the program. Fast."

Ryodan stalks off. Looking amused, Barrons heads off after him.

Fascinated by the perks of my new state—my own personal reality TV, I'm getting *all* the juicy dirt!—I hurry after them.

28

"Don't play with me 'cause you're playing with fire"

MAC

When we reach Ryodan's office, Barrons says he's got things to do and I'm abruptly divided, but I make a snap decision to stick with Ryodan. Although I'm dying to know what kind of "things" Barrons does when he goes off by himself (and intend to fulfill that fantasy very soon), I'm also riveted by the intimate look I'm getting at the man behind Chester's, who I'm beginning to realize is far more complex than I thought.

He protected Jo's feelings. He was done with her months ago and waited for her to dump him without ever betraying it. That's hard to pull off in any relationship. I can't reconcile the ruthless, bottom-lining man I know with the one who went out of his way not to hurt a human woman.

When he steps into his office, I follow, realizing only after the door slides shut that I'm stuck in here until he decides to leave again. When he pulls out his cell phone that shouldn't work and taps a number, I hope he's not summoning a woman to get the taste of Jo and Lor out of his mouth because I really don't want to watch Ryodan have sex.

Well, okay, so maybe I wouldn't be entirely adverse to that, if I didn't know him and have to see him all the time, but really. Not in the mood for more of the sex everyone else is getting to have at the moment. Between my new invisibility and extreme irritation at the only man I want to have sex with, my prospects are slim.

"Fade, get your ass down to Lor's room and untie Jo." He's silent a moment. "It's none of your fucking business why Jo's tied up there. Just do it. And I don't care what that woman says or does, I don't care if she's suddenly snatched up by a tornado and dropped straight on your dick, you will not fuck her." Another silence. "Yes, she's naked. No, that's not 'cool.' Fuck you, Fade. Forget it. Take one of the waitresses down. You will remain outside the door while she goes in and unties her. Then tell Jo she's fired." Silence. "I don't care what the waitress thinks. Fire her, too."

He ends the call, shoves the cell phone in his pocket, drops down into the large leather chair behind his desk, picks up the dark blade and starts toying with it again. I'd really like to know what his deal is with that knife.

When the door swishes open I debate leaving while I can.

While I stand there, pondering options, the Unseelie that Dani called "Papa Roach" stumps in, and I shiver with revulsion. I totally get why she nicknamed it that. Papa Roach is segmented, made by thousands and thousands of roachlike creatures clambering up on top of one another to form a larger being. They are the same bugs the waitresses permit beneath their skin to feed on their fat. Papa Roach, the collective, is purplish-brown, about four feet tall with thick legs, a half-dozen arms, and a head the size of a walnut. It jiggles like gelatin when it moves as its countless individual parts shift minutely to remain coalesced. It has a thin-lipped beak-like mouth and round, weirdly lidless eyes. As it moves into the room, a few of the roaches skitter off. I press back against the wall, creeped out by the nasty things, in no mood for a few of them to scurry over the toes of my boots. I imagine they're small enough to turn invisible, which could be a problem if anyone was looking.

Ryodan barks, "Keep your shit together when you're in my fucking office."

The bugs scurry back up Papa Roach, scale a leg, and settle into a knee.

I don't heave the sigh of relief I feel.

When Papa Roach speaks, I shiver again. Its voice is pretty much exactly what I'd expect a roach to sound like: a dry, malevolent, insectile rustle. "The one you call Jada has left the abbey. We lost her a few blocks from here."

"Kasteo."

"Hasn't spoken a word. The woman has only just begun to talk to him."

I wonder, What woman?

"The black hole at the church."

"Is minutely larger."

"The Unseelie Princes."

"Plot to take the spear from the woman and kill R'jan."

My hand goes instantly to my spear. This time, however, I'm not assaulted by images of death and destruction. My Book is oddly still.

"Their fortifications."

"Remain unchanged. They grow lax since meeting with you. Believe you think them leashed. Think they have an edge you don't know about. Believe you've overestimated yourself."

I expect Ryodan to press that issue but he says only, "R'jan's location."

"Three days ago moved into McCabe's old house and is fortifying it. It appears he plans to stay."

"Bring me precise details on his defenses. Within the hour. Sean O'Bannion."

"Spoke last night at Temple Bar. Offered jobs rebuilding the pubs and stores for pay, and made it clear he will accept only currency in exchange for goods."

"The Unseelie Princesses."

"So far we have seen only the one. Met recently with Jada. They conspire to trade services."

"For."

"Jada offered to kill the Unseelie Princes in exchange for the location of the Crimson Hag. The princess is considering it."

"Take the princess a message. She will trade services with me, not Jada. I will make it worth her while. The Highlanders."

I thought he was worried about her! Why the hell did he force me to stick around if he's willing to meet with her without me present?

"R'jan has provided them with three sifting Seelie to help them search in exchange for protection against his various enemies. Seems they have Fae lore he finds useful."

I listen, gaping. Ryodan's network of spies is standing right in front of me in a single entity comprised of thousands and thousands of sentient "bugs." He literally has the whole freaking city *bugged*. Papa Roach divests various "roaches," sends them scurrying beneath doors and into cracks to eavesdrop on everything that happens in Dublin and report back. No wonder Ryodan knows everything all the time!

"The Unseelie King."

"Does not appear to be in Dublin."

He's wrong about that.

"Mac."

"As if she's vanished."

I smirk.

"Dancer."

"Succeeds in evading us occasionally. Not certain how. He spends a great deal of time in the labs at Trinity performing various experiments. He has taken recent interest in a female musician."

"In what capacity."

"We have not seen them fuck."

"The cavern beneath the abbey."

"We are no longer able to enter. The doors have been closed. Not so much as a crack left to us."

Okay, what the heck? We tried and tried to close those doors. Who closed them, how and when?

"Recently you neglected to mention details of significance. If the environ at the abbey or either of the princes' lairs alter in any way, no matter how small, you will report it to me instantly."

"Understood."

Papa Roach waits, and when another demand isn't forthcoming rustles, "Our servitude is nearly up. If you wish to renew our contract again, it will cost you more. There are others who value our services now."

"For the first time in millennia you can walk among humans in your natural state, only because the Fae have come out and the world thinks you're one of them. Piss me off and I'll drive the Fae from this world, sending you back into the cracks and crevices and trenches of war in which you've scrounged for rotting carcasses since the dawn of time. You will renew your contract for the same terms. I have always seen to your needs."

I blink, stunned. Papa Roach isn't Fae? What the hell is it, then? What a vast, complicated world Ryodan manages!

Then I have a worse thought: Criminy, have all roaches since time immemorial been spies? Or only certain ones, and that's why every now and then you find one in your bathtub that just won't die no matter how much hair spray you coat it with or how hard you try to squish it?

Papa Roach makes a dry, grinding sound deep in its throat that's creepy as hell.

"Our needs have increased."

"You enjoy parasitic relationships with humans that were never permitted before."

"We wish it to be required that all humans host one of us."

I shudder.

Ryodan picks up the dark blade and toys with it. "We will discuss it at your next contract renewal."

Papa Roach's round eyes fix on the black blade, and its beak parts, revealing rows of tiny sharp teeth.

I suddenly think I know what the blade does. Kills whatever Papa Roach is.

"As you wish."

When Papa Roach leaves, Lor walks in.

Dressed.

I decide to stay a little longer and leave with Lor. Who knows what I might learn next?

"Sit," Ryodan barks.

Lor moves to the desk and drops down into a chair, shoving his blond hair back with a hand, looking wary. I don't blame him. Ryodan is unpredictable as hell. They don't call his way of dealing with things the "gavel effect" for nothing. He's famed for biding his time, gathering information, processing it, then when he makes a decision, the gavel falls and everyone that pissed him off or offended him or just breathed wrong dies.

"What's up with Dani?" Lor says.

Ryodan lays the knife on the desk. "Remember Fade telling us he'd found a kid who could move like us and was blowing through the streets, pretending to be a superhero."

Lor laughs. "Fuck, yeah. We all accused each other of breaking covenant and making her. Skinny redhead with balls the size of mine. I'd go watch her even when it wasn't my turn just to see what she'd do next. Kid's better than Netflix."

"I didn't give her a second thought until I found a warded house where Rowena did her dirty work. Old woman kept journals Hitler would've enjoyed. Book after book of notes about the experiments she performed. Dani wasn't her only unwilling subject. She recorded every detail. The drugs, the black arts, the manipulation and coercion, how she caged her, dehumanized her, turned a child into an animal, watchdog, fetch-it girl, assassin. Made her grateful for any crumb of kindness. Completely controlled her mother until—" Ryodan breaks off, a muscle twitching in his jaw.

Lor growls, "Until what?"

"Doesn't matter. Point is, the headmistress was in Dani's life long before she remembers it. There were a dozen volumes, filled cover to cover. When I finished reading them, I went hunting."

Ryodan—an avenging angel? Knock me over with a feather.

"What happened? Mac killed the old bitch."

Now that I'm hearing this, I'm sorry I didn't kill her sooner. And make it last longer.

"Not Rowena," Ryodan says. "I went hunting Dani. It was the kid I meant to kill. First."

There goes the feather. *This* is the man I fight with incessantly.

"That's fucked up, boss. That's beyond fucked up."

I nod vigorously, scowling.

"You went hunting Dani instead of Ro? You don't kill the victim. You kill the perp."

"I thought the kid's life was like that of another child I knew. Grown men can withstand things children can't. For centuries I took care of Barrons's son while he searched for a way to end his torment. For an eternity I shared their fucking pain. I couldn't put my nephew out of his misery, but I could spare the girl a hellish existence."

I'm slammed by a one-two punch of shocks and my mouth drops open. Nephew? Freaking *nephew*? Is he serious? Ryodan and Barrons are brothers? I study his face intently, looking for similarities. So, when Ryodan called him "brother" earlier, he really meant it. I'd thought it was just guy-bro-talk. Brothers in arms or something like that. I narrow my eyes with a scowl. That makes me and Ryodan almost like . . . family or something. Ew. The second shock is more palatable: there *was* something of avenging angel in his actions, after all. Mercy from Ryodan. Who'd have thought.

"Why the fuck are you telling me this? And why now? Figured you'd be chewing my ass over Jo not telling me shit you never talk about."

I was wondering the same thing. Ryodan doesn't explain himself. Ever.

"I'm telling you because for some unfathomable fucking reason Dani likes you. That means you may prove useful in getting her back. The more you know, the more you can help."

"Getting her back from where?" Lor demands. "What did the bitch do to her? Where are those journals? I want to see them."

"It wasn't just Rowena. And I suggest you leave it."

"I suggest you go fuck yourself."

"Once you called me king. Now you lie, fuck my ex, and tell me to fuck myself. Tread lightly, Lor. You may have changed. I have not."

"You're talking about my favorite human. I want

names. Details. I'll rip out their hearts. I'll flay their fucking hides."

"I already took care of them."

My hands are fists, nails digging into my palms. I force myself to unclench them so I don't drip blood on the floor. Other people abused Dani? Who? I want to kill them, too.

"Yet you let the old bitch live after you found out. What the fuck's with that?"

Something inhuman rattles deep in Ryodan's chest. "The moment Barrons got the *Sinsar Dubh,* I planned to lock Rowena away in a dark, hellish pit. Keep her alive so that if one day Dani remembered, she could exterminate her. Some crimes are so personal, blood-vengeance belongs only to the one who suffered them. It was the only gift I could give her."

"Dani doesn't remember? How's that possible?"

"She fragmented. Not sure if the old bitch managed to intentionally cause it or if it had already happened to some degree before she came on the scene and she just drove wedges in the door to lodge it open. When I chained Dani up in the dungeon, it wasn't because she'd killed Unseelie in my club. I was trying to discover what she recalled of Ro's experiments. I'd begun to suspect it was little. Skimming her mind was time-consuming and tricky as hell. Kid's got more locked doors in that mega-brain of hers than a high-security prison. Dani remembers some of it but it seems the worst memories were embedded in her other personality's psyche, or never fully absorbed. It was difficult to read her, even uncon-scious. There are things she may never remember. If we're lucky. Our supergirl carries her own kryptonite, right there in her head."

"You gotta be kidding me. My little darlin's a split personality?"

"Not so little anymore. And she calls herself Jada

now. She's the survivor, aware of Dani. Jada has ledgers and objectives. Dani has hopes and dreams. Dani doesn't know about Jada. She has what she thinks of as an 'Other' but doesn't realize it's a fully formed persona."

Lor shakes his head. "How the fuck did I miss it?"

How did *I* miss it? I narrowed my eyes, replaying memories, searching for clues.

"They're hard to tell apart. Nearly identical, but one feels, the other doesn't. One's on fire with life, the other's cold as ice. One butchers the English language. The other obeys it to the letter. Not a flicker of emotion, not an ounce of humanity. Their posture is subtly different. I've watched her change four times. She pulled back a fifth time, recently, outside the club while she was trying to figure out what the Hoar Frost King was after, as if she'd dipped in a toe but pulled out quickly. Each time she changed, she was unstoppable. The other has double her talent and abilities. You never saw it, then."

Lor rubs his jaw. "No. You ordered us to stay back, out of sight. We just thought she was a helluva fighter. Stone cold at times but that's my little honey. Couldn't be more proud of her." He grins but it quickly fades. "You said you went to kill her. Why didn't you?"

"The memories Dani retains are enough that she should hate the world. Kevlar her heart. Never trust anyone or anything."

"Sounds like someone I know."

"I feel."

"With your dick, maybe."

"Hands and tongue, too."

"So, why didn't you kill her?"

"I found her standing outside Temple Bar, watching street mimes. Eyes brilliant, up on her tiptoes, at the back of the crowd, one hand shoved in a pocket, the other cramming a cheeseburger in her mouth. Bouncing from foot to foot trying to burn off some of that excess energy she always has. There were guts from a recent Unseelie kill in her hair. Never had friends, went to school, celebrated a birthday or Christmas, none of those rites of passage by which humans mark their time and so highly prize."

I blink. Ryodan is talking about human experiences like he understands them? Like he's actually given one ounce of thought to a moment of it?

"Alone. Living on the streets. Dirty. Torn jeans. Two black eyes, bruises everywhere. Not one person in the world gave a bloody damn she was alive except to use her. And she knew it."

"That's why you didn't kill her? Because she was young and dirty and a beat-up, unwanted kid? World's fucking full of 'em."

"It was what she did next."

What could make the implacable, imperious Ryodan change his mind? This was a man of steel who made rules and enforced them without question.

"What?"

His face changes, eyes distant on a memory, and he smiles faintly. I realize I might not know him at all. Perhaps no one does.

"She threw her head back and laughed. The kid fucking laughed, eyes shining. Like there was no greater adventure she could possibly be on. Like life was turning out to be the most exhilarating, fantastic roller-coaster ride she could ever have imagined. Fuck the pain. Fuck the misery. In the middle of the hopeless, brutal hell her short existence on this Earth had been, that girl laughed," he finishes on a near whisper.

That was Dani. Nothing broke her. Ever. Not even if it meant splitting herself into pieces to deal with things, so she *could* laugh and want to go on living.

"You don't snuff a life like that," Ryodan says softly.

"You honor it. You take measures to protect it, even from itself when necessary, and keep it alive." The ghost of a smile vanishes and his face is once again a smooth, urbane mask. He clips, brisk and businesslike, "She was reckless, convinced of her own invincibility. She's no longer reckless and far more powerful. We currently have two primary objectives: stop the cosmic anomalies that threaten to destroy this world, and get Dani back. Not necessarily in that order. I expect your full attention on those two matters. Nothing else. I've others addressing my secondary concerns."

Ryodan stands up and walks around the desk, a signal even I can read for Lor to get up and leave. I'm surprised he's letting him. Lor's got hell to pay, and Ryodan is the devil that collects.

Taking his cue, Lor rises. "Sure, boss." His brow furrows like he's hunting for words. After a moment he adds, "Like I said earlier, I didn't go looking for Jo."

"But you plan to fuck her again."

Lor rubs his jaw, sighs but doesn't answer.

Ryodan changes into the beast faster than I believed possible. One instant he's a man—the next his clothing is in tatters on the floor.

A nine-foot-tall, horned, black-skinned slathering monster with feral crimson eyes slams his fist through the wall of Lor's chest and rips out his heart.

The beast holds the bloody thing up—God, it's still beating!—narrows its eyes then licks it, forked black tongue unfurling with grace around the delicacy.

Then he looks at Lor, who's jerking convulsively, gushing blood from a huge jagged-edged hole in his chest, framed by an explosion of bone fragments, taps him lightly on the shoulder and pushes him over.

Despite enormous fangs distorting his words, I have no problem understanding them.

"Never. Fucking. Lie. To. Me. Again."

Lor crashes to the floor, dead.

The beast drops Lor's heart on the floor where it lands with a wet splat, turns and swipes the wall panel with a prehensile, taloned claw, and stalks out.

I stand staring dumbly, then realize my chance to leave without risking exposure is leaving. As I race through the door after him he changes back into a man as quickly as he became the beast.

A naked man.

I close my eyes.

Well, most of the way.

29

"It's who we are,
doesn't matter if we've gone too far"

MAC

We're halfway down the hall and I'm hot on his heels, wondering how Ryodan manages to change so swiftly from beast to man, when it takes Barrons a full minute or two to complete the transformation. Then I move on to wondering exactly where Ryodan plans to go naked, thinking maybe I'm about to see the man's private quarters, which I'm admittedly anticipating, when my hair suddenly shoots straight up in the air, blasted by a brisk wind.

I know that gust of wind.

It's Dani, passing me in freeze-frame.

Ryodan recognizes it, too. She's got balls exploding in here when she knows he's around.

We spin instantly to follow her (me much more slowly, I'm beginning to despise my lack of speed compared to theirs) and I barely get out of the way in time to keep from being flattened by a very large, very naked man.

I skid back into the office a split second before the door hisses closed.

The room appears to be under siege by an army of

poltergeists. Drawers are flying open, papers exploding everywhere.

I'm stunned to see Lor's body is already gone. I knew they vanished when they died, I just didn't know how quickly it happened. It's as tidy as the way vampires "poof" on *Buffy,* which I never watched before in my life until a few months ago when I got obsessed with paranormal TV shows, as if I might glean useful clues from them. I frown. But Barrons's corpse didn't vanish that quickly in Faery the day Ryodan and I killed him. Then again, that shouldn't surprise me, nothing works the way you expect it to in Faery.

"If you're looking for the contract," Ryodan says, "I put it away where you won't find it. Give me Dani back and I'll tear it up."

Jada materializes in the middle of the study, cool and remote as ever. She has a long curved knife strapped in a sheath to one of her thighs, a Glock tucked in the front of her waistband, an automatic machine gun slung over a shoulder, pushed behind her back, and rounds of ammo draped across her chest. She looks fierce, savage, stunning.

Dani used to sport bruises from freeze-framing. Looks like Jada got that under control. The way she moves that sleek, long-legged body, grace could be her middle name. In black leather pants, combat boots, and a black tee, long auburn hair swept up high in a sleek ponytail, she reminds me of Angelina Jolie in *Lara Croft, Tomb Raider,* her face chiseled-porcelain beautiful, strong and icy. Besides a thin silver chain belt, her only other adornment is a silver and gold cuff. I stare fixedly at it, trying to remember where I've seen it before. Or one very similar to it.

Her gaze sweeps down over Ryodan's nude body, a muscle flexes in her jaw. She yanks her gaze back up and trains it on his face.

I press back against a wall, studying her, grateful she's no longer freeze-framing. It'd be far too easy to get smashed if they both start doing that Tasmanian devil thing again.

My heart sinks.

Jada *is* Dani.

There's no question in my mind. I can see the teenager in the woman's face now. It's there in her bone structure, in the way she carries herself, in the fiery hair she must flat-iron every time she washes it or gets rained on (which means she must be flat-ironing constantly, considering how much it rains in this city).

I can't believe I didn't see it before.

Actually, yes I can. Not only did I have no reason to expect Dani to abruptly age four or five years in a few weeks, the years from fourteen to nineteen or twenty are enormously transformative. Ugly ducklings become swans, sometimes swans lose their youthful beauty and become ducks. Fourteen to twenty is the most transfiguring rite of passage a man or woman completes, mentally, emotionally, and physically.

I press a hand to my chest, as if it might somehow ease the pain in my heart.

I did this.

I chased her through the portal and she lost years in there, where whatever she had to do to survive forced what was once a temporary split to become permanent, burying Dani pretty much the same way the Book would like to bury me.

I have to get her back. Unfortunately the only thing Jada wants to do to me is lock me up next to Cruce.

"The one that signed that contract is no longer here to honor it." Jada's gaze takes an involuntary dip over Ryodan's body again and her face tightens. I get that. His body is surreal, powerful, perfect. I see his kinship to Barrons now. Criminy. He's not hard—yes, I'm frigging looking, and I'm not about to feel bad about it because you try not looking at a hot, naked man standing in front of you when you're twenty-three, perfectly healthy, and full of a lot of aggression you'd like to vent. I think men don't realize women think dicks are beautiful. Not all dicks. But some men get the mother lode, just the right length and thickness covered with beautiful olive-toned, velvety skin that has a luscious pink undertone and makes the head of their dick look like a succulent lollipop, and since Ryodan is totally waxed or lasered or trimmed recently—

I catch myself about to audibly clear my throat. I glue my eyes to his face, where they will remain until I leave this room, so help me God. I'm staring at Barrons's brother naked. It makes me feel vaguely unfaithful somehow.

Ryodan stalks across the room, stops a few feet from her, close enough to unnerve, not so close that she won't—if there's as much red-blooded woman in her as I think there is—have as hard a time keeping her eyes locked on his face as I am.

Great, now I have to not look at his ass. With a distant part of my brain I admire that Jada/Dani doesn't comment on Ryodan's nudity, ask where his clothes are or demand he put some on. Ignoring it makes it irrelevant. No man wants his nudity to be irrelevant.

"One would think you wouldn't bother to come looking for it, then."

"It offends in letter only, not verse."

"You know it has power. Over even you. Should I choose to exercise it."

"Should you choose to exercise it, you'll die more quickly than I currently plan."

"You admit you're Dani, then."

"It would be inefficient for me to continue to deny

that which we both know was once true. 'Was once' are the key words there. Dani is dead."

"You've got that wrong. You're the one who's dead."

"I'm alive. She was never as alive as me. She was in constant pain. I terminated it."

"By terminating all emotion."

"I feel."

"Bullshit. The currency of life is passion, and as with any coin, it has two sides: pleasure, pain, joy, sorrow. Impossible to slip a single side of that coin into your pocket. You take all or nothing."

She cocks her head and says coolly, "Perhaps we are alike, you and I, and I prefer my pockets empty."

"My pockets are far from empty."

"Says the man whose face is etched by neither laugh nor frown lines. Feeling nothing is called traveling light. It's called freedom."

"It's called being dead inside. You will return her to me."

"I won't. She was too stupid to live."

"Is," he corrects. "And she's not. She's the one who's smart enough to live. You merely survive."

"One of us must. You were no help. You lost her the instant she stepped through the portal and entered Faery. You didn't save her. She waited, thinking you were different from those who used and betrayed her. She believed you would find her, come charging to her rescue. That belief was as misplaced as the monsters we faced were deadly. The day came she finally lost her faith in you, and I was there as I've always been there when she needed me, and she was grateful. I saved her. Not you. You failed her. Failed as in: did not accomplish the specified, desired objective; performing inadequately or ineffectively; neglecting to honor promises, implied or contractual—"

A muscle in his jaw twitches. "Like I need a fucking dictionary."

"It would seem you do. You broke her finger that night in Chester's. I've not forgotten. I forget no wrong done to her."

"It was unintentional. *Sidhe*-seer or not, I'm unaccustomed to young humans. Their bones are different."

"I'm no longer young."

"I'm bloody fucking aware of that."

" 'I'm aware' would have sufficed. 'Bloody fucking' is superfluous and contributes nothing to the sentence in either connotation or denotation."

"I'll bloody fucking decide what's bloody fucking superfluous."

"You're so . . . human. It's inefficient."

"Wrong on that score. And efficiency is no guarantee of survival. Nor is intellect. What it takes to be the last one standing is an unquenchable hunger to live. He who wants it the most wins. It takes fire, willingness to burn down to your motherfucking core."

"You're ice. Yet you live."

"Not as cold as you think."

"Omission or commission. You said you would break more bones that night."

"A necessary threat, one I knew she wouldn't test. I've rescued her in Dublin's streets more often than you. Saved her times uncounted without her knowing. She's not as unbreakable as she likes to believe. The day Jayne took her sword, I was there before Christian. It was I who nudged Christian in her direction."

"You do nothing without motive."

"She needed to see what he was becoming. Not hear it from me. She has never been unprotected, from the day I learned of her existence. First my men, then I, watched over her. But you know that. The night the gang of drunken men attacked her near Trinity, it wasn't you who got her out of that one."

"Only because she fought me instead of them. She should have killed them. I would have."

"Unlike you, she prefers not to kill humans."

"You make it sound like a virtue. Protecting those sheep. Rather you should knit sweaters from their skin and roast mutton of their flesh. Three nights ago I finished what you failed to complete those many years ago. They're dead now."

"There are lines. You've dragged her across enough. I'll do whatever it takes to preserve what humanity she retains, and guarantee she lives long enough to master her staggering power and intellect—"

"My staggering power and intellect."

"—while keeping you out of the driver's seat—"

"I belong in the driver's seat."

"—and giving her a chance to fly."

"They're my wings."

"It's her sky. You were made, not born. It's Dani's life."

"Was. She was a fool. She wept like a helpless child that night at Chester's while the entire club watched. Not because you broke her finger or threatened her but because you were alive and she was that happy to see you. She was always happy to see you. She lit up inside. You lost her. You let her be lost."

"I ripped this city apart for a month looking for her."

"That month was five and a half years for me."

Ryodan flinches almost imperceptibly.

"Five and a half years in Hell. Don't berate me for being. Thank me. She was weak. She needed me. I became."

"She was never weak. She was a child. Treated abominably. Yet she shined."

"I was never a child. I couldn't afford that luxury. She

made mistakes. She is dull. It is I who shine. You of all people should see that."

"That's why you've come today. To show me you're all grown up and display your dazzling new persona."

"As if I care what you think. I came for the contract, nothing more."

"Because you believe it's the only hold I have on you. You've been back for weeks and haven't tried to kill me. I'd imagine, considering how hard I was on Dani, I must rank high on your list of scores to settle. Yet you've avoided me. You fear me."

"I fear nothing."

"Or perhaps you can't quite bring yourself to kill me and have begun to wonder if my contract somehow mystically prevents you from harming me."

Jada tenses slightly, and I realize Ryodan's nailed it. Barrons told me a few months ago that Ryodan had coerced Dani into working for him, that he was being tough on her, trying to make her see that she wasn't indestructible, curb some of the recklessness that would one day get her killed. Jada would surely despise Ryodan for controlling Dani. So why has she been back in Dublin for weeks and not once tried to get even with him? That's not Dani's way at all, and since Jada appears to be Dani on steroids, well . . . I hold my breath, waiting for her to answer.

"Let me make it simple for you." Ryodan reaches beneath his desk, presses something, and a hidden panel slides soundlessly out.

"I would have found that," Jada says instantly.

He pulls out a sheet of paper and glances at it. "Said contract. Signed in blood. By Dani. In your hand. Binding both of you. You think this keeps you from killing me. You want to kill me, pick up the blade on my desk."

"You would only come back. When I kill you I will do so for good."

"Get a little practice. See what it feels like to drive a knife through my heart. Relish it. Watch the light fade from my eyes, stare into my dying, taste it, see how you like it. There's a moment in death that is unlike anything else in all existence."

"You think I don't know that. I began killing far younger than you."

"Not even close. I'm here now. So are you. Do it." He rips the contract in half, drops the pieces to the floor. "Contract void. Kill me. Dani."

Jada says nothing. Her gaze drifts down to the knife on his desk, then back to Ryodan, but not starting at his face. It makes it there only after a false start from his feet.

"Pick up the fucking knife," Ryodan orders.

"You don't order me around. I'm not she who once obeyed."

He steps forward, closing the space between them. I wonder how many of the Nine I'm going to watch die today.

Ryodan takes the knife from the desk, grabs her by the wrist and slaps the hilt into the palm of her hand. "I said kill me," he says softly.

And all I can think is, God this is a terrible bluff. He's trying to force Dani to stir behind Jada's implacable countenance, force her alter ego to do something he believes Dani won't let her do because she lit up whenever he was around.

She closes long, elegant fingers around the hilt. "Fine," she says coolly.

She draws back her hand and, aiming at his heart, stabs him.

At the last moment, however, her wrist stutters, jerks, and twists around. The blade skids sideways, flat to his chest.

She goes motionless, fist resting on his bare skin and they stare at each other. Emerald ice meets silver steel.

I angle myself sideways, spellbound, trying to get a read on what's going on by their expressions but, Christ, it's like trying to read two standing stones. I'm startled to realize Dani didn't merely grow up—she grew tall. The top of her head comes to Ryodan's jaw, and since I know he's six-foot-four, she's got to be all of five-foot-ten, plus two inches of thick combat boot soles.

They both begin to shift subtly as if they're fighting a silent war of the wills with their bodies. Ryodan's stance becomes even more aggressive, intimidating, coercing. But unlike Dani, who would have backed away, Jada molds herself farther into his space, demanding her share of it.

For nearly a minute they stand there like that, staring at each other, trying to force the other to yield in some small way.

It's Ryodan who breaks the volatile silence. "I'll give you a choice. Kill me."

"By definition 'choice' mandates a minimum of two possible avenues of action."

"I wasn't done. Or kiss me. But do one or the other. Before I do one or the other to you."

Jada stares at him a long moment, then slowly, deliberately, presses the full length of her body up against his naked one, black leather to nude man, soft, feminine curves to heavily muscled, scarred chest.

Ryodan doesn't move a muscle, just stands there.

She wets her lips and angles her head so that her mouth is a breath away from his, and I'm a mess of quivering frigging nerves in the corner because she just stays like that and her eyes fix on his mouth, and his fixes on hers and I think, Shit, this room is going to blow, then I think, Shit, this is Dani and Ryodan. But it's not.

It's two cataclysmic forces of nature that are brilliant and stubborn and strong, who cut their teeth on razor blades and live on a razor edge of violence at all times. I've learned a few things about the world, about myself, during my sojourn in Dublin. In the great pasture of life there are really only four kinds of creatures: sheep, as Dani likes to call them; shepherds who try to guide the sheep and keep them on the straight and narrow; sheepdogs who run them from field to field, prevent them from straying, and fight off the predators that come to slaughter and feast; and wolves, savage, fierce, and a law unto their own.

I know what I am. I'm a sheepdog. If my food supply ran out and I was stranded on a mountain with the flock, I would starve before I ate one of the sheep. Nature or nurture, I don't know. It doesn't really matter. I protect the flock. To my dying breath.

Ryodan's a wolf. He'd eat the whole damn flock if his survival depended on it.

Dani is a sheepdog, too.

Jada is a wolf.

Two wolves stand in this room, with a complicated past and an uncertain future, their lips a breath apart, and I'm not sure if they'll kiss or kill each other. Probably both.

Then Jada reaches up and cups the back of his head with one hand, pulls his head forward and down.

And presses her mouth to his.

Ryodan holds perfectly still, still as stone.

So do I. Holy freaking cow.

She kisses him, lips parted, slow and sexy, lightly touching his lips with her tongue, offering wonders that would rock his world, while delivering nothing. Open mouthed, seductive, warm, inviting and . . . dangerous. Even I can feel the explosive sexual energy held in check behind her bare feather of a touch. She's making sure he feels it, slapping him in the face with all she could offer—but isn't. I've kissed men like that before.

It's a challenge. It says "You think you have what it takes to handle me? Oh, honey, prove it."

Still, he doesn't move. Just stands there, letting her kiss him, making no response.

Against his lips she murmurs, "You'll never kill me."

Then Jada puts her arms around his neck and pulls him against her, melting against him until there is no space between their bodies. She turns her face slowly to the side and rests her cheek against his, her chin on his shoulder. Laces her fingers into his short thick hair.

His hands move to her waist, stop. Drop to his sides. They stand there like that, sort of hugging but not. Pressed together, staring past each other.

Intimate yet a million miles apart.

It's one of the most subtly erotic moments I've seen.

She closes her eyes and for a fleeting instant every bit of tension in the fine muscles of her face vanishes. If pressed to define the moment, I'd call it basking, a cat soaking up sun on an icy winter's day. Savoring something she's wanted for a long time, and I wonder, did she think of him while she battled whatever demons she faced for the past five and a half years, lost in Faery? Did she hear his voice in her head during her darkest hours? Did she find strength in the hard truths he'd battered her with? Does touching him make her feel the way I do when I press my body against Barrons—like coming home?

"I'm all you have left of Dani," she tells him softly. "Be very careful how you push me, Ryodan. I'm not a little girl. I could turn you inside out. Play you the way you play the rest of the world. You're not a singularity anymore. I've become your equal in every way."

Then she shoves him back and pushes past him with that long-legged gazelle walk, gracefully swipes the palm pad and glides out the door. He may think Jada doesn't feel, but there is pure fire in the way she moves. She's sexy, confident, strong. I've walked that way myself. It feels *good*.

I glance between him and the door, dying to stay, knowing I should go. I've seen more than my brain can process for one day.

He drops his dark head forward and stands there, unmoving.

As I slip out, just before it slides closed, I hear him murmur, "Ah, Dani, yes you have. As I always knew you would."

30

*"When you feel my heat, look into my eyes
It's where my demons hide"*

MAC

Jada leaves at normal speed—what Dani used to call walking like a Joe—and I follow her to the top of the stairs, trying to decide who, in my new ghostlike state, I want to haunt next.

I'm eager to see if Ryodan's wards can detect me should I decide to explore the lower levels of his underground fortress, or if the Book's cloak will keep me from tripping them. Worst-case scenario, I set one off and run. Then again, knowing Ryodan, enormous steel doors will come slamming down, barricading me in a tiny space of corridor until he releases some high-tech vapor-dye that paints me visible on his monitors, drags me out, and locks me up in his dungeon.

On the subject of the Book, it's been perversely silent since I arrived back in the city this morning. I'd pause to wonder why but I'm busy enjoying being invisible and not stalked at the moment, plus my head is spinning from all that I've learned. I'm beginning to see that my view of the world was very limited. Life is an iceberg and I've only been seeing the tip.

Jo had sex with Lor! Ryodan saw it happening, and it turns out he's actually got a code of ethics that accommodates humans. Lor might have a bit of a thing for Jo. That would be nice for her. I frown. Maybe. Then again she seemed pretty furious about the whole situation, and Ryodan fired her, so now, insult to injury, she's out of a job. Barrons and Ryodan are brothers! Ryodan's been keeping tabs on Dani for years. Papa Roach isn't Fae, serves as the urbane owner of Chester's spy network and has been doing so for thousands of years. All roaches are now suspect! Dani's always had a second persona and I never figured it out. Ryodan killed Lor. Jada kissed Ryodan! Criminy. Never saw that coming. Dani and Ryodan? Weird. Jada and Ryodan? Not weird at all. Sexy as hell. I'd been tense, heart hammering, waiting for that damn kiss. I'd *wanted* it to happen.

It's like my own private soap opera. Plus I've seen two of the Nine naked today. Nice bit of eye candy for a woman with a ferocious sweet tooth and no way to satisfy it.

Fade stops Jada at the top of the stairs, or rather Fade moves in front of Jada and she consents to briefly pause. I have no doubt she could blast past him and quite possibly outrun him.

"The boss wants me to ask if you remember the first iced scene he took Dani to see beneath the club."

Jada inclines her head.

"Boss said he thinks you should see it."

"I have no interest in his club. Less in his thoughts."

"He said to tell you if what's down there continues to grow, it'll destroy the world, and the same thing that's down there got left at every place that was iced," Fade delivers coolly. "Said to warn you not to touch it because they behave like black holes with event horizons. Whatever the fuck those are. Black holes I get."

"An event horizon is also called the point of no return.

In a sense of general relativity, it's the point at which the gravitational pull becomes so great escape is impossible. Some theorize quantum gravity effects become significant in the vicinity of such an occurrence."

"Whatever. Boss said some college kid thinks your brain is the only one that has a chance of cracking it."

I glimpse Dani in Jada then, not in a jauntily cocked hip, but a small, telltale straightening of her spine.

"You may tell Ryodan I will inspect it. But I won't work with his 'college kid.' That's non-negotiable."

"I'll tell him. We'll see what he says. Wait here and I'll get someone to take you down. I'm on bouncer duty."

When he turns away, Jada vanishes on a brisk wind.

I could have called that one. And I can predict she sure as hell isn't going down below. She'll find another place to examine.

Oh well, it's obviously not going to be Jada I haunt. She's gone with the wind. What next? As I descend the chrome stairs I'm startled to see Jo coming out of one of the restrooms dressed for work in the subclub where the waitresses wear short plaid skirts and baby doll heels, and burst out laughing before I can catch myself. The woman just keeps surprising me. Ryodan may have fired her. But Jo didn't quit. And from the expression on her face, she's not going to go easily if he tries to enforce it. I don't blame her. He doesn't get to fire her just because she slept with someone else. That's bullshit, and I'd tell him so myself if I wasn't currently relishing my invisibility.

Fortunately, my disembodied laugh gets swallowed up in the general din of the club.

I melt into the crowd, ducking and dodging as I go. I'm beginning to get the hang of this invisibility stuff.

I sort and discard various destinations. I don't trust myself to go spy on the Unseelie Princes. I'd be tempted to use my spear, and although I pretty much think any humans stupid enough to go there deserve to die, I have no guarantee my resultant killing spree would be confined to the grounds of the Escheresque gothic mansion.

I could head out to the abbey, slip in and eavesdrop. Go down below and check on Cruce.

I shudder. No thank you.

Search Chester's?

I've had enough of Chester's for one day. My brain is on overload, and there's really only one person I want to spy on now. He deserves it. I won't feel one ounce of guilt for invading his privacy. He invaded the fuck out of mine.

I slip from the club amid a cluster of drunken revelers and navigate the surprisingly busy streets back to the place I call home: Barrons Books & Baubles.

I find Jericho Barrons sitting in his study at the back of the bookstore watching a video on his computer. He exudes tall, dark, and dangerous, even dressed casually in faded jeans, an unbuttoned black shirt, and boots with silver chains. His hair is wet from a recent shower and he smells like clean, damp, deliciously edible man. His chest is nearly covered with tattoos, black and crimson runes and designs that look like ancient tribal emblems, his rock-hard six-pack abs on full display. His sleeves are rolled back over thick, powerful forearms, and the cuff that matches the one Ryodan wears glints in the low light, reminding me they are brothers, reminding me of Jada/Dani's cuff. There's something anciently elegant poured over the beast that is Barrons, Old-World-Mediterranean-basted barbarian. The interior lights are set to a soft amber glow and he sits in the darkness, all hot, sexy coiled muscle and aggression and, oh God, I need to have sex.

I shove that thought from my mind because it's highly

unlikely in the near future. No point in torturing myself when the world's been so busy doing it for me. I wonder what Barrons watches. Action/adventure? Spy movies? Horror? *Bewitched*?

Porn?

The sounds coming from the monitor are base, guttural. I ease into the study, walking like an Indian in the quiet, stealthy way Daddy once taught me on a camping trip: heel to toe, heel to toe.

Barrons touches the screen, tracing an image, dark gaze unfathomable.

As I move around the desk and glimpse the monitor, I bite back a soft, instinctive protest.

He's watching a video of his son.

The child is in human form, naked on the floor of his cage. He's in the throes of hard convulsions and there's blood on his face, ostensibly from having bitten his own tongue.

This isn't what Barrons's son looked like the only time I ever met him. Then, he seemed a lovely, helpless, innocent, and frightened child, and although it was but an act to lure me close enough to attack, it was one of very few times in his tortured existence he'd looked normal. I still remember the anguish in Barrons's voice when he asked me if I'd seen him as a boy, not the beast.

As I watch, his son begins to change back into his monstrous form, and it's a violent, excruciating transformation, even more torturous to watch than when Barrons turns back into a man.

The beast his son is becoming on-screen makes the rabid beast-form of Barrons that stalked me on a cliff in Faery look like a playful puppy.

Shortly after his son tried to eat me, Barrons told me he used to keep cameras on the boy at all times, reviewing them endlessly for a single glimpse of him as the child he'd fathered. Over the millennia, he saw him that way on only five occasions. Apparently this was one of them.

Why is he watching it now? It's over. We freed him. Didn't we? Or did the oddly malleable universe in which I seem to find myself lately find some way to reshape that, too?

The tips of his fingers slide from the screen. "I wanted to give you peace," he murmurs. "Not erase you from the cycle forever. Now I wonder if it was my pain or yours I sought to end."

I wince and close my eyes. My life hasn't been completely blithe and carefree. When I was sixteen, my adopted paternal grandfather was diagnosed with lung cancer that metastasized to his liver and brain. Daddy's grief cast a palpable shadow over the Lane household for months. I'll never forget the crippling headaches Grandpa suffered, the nausea from chemo and radiation. I watched Daddy wrestle with decision after decision, ultimately withholding IV antibiotics to treat the pneumonia that took Grandpa more quickly and far more gently.

Barrons is voicing the legitimate question of anyone who's ever agreed not to resuscitate, to cease life-sustaining measures for a loved one, to accept a Stage 4 cancer patient's decision to refuse more chemo, or euthanize a beloved pet. Throughout the caretaker experience, your loved one's presence is intense and exquisitely poignant and painful, then all the sudden they're gone and you discover their absence is even more intense and exquisitely poignant and painful. You don't know how to walk or breathe when they're no longer there. And how could you? Your world revolved around them.

I should have seen this coming. At least I have the comfort of believing Alina is in heaven. That maybe someday I'll gaze into a child's eyes and see a piece of my sister's soul in there, because the fact is I *do* believe we go on. Then again, maybe I'll never see a trace of her, but I still feel her. I don't know how to explain it. It's as if she's only a slight shift of reality away from me sometimes, in what I think of as the slipstream, and if I could only slip sideways, too, I could join her. And one day I think I *will* slip sideways and get to see her again, if only as ships passing on our way to new destinations in the same vast, magnificent sea.

Perhaps it's a sentimental delusion to which I cling so I don't drown in grief.

I don't think so.

Barrons says softly, "Eternal agony or nothing. I'd have chosen agony. I gave you nothing. You weren't cognizant. You couldn't make the choice."

What do we crave for those terrible decisions we're forced to make in the course of an average lifetime?

Forgiveness. Absolution.

There's no possibility Barrons will get it, in this lifetime or any other.

We K'Vrucked his son to grant him rest. We didn't merely kill him, we annihilated his very being. As the *Sinsar Dubh* put it, a good K'Vrucking is more final than death, it's complete eradication of all essence, of what humans like to think of as a soul.

I don't know that I believe in souls, but I believe in something. I think each of us has a unique vibration that's inextinguishable, and when we die it translates into the next phase of being. We may come back as a tree, or a cat, perhaps a person again, or a star. I don't think our journey is limited. I look up at the sky, ponder the enormity of the universe and simply know that the same well of joy that birthed so much wonder gave us more than a single chance to explore it.

Not so with his son. The child is no longer in pain because he is no longer. No heaven, no hell. Just gone.

As Barrons said, erased. Unlike me always sort of sensing Alina out there, Barrons can't feel him anymore.

Who knows how long he took care of his child, searched for the way to free him, sat in his subterranean cave watching him, cultivating the hope that he would one day find the right spell, or ritual or god or demon powerful enough to change his son back.

A few months ago the never-ending ritual that had shaped his existence for thousands and thousands of years ended.

As did the hope.

And the true, long overdue grief began.

I know a simple truth: mercy killing doesn't hold one fucking ounce of mercy for those that live.

I wonder how many times he's caught himself walking toward his son's stone chamber, as I caught myself walking down the hall to Alina's bedroom with something I just had to tell her, this very moment, on the tip of my tongue. The hundredth time I did it, I realized it was either go join Dad in his black hole of depression, drink myself quietly to death at the Brickyard and die by the age of forty from liver disease—or fly to Dublin and channel my grief into a search for answers. Death is the final chapter in a book you can't unread. You keep waiting to feel like the person you were before that chapter ended. You never will.

I open my eyes. Barrons is staring at the screen in silence. There's no sound in the bookstore. Not a drip of water from the distant bathroom sink in the hall, no white noise from an air vent, no soft hiss of gas from the fireplace. Grief is a private thing. I respect that and I respect the man.

I begin to ease out of the room slowly.

When I back into the ottoman I forgot was there, the legs scrape across the polished wood of the floor.

Barrons's head whips up and around, pinpoints the precise spot in which I stand.

For a moment I consider trying to be his son's ghost for him. Give him what he'd think was a sign, ease his pain with as kind and white a lie as they come.

I know better.

Barrons is all about purity. If he ever learned the truth—and Barrons has a way of *always* learning the truth—he'd despise me for it. I'd have given him a gift, only to snatch it away again, and counter to mainstream cliché, for some of us it's kinder to never have a thing at all than to have it and lose it.

Some of us love too hard. Some of us don't seem to be able to hold that vital piece of ourselves back.

His nostrils flare as he inhales, cocks his head, and listens. He presses the Off button on the monitor. "Ms. Lane."

Though he can't see me, I scowl at him. "You don't know that for certain. You guessed. I've been hanging around you a lot today and you didn't know it."

"The *Sinsar Dubh* protected you at the last minute. You were going to let the *sidhe*-seers take you rather than risk killing them."

"Uh-huh."

"I believed it had sifted you elsewhere, and it was taking time for you to get back."

"Nope. Just made me invisible and told me to run."

Pleasantries exchanged, I search for something to say that is about anything but his son. I know Barrons. Like me, he'd prefer I'd never seen him grieving.

He'll sit and stare at his computer screen however many times he must, just as I indulge the OCD facets of my grief and, with each month that goes by, find there are three or four, sometimes as many as five additional days between those upon which I am compelled to drag out my photo albums and brood. At some point there will be ten, twenty, then thirty. Time will scar my wound and I'll emerge from my fugue tougher, if not healed.

I decide to bitch. That'll take his mind off things.

"You know, I just don't get it. Every time I solve a problem, the universe lobs another one at me. And it's always bigger and messier than the last. Am I being persecuted?"

He smiles faintly. "If only it were that personal. Life fucks you anonymously. It doesn't want to know your name, doesn't give a shit about your station. The terrain never stops shifting. One minute you think you've got the world by the balls, the next minute you don't know where the fuck the world's balls are."

"Sure I do," I say irritably. "Right next to the world's big fat hairy asshole, upon which I seem to be stuck in superglue lately, waiting for it to have its next case of explosive diarrhea."

He laughs. A bona-fide laugh, and I smile, grateful to have lifted a bit of sorrow from that dark, forbidding countenance. Then he says, "Move."

"Huh? Why? You can't even see me."

"Off the asshole."

"Easy for you to say. How am I supposed to do that?"

"Study the terrain. If you can't move yourself, find something that moves the world."

"Tall order. Isn't it easier to move myself?"

"Sometimes. Sometimes not."

I think about it a moment. "If Cruce was free, I'd become a secondary concern. *He'd* be on the asshole."

"Which would put pretty much the entire world on the asshole with him."

"But *I'd* be out of the way."

He shrugs. "Do it."

"You don't mean that." I'm not so certain he doesn't. Barrons would probably just go along for the ride, finding no end of things to enjoy along the way. Move the world. How can I move the world? "Make me like you," I say. "Then I wouldn't mind being visible again because I wouldn't have to worry about them catching me."

"Never ask me that."

"Jada—Dani is like you."

"Dani is a genetically mutated human. Not like us at all. There's a price for what we are. We pay it every day."

"What kind of price?"

He doesn't reply.

I try a side approach. "Why does it take you so much longer than Ryodan to transform from beast back to man?"

"I enjoy the beast. He enjoys the man. The beast has little desire to resume human form, resists it."

"Yet you live mostly as a man. Why?"

Again he doesn't reply. I resume pondering my position on the asshole and how to get off it.

"Fuck me," he says softly.

I stare at him through the dim light as instant lust eclipses anger, will, time, place. My knees weaken in anticipation of ceasing their function, ready to drop me back on the floor so I can wrap my legs around Barrons when he spreads his big hard body over me. Master to slave: when he says "Fuck me," my body softens and I get wet. It's visceral. Inescapable. I love the way he says "Fuck me," as if his body will explode if I don't touch him, slam down on him and take him inside me, meld our flesh together in that place we both find the only peace we ever know. Out of bed, we're a storm. In bed, we find the eye. The detritus of our world, of our complex and difficult personalities, gets swept up into the various supercells eternally raging around us and vanishes.

I want to. Especially after what I just saw. But that he suffers doesn't absolve him for an action he shouldn't have taken. "Why?" I say pissily. "So you can erase my memory again?"

"And there it is. Go ahead, Ms. Lane. Air your grievances. Tell me what a big bad bastard I am that I tucked away a truth you couldn't face and gave you time to come to terms with it. But reflect on this: it wasn't the only time. You did the same when you were Pri-ya. Twice I got under your skin, and both times you couldn't shut me out fast enough."

"Bullshit. You don't get to cast it in some sunny, kind light when there's nothing sunny and kind about it." I don't acknowledge his second comment because he has a somewhat valid point and this is about my irritation, not his.

"I didn't say it was sunny and kind. It was self-serving, as is all I do. One would think by now you know who I am."

"You had no right."

"Ah, the morally outraged cry of the weak: You're not 'allowed' to do that. One is *allowed* to do anything one can get away with. Only when you understand that will you know your place in this world. And your power. Might is right."

"Ah," I mock, "the morally bankrupt howl of the predator."

"Guilty as charged. I'm not the only one that howled that night."

"You don't know for certain that I wouldn't have—"

"Bullshit," he cuts me off impatiently. "You don't get to pretend you would have done anything but despise me. It was already there in your eyes. You were young, so bloody young. Untouched by tragedy until your sister's death. You came to Dublin, avenging angel, and what's the first thing you did? Fucked the devil. Oops, shit, eh? You felt more alive with me that night than you've ever felt in your life. You were fucking *born* in that run-down rented room with me. I watched it happen, saw the woman you really are tear her constrictive, circumscribing skin right down the middle and strip it off. And I'm not talking about fucking. I'm talking about a way of existence. That night. You. Me. No fear. No holds barred. No rules. Watching you change was an epiphany. How did it feel to come alive in the city that killed your sister? Like the biggest fucking betrayal in the world?"

I snarl like an enraged animal. Yes, yes, and *yes*. It abso-fucking-lutely did. Alina was cold in a grave and I was on fire. I was *glad* I'd come to Dublin, glad I'd gotten lost and stumbled into his bookstore, because something in me that had slumbered all my life was waking up. How can you be *glad* you came to the city that killed your sister? How can you feel exhilarated to be alive when she's dead? How could I let anything ever make me feel good again?

"You couldn't deal with it, and you couldn't despise yourself any more than you already did, so you turned it on me. You want to hate me for taking that memory and stashing it away for a while, go ahead."

I snap, "I don't want to hate you for it. I want to find a way to forgive you for it. And *that's* what scares me. You took my memory, my choice to deal with or refuse to deal with what happened. You took a slice of my reality."

"I'll say this one more fucking time: I couldn't have taken it if you hadn't been so willing to throw it away. The brain is a complex thing. It inscribes, it etches, it's bloody well sticky. The memory was always there, that's how you found it. I merely kicked it beneath a rock. You put the entire force of your will behind my kicking it. You *helped* me hide it. I relieved you of what you considered a despicable stain in your mind. Best fucking night of my existence." He laughs and shakes his head. "And you couldn't get rid of it fast enough. I didn't want to hide the memory from you. I wanted to cram it down your goddamn throat. I wanted to force you to face it, to want it, to want me, to be willing to fight for what was possible between us with the same single-minded devotion as you fucked. Well, Ms. Lane, you've got your precious memory back. Will you throw me away now?"

I'm horrified to realize that's the choice. Keep him or don't. Stay or go. How do you trust a man who took one of your memories from you? How do you convince yourself he won't do it again? And if I did convince myself of it, wouldn't I pretty much *be* that lamb in a city of wolves he'd accused me of being that night? Believing what I wanted to believe, over the far more likely truth: recidivism is human nature.

We are what we are. Actions speak.

He intuits my thoughts without even being able to see my face. "Yes. Actions speak. Analyze mine. Not long after I used Voice on you to tuck away your memory of that night, I began teaching you Voice, knowing you would be immune to me ever using it on you again. I leveled the playing field. In a court of justice, one might consider that atonement for a—" He breaks off and laughs softly. "—crime of passion. And that, my dear complicated fucking Ms. Lane, is the closest thing to an apology you will ever get from a man who apologizes to no one. Take it or leave it."

He's up, past me, and out the door before I can even reply.

3¹

"Like an army falling one by one by one"

MAC

Fact: you can never know another person completely.

Fact: you are born alone and die alone.

Fact: there is no such thing as safety. Only vigilance, determination to survive, and a willingness to be ruthless about it.

Fact: love is not perfect.

Fact: neither am I.

Those five facts are the bile with which I digest the events of my day.

I marvel, as I sprawl on the chesterfield in front of my favorite gas fireplace aft of the bookstore, at the way my thought processes have refined. There used to be so many pit stops and detours between my mental points of departure and their eventual destinations, but now it goes kind of like this: Do I love him? Yes. Is he perfect? No. Am I? No. Will I leave him? No. Okay, that's resolved. Time for a nap.

*   *   *

I wake when the doorbell tinkles, roll over, rub my eyes, and shove my hair out of my face. I slept hard. It occurs to me that I didn't rehang the bell after Ryodan ripped it off the frame. Barrons must have done it.

First thing I do when I open my eyes is look down at my hand. Yup. Still invisible. Awesome! I'm in no hurry to give this up. Besides, I feel deep couch marks all over my right side, from my arm up to my cheek. I've been tufted. I hate walking around with sheet creases and now I have little sphincter-like explosions all over the side of my face.

I become aware of a slow burn in the pit of my stomach and leap up to an instant crouch, biting back a growl.

I smell Unseelie Prince.

I duck low to remain concealed behind the silhouette of the couch and begin inching quietly back toward the private-residence half of the bookstore, then remember they can't see me. Duh.

I straighten up and peer through the low light, wondering what the hell my rapists are doing in my home.

I blink. They're standing in the entry with Fade, Dageus and Drustan MacKeltar, and R'jan, who is attended by the new Seelie advisor-vote Ryodan recently approved.

The doorbell chimes two more times in quick succession as Barrons and Jada step in, dusting rain from their shoulders.

What the hell?

"Why did you ask me to come?" Jada says to Barrons. "And what are they doing here?" She narrows her eyes at the princes who hiss and posture aggressively.

"I didn't."

"I received your message."

"I didn't send one."

Jada moves to leave. Barrons places a hand on her arm and she turns slowly back and looks up.

He says, "I would prefer you stay."

I narrow my eyes. What is Barrons up to?

She stares at him for a moment then says, "I will honor your request. Once. In the future you will honor one for me."

"A simple request of attendance. Nothing more."

She inclines her head.

Right, she's nice to Barrons but not me.

I like Jada. She's strong. Smart. Lethal. Too bad she used to be Dani. Too bad she has no heart. I want Dani back. But I wouldn't mind keeping Jada, too, once she gets with the program that reads: Mac is good, don't hunt her. Speaking of why she's hunting me—where the heck has the *Sinsar Dubh* gone? Three princes are standing here and I'm not hearing a single suggestion that I go postal and kill everyone in sight. The Book has been so quiet it's starting to make me nervous.

Then the Unseelie Princes are asking why Barrons sent a message threatening to remove them from the council if the princes didn't meet him here, and R'jan starts snarling about the threat he received from the Highlander to withdraw their protection if he didn't come, and I smell Ryodan's hand in things before I even catch a glimpse of him approaching through the rain beyond the beveled glass diamond panes of the front door.

When the urbane owner of Chester's stalks in, the accusations escalate, all now directed toward him and his sleight of hand.

"Had I summoned, you wouldn't have come," Ryodan says to Rath, then barks, "Upstairs, at the table. All of you."

Yeah, right. He just tried to order nine of the most

uncooperative beings I know to cooperate en masse. It's not going to happen.

Everyone starts growling and arguing again. Ryodan vanishes. Then R'jan's new advisor is gone.

Long moments spin out while R'jan looks around wildly.

After nearly thirty seconds Ryodan reappears and tosses the body of R'jan's new advisor at his feet. Dead. I almost laugh aloud at the look of consternation on R'jan's face.

The Seelie Prince snarls, "You will cease doing that! You killed our fucking advisor! That is twice now you've insulted us with—"

"Little point devising new tactics when the old ones just keep working. Pull your head out of your ass and see it coming. The next one to die is you, then Rath. Get the fuck upstairs."

Jada moves for the door.

Barrons says, "You will remain. Honor your pledge."

A muscle works in her jaw but she slowly turns back around. "You have five minutes of my time."

"Five is all I need," Ryodan says.

Jada gives him a cool smile. "That's what I've heard."

I smirk.

Ryodan opens his mouth to reply then astounds me by closing it. I was ready for one of his frankly sexual remarks. I was rather looking forward to it. She deserved it for that one. From the look on Jada's face, she was anticipating one, too.

He says nothing. Interesting. Is it because she's Dani? Or because she's not Dani at all?

"Move your asses, all of you," Fade orders.

When they ascend, growling and snarling the whole way, I hurry up the stairs behind them, to camouflage any telltale squeaks the planks might make as they shift beneath my weight if I wait until they all reach the top.

Barrons, Fade, Ryodan, and the two Highlanders cram into seats along one side of the square and it's almost comical to see the five enormous men packed shoulder to shoulder, leaving the Unseelie Princes and R'jan to split the other two. I wonder where Sean is; if he was similarly summoned and chose not to appear or if Ryodan omitted him deliberately.

Jada stands, legs spread, arms folded. Tonight she has a knife strapped to each thigh, in addition to an assortment of bulges at her ankles, pockets, and waistband. I carry concealed myself, so have no trouble picking out extra magazines and grenades. There's blood on her shirt. I wonder who or what she killed tonight, and how many. I miss fighting back-to-back with her.

"Why have you called us here?" R'jan demands. "And where is the O'Bannion?"

I take a position opposite Jada, with the table between us, unconsciously mimicking her posture, studying her curiously. Still dressed in black, still coolly beautiful, something nags about her appearance. My gaze drifts from her head to her feet then back. Her cuff glints silver. Where have I seen it before?

"O'Bannion is irrelevant to the matter we're discussing tonight."

The Seelie Prince scowls, no doubt wondering if there have been meetings held without him present, without his knowledge. "And the human that runs the abbey?"

"I run the abbey," Jada says.

"There is one thing upon which we can agree," Ryodan says, "and that is we would all prefer the Crimson Hag dead."

"That is why you brought us here? To discuss the Hag?" Rath says. "She is occupied. We do not care about her."

"You will aid in destroying our mutual enemies or you are the enemy," Ryodan says.

Jada says, "No one knows the Hag's location."

"The Unseelie Princess has located her," Ryodan says.

"You know this how?" Jada says.

"You know where Christian is?" Dageus explodes. "Why the bloody hell are we sitting here?"

Ryodan says to Jada, "The Unseelie Princess is now in my employ. Never think to control my city. You have the *sidhe*-seers. That is all you have."

"The princess is not pureblood," Kiall says coldly. "You will never admit her to our table."

I wonder what he means by that. Even I sensed the difference. But what?

"You will share a table with anyone I choose, mongrel or otherwise," Ryodan says.

"I said, where the bloody hell is Christian?" Dageus says again.

"I would see Christian freed. You may present your proposition." Jada's voice is void of inflection. If she's irritated that Ryodan usurped her plan, she betrays none of it. The fire I saw in his office is now ice.

"His location is difficult to reach," Ryodan says. "The three princes will sift three of us in. Using one of them as bait and Mac to divert—"

WTF? I bristle.

"You think we will be your fucking bait?" Kiall snarls.

"—we will put the Hag down for good and free the Keltar," Ryodan says.

"In addition to me, who are the other two sifting in?" Jada says.

"Aye, exactly who the bloody hell do you think is going?" Dageus growls.

"We will cooperate with this plan why?" Kiall says.

"With your new brother back and the Hag dead . . ." Ryodan lets it hang. He doesn't need to say more. They would be enormously powerful.

"He is not their brother," Drustan says softly. "And never will be."

Kiall says, "In every sense that matters, Highlander."

"Why should the Seelie give a fuck?" R'jan growls.

"A prince with no royal allies, you are the Hag's most logical next target. If that is not enough to persuade you, Mac is in the room with us and will kill any of you that don't cooperate with my plan. You won't see it coming because she's invisible. Say hello, Mac."

Jada's head whips from side to side, scanning the room.

I can't freaking believe Barrons told Ryodan I'm invisible! And I can't freaking believe Ryodan thinks he's going to use me as his private weapon! My jaw clenches. That man makes me almost as crazy as Barrons does. No wonder. They're related.

"You *do* wish to rescue Christian, don't you, Ms. Lane?" It's a soft warning from Barrons.

He doesn't know I'm here. He's assuming. And as the man once told me himself: assume makes an ass out of u and me. I clench my jaw harder. Let them talk to air. Let others think them mad.

Jada continues searching the room intently. I can practically see her ears perked up like a hunting dog. If I'm stupid enough to say something, she'll be on me in an instant.

To Jada, Ryodan says, "If you think to attack Mac for a reason I'm certain you don't want to discuss right now, it'll be war between us. If you're half as intelligent as I think you are, you know such a war would be futile, pointless, and catastrophic." To the princes, he says, "We will work together to destroy our mutual enemies. Only then will we kill each other, making it easier for the one who remains to control the world."

Rath and Kiall look at each other and nod. "That is the first wise thing you've said, human."

Ryodan cuts Kiall a hard look. "Call me human again and you die."

Kiall is silent a moment then inclines his head. "Mongrel will do. For now."

Ryodan smiles faintly but it doesn't reach his eyes. "Mongrel is preferable to human."

"Another wise comment. But we will not be 'bait' for the Hag."

"Nor will I," R'jan growls.

"Whoever agrees to be bait will get another vote at the table."

"Who the fuck put you in charge of the table anyway?" Kiall demands.

"In addition to the advisor you killed?" R'jan says quickly.

"None of you are touching me long enough to sift," Rath says. "I am not one of your fucking ferries."

"Yes."

"That would give him three and us two," Kiall growls.

"A tie, when you rescue your brother," Ryodan points out.

"A Keltar druid will bloody well not be joining the Unseelie Princes," Dageus says.

Ryodan says nothing. Merely waits.

"You have no investment in Christian," Jada says.

"I have an investment in the Keltar. They wish him freed."

"I don't believe Mac is here," Jada says.

"Ms. Lane, speak," Barrons orders.

Ruff, I don't say, feeling like a dog ordered to bark. Not speaking. I'm not getting used like this. They didn't even consult with me. Like my vote doesn't even matter.

"You will also have a vote at our table, Mac," Ryodan says. "Or do you plan to continue abandoning your city in her time of need?"

"Oh, fuck you," I snap. "I didn't plan to abandon it at all. I've had a few problems of my own to contend with."

Every head in the room whips to my general direction.

I duck, tumble, and roll instantly. When I look back, Jada is standing precisely where I was an instant ago.

Ryodan is behind her with an arm around her throat. Barrons is standing in front of her. I don't envy her, sandwiched between those two men.

Or wait, maybe I do.

Jada puts a hand on Ryodan's wrist, executes a maneuver too sleek and fast for me to follow and is abruptly standing next to him, unrestrained. "You know what Mac is. She cannot be trusted."

Barrons moves to her left, sandwiching her between them again.

"I do know what Mac is. Your best friend. Dani," Ryodan says, and it hurts my heart because if I'd really been her best friend, I wouldn't have run her off into who knows what that turned her into Jada permanently. I understand now what Ryodan wasn't telling me that night in the Hummer. Dani didn't kill Alina. Jada did—coerced by Rowena with her vile black arts. And Jada is savagery born of unconscionable savagery done to her. I close my eyes, mourning Dani, the girl who staunchly, bravely, took the blame for killing my sister. If Ryodan is right, Dani doesn't know for certain that she did. Merely suspects it. If Ryodan is wrong, then somehow Dani was forced to see what Jada was forced to do. I don't know which thought pains me more.

Kiall narrows his eyes. "Dani. This human woman who stands before us now was once the young female with the sword?" Reverting for a moment to full, mad Unseelie Prince, he swivels his head and fixes Jada with an empty stare, iridescent eyes flashing as he realizes what that means. "Both the sword and the spear are in this room with us. That is unacceptable." He begins to chime, harshly, gutturally.

"Now you understand why I'm in charge," Ryodan says.

Jada says coolly, "Because we have the weapons and you *think* you have us?"

"We are far more lethal weapons," Ryodan corrects, "and we have you."

"No one has me or ever will. I assure you, if Mac or I cooperate with you on any matter, it's because we want something. No other reason." Still sandwiched between Barrons and Ryodan, she cuts a look in my general direction. "What do you want, Mac?"

Oh, wow, that's a long list. My sister back. Dani the way she was. The *Sinsar Dubh* out of me. To be able to trust Barrons again. The black holes in our world gone. And that's just for starters.

I keep it simple. Someone needs to be the voice of reason in this room.

"I want Christian rescued," I say. "I agree to put aside all grievances in pursuit of that end. Do you?" I pause a moment, then say carefully, "Jada." I resume studying her, nagged by something I just can't quite—oh, holy shit. Her clothing hugs her curves, leaving no room for her to carry anything larger than a gun, knife, or grenade concealed. Jada doesn't have the sword. At least not on her. I mentally review each time I've seen her: nope, she's never been carrying it. The Dani I know would never stand in the same room with any Fae princes without it.

After a long moment she inclines her head. "I will agree to that. For now. Ryodan, you may tell us your plan."

I glance back at her cuff. No sword, but a shiny new cuff. What would make Dani feel invincible in the presence of Fae royalty? Not at all worried that they might control her with their sexual thrall, a thing they once did; the only time I ever saw Dani cry. If she lost her sword in Faery, what would she want instead—besides my spear, and if she'd interred me at the abbey, she could have taken it.

The truth hits me with the intensity of a two-by-four to my skull.

"Your cuff," I blurt, stunned. I was offered it on several occasions. Never looked at it long because I wanted it so damn much I could taste it. "It was Cruce's." My gaze flies to her face. "And it was on his arm when he got iced!" The cuff protects the wearer from Seelie and Unseelie and, according to Cruce, other assorted nasties. If his claims about it are true, with it, Jada could literally walk through a wall of Shades and pass untouched. I stare at the cuff longingly.

"Cruce?" Rath growls.

"He was destroyed long ago," Kiall hisses.

"Remember the fourth when we fucked her in the street," Rath murmurs to Kiall. "We detected a presence but couldn't see it."

"You said 'iced.' By the Gh'luk-ra d'J'hai? Cruce is alive?" Kiall demands.

"Duh, iced means dead," I say coldly, in a belated attempt to exercise damage control. Their idle comment about fucking me in the street was like a shot of adrenaline to my heart. I inhale slowly, exhale even more slowly, waiting for the Book to goad me. There's only silence.

Kiall sneers. "I do not believe even the one you called the Hoar Frost King could destroy our brother. Where is he? You will tell us now." The Unseelie Princes lunge to their feet, staring directly at the spot I used to be standing in.

I'm a dozen feet away, half concealed behind a bookcase, hand pressed to my lips, wishing I could scrape most of my words back into my mouth tonight.

"Her brain vanished when her body did," Ryodan says to Barrons.

"Apparently," Barrons says.

"That's not true," I say hotly. "The realization startled me. I blurted. Excuse the hell out of me for being stunned to realize the one who was so busy incriminating me for trafficking with the *Sinsar Dubh* was also trafficking with the *Sinsar Dubh*. And why isn't anyone looking accusingly at Jada?" I want to know how the heck she got that cuff off the frozen prince. That worries me. A lot.

"The *Sinsar Dubh*," Kiall says softly, eyes gleaming. "It is here as well? In Dublin? Where?" He and Rath begin to chime hollowly. I can imagine their alien conversation and it's all my fault: *Our brother is alive and the* Sinsar Dubh *is near, we can bring them together and rule the world!*

They don't know their brother *is* the *Sinsar Dubh* and would destroy them before teaming up with them.

"And she just keeps making it worse," Ryodan marvels.

"She *is* the *Sinsar Dubh*," Jada says coolly. "She has it inside her."

"And Dani just joined her," Barrons observes, fascinated.

"As one of our Pri-ya," Kiall murmurs to Rath, like I'm not standing right here, listening, "we could control both her and the power of the Unseelie King."

"Pri-ya doesn't work on me anymore. And nobody controls the *Sinsar Dubh*," I say irritably, then snap at Dani, "I can't believe you just ratted me out like that!" I duck and roll again, soundlessly relocating as Rath and Kiall begin to prowl the room looking for me.

"You did it first," Jada says. "The cuff is an invaluable weapon. Dangerous to leave where it was."

"You lost your sword. Admit it."

"I know precisely where it is."

Maybe she does. But wherever it is, for some reason she can't get to it.

"We shall see," Rath threatens me. "Perhaps it merely takes longer now."

I open my mouth to ask how Dani got the cuff and if the removal of it in any way compromised the integrity of Cruce's prison, then clack my teeth together before I say anything else spectacularly stupid. At the moment, the Unseelie Princes think I am the Book. Last thing I want them to know is that their long lost brother is, too.

As the princes continue stalking, I warn them, "I have the spear. Touch me, you're dead." They don't know it's a bluff. I draw my spear in this room, and who knows what will happen? I duck, roll, stay low.

"Where is Cruce?" R'jan demands.

No one says a word. There were only three "Seelie" present the night we interred the *Sinsar Dubh*: V'lane, who was actually Cruce; Velvet, who is dead; and Dreelia, who's apparently told no one among her court what happened. Wise woman.

"You invite us to this table yet treat us as slaves. You lie, deceive, and manipulate," Rath snarls.

"Oh, gee, we act like far more civilized versions of you," I mock.

"You have information you do not share," Kiall fires back. "We are no longer allies. Fuck you." He and his brother vanish.

"Uh, did they just sift out?" I say, looking around warily, ready to duck and roll again in a heartbeat.

"We are no longer so predictable," R'jan purrs.

"Predictable enough," Ryodan says.

R'jan sifts out an instant before Ryodan gets to him.

"My head is not up my ass. The advisor was disposable. We knew you kept secrets. We kept our own." The
Seelie's words linger on the air, disembodied. "Your
wards no longer work on us."

"Your wards don't work?" I say incredulously.

"So they think," Barrons murmurs.

"Och, that was bloody grand," Drustan growls.
"We've no sifters."

"Aye," Dageus agrees. "So now what's the fucking
plan?"

Ryodan smiles faintly. "That was the plan."

I gasp when the Unseelie Princess from whom I'm
supposedly protecting the Nine sifts into the room, materializing directly behind Barrons and Ryodan.

She takes each by an arm.

Then all three of them are gone.

3²

"I ain't scared of your teeth, I admire what's in 'em"

MAC

The problem with having all chiefs and no Indians in your teepee is that unless you're the chief dictating the current warpath, or in tight with that chief, you have no bloody idea what's going on.

I'm not in tight with Ryodan, and apparently not with Barrons either.

I have news for them: if they think I'm going to be one of the squaws in their chauvinistic tent, they're wrong.

Dageus and Drustan left the bookstore, less angry than I expected them to be, with Dageus making a comment about heading back to wherever it is they're staying to spend time with his wife, and I got the impression they were either in on the plan or had reason to believe Ryodan and Barrons were actively furthering their aim of rescuing Christian. The Keltar remind me of Ryodan, men accustomed to patiently mounting complicated campaigns in pursuit of long-term goals. I suspect they see a few chess moves ahead better than I do. At the moment. I'm learning.

I have no clue if Jada/Dani was in the know or as

miffed as me. Her cold, beautiful face had betrayed nothing. I'd slipped behind a bookcase and held perfectly still until I heard the doorbell tinkle as she left, then remained motionless an additional interminable ten minutes to be certain she wasn't faking an exit while crouching silently near, a tiger ready to pounce the moment I moved so she could try to take my spear and lock me up beneath the abbey.

Eventually I'd eased out and taken a thorough look around. She was gone, ostensibly no more anxious to spend time with me than I was with her.

Now, sitting in front of the fireplace, munching a bag of slightly stale chips, I wonder why, in whatever chess game they're playing, Barrons and Ryodan would want to make the princes think their wards didn't work on them any longer.

I smile faintly. I *am* getting better at this. Soon I'll be devising the plans, instead of merely decoding them while they're being implemented without me.

Because the princes would relax.

Encouraging them to further lower their defenses, Ryodan made them believe they were essential to his plan, and power goes to an Unseelie Prince's head faster than night comes slamming down in Faery.

When one feels threatened, one clears the house before going to bed, but when one feels safe—a foolish thing to ever believe—one doesn't compulsively check all windows and doors, or is perhaps busy celebrating what one perceives as a victory over one's enemy.

And that's precisely when the enemy strikes.

Barrons and Ryodan went after the princes.

Ryodan usurped the contract Jada sought: offered to kill the princes in exchange for Christian's location, and after what I heard him asking Papa Roach in his office, I suspect he upped the ante, offering R'jan to the princess as well, thus allying himself with the *only* royal remaining in Dublin. At least for a time. Why bother dealing with three Fae princes when you can deal with a single Fae princess?

They went after my rapists without me.

I murmur, "Son of a bitch." Now I'm pissed at Barrons about two things.

An hour later when the doorbell tinkles, I don't bother turning around. On the chesterfield, with my back to the door, I know it's Barrons. I feel him.

"If you came back to tell me you killed the princes, I'm never speaking to you again."

I half expect him to say, *Good. I wondered when you'd finally shut up.*

The only reply is a deep, atavistic rattling noise, and I tense. It's primitively terrifying on a cellular level. It's not Barrons behind me.

It's the beast version of the man.

I hear the scrape of taloned claws on the floor as he prowls into the bookstore, the prehistoric panting around what sounds like a death rattle caught in its chest. The beast version of Barrons *is* death: a primeval executioner at the top of his game. Although I've seen him transform partially on multiple occasions, I've only seen him wearing its full skin twice. Both times I was acutely aware that I was in the presence of a thing not at all human, governed by vastly different imperatives, a beast that had no mercy for anything but others of its kind.

It's behind me, beside me, then the creature passes the couch and hulks into my line of vision.

I sit motionless, staring up at it. Nine feet tall or more, its skin is ebony, it's nude and enormously male. Massively muscled, with thick veins and tendons, it has crimson eyes with inhuman, slitted, vertical pupils.

Three rows of long, deadly horns at bony intervals frame each side of its head and there are bits of bloody things stuck on them.

Its prominent, crested forehead is a throwback to ancient times. It has long, lethal black fangs, and when it snarls—as it's doing now—like a lion, it becomes all teeth and deep, rumbling roar.

It's horrifying, it's bestial, yet in this form I still find Barrons savagely beautiful. I'm envious of how well he's engineered to survive, to conquer, to outlast apocalypse.

I remain completely still. I'm invisible.

It whips its head to the left and looks directly at me, peering down through matted hanks of black hair.

Well, shit, I realize, I'm making butt-cheek-shaped indents on the soft leather.

It's holding the severed heads of Kiall and Rath, still dripping a bluish-black blood.

"Some crimes," I quote Ryodan stiffly, "are so personal, blood-vengeance belongs only to the one who suffered them."

The beast snarls at me and gouges the floor with a taloned foot, ripping long gashes into the priceless rug. Crimson eyes flash. So much for the damage my heels do. I'll remind him of this the next time he comments on my shoes.

"I wanted to be the one that killed them," I say, in case I hadn't made myself perfectly clear.

It roars so loudly, the windows rattle in their panes, then stalks forward, shaking the severed heads at me in wordless rebuke, crimson eyes flashing.

I stare into the princes' faces. Eyes rolled back in their heads, their mouths open on screams. Faces don't freeze like that unless pushed to breaking, where death itself becomes the kindness.

Around enormous fangs, the beast snarls, "You had

ample time. You didn't. Your time ran the fuck out." Its horns begin to melt and run down the sides of its face. Its head becomes grossly misshapen, expands and contracts, pulses and shrinks before expanding again—as if too much mass is being compacted into too small a form and the beast is resisting. Massive shoulders collapse inward, straighten then collapse again. The princes' heads thud wetly to the floor. The beast gouges deep splinters of wood up through what used to be a priceless rug, as it bows upon itself, shuddering.

Talons splay across the rug and become fingers. Haunches lift, slam down, and become legs. But they aren't right. The limbs contort, the bones don't bend where they should, rubbery in some places, knobbed in others.

Still it bays, but the sound is changing. Its misshapen head whips from side to side. I catch a glimpse through matted hair of wild eyes glittering with moonlight, of black fangs and spittle as it snarls. Then the tangled locks abruptly melt, the sleek black skin begins to lighten. It hits the floor, convulsing.

I can't help but compare it to the sudden swiftness with which Ryodan transforms. Although both can become the beast quickly, Barrons's reversion to human is lengthy.

I enjoy the beast, Barrons had said. *Ryodan enjoys the man.*

Although both are animal, they prefer to stalk different terrains. Ryodan dons the concrete and glass of the urban jungle like a second skin. Barrons glides into the dark, primitive, forested jungle with the lusty hunger of a long-confined, feral lion escaped from a zoo.

Suddenly it shoots up on all fours, head down. Bones crunch and crack, settling into a new shape. Shoulders form, strong, smooth, bunched with muscle. Hands brace wide. One leg stretched back, the other bent as it tenses in a low lunge.

A naked man crouches on the floor.

Barrons lifts his head and stares straight at me, a few feet above my indent on the sofa. "It was my crime, too. I may not have been there to see it, but I've seen it in my head every fucking day since."

"I was the one that got raped."

"I was the one that failed to save you."

"And because you blamed yourself—"

"I wasn't the only one blaming me."

"I didn't blame you for not saving me," I growl. "It's nobody's responsibility to save me but mine."

"You blamed me for letting them live."

"I did—" *not* is what I intended to say. But I'm startled to realize that he's right.

Deep down I was harboring a grudge. I'd despised that Barrons hadn't killed them the instant he learned what they'd done to me.

"I wanted to," he says tightly. "They were fucking linchpins."

V'lane had needled me that Barrons permitted my rapists to live, to go on after the hellish things they'd done to me. I'd hungered for him to go bloodlust crazy for vengeance, to do precisely what he'd done tonight, rip their heads off and bring them to me in a silent *I may not have saved you but I fucking avenged you*. All this time some part of me was measuring him by his failure to retaliate on my behalf, holding a piece of myself back. How could he not want them dead?

He's right about the other part, too. I could have hunted the princes months ago. I didn't want to. They changed me. Before the rape, I was good, genuinely never had a mean thought. If I hurt someone, it was by accident and I felt bad about it. But when they were done with me, there was something new inside me:

something ruthless and feral and beyond law that hungered to be the one *perpetrating* the savagery, because when you *are* the savage, no one messes with you. I'd wanted to be bad. It's safer to be bad.

When someone hurts you—and I'm not talking about forgivable offenses, some things are irrevocable and demand recompense—you have two choices: slice them out of your life or slice them into delicious, bloody pieces. While the latter would be infinitely more satisfying in an immediate, animalistic way, it changes you. And, although you think the memory of the battle won will be a pleasure—if it is a pleasure, you've lost the war.

They raped me. I survived. I moved on. I wanted someone else to be the animal I didn't want to become.

I could have cold-bloodedly stalked into their goth mansion months ago. I would have enjoyed mutilating and torturing them, killing them slowly. Savored every minute of it. Painted my face with their blood, reveling in my dominance.

But it wouldn't have been a sheepdog that walked out that gothic, towering front door.

It would have been a wolf.

"Wolves don't kill with hate," Barrons says. "They kill because it's what they do."

"What are you saying?"

"Only humans kill with hate. When you kill, you must kill like an animal."

"I don't understand."

"What happens when a sheepdog gets bit by a wolf?"

"Duh. It becomes a wolf."

"No. It becomes a sheepdog that fights with the savagery and lawlessness of a wolf."

"Debatable." I feel like a wolf inside and I don't know what to do with it. I think my soul was turned. It worries me.

Two of the princes who raped me are dead, their heads lying at my feet. The third one, Dani killed months ago. The fourth one—about whom Barrons knows nothing—is imprisoned behind bars of ice.

I have a bad feeling if he ever gets out, I might grow those fangs I don't want.

"The princess is waiting for their heads," Barrons says. "She will not give us Christian's precise location until she receives them."

I sigh and say something I never thought I'd hear myself say to a completely, beautifully, naked Barrons. "Get dressed. I'm ready."

As he leaves the room, I glance at the severed heads, the tortured expressions, and I feel a festering, messy wound inside me finally begin to grow a thin covering of healing skin.

It's over. With the deaths of those who so deeply cut me, I can finally put the horror to rest.

I add softly, "And thank you."

Walking invisible behind Barrons through Chester's many subclubs is annoying as hell. When I rode his wake before, between being aggravated with him and intoxicated by my new supersleuthing state, I hadn't spared a glance beyond his wide shoulders.

Tonight I'm looking. Tonight I see the dozens and dozens of heads rotating to follow him as he passes, the blatantly sexual looks the women give him (and more than a few men!), and I growl with irritation.

"Problem, Ms. Lane?"

"Nope," I mutter, then voice something I can't quite wrap my brain around. "Why are you and Ryodan willing to help rescue Christian?"

"Beats looking for a bloody spell all the time," he says dryly.

"Aha, I knew I forgot to tell you something! I saw the Dreamy-Eyed Guy in Chester's and again on the street. We don't need to keep looking. The king is hanging around Dublin again."

"You continue to cling to the absurd hope he'll free you from your burden, no harm, no foul. Doesn't look like much of a burden at the moment, Ms. Lane. Rather seems you're enjoying it."

Criminy, that woman is flashing him her boobs! Slanting him a come-hither look, gyrating seductively to the music, pulling up her shirt (no, there's not a damn thing but skin and perky nipples underneath), gaze moving hungrily from his face to his crotch as she prowls closer.

I veer to the right and jostle her before she gets to him, knocking her off balance. She has no idea what hits her. She stumbles into a chair then crashes into a table, drinks go flying, and she lands in a tangled heap on the floor. A bottle of beer mysteriously tips itself over and pours all over her head.

Now she looks like a drowned rat. "It does have perks," I agree.

"Little testy tonight?"

"That woman's boobs do not belong in your face."

"It's not as if I can see yours at the moment."

"Well, you're damn well going to feel them. Soon."

"One hopes," he murmurs.

"So, why is Ryodan willing to get involved in all this again?" I circle back to my earlier question. "I thought he couldn't stand Christian."

"Jada will go after the Highlander herself if she discovers where he is. Ryodan won't let that happen."

"He cares about her. A great deal."

Barrons says nothing, but I didn't expect him to.

When we step into Ryodan's office, Barrons removes

the princes' heads from a duffel bag and tosses them onto the desk next to R'jan's.

I never knew I could be happy to see three gruesome, severed heads. More princes will no doubt be made, transformed from whatever raw material the Fae realm likes to pick up and use. But at the moment the only two princes that remain are Christian and Cruce.

"Risky as fuck," Ryodan says, staring down at the heads.

"What?" I ask.

"Killing them now," Barrons replies. "Their continued use as linchpins was debatable. Their absence problematic."

"Well, at least now we can get the women out of their mansion, help the ones they turned Pri-ya," I say.

Ryodan says, "More princes will be made."

"Yeah, but they'll have to do something like eat Unseelie flesh. And participate in a botched ritual."

"Any here that haven't eaten Unseelie flesh, raise your hand," Barrons says dryly. He glances down through the glass floor. "Ask the same question down there."

"Humans are eternally performing botched rituals," Ryodan says. "Every fucking time they use a Ouija board. Among other things."

"Really, a Ouija board?" I knew it! The macabre board game played with unseen participants always made me uneasy. Someone tells you, *Here, I'm giving you a door to death,* and you *play* with it? Not me. No clue what's on the other side but I'd bet it sure as hell isn't going to be my dead sister. No matter how much I'd like to think so.

By such criteria, half this city could start turning Fae.

"Barrons could become Rath. I could become Kiall," Ryodan says.

I protest instantly, "You two are immune—"

"Not to the princess's magic. Not to K'Vruck,"

Barrons points out. "When the Fae royal court is reduced, someone or something will always be altered to complete it. Who's to say we're immune to being transformed?"

I refuse to entertain the possibility. "Speaking of the princess," I ask Ryodan, changing the subject, "how are you controlling her?"

"How are you controlling the *Sinsar Dubh*," Ryodan mocks.

"Day by day," I say coolly. "And I'm doing just fine."

Ryodan smiles faintly. "Welcome to war games, Mac, where the terrain never stops changing and he who adapts fastest wins."

None of us adapt fast enough in the next moment. But then we have absolutely no warning.

The Unseelie Princess sifts in, snatches the princes' heads, and sifts out before my brain manages to process what my eyes just saw.

"Son of a bitch," Barrons snarls.

"Don't make me hunt you, Princess," Ryodan warns softly. "You'll become my sole target, my obsession, my compulsion, my undying homicidal fantasy, the object of my every fucking thought and inclination, and the more time I have to contemplate what I'm going to do to you when I find you—"

Christ, he's freaking even me out. I'd never want to be that to him.

A disembodied voice snaps, "As you do not intend to kill the final prince, the Compact between us is complete. We will spare no further aid to rescue one of our enemies." A scrap of paper materializes and floats to the desk.

"You will sift us there," Ryodan barks.

She doesn't reply. The princess is gone.

Barrons picks up the paper. I peer around him and see that it's a piece of a map. In the middle of a vast mountain range is a tiny red dot. I scowl. "Austria? Christian's in freaking *Austria*?"

"Dreitorspitze," Ryodan murmurs. "Of course. Near enough to Dublin to return for prey, yet difficult to reach."

If I were in a video game, I ponder irritably, there are two powers I'd be stalking: the cuff of Cruce and the highly useful ability to sift. Austria is hours away by plane, a full day or more by car. With so many fragments of Faery floating around out there since the walls fell, no one takes a plane up anymore. Not even Barrons and his men. It's too risky. Driving is enough of a challenge, especially if it's rainy or foggy, but at least you can see the dangerous reality warps coming in a car and have a chance to avoid them. "So, what now? We try to find more sifters?"

"Bloody hell," Ryodan says to Barrons, "she watched too much *Bewitched* as a kid."

Barrons shoots a dry look over his shoulder at the location of my voice. "We do it the old-fashioned, tedious, human way, Ms. Lane. Drive."

33

"Stuck in the middle with you"

MAC

Thirty-five interminable, testosterone-soaked, cranky hours later, the six of us—me, Barrons, Ryodan, Jada, and the Keltar twins—arrive in a small town at the foothills of the Dreitorspitze mountain range, just before dawn. We stop briefly to siphon more petrol on a narrow street blocked by abandoned vehicles, filling the tank and two cans in the back of the Hummer so we'll be prepared for a fast getaway.

The past day and a half is a surreal, grim blur in my mind, and if I'm lucky it'll stay that way. It's one thing to know with your brain that half the world's population is gone, and entirely another thing to see it.

As we drove through England, France, and Germany, I'd stared out at the destroyed cities and riot-torn towns, the miles and miles of Shade-stripped landscape, derelict buses and cabs, bent and twisted streetlamps, the diminished presence of wildlife. Those humans that survived have gone to ground, holed up in barricaded homes or gathered in tightly guarded apartment buildings and hotels. Gangs are rampant, their graffiti wars painted on abandoned buildings, community centers, and underpasses. The few people we encountered in the streets when we stopped to siphon gas, or in the stores we paused to loot, were heavily armed and kept a wary distance. It appears Dublin is rebounding far more quickly than most cities. In three countries, I've seen no sign of people working together to rebuild, like Mom's Green-Up group.

When I was eleven, the town a few miles east of Ashford got hit hard by a tornado, twenty-three dead and hundreds of homes destroyed. Our parents took Alina and me to help with the cleanup, food and clothing donations, and rebuilding. Though some of their friends couldn't believe they let their kids see such horrifying devastation, we'd been glad they did, happy to help, and there'd been plenty for us to do. I still remember seeing Southwest Maple Avenue for the first time after the storm, with the quaint antique shops, pizza parlor, elaborate playground, and my favorite old-fashioned ice-cream store, destroyed, reduced to a shambles of crushed, flattened buildings, twisted slides, and fallen wires, with debris everywhere. It had made me feel dizzy and disoriented.

I've felt that same disorientation on this drive, multiplied exponentially.

The world is no longer the same. My world, like *my* Dani, is a thing of the past. I understand now why Ryodan prizes adaptability. I can't imagine how many times their world changed dramatically overnight, with civilizations rising, falling, new ones being born. Over countless millennia, the armies they allied themselves with were defeated or did the defeating, and a new world order was born, again and again.

They've seen endless cyclical changes. That's one hell of a wave to keep riding and coming out on top.

Or even coming out with your sanity. I feel grief for

what we had, I mourn the Paris in the springtime I never got to experience, the bustling London I didn't get to explore and now never will. I rue the world that's gone.

I could get lost in pining for the way things used to be.

Or I could adapt and learn to ride the changes like they do, with eagerness to see what the new day has in store and unquenchable lust for life, however it unfolds. I understand now why Ryodan stays so invested in his day-to-day world and keeps them all together. Everything else falls away except for the family you're born into, choose, or make; the circle of love you'll die to protect and keep near you. The only thing that keeps us rooted in the past is our refusal to embrace the present. I can almost see the old Dani flashing me a gamine grin and saying, *Dude, you gotta hug it with both arms and legs and hold on tight! The present is all we've got. That's why they call it a present!*

Icy, fierce Jada is all that's left of my Dani.

I've thought about that a lot on this ride. Trying to make peace with it, figure out how to move forward with her. Stop beating myself up for chasing her into the Hall of All Days, and wondering if I can reach what's left of Dani inside, if anything is. I study her when I get the chance, searching for some trace of the teenager in her face, her posture, and finding none. I remember the last fight we had, when I pulled her hair and she bit me. I smile faintly, wondering if we'll ever have such a silly fight again, hoping we might just because it would mean she was reachable. Yes, Alina was murdered. By a young girl who was forced to kill her. A girl who'd already fragmented to adapt, who was further fragmented intentionally by the one who should have saved her, protected her.

I should have seen what was going on with her but didn't, blinded by my own pain. I unintentionally drove her further into the fragmentation. I imagine Dani might have known Alina, even liked her, and been forced to end her life. I really know nothing of the details. I wonder if she found my sister the same way she'd tracked me down near Trinity, driven by curiosity and loneliness. I wonder if the two of them talked. I'd like to see the rest of Alina's journals one day. Jada must know where they are because Dani once surreptitiously sent me pages from them—the ones that told me how much my sister loved me. I'm glad Jada has the cuff of Cruce, although I'd prefer it myself. I don't want her on the streets without a sword or a shield. I'd worry too much.

Jada thinks she's the victory for Dani, but Ryodan's right. Feeling nothing is being dead inside, especially for someone like Dani who used to feel everything so intensely. The only victory here would be Dani back in charge, strengthened by Jada's traits. I wonder if Jada's existence is part of what made Dani impulsive and reckless, as if the facets of her personality were neatly dissected down the middle: the adult survivor traits apportioned to one side, the unabashed child to the other. The more controlled Jada was, the wilder Dani could be.

All the anger I harbored is gone, leaving only a locked, barricaded door between us, with no keys in sight. I intend to hammer the hell out of that door. I'm not losing her when she's right in front of me. But it'll take a committed, well-thought-out campaign to breach the icy commando's defenses and find the young woman within. I know part of the reason Ryodan insisted on bringing her along was to force Jada to be around Barrons and me, people Dani spent time with and cared about. If anything might stir emotion inside her, it's me, good and bad.

Ryodan finishes filling the gas tank, opens the door, and gets back in.

"Ow! If you sit on me one more time," I growl at him, "I'm going to kill you."

"Good luck with that. Don't fucking move every time I get out. You're on my side of the seat again."

"Watch out for my indent," I say crossly.

"Hummer, Mac. Nothing causes indents. Except grenades."

"I have several of those," Jada says. "Persist with your pointless bickering, I'll share one. Pin out."

I ignore her. "I'm cramped. I needed to stretch."

"So, get out when I do."

"I'm afraid you'll leave me behind since you can't see me."

"I'd leave you behind if I *could* see you."

"Christ, would the two of you just shut up?" Dageus growls. "You've been at it for hours. I think I have a headache."

"We've been sharing two freaking feet of space for a day and a freaking half," I say sourly. "What do you expect?" I'm beginning to wonder just how long the Book plans to keep me invisible. I'm still enjoying the hell out of it but have no desire to remain unseen forever.

"How can you *think* you have a headache?" Drustan says irritably. "Either you do or you don't."

"I can't bloody well think in the backseat, so how would I bloody well know? I drive. I don't ride."

Barrons laughs, and I remember him saying something similar once: *Who's driving this motorcycle and who's in the sidecar? I don't even own a bike with a pussy sidecar.* He turns sharply and we begin our off-road ascent, slowly clambering over the rocky terrain.

"You used to ride horses," Drustan says.

"I was bloody well controlling the bloody reins."

"Focus on the mission," Jada says flatly. "Discomfort is irrelevant. Bloody means bleeding or having bled. Accuracy is expediency. You've not heard me complaining."

"We've not heard you talk at all," Drustan says. "You speak less than that one." He gestures at Barrons, who just so happens to be driving and has been doing all of the driving since we left Dublin, barely talking to anyone, not even me except for an occasional silent message he shoots me with his eyes. Since he can't currently see me, my ocular replies are lost on him. "Unless to correct our bloody grammar," Drustan adds.

"Communication is difficult enough when all parties to the discussion strive for clarity," she replies coolly. "Employ precision."

"Precision" and "expediency" rank right up there with "grace" as Jada's middle freaking names. I puked on the ferry. She sure didn't. I caught the lovely, not-one-hair-out-of-place Jada scornfully regarding my projectile over the side. We were all testy and tired and the passage was stormy and I don't have sea legs.

Now we're in Austria and it's cold, and although I dressed warmly, anticipating a mountainous climb, I wish I'd put on more layers. I've been in a Hummer H1, modified for comfort—as if such a thing is possible in a Hummer—for a day and a half straight, sharing the front seat, half astride its enormous console with Barrons and Ryodan on either side. They put Dageus and Drustan in the backseat, and Jada behind them, to keep her and me as far apart as possible, although, loath though I am to admit it, she's the most even-tempered of us all, relaxed, focused, and apparently undisturbed by any facet of her current physical conditions.

Sprawled like a long-legged, curvy commando in the far back on top of rappelling gear, gloves, grappling hooks, and other assorted supplies, and aside from eating protein bars and jerky constantly, Jada looks smoothly in her element.

The interior of the Hummer smells of beef jerky. And testosterone. It's been the most trying road trip I've ever been on.

Before plotting our course, we'd studied Ryodan's map of the many places that were iced, so we could avoid treacherous black holes. Between dodging untethered IFPs—other countries lack the Nine to tidy up for them—detouring around blocked roads and freeways, having to find petrol for the ferry, and siphoning abandoned vehicles for more gas, this drive has made sifting a thousand times more desirable than it already was.

Along the way, amid the eternal grousing that happens when you pack six alphas of varying temperaments—who can work together for a common goal but would probably kill one another—into a sardine can, we've been discussing possibilities and plans.

The princess scrawled a picture at the bottom of the scrap of map. After much debate we all managed to agree Christian is somehow attached to the side of a mountain in the Dreitorspitze range, but we have no idea how high or low. We just have to find the right mountain, scale the face of it, and get him down. Oh, and kill the Hag so she doesn't rain down death on all of us as we try to escape.

Simple, right?

We agree that our primary goal is to rescue Christian, secondary to kill the Hag. However, any way we look at it, both need to happen. The Hag can fly alarmingly fast for short bursts of distance, although Ryodan claims she can't sustain it for long according to his sources. Considering how creepy-crawly and numerous his sources are, I believe he knows what he's talking about. If we have to climb up for Christian, it won't be quite as dangerous. But if we have to go down for him from above, once we free him we'll all be on top of a mountain, with no cover, and one very pissed off Hag circling. Unless she's somewhere else, hunting something else, if we could get so lucky. Fact is, we won't know anything until we see the scene.

"We need sifters," I say for the dozenth time.

"Wake the fuck up, Mac," Ryodan says, "there aren't any. Few of the Fae can sift, and we've killed most of the ones that can."

"Maybe you should have thought of that before you killed the princes."

"The princess refused to disclose their location until we did."

"Dree-lia can sift," I point out.

"Have you any idea where to find her, lass?" Dageus says. "None of the Seelie are responding to our summons."

"We could go into Faery and hunt for them," I say. I scowl when the lumbering Hummer nearly tosses me into Ryodan's lap, and brace myself better on the console.

"Aye, and potentially lose years of our time trying to locate her," Drustan growls. "Leaving Christian on the cliff, dying over and over. Bad plan."

"We don't need sifters," Jada says. "I can do this."

"*We* can do this," Dageus says. "'Tis the only option. We won't be returning to Christopher without his son. He'll be bloody well furious enough that we left without him."

We'd told no one what we'd learned of Christian's whereabouts and stole off like thieves in the night to prevent the other Keltar from joining us. The larger our party, the greater the risk. After twenty minutes of heated debate, with Ryodan insisting Jada be included, we'd narrowed our rescue attempt to six participants, picked her and the Keltar up, and left Dublin immediately. I'd argued against the Keltar. Both Barrons and Ryodan had insisted we take backup.

"We're close enough for now," Barrons says, as we slow to a stop beneath a rocky outcropping that should keep us hidden from above. When he turns the engine off, Ryodan takes a pair of binoculars from the dash and gets out, quietly closing the door.

I finally have the whole seat to myself!

I sink into it gratefully and stretch my legs as we settle back to wait for the details of his reconnaissance mission to finalize our plan.

Three hours later Ryodan's back with a second SUV, and bad news. Christian is indeed chained to the side of a mountain, about a half mile from here, a thousand feet above a rocky crevasse. Although Ryodan located a spot accessible by vehicle where we can conceal it near the Highlander's location, as we feared, there's no way to get to him from below.

Ryodan estimates he's roughly two hundred feet from the top of the sheer stone face. There are cables driven into the backside of the mountain, a modified path for hikers. Ascent is possible. Descent will make us targets, except for me, of course.

Unfortunately, when I touch people, they don't turn invisible like my clothing and food, so I can't get everyone back down that way. Nor do I have any desire to have these particular five people clutching pieces of me for hours.

"Why did you acquire another vehicle?" Drustan asks.

"Backup plan. If something goes wrong and we need to split up."

"Wise decision," Dageus says.

According to Ryodan, the Hag has built herself a nest on a splinter of rock opposite Christian, about a quarter of a mile away from where he's chained. While Ryodan watched, she swooped in, flayed him from breastbone to groin, then returned to her nest to resume her gruesome knitting.

"Exercise in futility. One would think she'd cease doing it," Jada says.

"All is not governed by logic," Ryodan says. "Though you like to pretend it is."

"Fools and the dead are not governed by logic. Survivors are."

"There are biologic imperatives, like it or not," he says. "Eating. Fucking. For humans, which you are, sleeping. For her, knitting."

"I eat. And sleep. Fucking is only relevant if one intends to reproduce. I don't."

"Christian," I remind. "Stay on point."

"The point is I don't need any of you," Jada says. "Give me the spear. I'll return in two hours."

We all ignore her.

Ryodan says, "The bitch actually lances him then sits on him like an insect on a cocoon, taking her time collecting his guts."

"Bad for him, good for us," I say. "The problem with the Hag has always been getting past those damn legs she uses as weapons. That's how we get close enough to kill her."

"What are you suggesting, lass?" Drustan says.

Jada says swiftly, "I'll kill the Hag first, then rescue Christian."

Ryodan says, "The Hag is nested like an eagle on a splinter of stone, impossible to scale."

"I could," I say. "I'm invisible."

"Physically impossible," he clarifies, "it's hundreds of feet, straight up. Nobody's climbing that needle. That's why she chose it. We're going to have to kill her somewhere else."

"I'm the logical choice to kill the Hag," Jada says. "I have the cuff of Cruce. She can't harm me."

"I will make the descent down the face of the cliff, *invisible,* and give Christian the spear," I say coolly.

"The Hag hunts by echolocation; she targets her prey by sound," Jada says. "Visibility is irrelevant."

"Fallacy," Ryodan says. "Although she has no eyes, she employs both visual and auditory guides. When she targeted Christian on the abbey's grounds, he wasn't making noise."

"You don't know for a certainty she can see," Jada disagrees.

"You don't know for a certainty she can't," he says.

I say, "Once I give him the spear, the next time the Hag attacks, Christian can stab her while she's resting on him. Then we free him. I'll wear the cuff to be certain I won't be harmed if she attacks while I'm climbing down to give him the spear."

"You'll wear the cuff the day you can take it from me," Jada says coolly.

"You'll use the spear the day you can take it from me," I return just as coolly.

"It's a solid plan," Drustan says to Jada. "More so than yours."

"Agreed," Ryodan says.

Jada says, "You fail to consider anatomical limitations. Ryodan said Christian is chained, both hands, arms spread wide. With which free hand do you expect him to stab the Hag?"

I open my mouth then shut it. Well, damn. "How are the chains fastened?" I ask Ryodan.

"From what I could see, driven in with metal rivets."

I shrug. "I pry one free."

"You aren't strong enough," Jada says.

I bristle. "First of all, I am, but second, I have a few bottles of Unseelie flesh on hand for just such emergencies." Loath though I am to eat it again, I never leave home without it. All weapons, necessary.

"Walking on the wild side, Ms. Lane?" Barrons murmurs.

"And you think the Hag won't notice someone freeing one of his hands," Jada mocks. "Or that he's suddenly hanging from only one."

"We go at nightfall. He may be strong enough to hold himself by clutching rock, or I drive a spike in for him. It's doable. How quickly is Christian healing?" I ask Ryodan. If he's in bad shape, hanging on could be difficult. "When do you think the Hag will next attack him?"

"Hard to say. I didn't linger."

"I'm the one he sacrificed himself for," Jada says. "I'm the one who will rescue him."

"Illogical and emotional," I say acerbically. "Debt owed does not determine best woman for the job. Besides, I'm immune to the thrall of a Fae prince."

"As am I," she says. She raises her arm and flashes that darned cuff at me that I really wish I had.

"You know I'm right," I say. "The plan with the greatest odds of success is the one I just detailed. And I don't need your bloody cuff. I can do it without it."

I glance at Barrons, who's looking in my general direction. His eyes say, *You're comfortable with this?*

"Yes," I say. I love that about him: he's alpha to the bone but when the stakes get high, he doesn't go all apeshit crazy trying to keep me out of the game. When I choose my place to stand, he supports me standing there.

"It's no' about who saves Christian and kills the Hag. It's about saving him. Period," Drustan says quietly.

I say, "And like it or not, Jada, my invisibility is the edge we need. If I go down, there's only a cable hanging over the cliff at night. If you go down, there's a cable and a whole five feet ten inches of human body visible."

Everyone but Jada murmurs agreement.

"And if the *Sinsar Dubh* decides to seize a perilous moment to wrest control of you?" Jada says.

"Aye, how is it you have the Book?" Drustan says. "Is it similar to Dageus and the Draghar?"

"It is," I tell him. "And it can only take control of me if I kill. That's why I'm handing Christian the spear."

"Even if it's an Unseelie you kill?" Dageus says.

"You've killed and lost control before," Jada says. "I saw her. The Gray Woman. And the Garda you killed. I saw your shrine."

"Which is why I'm handing Christian the spear," I repeat irritably.

"I won't be spotted scaling the cliff," she says. "I'm wearing black and will darken my face."

"Dude"—I use the word deliberately—"I am wearing an invisibility cloak."

"Ryodan and I will make the climb with Ms. Lane at dusk," Barrons says. "Jada, you will remain here with the Keltar."

"The bloody hell we will," Dageus explodes.

"Bullshit," Drustan agrees.

"No," Jada says flatly.

"You only increase the odds of us being heard or seen as we make the climb."

"He's blood. Like it or not, we attend," Drustan says softly.

"Not even you can foresee the myriad possibilities," Jada says to Barrons. "I didn't come this far to remain behind. The Hag might kill you both, leaving Mac dangling on the cliff. Any number of things could go wrong. There are reasons the military takes backup when they go on a dangerous mission. There are reasons you brought us. Don't second-guess the decision you made now."

I can't say in front of the Keltar, yes, but Barrons and Ryodan will come back. Dageus and Drustan won't.

"We could all be killed, lass," Dageus says to Jada. "Any time. Any place. Think you that means a man should never go to war? War is a natural way of life."

"*I said the three of you will remain in the car,*" Barrons says, and his voice resonates in the confines of the vehicle like a thousand layered voices.

Dageus laughs. "Aye, right, try that one on two druids trained in Voice since birth."

Drustan snorts.

Even Jada appears unaffected. Damn, the woman is impervious as Ryodan.

"Looks like we're all going," I say dryly.

We spend another miserable eight hours packed in the car waiting for nightfall. I consider trying to slip off for a private moment with Barrons but instead we end up playing musical seats. Twenty minutes after we agreed on our plan, Jada tried to freeze-frame out with gear. She's been firmly sandwiched between Barrons and Ryodan in the backseat ever since, with Dageus and Drustan in the front and me sprawled out on top of the gear, brooding out the rear window. At least I got a little sleep.

Night descends.

And a full moon rises. No clouds. Not one fluffy little bit of mist in sight. The moon is rimmed with crimson, casting the entire mountainous landscape an eerie blood-black hue.

"Son of a bitch," Dageus curses.

"We could wait a week, or for a cloudy night," I say.

"Nay," Dageus says. "'Tis now or never. We do this tonight."

Drustan eyes him curiously. "Ken you something of these events from your travels in time?"

Dageus mutters darkly, "Only that things get worse the longer it takes us to save him. Much, much worse."

Dageus starts the Hummer and follows Ryodan's directions, lumbering slowly toward our destination so as not to rev the engine and make more noise, then parks beneath another rocky outcropping.

"You will cooperate with our plan," Ryodan tells Jada. "And you will not deviate."

"I accept that," she says with slow precision, "for one reason only. As all of you have agreed upon it, should I deviate, it would jeopardize the mission and all participants. I am not the rash child you once knew. You have my compliance. For this event." She pauses a moment then adds softly and with the first trace of humanity I've seen in her cool countenance, "Never has anyone willingly taken such agony upon themselves to spare me a difficult choice. Christian was my hero when I needed one. I'll see him freed and the Hag killed."

I glance at Ryodan. A muscle is working in his jaw. Oh, yeah, he didn't like that hero comment.

Then we're all getting out and loading up cables and hooks and spikes and lacing our hiking boots tightly.

34

"Walking the cliff's edge, going over, going over"

MAC

If I allow myself a moment of completely serious sincerity, though I often bitch about my current companions, I wouldn't trade them for the world.

None of them.

Over time I've developed a grudging admiration and respect for Ryodan. Recent events have further honed it into something close to affection. He's become the older, irritating brother that drives me crazy, but I'd defend him the instant someone else tried to criticize. I'll never let him know that. I'm glad he keeps the men together. Someone needs to. I've also finally acknowledged to myself that I think he's one hell of a sexy man. I thought so even before I met him, merely from his voice on the phone, the mysterious IYCGM. I'd resisted liking him with the same fervent intensity I'd devoted to disliking Barrons. I'd known from the first I could like them both more than I wanted to.

Dageus and Drustan are very similar to Barrons and Ryodan; strong men, tough, sexy, and fascinating in a human way that if I'd not met Barrons first, and they'd not been married, I'd have fallen hard for one of them. Of the two, Drustan is the stable, solid, reliable one. He exudes a palpable sense of calm competence, even in the midst of confusion. Dageus is the wild card, with a dark edge to him that's an enormous turn-on. And their rich, husky Scots brogue is to die for.

Barrons, well, it goes without saying but I'll say it: he's the best of the best. The strong, silent, dangerously attractive type that harbors a private, vast, brilliant inner landscape of knowledge, wisdom, and experience, and watches, always watches, learns, adapts, evolves. A woman takes one look at the dark, carnal complexity that is Barrons and thinks: Damn, if that man chose me, took me into his inner circle, I'd never stray, never betray him. Beastly and brutal? Sure. Merciful when the situation demands it? Absolutely. Demanding? None more so. Exciting? Holy shit, yes. Respectful of my needs to make my own decisions? Most of the time.

The memory theft incident is a notable exception—and believe me, I'm not done bitching about it. It's a good thing he leveled that playing field. I need to know he can't do it to me again, although I suspect he wouldn't even if he could. He did have a few valid points. I shut him out every time he got close to me. Rejected him at every turn. I marvel at how well he restrained himself over the subsequent months after that night together. If I'd known what incredible sex we'd had and he kept rejecting me, I'd have gotten more than a little pissy. I'd have half hated that I'd taken his memory away, but it would have been too late to undo it . . . so . . . maybe I would have taught him to resist that trick so it could never happen again. I get the impression he's sometimes stymied, trying to figure out how to cope with me. From what I know of him, he was alone for a long time before me, Fiona the exception, and she was little more than an acquaintance with benefits.

Jada. I like the wench. Brilliant, strong, focused, gifted. I can't think of many other people I'd want fighting at my back—if only I could believe she wouldn't stab me in it at the first opportunity. Hate her for taking Dani, but if the kid had to come back as someone else, well, she couldn't have come back more kick-ass.

I sneak a look at her then remember I don't have to sneak anything. She really is beautiful. I smile faintly. Good for Dani. I always told her she would be. And there's no doubt Ryodan thinks so, too. God, he's got his hands full with that situation. He was practically raising the kid, now she's a grown, fire-and-ice woman. Trouble behind, trouble ahead.

I'm looking forward to watching it play out.

The climb up the side of the mountain goes smoothly. Though patches of brilliant snow shimmer in the moonlight, we stick to the dark, rocky areas that thawed in the heat of the day's sun, the better to blend.

Everyone blackened their faces before climbing, not that any of them have fair skin but Jada. We're all in good physical condition, which renders the cable pulls that were pounded in for tourists unnecessary. At least the Hag picked a popular mountain to stake Christian on the opposite side of. We'd have been in a world of shit if she'd chosen Everest. Fortunately, Everest is too far from Dublin for her purposes. From her attempts to abduct the other Unseelie Princes—who she presumably doesn't know are dead—she'd planned to eventually stake all of them to the side of Christian's cliff.

I shudder. Gruesome.

As we begin the final stretch, I ponder the Book's unnatural silence. I keep waiting for it to begin talking again, throw a few vile images at me, turn me visible at a critical moment, anything. I don't understand why it's gone so silent. It's almost as if it's actually *gone*.

It makes me nervous.

In time, I might begin to forget it's there and wonder if that's the *Sinsar Dubh*'s plan. To lull me into lowering my guards, like Barrons and Ryodan did with the princes.

As we navigate a narrow crevice between boulders, Ryodan says in a rough whisper, "When you get close to Christian, talk to him before you touch him. He's a hair-trigger. You can't afford to have him jerk and drop the spear. I don't want any of us to have to climb this bloody cliff twice. Prepare him. He must be able to hold onto it and hold himself on the cliff until she comes again."

In a low voice, I say, "What if it takes days?"

"Though it would mean he's died fewer times, let's hope it doesn't," Dageus whispers grimly.

Barrons says softly, "You must judge his condition when you get there. If he's too weak, come back up."

"I disagree. If you time it wrong," Jada whispers, "we could be here for weeks. He's strong. He'll hold."

"Aye. He is Keltar," Drustan says quietly. "He will hold."

"Kairos," Dageus says, "this eve reeks of it. The time is now."

We continue the ascent in silence. We all know our tasks and have agreed upon a number of contingency plans. I'm already wearing my rappelling harness. Barrons and Ryodan will hook me up and lower me over the side when we reach the top. When I see Christian, I'll make the call. Jada, Dageus, and Drustan are our lookouts. They'll have binoculars trained on the Hag's nest the entire time.

As we ascend the snowy peak, the others drop to low crouches near the ground.

Barrons leads the rest of them, sticking to the barren patches. The moon silvers the mountain with a faint merlot tinge. Invisible, I stride to the cliff's edge, battling a stiff breeze. I inhale deeply of the crisp cold mountain air. Far to the north I see the needlelike spire where the Hag roosts. Ryodan's right. Nobody could climb it. Not with her sitting on top of it as she is now, back to us, knitting feverishly away, bloody, snaky hair spilling down her back and bloody, snaky guts from her gown dripping over the side. Even with her gone, it would be a dangerous feat. Although as a potential plan B, we might wait for her to leave and try it, if plan A fails. If I could get into her nest and lie in wait, invisible . . . wait, I don't dare stab her. But then again, if everyone else rescued Christian and abandoned me here until I got control of myself again . . .

Hopefully it won't come to that.

"Are you ready?" Barrons says in a rough whisper.

I nod, then append it with a "Yes." I keep forgetting they can't see me, since I can see them.

"Where are you? Touch me."

I slip my hand into his, and for a moment he just stands there, looking down at where I am, then he closes his eyes and laces strong fingers with mine. I hear exactly what he's not saying in them: *You better bring your ass back to me, woman.*

I reply with mine, *Always.*

He laughs softly then somehow finds my face and kisses me, light and fast, and I taste him on my lips, need him again, hard and fast and soon.

Then he and Ryodan are groping around on me, hooking pulleys to my rings, preparing me for my first-ever rappelling trip down the side of a twelve-hundred-foot cliff.

Going over the side is the hardest part. The wind is cutting up here, pelleting in stiff gusts. I close my gloved hands on the cable as I ease over the edge, feeling about for footing. I eye the thin cable dubiously. It's all that's keeping me connected to life. I'm not sure even *I* could survive a twelve-hundred-foot fall. I know I wouldn't like the recovery from it. "Are you going to hook it around something?" I whisper.

"Ryodan already secured it to a rock. You're safe. We've got you," Barrons replies. "If something goes wrong, you have only to pull yourself up."

"Your primary objective is getting Christian out of here," Dageus whispers. "Doona fash yourselves with the rest of us." Then he adds something in another language.

Drustan says, "Gaelic. A blessing in the old way."

"Thanks," I murmur.

"If you prefer, I will go," Jada says.

I hear something different in her voice and look up, past Barrons, and catch my breath. It's the first trace of Dani I've seen. Jada looks worried. About me.

I smile, but she can't see it, and say, "I know you would. And I appreciate it. But I've got it. Just keep an eye on the Hag for me."

"You have to kick off, Mac," Ryodan says softly. "Go down a dozen feet, push out gently, drop twenty feet or so, regain the face and repeat."

"Don't push out hard," Jada whispers. "Get your climbing legs. Descend slowly at first." She doesn't add *and do not puke* but I hear the unspoken recrimination in her voice.

I glance down and am instantly sorry I did. I almost puke. I'm hanging above a sheer drop. *I can do this*, I tell myself. *I can do this*.

"Did you eat Unseelie, lass?" Drustan whispers.

"Got it on me. Hits fast as a shot of adrenaline."

"Go," Barrons says. "We don't know what shape he's in or when she'll next stir."

I keep my eyes locked on his dark face as I force my feet to do the counterintuitive on a cliff and kick myself off it.

My first drop takes me a short ten feet. The instant I feel myself free-falling, I grab the cable and squeeze. My gloves grip hard and yank me to an abrupt halt. I take a deep breath, exhale, and try again. This time I drop about fifteen. My heart is racing and lodged high in my throat.

Each time I kick off, I feel a little more secure, trust that my cable is solid and I'm not going to fall. After my fifth try, I force myself to glance down and see where Christian is, and estimate he's still about eighty or so feet below me. I decide to start talking to him when I'm a dozen feet away. I glance up and see three heads looking down but the moon is behind them so I can't make out their features.

When I'm twenty feet or so from Christian's head, I feel a tight snap of the cable, a prearranged warning if anything in our current situation changes. Shit, I think, glancing around wildly, half expecting the Hag to erupt from directly behind me and somehow pierce me with her lance even though I'm invisible.

My blood chills. I *am* still invisible, right? The Book would have no reason to expose me now. I glance up at my gloved hand then down at my body. Yup, still invisible. Then what? I brace myself on the rock and turn to look at the Hag's nest.

My heart sinks. She's stirring, standing, bloody dress dripping over the side of the spire, black holes where her eyes should be trained in our direction.

She's tense, preparing for flight.

Son of a bitch.

She's coming.

35

*"Off into the sunset,
living like there's nothing left to lose"*

MAC

I glance up but don't see anyone at the cliff's edge. Only a thin black cable snaking over the side.

Good. That means they warned me and sought cover, as was our contingency plan.

I glance down. If the Hag comes for Christian now, I'm perched on the side of the cliff a mere twenty feet above where she plans to hunker down and flay the Highlander. I'll have to hang here, wait for her to finish, then climb back up and wait until Christian heals a little to try again.

Unless she's going somewhere else. Could I be so lucky?

I glance back over my shoulder, peering through the moonlit night. She's still standing in her nest, macabre gown of guts dripping over the edge, swaying from side to side in an eerily reptilian manner, nose in the air, head tilted as if listening intently.

Surely she didn't hear the sound of my boots hitting the side of the cliff over all this wind and from a quarter of a mile away.

Did she? I have no idea the acuteness of her echo-location skills.

I hang there, debating options. I don't need to kick out anymore. I can inch down another ten feet, whisper to Christian, give him the spear, kick out to draw her near him. Then pull myself up out of the way really fast.

Or . . . I could hang here while she kills him again, wait and inch back up.

Only to inch back down later.

I *so* don't want to do this again. The way I see it, the odds of failing are directly proportionate to the number of attempts, increasing each time.

What would Jada do?

That's a no-brainer.

I steal another glance at the Hag.

She's still standing in her nest. Not hearing any vibrations. As long as she doesn't, we should be fine.

I begin to inch slowly downward.

When I'm ten feet from Christian's head, I say softly, "Christian, it's me, Mac. Don't talk loud. Keep it low."

I have to repeat it several times before I hear a guttural groan.

My head instantly whips to the Hag but she's still standing, unmoving.

"We're here to save you. I'm bringing you the spear. I'm going to pry one of your hands free," I say in a low voice. No way I can try to drive a spike in now. She'd hear it for sure. It's going to be risky enough prying one of the rivets out. "You'll have to hold on until she comes for you again. Hide the spear." As soon as I say that, I think, Where exactly do I expect him to hide it? The man is naked.

I'm beginning to realize we overlooked a few critical details in our plan.

I hang there, boots carefully braced on a tiny, narrow ledge on the sheer cliff face, being buffeted by a stiff, cutting wind, suspended by nothing but my frightfully thin cable (yes, I read the weight rating; it doesn't make me feel any better), and force myself to take one hand off it to rummage around in the pocket of my jacket for a bottle of Unseelie flesh, neatly sliced and diced months ago. I keep them hidden all over the bookstore. I'll take every advantage I can get right now. I half expect the *Sinsar Dubh* to either prevent me from using it or try to amp it up in some nasty way. Biting back revulsion, I gingerly work the lid free and ease the wriggling contents into my mouth.

My body stiffens as it hits me like a thunderbolt.

Energy, sexuality, vitality, and strength burn in my veins. No wonder so many people are so addicted to it. I feel strong. I feel alive. I feel invincible. I remember eating it once before and taunting Barrons to hit me, punch me, fight with me.

I ease down a few more inches. So far no malevolent commentary from the Book and no apparent negative side effects. If you exclude a ferocious desire to eat it again once it wears off.

"Christian, can you hear me?" I whisper.

"I . . . hear you," he says weakly. "Mac . . . I smell . . . Unseelie flesh. You . . . eating it? Ken you what . . . vile stuff . . . does . . . to you."

Despite the agony in his voice, I swear I hear a faint note of teasing.

"Are you strong enough to hold yourself up for a little while if I free one of your hands?"

"Aye," he whispers. "Give me . . . the bloody spear . . . kill the . . . bloody bitch. Can't see . . . you. Naught but . . . black and moonlight. Am I . . . blind?"

"I'm invisible."

"Och, and . . . why wouldn't you . . . be." He sort of laughs but it turns into a blood-chilling moan of pain.

"How long do you think you can hold yourself if I get your hand on an outcropping of rock?"

He's silent and I get the sense he's resisting the urge to snarl *Forever*, trying to gauge what he believes he can actually do. Finally he says faintly, "A few minutes . . . no more. I'm gutted . . . nigh dead. Keep . . . blacking out."

"Shit," I mutter. From this angle I can't see past his head.

I feel another sharp pull on the cable, twice, three times, and my blood runs cold with dread. Three times means she's taken flight.

It's now or never. I have to hurry. And I'm going to be sitting mere feet away when it happens.

"I'm going for your left hand, Christian."

"She's . . . on her way."

"I hear her." She has no wings, who knows how the hell she flies? But she makes a sharp whining sound as she displaces air. She'll be on us in ten seconds if she comes straight for him. I kick out—why not, she's already coming?—and drop to rest below his left hand. I pull the spear out, wedge the tip beneath the pylon and get ready to pry it free. "Grab my arm with your fingers. You must hold on when I pry it out."

"I'll . . . pull you . . . down."

"You won't. I ate Unseelie."

"You . . . never . . . learn." His fingers close around my wrist.

I establish the most secure toeholds available, which is virtually nothing, as sheer as the rock is where she hung him, and pry with one swift, hard jerk.

The rivet shoots out, goes flying off into the air behind me, and begins the long plunge to the canyon below. Christian's grip on me tightens, and my feet slip off the nearly nonexistent ledges.

I plummet like a stone, in full free fall.

I grab the cable with both hands and squeeze as tight as I can, jerk it too hard, bounce upward and crash into the rocky bluff.

Wiping blood from my face, I glance up. Christian is a good thirty feet above me, hanging by a single arm at a telltale slant.

I look down. The Hag is gone, apparently chasing the sound of the rivet hitting stone.

It's a darn good thing I ate Unseelie flesh. Without it I'm not sure I would have been able to stop myself from plunging down to join the rivet. Dark energy pounds in my head, my heart, giving me many times my normal strength and energy.

I hang there a second, looking up, studying the cliff, picking out my toeholds, plotting my climb back up before beginning the steep ascent.

When I'm even with Christian, I see his body for the first time and gasp. He's sliced from breastbone to groin, skin flapping, parts of flesh hanging out, regrowing.

How the hell has he even been talking?

"She sees me . . . hanging by one arm, she'll lance . . . me from a . . . distance."

"I'm going to ease your hand onto a piece of rock. Hold like your life depends on it."

He groans. "Mere minutes, lass . . . no more . . . pain immense."

I hear the familiar, dreaded whine of the Hag's flight and scramble to get his fingers fastened onto a rocky ledge. "You got it?"

"Aye. Need . . . spear."

If she sees it, she'll never come near him. "I'm crouching on the wall, just above your hand. When she gets here, I'll wrap your fingers around it. It won't become visible until I let go of it."

"You'll . . . be. . . . lanced."

"I won't," I say flatly. "Shut up and focus." I use the cable to raise myself a few feet, praying he can hold on.

After a moment, he growls, "Where . . . is . . . she?"

Suddenly I hear shouting above us, and Jada screaming at someone to take cover.

"Fuck this," I snarl. I take my spear and slam the hard steel against the face of the cliff, to distract her, lure her to us.

It works.

She suddenly shoots out above us and hangs in the air, gut gown snaking over the edge, peering down.

"Right here, bitch," Christian snarls.

She draws back like a cobra about to strike.

And does.

With one of her insectile lancelike legs, she severs my cable.

Time suspends and everything seems to unfold in slow motion. I'm staring up, watching the cable snake in coils over the edge for what feels like a full minute, excruciatingly aware I'm a thousand feet above a deadly rocky canyon floor, crunching thoughts furiously: How fast will I fall? Will I die? Will I bounce off an outcropping and break every bone before I even hit bottom? How bad is this going to hurt? Have I been good? Was my life worth anything? What did I accomplish in twenty-three years? I haven't had nearly enough sex with Barrons.

I know a mere instant passes, but I understand what people mean when they say their life flashes before their eyes. In vivid detail I see the finest moments I've experienced, the ones I regret, my bravest times and my most cowardly, followed by the many experiences I'd hoped to have and now perhaps never will.

All of it crashes into my brain as I take that horrific first moment of free fall, and in spite of myself, my mouth stretches wide on a scream as I try desperately to brace myself for whatever's to come: a brutally painful recovery or a happy reunion with Alina in heaven, because if I go to Hell, I'm breaking out. I will *not* be separated from my sister forever. I haven't been that bad. Besides, I just ate Unseelie, which means I can kick some serious demon ass busting loose.

I slam into what feels like a seesaw between my legs and suddenly I'm choking and sputtering, trying to breathe.

"Good . . . fucking thing you . . . screamed," he rasps. "I've . . . got you . . . but can't hold . . . long." I realize he let go of the rock, kicked his leg in the general direction of where he heard me (my pelvic bone is going to be sporting one heck of a bruise) and grabbed blindly for any part of me, ending up with the front of my jacket. He's hanging by one hand. Strangling me with my coat with the other.

He murmurs, "And that's . . . what . . . Dageus meant."

"What?" I ask as I flail wildly, finally get my legs wrapped around him and clamber up his body, trying hard not to clutch at any torn flesh in the process. It's a messy, slippery business.

"About my opportunity. Bloody hell, she's . . . coming!"

I can't let go of him or I'll fall. If I don't let go of him, I'll get lanced when she stabs him. I sincerely doubt she's going to get close enough to us, with all the intruders she's spotted on her mountain, for either of us to stab her.

I'm not leaving without what I came for. We'll finish the Hag later.

I hiss, "Can you sift?"

"Iron. Manacles. Can't. Too . . . wounded . . . anyway."

Terrific. I can pry the rivets out but my spear is useless for cutting the manacles off his arms. I'd wondered how she was preventing an Unseelie Prince from sifting. With iron, the same way Inspector Jayne does with the Unseelie he captures and keeps until someone slays them. Speaking of which, his cages must be crammed to overflowing.

I'm not dying on this cliff.

I wrap one arm tightly around Christian's neck, force myself up and to the left, dig my spear beneath the rivet holding his right hand. It won't budge. There's too much weight hanging on it. I dig the tip of the spear in deeper, start rocking it back and forth beneath the rivet, using my Unseelie-flesh-enhanced strength.

He looks up, growls, "What . . . the . . . fuck . . . Mac! No!"

The rivet suddenly shoots from the cliff like a missile being launched, and for the second time I go into a full free fall.

I hold on to him tightly and scream, "Fly, Christian! *Fucking fly!*"

36

*"Forever trusting who we are and
nothing else matters"*

MAC

Once again, nothing goes as I expect it to.

I can't call what Christian does flying, and he confounds me by going *up* not down. I expected him to, at worst, be able to unfurl his wings and use them as a sort of hang glider, to soar us to the floor of the gorge without killing us. Instead he scrabbles higher with short, fierce bursts of his wings, digging and clawing at the side of the cliff, using them like appendages, a hawk that can't fly, scrambling desperately upward.

Closer to the freaking Hag.

"Why the hell don't you go *down*?" I shout.

I hear roaring on top of the cliff, a scream and the rapid burst of gunfire.

The Hag shrieks and explodes up into the night sky. A whip cracks, followed by another banshee-like wail.

"Shut . . . the fuck . . . up," Christian grits.

I've got both arms clamped around his neck, hanging on for dear life, getting repeatedly bashed against the side of the cliff with each scraping lunge of his wings.

My shirt is being ripped to shreds and the back of my head and spine are taking a brutal beating.

"Keep her away from them until they reach the top," I hear Ryodan bark.

"I'm trying to," Jada fires back. "She moves erratically. It's hard to compute."

"Stop fucking trying to compute and *feel*," he snarls. "She's not a machine. She's a goddamn pissed-off, bloodthirsty woman."

I hear more cracks from the whip. The sound is bounced back and intensified by the surrounding mountains. I decide they must be using it to mess with the Hag's echolocation.

"Behind the bitch, not to the side," Ryodan orders.

"You're almost there, lad," Dageus shouts down at us. "Grab the bloody cable." He's hanging over the cliff's edge swinging a length of thin black cord at us.

But Christian's desperately trying to sustain our altitude and in no position to reach for it. I grope wildly for the cable, praying I have enough strength to pull us up because each time I get slammed into the cliff my vision goes a little dark and I can feel Christian growing weaker. Not even my Unseelie flesh rush is enough to stand this constant battering.

Looks like we may end up trying to hang glide after all.

"She's coming back," Barrons shouts. "Get the fuck away from the cliff's edge, Highlander."

I hear the whip cracking furiously again, and Barrons roars, a horrible, guttural sound, and I cringe to the bottom of my soul because I know without needing to see it that Barrons just got lanced. Doesn't matter that I know he'll be back. It's one less person to protect the Keltar and Jada, and I despise the sound of that man dying. I have no doubt he stepped in the way to protect someone.

"Fuck." Dageus snarls down at us. "Bloody grab the bloody cable."

Then Drustan is beside Dageus and I hear Jada and Ryodan taunting the Hag, more gunfire and the sound of the whip cracking as they try to buy us time to get to solid ground.

I kick upward and Christian grunts with agony when my boot catches him in the stomach, but I close my fingers around the cord.

Moving quickly, Drustan and Dageus begin to pull us up.

We're nearly there when Jada and Ryodan start shouting again, then suddenly something explodes out of the front of Dageus's chest and he goes rigid, yanks upright and makes a soft grunt of shock and pain.

It takes my brain a second to process what just happened.

The Hag just lanced Dageus from behind.

Christian howls with such animalistic, inhuman fury that it chills my blood. It occurs to me how ironic it is that four of us on this mountain possess immense power but can't use it. Barrons and Ryodan won't turn into the beast in front of strangers. My inner Book has gone dead silent. Christian is too weak to use his Unseelie magic.

His wings begin that awful scrabbling again but it only slams me hard into the side of the mountain. I squeeze with all my might, struggling to merely maintain my grip on the cable with one hand and Christian with the other, but Dageus is no longer holding our weight and we begin to slip slowly, inexorably, downward.

"Pull them the fuck *up*," Dageus growls at Drustan, blood gushing from his mouth. Then he's airborne, impaled on the Hag's leg. She shoots out over the canyon as Drustan, joined by Ryodan and Jada, yank us to the top.

Christian collapses, rolls, and stares into the night sky over the gorge. Painted crimson and silver by eerie moonlight, the Hag hangs above the gorge, Dageus clutched in her gruesome, bloody embrace.

"Fucking bitch!" Christian pushes to his feet, but Drustan tackles him and prevents him from leaping off the edge to attempt to fly, something we both know he can't do right now.

"You will not make my brother's sacrifice for naught, lad!"

The Hag shoots across the chasm, smashes Dageus into the far cliff once, twice, three times before violently shaking her leg to dislodge the unmoving Highlander.

Dageus plunges silently down, a dark speck, vanishing into the shadows as we all watch in horrified silence.

The Hag whirls midair and rockets back across the chasm, straight for us, head down, unfinished gut-gown streaming out behind her.

Then Jada is shoving Drustan away from Christian. "Get down and stay down," she hisses at him. She drags Christian to his feet and steps in front of him and commands, "Mac. Spear. Now."

There's no time to argue. Barrons is down and Dageus just gave his life to save us. I want vengeance. Nothing else matters. I move to her side, place my hand against hers and make sure she feels the cold metal of the blade between us. "I'll let go at the last minute so she doesn't see it. Don't you dare fucking miss or I'll kill you myself."

She doesn't dignify my threat with a response.

Christian tries to push Jada out of the way, snarling that no one else is dying for him on this cliff. Jada shoves back, pushing him behind us.

The Hag dives headfirst, slicing through the night,

mouth twisted with rage, black holes where her eyes should be narrowed in fury.

Jada freeze-frames us and suddenly we're standing twenty feet away. My spear is no longer in my hand. While I was discombobulated from being freeze-framed, which she knows makes me feel sick, she took it from my grasp.

"What are you doing?" I explode.

"Not letting you die, Mac." She shoves me so hard and unexpectedly that I go sprawling face-first to the ground.

Christian howls and I don't need to look to know he just got lanced. When I peel myself from the rocks, wipe snow from my face, and look back over my shoulder, I see the Hag has impaled him and is preparing to fold her knitting-needle legs together around him and soar off into the sky.

Ryodan and Jada exchange a glance and she tosses him her whip.

He cracks it in the air behind the Hag, impeding her flight, and goads, "Come and get me, bitch. I don't die either." He moves closer, snapping the whip so fast I can't even see it, keeping her penned into a small space of air. Unlike Jada, he seems to have no problem anticipating her airborne lunges.

The Hag levels her free leg at his head. He dances around, ducking and dodging like a boxer on meth, cracking the whip repeatedly. "But you know that. You killed me once before." He's become a blur, and I wonder if he's actually going to be able to get close enough to kill her however it is the Nine do.

Then Jada materializes between the Hag and Ryodan with the abruptness of a Fae sifting in and I realize that was never his plan.

With that one shared glance, he and Jada made another one.

Ryodan was the distraction.

Jada closes her hands around the leg upon which Christian is impaled and with the grace of a circus acrobat swings herself up, spear tucked into the waistband of her camo pants.

The Hag rears back, violently shaking her leg, trying to dislodge her, but Jada doesn't let go. When she reaches the writhing, bloody mess of a gown, she uses the guts as ropes to vault herself up, grabs the Hag by the hair, yanks back her head and slits her throat from ear to ear.

Blood sprays everywhere and the Hag's head lolls back. Jada shoves the spear deep into the bone and gristle of her corset, expression fierce, savage.

The three of them crash to the ground in a heap.

The Crimson Hag is dead.

37

*"And the shadow of the day will
embrace the world in grey"*

MAC

Ours is a somber group that descends the cliff, battered, weary, and bleak.

I now understand the meaning of the phrase "hollow victory."

In the past, each time we did battle with the enemy, although there were losses, none cut so deeply, so close to the heart.

I realize belatedly that for some time now I've counted the Keltar as one of us: indomitable soldiers, battling tirelessly against evil, fighting the good fight, always surviving to wage war another day. I counted on it.

One of the good guys died tonight.

A man with family.

A legend of a Highlander.

There's no hope Dageus survived the brutal gutting, the crushing blows against the cliff, and the subsequent twelve-hundred-foot fall.

Like the Hag, Dageus MacKeltar is dead.

Drustan doesn't speak a word, supports Christian on one side, with Jada on the other, and they half carry, half drag the now unconscious prince down the mountainside.

When we reach the bottom and load him carefully into the Hummer, Drustan murmurs, "Och, Christ, how am I to tell Chloe? They fought so hard to remain together. Now she's lost him for good." He whispers something over Christian in Gaelic then turns to leave.

Ryodan steps into his path, blocking it. "Where do you think you're going, Keltar."

"Unlike you, I'll no' be leaving without retrieving what remains of my brother's body for burial."

He's referring to Ryodan hastening us from the mountaintop without pausing to collect Barrons, which I know he did so Drustan and Jada wouldn't see him vanish but no doubt appeared callous to the others.

Drustan's gaze is bleak, haunted. "Too many times he took the burden upon himself to save us. I'll see him buried properly, in the old ways, on Keltar ground, in Scotia. If the Draghar still inhabit his body, certain rituals must be performed. If not, aye, well, bloody hell if not, they're free again."

"I've no intention of returning to Dublin without Barrons," Ryodan says. "I will collect your brother's body as well. Christian needs you. Your clan needs you now."

I search his face and am surprised to see something patient and understanding in those cool silver eyes.

"I know the sorrow of losing a brother," Ryodan presses. "I'll bring him back. Go."

I wonder about Ryodan and Barrons. Did they once have other brothers? Did they lose them before they became what they are, or afterward? How? I want to know about these two, understand them, hear their tales.

I doubt anyone ever does.

Drustan glances between Christian and the shadowy

entrance to the gorge, visibly torn, unwilling to do anything that might risk that for which his brother gave his life, equally unwilling to leave his brother's body behind.

"Come, Drustan," I say gently. "The living need you now. If Ryodan says he'll bring his body back, he will."

Ryodan says to me, "It may take time to find . . . all of him. Take Christian to Chester's. Sequester him where we protected the Seelie Queen. He'll be safe there while he heals."

As Ryodan turns to go, Jada says, "I'll come with you."

"You will return with the others and protect them."

"I'm not she who once—"

He cuts her off fast and hard. "I know who the fuck you are," he clips the words out coldly. "You're the only one that doesn't. Dani could have anticipated the Hag's movements. You could not. *Jada*."

Ryodan vanishes into the night without another word.

I wince. That was harsh. Whether or not it was true.

The three of us join Christian in the Hummer and begin the long silent ride home.

38

"How I wish, how I wish you were here"

MAC

After seeing Christian and Drustan safely inside Chester's, I'm surprised when Jada doesn't immediately stalk off. *With* my spear, which I'm stunned to realize I'd forgotten about. But the three-day ride was depressing, Christian largely unconscious, Drustan deeply grieving, and neither Jada nor I in any mood to talk. I suspect my invisibility makes me feel safer, plus I'm still pumped by the final stages of Unseelie-flesh-high. Regardless, once she'd tucked the spear away somewhere, I'd not thought about it again.

Now I'm doubly surprised she didn't rush off. Why linger and give me time to demand she return it? Jada does nothing without purpose.

We stand in taut silence outside Chester's, eyeing the long line of people waiting to get in with distaste, and I'm reminded of the old Dani, how we would have sauntered off into the night to slay Unseelie and reduce the number of predators in our city, dozen by dozen, hoping to one day save these mindless lemmings from the apparently irresistible lure of flinging themselves off the proverbial cliff inside the club.

Neither of us has showered in nearly a week. I suspect if I could see myself, I'd look a fright. A week out, Jada still looks spit-and-polish perfect. I sigh, wondering if I'm going to have to fight to get my spear back. Truth is, I'm not entirely sure I can take it from her. Nor do I want to have to.

I opt for the direct approach. "Give me my spear, Jada."

She glances in my general direction. "You can't use it."

"It's mine. That's enough of a reason."

"Inefficient. Someone should be able to use it. I'm the obvious choice."

I'd like to deny the validity of her words but I can't. Given the risks, I'm unwilling to wield it. I can't walk these streets and slay, and the sheer number of newly arrived Fae inside Chester's tonight was staggering.

Without the sword—I wonder again where it is, that she can't get to it—Jada can't kill them. Seems a hell of a waste of lethal womanpower in this city.

Still, if the *Sinsar Dubh* decides to suddenly make me visible, I'm going to want it, need it.

"What happened after I chased you into the hall?"

"Like the one you called Dani, the past is irrelevant. I'm here now. That's all that signifies."

"What are your plans for the abbey?"

"None of your concern."

"Once, we worked together."

"Once, I was someone else."

"What about the Book I carry?" I want to know if I have to watch my back every second of the day. I want to know how Jada thinks, if there are weaknesses in her mental defenses where I'm concerned.

"I'll contend with Cruce. Barrons and Ryodan are enough to contend with you."

"You're granting me free passage." I choose my words carefully, using the same words I spoke the night I made a pact with the Gray Woman to save her life, the night I discovered what she'd done with Alina, probing to see if I can elicit an emotional response.

"For now," she says tonelessly.

Still, she stands in the street looking at me as if she's waiting for something. I can't fathom what.

"Have you seen Dancer since you've been back?" I take another shot at provoking emotion.

"I don't know Dancer."

"Yes you do. Dani was crazy about him."

"You could have ended your second sentence after the initial three words."

Okay, now she's starting to piss me off, insulting the tenacious, brilliant teen that battled tirelessly for our city. "What do you want, Jada?" I say flatly. "Why are you still standing here?"

She wrinkles her nose as if her next words leave a foul taste on her tongue. "Do you believe Dani could have anticipated the Hag's movements better than I could?"

I catch my breath. There it is. Why she remained. She despises asking me, yet can't resist. Apparently Ryodan's criticism has been burning like sullen fire in her gut ever since he leveled it at her. Who better to ask to confirm or deny it than me? I knew Dani better than most. That she even asks it shocks me. Jada has opened herself to an opinion. My opinion.

I don't like this question. I don't want Dani harboring more guilt or self-recrimination. I've not forgotten, and will never be able to forget, her cry that she deserved to die. I wonder what happened to her when she was young, what Ryodan knows about her, what "kryptonite" she carries in her head that he believes could destroy her. I wonder if he's wrong, and Dani actually knows it and was relieved to turn the reins over to a remote, unfeeling part of herself. I wonder what happened to her in the Silvers, what she endured that made her transform fully into this icy other.

I study Jada in silence, realizing her question might be a small crack in the dominant personality's facade. Then again, it might merely be a desire to reconfigure herself into the most efficient weapon possible. I don't know much about dissociative disorder, but between trying to figure out how to stop the black holes that threaten our world, hunt the Unseelie King to get rid of this Book, and find Barrons because I need him like a bandage to my wounds, I intend to learn.

I wonder how Jada subdued Dani so completely. Similar to the way I subdue the Book? Does Dani whisper daily, struggling to break free, or is she imprisoned somewhere deep inside, in a small dark cell, her exuberant, passionate voice echoing in a tight vacuum, not heard even by Jada? Worse, has she given up?

"Are you still there?" Jada says.

"I don't blame you for killing my sister, Dani," I say softly. "I forgive you." My heart feels abruptly, enormously lighter. Saying those words released an awful compressed knot behind my breastbone. I clear a throat suddenly thick with unshed grief, for the loss of Dani, for Dageus, for the way things turned out. I wish I'd been able to say these things before I chased her through the portal. "I love you," I tell Jada, hoping somehow my Dani hears me. "I always will."

"Irrelevant and maudlin. I asked you a question. Answer it."

"Yes. She could have anticipated the Hag's movements better," I say flatly. "Dani has a fire you lack. Her gut instincts are flawless, she is brilliant."

Jada's eyes narrow and her nostrils flare. "I'm flawless. I'm brilliant."

"Give me my spear."

She cocks her head as if holding an internal debate, then slips the cuff of Cruce from her arm and holds it in the general direction of my voice. "Logic dictates a different course."

Oh no, it doesn't. Logic dictates she keeps both. Not give away something she isn't required to relinquish. Interesting.

"Take the cuff," Jada insists. "It makes sense."

"How does letting you keep *my* spear make sense?"

Emerald eyes bore into the space where I stand, as if she's trying to hammer me into her desired shape with the sheer intensity and implacability of her gaze. "I kill. It's what I do. It's who I am. It's who I've always been. I will never change. Stay out of my way. Or your free passage will be rescinded."

The cuff tinkles to the cobbled pavement at my feet.

Jada is gone.

39

"What are you waiting for?" the Seelie Queen demands, trying but failing to conceal her fear behind an imperious facade. "Seal our pact and attend Dublin."

She dreads kissing him.

Once, she couldn't kiss him enough.

The Unseelie King completes the complex process of reducing himself, compressing fragments into various, new human forms those who live in Dublin have not seen him wearing.

He never attends a world twice in the same human bodies once they've been identified. Humans recall him, bring petitions, crucify him with incessant, foolish demands. *Give us laws, chisel them in stone, tell us how to live!*

Absurd, floundering humanity, spreading from planet to planet like a plague, colonizing the stars, he finds it astounding how long they have managed to persist.

Once, he told them the truth.

Chiseled a single commandment upon a slab of stone: *That* is *how to live: in the choosing. There are no rules but those you make for yourself.*

The man to whom he'd entrusted the tablet promptly shattered it, chiseled ten precise commands upon two stone slabs and carried them down a mountain with the pomp and circumstance of a prophet.

Religious wars ravaged that world ever since.

It is possible that day, those tablets, are why he feels an unwelcome twinge of responsibility for that planet. He should never have chiseled.

He shakes off his brood and looks down at the concubine. He made himself taller and wider than she, and is now appropriate for her size, sporting the same visage he wore the day they met, nearly a million years ago.

She recalls no detail of their time together. He remembers enough for both of them. He wears the same attire.

He pushes open her cloak, closes his hands on her waist, and transports them through space and time to another location where he swiftly erects barricades and walls and seals off the prison in which he will leave her while he pretends to try to save a world beyond saving.

He inhales deeply of memory-residue on the air, the scent of sex on skin, of wings glossed with sweat, of sheets damp with passion. He has not been here in a long time.

Once their boudoir of light and shadows, of fire and ice, was the only place he wanted to be.

Till the day he found her dead inside their sacred place and madness claimed him.

Against a frosted crystalline wall, the white half of the chamber features a round bed on a diamond-crusted dais, draped in silks and snowy ermine throws. Fragrant ivory petals are scattered across the furs, perfuming the air. The floor is covered with plush white carpets before an enormous alabaster hearth filled with white and gold logs from which dazzlingly bright flames pop and crackle. Thousands of tiny diamond-bright lights float lazily on the air, twinkling. Her half is bright, joyous, a sunny day at high altitudes, the ceiling of her chamber a brilliant blue sky.

He turns his head and looks beyond the enormous gilt-framed mirror, the first Silver he ever created.

His chamber is the size of a human sports arena, draped in black velvet and furs, filled with darkly spiced ebony petals. Between sheer slabs of dark ice, a bed stretches. On one wall, a blue-black fire sends exotic flames licking up to the ceiling where they terminate in dark stars amid fantastic nebulae shimmering with blue vapors.

For a moment he sees her there, on his bed, falling back on the dark, glossy furs, laughing, dusky ice frosting her hair, a handful of velvety petals fluttering down to land on her bare breasts.

Sorrow fills him.

He had so many ambitions.

She had but one.

To love.

"What is this place? Why have you brought me here?" she demands.

He doesn't tell her it is here he spent the finest hours of his existence.

He will leave her soon, trapped in the memory-residue of the place, a spider in a web sticky with his love.

Here, she will watch them. Laugh and dream and fuck and create. Here, she will taste their passion, know their joy.

If, after seeing it, she still insists upon her freedom, he may consider granting it. May consider her lost to him forever.

But most likely not.

He does not tell her any of that.

She inhales sharply. "You would let me go?"

"Finest hours," he says. "You must have heard that part, too."

"I heard also that you believe this world you claim you can save is doomed."

He does not answer, merely stands, enjoying the warmth of her body near his, the sweetness of her breath on his face.

She disparages, "You would deceive me for a single kiss."

"I would raze worlds for a single kiss."

"Try saving one, for far more than that."

"The fabric of their Universe is damaged. Without the song, it is not possible."

She says, "You are the Unseelie King. You will find a way."

"That sounds suspiciously like faith in me," he mocks.

"You see faith where only a challenge has been issued. Will you fail?"

He lowers his head again, until their lips are nearly touching. "Kiss me as if you remember me. Inspire this wild god as once you did. Incite poetry and fire with your passion and perhaps I'll find a way."

She looks up at him and shivers, then places her small, lovely hands on his face and it's his turn to shudder. She's touching him. Of her own volition. Music dances on his skin, translating from her palms into his very being. A stolen touch can never compete with a voluntary touch of hunger, passion, desire. The aria of choice is joyous, the cacophony of force brutal, ugly, and cold.

She kisses him reluctantly, barely brushing her warm lips to his icy ones.

This time, unlike so many others, he doesn't take charge, or seek to deepen the kiss. Merely stands after the agony of half a million years of grieving this woman, basking in his first moment free of pain. Breathes it, inhales it, allows the particles of his being the chance to become for a single glorious moment something other than drawn in tightly upon himself in a frozen, eternal shudder of denial and crushing loss. Regret is poison that kills the soul.

She cries out against his lips, draws back and looks up at him. "Such grief! It is too much. I cannot endure it!"

"If you believe nothing else I tell you, my queen, believe my pain. Consider the cause."

Then he is gone.

40

"There's a beast and I let it run"

MAC

Five days later, a full eight days since Barrons was killed on the top of the mountain, he's still not back and I'm edgy as hell and only a minor part of it is due to being in the full throes of Unseelie-flesh withdrawal. The fact that I know he always comes back doesn't mean I can't still think of a gazillion reasons to worry.

I don't know where the Nine are "reborn." I don't know how far away it is. I don't even know if it's on this planet. What if he gets stuck in an IFP? What if he tries to hurry, risks taking a plane and encounters a black hole? Would it kill him again and he'd be reborn, or like K'Vruck, does this strange new Fae-fabricated development on our world possess the ability to really, truly kill him?

In the past, it's taken him as few as four days to return. However, it took him nearly a month to make it back to Dublin after Ryodan and I killed him on that cliff in Faery. It's the second time he's died on a cliff. I make a mental note to avoid cliffs with Barrons in the future.

I won't survive another three weeks. I'm driving myself crazy.

I'm still invisible and beginning to feel like the real emotional and mental me is getting sketchy around the edges, with no one to see me, and no reflection in the mirror. I've begun to worry I might fade entirely away.

I don't have the heart to visit my parents and try to explain why I'm invisible.

The Book still hasn't stirred once, not since the day it made me vanish, which continues to freak me out. I've begun to wonder if something happened to it. Surely it doesn't plan to leave me invisible forever. While I love the power and safety from my enemies it confers, I'm getting a little tired of looking in the mirror and seeing nothing. I like seeing me. I like Barrons seeing me, watching his dark eyes get heavy-lidded and hot with desire.

I can't put on makeup. I tried to blow my hair dry a few days ago and succeeded only in scorching my eyebrows and drying out my eyes. It's been weeks since I did my nails. I can't even see them to take the polish off. Yesterday I was struck by a sudden fear I was going to get fat and wouldn't even know it. I had to dash out and find a scale in a nearby house and weigh myself. Unfortunately, every time I stepped on it, I turned the scale invisible, too. You don't realize how reassuring it is to see yourself every day until you can't anymore. Last night, while pacing the bookstore, I found a book called *The Invisible Man* and decided to read it to see how he handled things, but I couldn't bear the suspense of his struggles so I skipped to the end.

Then I tossed the freaking book across the room.

Oh, yeah, don't want to stay this way forever.

I've taken to haunting Chester's at least once, sometimes twice, a day looking for Ryodan, eavesdropping for word of Barrons, but I haven't caught a glimpse of the owner of Chester's since two nights ago when he brought the Highlander's body back. What little of it he was able to recover. Last time I was there, it appeared Fade was running the club.

The Keltar returned to Scotland the moment they had Dageus's remains, taking Christian with them, and I'd finally seen the elusive Colleen—that was a woman I was looking forward to meeting again, under better circumstances—to hold a High Druid burial with all the living Keltar in attendance. I'd stood watching as they left, hearing mournful bagpipes in my head, tempted to attend, unwilling to leave my city and miss Barrons's return.

Five days and four long silent nights in the bookstore. I don't sleep in our lair beneath the garage when he's not here. It makes me feel small and alone. I've been tossing restlessly on the chesterfield, waiting for the bell to tinkle.

I fidget with the cuff I slipped on my wrist shortly after Jada dropped it. At least now neither Seelie nor Unseelie can harm me. If Cruce is to be believed.

On the topic of Cruce, I wonder what's happening at the abbey, if Jada really has been able to stop the transformation of our mother house, and if she was the one that closed the doors to the cavern where he's imprisoned. I wonder what things she learned, lost in the Silvers for five and a half years. I'd head out there to see for myself but am currently obsessed with remaining close to the bookstore. In a few more days I might get resigned to the waiting and go take a look around.

The moment Jada had my spear she went on a killing spree. The next day the *Dublin Daily* reported hundreds of Fae dead.

And the next.

And the next.

I suspect she was making up for her failure to protect the Highlander.

Jada wasn't lying. She certainly does kill.

Eavesdropping at Chester's yesterday, I heard Fae have begun projecting glamour again, concealing their otherworldliness, in an effort to blend with humans, elude Jada's lethal spear.

Which makes *sidhe*-seers even more critical now.

I blow out a frustrated breath. I haven't been by Chester's since last night. Time for my rounds. "Come on, Barrons," I mutter. "Get your ass back here." I leave a note on the table by the couch in case he returns and bang out the door into the night.

I slip into Chester's when a group of drunken revelers stumble out. I pause a moment at the balustrade, looking down over the many subclubs, but see no sign of Ryodan. I don't bother looking for Barrons. I know he'd return to the bookstore, to me, before he went anywhere else.

There's Jo, looking dainty and pretty, hair spiky and tousled around her face, waitressing in the short tartan skirt, baby doll pumps, and crisp white blouse uniform of the kiddie subclub. I'm glad to see she didn't let Ryodan drive her away.

Sean O'Bannion sits with four big, tough-looking men, heads close together, talking quietly at the Sinatra bar. I wonder if Kat's back from wherever she went, if she's okay, if they're still together.

Over by the stairs are Lor and another of the Nine I've not seen before, tall, dark, cute as hell, and hot in a Jason Statham way, with a full dark shadow beard and intense eyes. I smile faintly when Lor's gaze repeatedly sweeps the many clubs, to linger on Jo. His mouth changes when he watches her. I know that look. He's thinking about fucking.

Barrons. God. I need that man to come back.

Fade is patrolling, watching everything, ready for the slightest disturbance.

I slip down the stairs and head across the club, walk slowly and carefully between Lor and the Jason Statham bouncer so as not to create the slightest breeze, and hurry up the chrome staircase to the private floors.

I'm not leaving tonight without snooping a bit. If I set off an alarm, so be it. I'm restless, bored, and invisible. A dangerous thing for any woman to be.

I ponder what I most want to see: the mysterious sex club the Nine are rumored to have? Nope. It would just get my already twisted, neglected panties in a worse twist. Try to find their private residences? Hmmm. That might be interesting. Steal Ryodan's dark blade so I could control Papa Roach?

Wow. I'm stilled by the marvelous thought.

If he's in there, I'll just pretend I was looking for him to ask if he'd seen Barrons yet.

Ditto, if one of the others is in there.

I can't believe I didn't think of this before! All weapons, good.

I head straight for his office, peer up and down the hallway to make sure no one's looking, press my hand to the panel and slip inside.

It's empty.

Just me and Ryodan's high-tech, two-way glass headquarters lined with gadgets, and high at the perimeter those countless hi-def cameras upon which he watches the sordid and varied details of his club. The arrogance of the man, thinking his bouncers at the bottom of the stairs guarantee sufficient security.

I head straight for his desk. The knife is no longer there. Like the office, it too is empty. I stand, looking around, trying to spot it, then fiddle with the bottom of his desk to open the hidden panel where he'd stored Jada's contract, deciding he probably put it away for safekeeping.

When the panel slides out, I'm disappointed to find it empty. I move around to the other side of his desk and drop down into his chair, trying to think like him, decide where I would put it if I were Ryodan.

I consider the hidden panel. If I were him, I'd have a panel on this side of the desk, too. I reach beneath the drawer, groping for anomalies in the smooth wood.

There are none. I press gingerly, walking my fingers gently around on the bottom of the desk, down the legs, around the many carvings.

Got it!

A tiny notch in the center of an ornate scroll.

When the second panel slides out, I'm once again disappointed. No knife. Just rows and rows of square black buttons like those on a computer keyboard. None of them are labeled. Just smooth black buttons. I have no clue what they're for.

I poise a finger above one of them, debating. Knowing Ryodan, I could inadvertently blow the whole club if I push the wrong one.

I sigh. Surely not. Surely he'd make it red if it was the destruct button, right?

Holding my breath, I poke the first one on the left.

Nothing happens.

I glance around the office quickly to see if some other hidden panel suddenly slid silently out. As far as I see, nothing has changed. I punch the one next to it.

Again nothing.

I punch four more in quick succession.

Not a damn thing. What the hell are these buttons for?

I blow out an exasperated breath, lean back in his

chair, prop my feet on the desk, fold my arms behind my head and close my eyes, imagining I'm him, trying to fathom what he might want so close at hand.

I pretend I'm Ryodan, sitting in his office, where he watches the world on his monitors, where he receives reconnaissance, where he controls and nudges the fine details of his kingdom.

Still stymied, I open my eyes and stare around the room.

The monitors. Holy cow. There must be places in his club he likes to keep tabs on that he prefers no one else see.

I kick my boots off the desk and sit up straight. This time when I begin punching buttons, I keep a close eye on the screens on the wall directly in front of me.

Aha! Just as I thought, these control his private cameras! The ones that monitor places visitors don't get to see.

The first one on the left makes the image of the main stairs speckle out on the seventh screen from the right and reveals their kitchens.

Oops, guess he knows I was regularly raiding them while I stayed here.

A white-haired man with burning eyes stands at the counter, eating . . . oh, no. I didn't want to see that. I punch it off hastily.

The second button wipes out a shot of the kiddie sub-club (apparently he liked to keep an eye on Jo) to reveal a dark, shadowy room, ornately paneled with a lovely transom ceiling. It's empty.

I keep my eyes trained on the cameras at the ceiling in front of his desk. The third button causes the live feed of the Sinatra subclub to vanish, replacing it with an overhead shot of a state-of-the-art gym, paneled with mirrors.

Kasteo is stretched out on a weight bench, pumping

iron, massive muscles rippling as he does deep, wide flies. He's bare-chested and as heavily scarred as the others.

To his left, nearly lost in shadow, a woman lies, similarly supine, mimicking his movements with smaller dumbbells.

I gasp, and push slowly to my feet. I don't believe my eyes. I hurry around the desk and stand directly beneath the monitor a few feet above my head. "Kat?" I exclaim softly. "Kat is working out with Kasteo? What the hell?" Is she here of her own choice? Did Kasteo abduct her? Did Ryodan lock her away with him? He'd pretended not to have any idea where the missing headmistress had gone!

I watch for a few moments then hurry back around the desk. I want to know everything. This is unbelievable.

I punch the next button. A shot of the balustrade at the entry vanishes and I see a long shadowy corridor. Lor is stalking down it, and I wonder where he's going in such a hurry. I lose him and punch the next button. As I'd hoped, I'm able to follow him down the hallway. I punch three more buttons tracking him through what I realize must be the servers' wing. When I punch the fifth, I gasp again as Lor reaches out, grabs Jo from behind and spins her around. I see their mouths moving, she's angry, he's pissed, too, but I can't hear a word. I study the panel irritably, feeling cheated by my reality TV, trying to locate a volume button but no such luck. When I glance back up, Lor has Jo turned around, facing the wall, shoved against it. He's holding both her hands in one of his, trapped against the cool glass surface.

I can see her profile. She's not angry anymore. She's turned on as hell.

With his other hand he undoes his belt, shoves her short skirt up, and before I can give them the privacy the moment demands, he's up against her, pushing inside her.

Her back arches, head drops back, and the look on her face is—

"Just as I suspected, everybody is having sex but me," I mutter irritably.

I punch the screen off and hurry to the next one.

And stare blankly at the screen for a long, pained moment.

"No," I finally manage to say. "He would *not* come back here first. He would come to me."

But he wouldn't. And he didn't.

Barrons is back.

Standing in a room I can't place, a deep gash of a stone chamber. I think, Please tell me it's not the sex club I've heard so many rumors about. Please tell me I'm enough.

Ryodan moves into view.

Where are they? What are they doing? Why didn't Barrons come to me, tell me he was back?

I watch the screen, never taking my eyes from it. Minutes creep by and nothing changes. They don't even appear to be talking. Just watching something.

I shake myself from my trance and punch the next button.

The Rhino-boy club disappears, revealing another dimly lit stone room.

A shadow moves in the darkness.

What the hell is down there?

What are they watching?

The thing separates from the shadows, stumbles toward the light, cringes and stumbles back again.

I suddenly can't find enough oxygen in Ryodan's office to breathe.

My hand flies to my mouth as I stare, staggered.

Dageus MacKeltar is not dead.

PEOPLE

SIDHE-SEERS

SIDHE-SEER **(SHEE**-SEER**)**: *A person on whom Fae magic doesn't work, capable of seeing past the illusions or "glamour" cast by the Fae to the true nature that lies beneath. Some can also see Tabh'rs, hidden portals between realms. Others can sense Seelie and Unseelie objects of power. Each sidhe-seer is different, with varying degrees of resistance to the Fae. Some are limited; some are advanced, with multiple "special powers." For thousands of years, the sidhe-seers protected humans from the Fae that slipped through on pagan feast days when the veils grew thin, to run the Wild Hunt and prey on humans.*

MACKAYLA LANE **(O'CONNOR)**: Main character, female, twenty-three, adopted daughter of Jack and Rainey Lane, biological daughter of Isla O'Connor. Blond hair, green eyes, had an idyllic, sheltered childhood in the Deep South. When her biological sister, Alina, was murdered and the Garda swiftly closed the case with no leads, Mac quit her job bartending and headed for Dublin to search for Alina's killer herself. Shortly after her arrival she met Jericho Barrons and began reluctantly working with him toward common goals. Among her many skills and talents, Mac can track objects of power created by the Fae, including the ancient, sentient, psychopathic book of magic known as the *Sinsar Dubh*. At the end of *Shadowfever* we learn that twenty years before, when the *Sinsar Dubh* escaped its prison beneath the abbey, it briefly possessed Mac's mother and imprinted a complete copy of itself in the unprotected fetus. Although Mac succeeds in reinterring the dangerous book, her victory is simultaneous with the discovery that there are two copies of it, she *is* one of them and she will never be free from the temptation to use her limitless, deadly power.

ALINA LANE (O'CONNOR): Female, deceased, older sister to MacKayla Lane. At twenty-four went to Dublin to study at Trinity College and discovered she was a *sidhe*-seer. Became lovers with the Lord Master, also known as Darroc, an ex-Fae stripped of his immortality by Queen Aoibheal for attempting to overthrow her reign. Alina was killed by Rowena, who magically forced Dani O'Malley to trap her in an alley with a pair of deadly Unseelie.

DANIELLE "THE MEGA" O'MALLEY: Main character. An enormously gifted, genetically mutated *sidhe*-seer with an extremely high IQ, super strength, speed, and sass. She was abused and manipulated by Rowena from a young age, molded into the old woman's personal assassin, and forced to kill Mac's sister, Alina. Despite the darkness and trauma of her childhood, Dani is eternally optimistic and determined to survive and have her fair share of life plus some. In *Shadowfever*, Mac discovers Dani killed her sister, and the two, once as close as sisters, are now bitterly estranged.

ROWENA O'REILLY: Grand Mistress of the *sidhe*-seer organization until her death in *Shadowfever*. Governed the six major Irish *sidhe*-seer bloodlines but rather than training them, controlled and diminished them. Fiercely power-hungry, manipulative, and narcissistic, she was seduced by the *Sinsar Dubh* into freeing it. She ate Fae flesh to enhance her strength and talent, and kept a lesser Fae locked beneath the abbey. Dabbling in dangerous black arts, she experimented on many of the *sidhe*-seers in her care, most notably Danielle O'Malley. In *Shadowfever* she is possessed by the *Sinsar Dubh* and used to seduce Mac with the illusion of parents she never had, in an effort to get her to turn over the only illusion amulet capable of deceiving even the Unseelie King. Mac sees through the seduction and kills Rowena.

ISLA O'CONNOR: Mac's biological mother. Twenty-some years ago Isla was the leader of the Haven, one of seven trusted advisors to the Grand Mistress in the sacred, innermost circle of *sidhe*-seers at Arlington Abbey. Rowena (the Grand Mistress) wanted her daughter, Kayleigh O'Reilly, to be the Haven leader, and was furious when the women selected Isla instead. Isla was the only member of the Haven who survived the night the *Sinsar Dubh* escaped its prison beneath the abbey. She was briefly possessed by the Dark Book but not turned into a lethal, sadistic killing machine. In the chaos at the abbey, Isla was stabbed and badly injured. Barrons tells Mac he visited Isla's grave five days after she left the abbey, that she was cremated. Barrons says he discovered Isla had only one daughter. He later tells Mac it is conceivable Isla could have been pregnant the one night he saw her and a child might have survived given proper premature birth care. He also says it is conceivable Isla didn't die, but lived to bear another child (Mac) and give her up. Barrons theorizes Isla was spared because the sentient evil of the *Sinsar Dubh* imprinted itself on her unprotected fetus, made a complete second copy of itself inside the unborn Mac and deliberately released her. It is believed Isla died after having Mac and arranging for her friend Tellie to have both her daughters smuggled from Ireland and adopted in the States, forbidden ever to return to Ireland.

AUGUSTA O'CLARE: Tellie Sullivan's grandmother. Barrons took Isla O'Connor to her house the night the *Sinsar Dubh* escaped its prison beneath Arlington Abbey over twenty years ago.

KAYLEIGH O'REILLY: Rowena's daughter, Nana's granddaughter, best friend of Isla O'Connor. She was killed twenty-some years ago, the night the *Sinsar Dubh* escaped the abbey.

NANA O'REILLY: Rowena's mother, Kayleigh's grandmother. Old woman living alone by the sea, prone to nodding off in the middle of a sentence. She despised Rowena, saw her for what she was and was at the abbey the night the *Sinsar Dubh* escaped more than twenty years ago. Though many have questioned her, none have ever gotten the full story of what happened that night.

KATARINA (KAT) McLAUGHLIN (McLOUGHLIN): Daughter of a notorious crime family in Dublin, her gift is extreme empathy. She feels the pain of the world, all the emotions people work so hard to hide. Considered useless and a complete failure by her family, she was sent to the abbey at a young age, where Rowena manipulated and belittled her until she became afraid of her strengths and impeded by fear. Levelheaded, highly compassionate, with serene gray eyes that mask her constant inner turmoil, she wants desperately to learn to be a good leader and help the other *sidhe*-seers. She turned her back on her family mafia business to pursue a more scrupulous life. When Rowena was killed, Kat was coerced into becoming the next Grand Mistress, a position she has felt completely unfit for. Although imprisoned beneath the abbey, Cruce is still able to project a glamour of himself, and in dreams he seduces Kat nightly, shaming her and making her feel unfit to rule, or be loved by her longtime sweetheart Sean O'Bannion. Kat has a genuinely pure heart and pure motives but lacks the strength, discipline, and belief in herself to lead.

Jo Brennan: Midtwenties, petite, with delicate features and short, spiky dark hair, she descends from one of the six famous Irish bloodlines that can see the Fae (O'Connor, O'Reilly, Brennan, the McLaughlin or McLoughlin, O'Malley, and the Kennedy). Her special talent is eidetic or sticky memory for facts but unfortunately by her midtwenties she has so many facts in her head, she can rarely find the ones she needs. She has never been able to perfect a mental filing system. When Kat clandestinely dispatches her to get a job at Chester's so they can spy on the Nine, Jo allows herself to be coerced into taking a waitressing job at the nightclub by the immortal owner, Ryodan, and when he gives her his famous nod, inviting her to his bed, she's unable to resist even though she knows it's destined for an epic fail.

Patrona O'Connor: Mac's biological grandmother. Little is known of her to date.

THE NINE

Little is known about them. They are immortals who were long ago cursed to live forever and be reborn every time they die at precisely the same unknown geographic location. They have an alternate beast form that is savage, bloodthirsty, and atavistically superior. It is believed they were originally human from the planet Earth but that is unconfirmed. There were originally ten, counting Barrons's young son. The known names they currently go by are Jericho Barrons, Ryodan, Lor, Kasteo, Fade. In Burned *we discover one is named Daku. There's a rumor that one of the Nine is a woman.*

JERICHO BARRONS: Main character. One of a group of immortals who reside in Dublin, many of them at Chester's nightclub, and is their recognized leader, although Ryodan issues and enforces most of Barrons's orders. Six feet three inches tall, black hair, brown eyes, two hundred forty-five pounds, date of birth October 31, allegedly thirty-one years old, his middle initial is Z, which stands for Zigor, meaning either "the punished" or "the punisher" depending on dialect. He is adept in magic, a powerful warder, fluent in the druid art of Voice, an avid collector of antiquities and supercars. He despises words, believes in being judged by one's actions alone. No one knows how long the Nine have been alive, but references seem to indicate in excess of ten thousand years. If Barrons is killed, he is reborn at an unknown location precisely the same as he was the first time he died. Like all of the Nine, Barrons has an animal form, a skin he can don at will, or if pushed. Barrons had a son who was also immortal, but at some point in the distant past, shortly after Barrons and his men were cursed to become what they are, the child was brutally tortured and became a permanent, psychotic version of the beast. Barrons kept him caged below his garage while he searched for a way to free him, hence his quest to obtain the most powerful book of magic ever created, the *Sinsar Dubh*. He was seeking a way to end his son's suffering. In *Shadowfever,* Mac helps him lay his son to final rest by using the ancient Hunter, K'Vruck, to kill him.

RYODAN: Main character. Six feet four, two hundred thirty-five pounds, lean and cut, with silver eyes and dark hair nearly shaved at the sides, he has a taste for expensive clothing and toys. He has scars on his arms and a large, thick one that runs from his chest up to his jaw. Owner of Chester's and the brains behind the Nine's business empire, he manages the daily aspects of their existence. Each time the Nine have been visible in the past, he was king, ruler, pagan god, or dictator. Barrons is the silent command behind the Nine, Ryodan is the voice. Barrons is animalistic and primeval, Ryodan is urbane and professional. Highly sexual, he likes sex for breakfast and eats early and often.

LOR: Six feet two inches, two hundred twenty pounds, blond, green eyes, with strong Nordic features, he promotes himself as a caveman and likes it that way. Heavily muscled and scarred. Lor's life is a constant party. He loves music, hot blondes, and likes to chain his women to his bed so he can take his time with them, willing to play virtually any role in bed for sheer love of the sport. Long ago, however, he was called the Bone-crusher, feared and reviled throughout the Old World.

KASTEO: Tall, dark, scarred, and tattooed, with short, dark, nearly shaved hair, he hasn't spoken to anyone in a thousand years. There is a rumor floating around that others of the Nine killed the woman he loved.

FADE: Not much is known about him to date. During events in *Shadowfever* the *Sinsar Dubh* possessed him briefly and used him to kill Barrons and Ryodan then threaten Mac. Tall, heavily muscled, and scarred like the rest of the Nine.

FAE

Also known as the Tuatha De Danann or Tuatha De (TUA day dhanna or Tua DAY). An advanced race of otherworldly creatures that possess enormous powers of magic and illusion. After war destroyed their own world, they colonized Earth, settling on the shores of Ireland in a cloud of fog and light. Originally the Fae were united and there were only the Seelie, but the Seelie King left the Queen and created his own court when she refused to use the Song of Making to grant his concubine immortality. He became the Unseelie King and created a dark, mirror image court of Fae castes. While the Seelie are golden, shining, and beautiful, the Unseelie, with the exception of royalty, are dark-haired and -skinned, misshapen, hideous abominations with sadistic, insatiable desires. Both Seelie and Unseelie have four royal houses of princes and princesses that are sexually addictive and highly lethal to humans.

UNSEELIE

UNSEELIE KING: The most ancient of the Fae, no one knows where he came from or when he first appeared. The Seelie don't recall a time the king didn't exist and, despite the court's matriarchal nature, the king predates the queen and is the most complex and powerful of all the Fae—lacking a single enormous power that makes him the Seelie Queen's lesser: she alone can use the Song of Making, which can call new matter into being. The king can create only from matter that already exists, sculpting galaxies and universes, even on occasion arranging matter so that life springs from it. Countless worlds call him God. His view of the universe is so enormous and complicated by a vision that sees and weighs every detail, every possibility, that his vast intellect is virtually inaccessible. In order to communicate with humans he has to reduce himself into multiple human parts. When he walks in the mortal realm, he does so as one of these human "skins." He never wears the same skins twice after his involvement in a specific mortal episode is through.

DREAMY-EYED GUY: (aka DEG, see also Unseelie King) The Unseelie King is too enormous and complex to exist in human form unless he divides himself into multiple "skins." The Dreamy-Eyed Guy is one of the Unseelie King's many human forms and first appeared in *Darkfever* when Mac was searching a local museum for objects of power. Mac later encounters him at Trinity College in the Ancient Languages Department, where he works with Christian MacKeltar, and frequently thereafter when he takes a job bartending at Chester's after the walls fall. Enigma shrouded in mystery, he imparts cryptic bits of useful information. Mac doesn't know the DEG is a part of the Unseelie King until she and the others are reinterring the *Sinsar Dubh* beneath Arlington Abbey and all of the king's skins arrive to coalesce into a single entity.

CONCUBINE: (originally human, now Fae, see also Aoibheal, Seelie Queen, Unseelie King, Cruce) The Unseelie King's mortal lover and unwitting cause of endless war and suffering. When the king fell in love with her, he asked the Seelie Queen to use the Song of Making to make her Fae and immortal, but the queen refused. Incensed, the Seelie King left Faery, established his own icy realm, and became the dark, forbidding Unseelie King. After building his concubine the magnificent shining White Mansion inside the Silvers where she would never age so long as she didn't leave its labyrinthine walls, he vowed to re-create the Song of Making, and spent eons experimenting in his laboratory while his concubine waited. The Unseelie Court was the result of his efforts: dark, ravenous, and lethal, fashioned from an imperfect Song of Making. In *Shadowfever*, the king discovers his concubine isn't dead as he has believed for over half a million years. Unfortunately, the cup from the Cauldron of Forgetting that Cruce forced upon the concubine destroyed her mind and she doesn't retain a single memory of the king or their love. It is as if a complete stranger wears her skin.

CRUCE: (Unseelie, but has masqueraded for over half a million years as the Seelie Prince V'Lane) Powerful, sifting, lethally sexual Fae. Believes himself to be the last and finest Unseelie Prince the king created. Cruce was given special privileges at the dark court, working beside his liege to perfect the Song of Making. He was the only Fae ever allowed to enter the White Mansion, so he might carry the king's experimental potions to the concubine while the king continued with his work. Over time, Cruce grew jealous of the king, coveted his concubine and kingdom, and plotted to take it from him. Cruce resented that the king kept his dark court secret from the Seelie Queen and wanted the dark and light courts to be joined into one, which he then planned to rule himself. He petitioned the king to go to the Seelie Court and present his "children" but the king refused, knowing the queen would only subject his imperfect creations to endless torture and humiliation. Angry that the king would not fight for them, Cruce went to the Seelie Queen himself and told her of the dark court. Incensed at the king's betrayal and quest for power that was matriarchal, the queen locked Cruce away in her bower and summoned the king. With the help of the illusion amulets Cruce and the king had created, Cruce wove the glamour that he was the Seelie Prince, V'lane. Furious to learn the king had disobeyed her, and jealous of his love for the concubine, the queen summoned Cruce (who was actually her own prince, V'lane) and killed him with the sword of light to show the king what she would do to all his abominations. Enraged, the king stormed the Seelie Court with his dark Fae and killed the queen. When he went home to his icy realm, grieving the loss of his trusted and much-loved prince Cruce, he found his concubine was also dead. She'd left him a note saying she'd killed herself to escape what he'd become. Unknown to the king, while he'd fought with the Seelie Queen, Cruce slipped back to the White Mansion and gave the concubine another "potion," which was actually a cup stolen from the Cauldron of Forgetting. After erasing her memory, he used the power of the three lesser illusion amulets to convince the king she was dead. He took her away and assumed the role of V'lane, in love with a mortal at the Seelie Court, biding time to usurp the rule of their race, both light and dark courts. As V'lane, he approached MacKayla Lane and was using her to locate the *Sinsar Dubh*. Once he had it, he planned to acquire all the Unseelie King's forbidden dark knowledge, finally kill the concubine who had become the current queen and, as the only vessel holding both the patriarchal and matriarchal power of their race, become the next, most powerful, Unseelie King ever to rule. At the end of *Shadowfever,* when the *Sinsar Dubh* is reinterred beneath the abbey, he reveals himself as Cruce and absorbs all the forbidden magic from the king's Dark Book. But before Cruce can kill the current queen and become the ruler of both light and dark courts, the Unseelie King imprisons him in a cage of ice beneath Arlington Abbey.

UNSEELIE PRINCES: Highly sexual, insatiable, dark counterpart to the golden Seelie Princes. Long blue-black hair, leanly muscled dark-skinned bodies tattooed with brilliant complicated patterns that rush beneath their skin like kaleidoscopic storm clouds. They wear black torques like liquid darkness around their necks. They have the starved cruelty and arrogance of a human sociopath. There are four royal princes: Kiall, Rath, Cruce, and an unnamed prince slain by Danielle O'Malley in *Dreamfever*. In the way of Fae things, when one royal is killed, another becomes, and Christian MacKeltar is swiftly becoming the next Unseelie Prince.

UNSEELIE PRINCESSES: The princesses have not been heard of and were presumed dead until recent events brought to light that one or more were hidden away by the Unseelie King either in punishment or to contain a power he didn't want loose in the world. At least one of them was locked in the king's library inside the White Mansion until either Dani or Christian MacKeltar freed her. Highly sexual, a powerful sifter, this princess is stunningly beautiful with long black hair, pale skin, and blue eyes. In *Burned* we learn the Sweeper tinkered with the Unseelie Princess(es) and changed her (them) somehow. Unlike the Unseelie Princes who are prone to mindless savagery, the princess is quite rational about her desires, and logically focused on short-term sacrifice for long-term gain. It is unknown what her end goal is but, as with all Fae, it involves power.

ROYAL HUNTERS: A caste of Unseelie sifters, first introduced in *The Immortal Highlander*, this caste hunts for both the king and the queen, relentlessly tracking their prey. Tall, leathery skinned, with wings, they are feared by all Fae.

CRIMSON HAG: One of the Unseelie King's earliest creations, Dani O'Malley inadvertently freed this monster from a stoppered bottle at the king's fantastical library inside the White Mansion. Psychopathically driven to complete her unfinished, tattered gown of guts, she captures and kills anything in her path, using insectile, lancelike legs to slay her prey and disembowel them. She then perches nearby and knits their entrails into the ragged hem of her blood-red dress. They tend to rot as quickly as they're stitched, necessitating an endless, futile hunt for more. Rumor is, the Hag once held two Unseelie Princes captive, killing them over and over for nearly one hundred thousand years before the Unseelie King stopped her. She reeks of the stench of rotting meat, has matted, blood-drenched hair, an ice white face with black eye sockets, a thin gash of a mouth, and crimson fangs. Her upper body is lovely and voluptuous, encased in a gruesome corset of bone and sinew. She prefers to abduct Unseelie Princes because they are immortal and afford an unending supply of guts, as they regenerate each time she kills them. In *Iced*, she kills Barrons and Ryodan then captures Christian MacKeltar (the latest Unseelie Prince) and carries him off.

FEAR DORCHA: One of the Unseelie King's earliest creations, this seven-foot-tall, gaunt Unseelie wears a dark pinstriped tailcoat suit that is at least a century out of date and has no face. Beneath an elegant, cobwebbed black top hat is a swirling black tornado with various bits of features that occasionally materialize. Like all the Unseelie, created imperfectly from an imperfect Song of Making, he is pathologically driven to achieve what he lacks—a face and identity—by stealing faces and identities from humans. The Fear Dorcha was once the Unseelie King's personal assassin and traveling companion during his liege's time of madness after the concubine's death. In *Fever Moon,* the Fear Dorcha is defeated by Mac when she steals his top hat, but it is unknown if the Dorcha is actually deceased.

HOAR FROST KING (GH'LUK-RA D'J'HAI): (aka HFK) Villain introduced in *Iced,* responsible for turning Dublin into a frigid, arctic wasteland. This Unseelie is one of the most complex and powerful the king ever created, capable of opening holes in space-time to travel, similar to the Seelie ability to sift but with catastrophic results for the matter it manipulates. The Hoar Frost King is the only Unseelie aware of its fundamental imperfection on a quantum level, and like the king, was attempting to re-create the Song of Making to fix itself by collecting the necessary frequencies, physically removing them from the fabric of reality. Each place the Hoar Frost King fed, it stripped necessary structure from the universe while regurgitating a minute mass of enormous density, like a cat vomiting cosmic bones after eating a quantum bird. Although the HFK was destroyed in *Iced* by Dani, Dancer, and Ryodan, the holes it left in the fabric of the human world can only be fixed with the Song of Making.

GRAY MAN: Tall, monstrous, leprous, capable of sifting, he feeds by stealing beauty from human women. He projects the glamour of a devastatingly attractive human man. He is lethal but prefers his victims left hideously disfigured and alive to suffer. In *Darkfever,* Barrons stabs and kills the Gray Man with Mac's spear.

GRAY WOMAN: The Gray Man's female counterpart, nine feet tall, she projects the glamour of a stunningly beautiful woman and lures human men to their death. Gaunt, emaciated to the point of starvation, her face is long and narrow. Her mouth consumes the entire lower half of her face. She has two rows of sharklike teeth but prefers to feed by caressing her victims, drawing their beauty and vitality out through open sores on her grotesque hands. If she wants to kill in a hurry, she clamps her hands onto human flesh, creating an unbreakable suction. Unlike the Gray Man, she usually quickly kills her victims. In *Shadowfever*, she breaks pattern and preys upon Dani, in retaliation against Mac and Barrons for killing the Gray Man, her lover. Mac makes an unholy pact with her to save Dani.

RHINO-BOYS: Ugly gray-skinned creatures that resemble rhinoceroses with bumpy, protruding foreheads, barrel-like bodies, stumpy arms and legs, and lipless gashes of mouths with jutting underbites. Lower-caste Unseelie thugs dispatched primarily as watchdogs and security for high-ranking Fae.

PAPA ROACH: Made of thousands and thousands of roachlike creatures clambering up on top of one another to form a larger being. The individual bugs feed off human flesh, specifically fat. Consequently, post-wall, some women allow them to enter their bodies and live beneath their skin to keep them slim, a symbiotic liposuction. Papa Roach, the collective, is purplish-brown, about four feet tall with thick legs, a half-dozen arms, and a head the size of a walnut. It jiggles like gelatin when it moves as its countless individual parts shift minutely to remain coalesced. It has a thin-lipped beaklike mouth and round, lidless eyes.

SHADES: One of the lowest castes, they started out barely sentient but have been evolving since they were freed from their Unseelie prison. They thrive in darkness, can't bear direct light, and hunt at night or in dark places. They steal life in the same manner the Gray Man steals beauty, draining their victims with vampiric swiftness, leaving behind a pile of clothing and a husk of dehydrated human matter. They consume every living thing in their path from the leaves on trees to the worms in the soil.

SEELIE

AOIBHEAL, THE SEELIE QUEEN: (see also the **Concubine**) Fae queen, last in a long line of queens with an unusual empathy for humans. In *Shadowfever,* it is revealed the queen was once human herself, and is the Unseelie King's long-lost concubine and soul mate. Over half a million years ago, the Unseelie Prince Cruce drugged her with a cup stolen from the Cauldron of Forgetting, erased her memory and abducted her, staging it so the Unseelie King believed she was dead. Masquerading as the Seelie Prince V'lane, Cruce hid her in the one place he knew the king of the Unseelie would never go—the Seelie Court. Prolonged time in Faery transformed Aoibheal and she became what the king had desperately desired her to be: Fae and immortal. She is now the latest in a long line of Seelie Queens. Tragically, the original Seelie Queen was killed by the Unseelie King before she was able to pass on the Song of Making, the most powerful and beautiful of all Fae magic. Without it, the Seelie have changed.

DARROC, LORD MASTER: (Seelie turned human) Once Fae and trusted advisor to Aoibheal, he was set up by Cruce and banished from Faery for treason. At the Seelie Court, Adam Black (in the novel *The Immortal Highlander*) was given the choice to have Darroc killed or turned mortal as punishment for trying to free Unseelie and overthrow the queen. Adam chose to have him turned mortal, believing he would quickly die as a human, sparking the succession of events that culminates in *Faefever* when Darroc destroys the walls between the worlds of Man and Fae, setting the long-imprisoned Unseelie free. Once in the mortal realm, Darroc learned to eat Unseelie flesh to achieve power and caught wind of the *Sinsar Dubh*'s existence in the mortal realm. When Alina Lane came to Dublin, Darroc discovered she was a *sidhe*-seer with many talents and, like her sister, Mac, could sense and track the *Sinsar Dubh*. He began by using her but fell in love with her. After Alina's death, Darroc learned of Mac and attempted to use her as well, applying various methods of coercion, including abducting her parents. Once Mac believed Barrons was dead, she teamed up with Darroc, determined to find the *Sinsar Dubh* herself and use it to bring Barrons back. Darroc was killed in *Shadowfever* by K'Vruck, allegedly at the direction of the *Sinsar Dubh,* when the Hunter popped his head like a grape.

SEELIE PRINCES: There were once four princes and four princesses of the royal *Sidhe*. The Seelie Princesses have not been seen for a long time and are presumed dead. V'lane was killed long ago, Velvet (not his real name) is recently deceased, R'jan currently aspires to be king, and Adam Black is now human. Highly sexual, golden-haired (except for Adam who assumed a darker glamour), with iridescent eyes and golden skin, they are extremely powerful sifters, capable of sustaining nearly impenetrable glamour, and affect the climate with their pleasure or displeasure.

V'LANE: Seelie Prince, Queen of the Fae's high consort, extremely sexual and erotic. The real V'lane was killed by his own queen when Cruce switched faces and places with him via glamour. Cruce has been masquerading as V'lane ever since, hiding in plain sight.

VELVET: Lesser royalty, cousin to R'jan. He was introduced in *Shadowfever* and killed by Ryodan in *Iced*.

DREE-LIA: Frequent consort of Velvet, was present when the *Sinsar Dubh* was reinterred beneath the abbey.

R'JAN: Seelie Prince who would be king. Tall, blond, with the velvety gold skin of a light Fae, he makes his debut in *Iced* when he announces his claim on the Fae throne.

ADAM BLACK: Immortal Prince of the D'Jai House and favored consort of the Seelie Queen, banished from Faery and made mortal as punishment for one of his countless interferences with the human realm. Has been called the *sin siriche dubh* or blackest Fae, however undeserved. Rumor holds Adam was not always Fae, although that has not been substantiated. In *The Immortal Highlander,* he is exiled among mortals, falls in love with Gabrielle O'Callaghan, a *sidhe*-seer from Cincinnati, Ohio, and chooses to remain human to stay with her. He refuses to get involved in the current war between Man and Fae, fed up with the endless manipulation, seduction, and drama. With Gabrielle, he has a highly gifted and unusual daughter to protect.

THE KELTAR

An ancient bloodline of Highlanders chosen by Queen Aoibheal and trained in druidry to uphold the Compact between the races of Man and Fae. Brilliant, gifted in physics and engineering, they live near Inverness and guard a circle of standing stones called Ban Drochaid (the white bridge) that was used for time travel until the Keltar breached one of their many oaths to the Queen and she closed the circle of stones to other times and dimensions. Current Keltar druids: Christopher, Christian, Cian, Dageus, Drustan.

Druid: In pre-Christian Celtic society, a druid presided over divine worship, legislative and judicial matters, philosophy, and education of elite youth to their order. Druids were believed to be privy to the secrets of the gods, including issues pertaining to the manipulation of physical matter, space, and even time. The old Irish "Drui" means magician, wizard, diviner (Irish Myths and Legends).

CHRISTOPHER MACKELTAR: Modern-day laird of the Keltar clan, father of Christian MacKeltar.

CHRISTIAN MACKELTAR: (turned Unseelie Prince) Handsome Scotsman, dark hair, tall, muscular body and killer smile, he masqueraded as a student at Trinity College, working in the Ancient Languages Department, but was really stationed there by his uncles to keep an eye on Jericho Barrons. Trained as a druid by his clan, he participated in a ritual at Ban Drochaid on Samhain meant to reinforce the walls between the worlds of Man and Fae. Unfortunately the ceremony went badly wrong, leaving Christian and Barrons trapped in the Silvers. When Mac later finds Christian in the Hall of All Days, she feeds him Unseelie flesh to save his life, unwittingly sparking the chain of events that begins to turn the sexy Highlander into an Unseelie Prince. He loses himself for a time in madness, and fixates on the innocence of Dani O'Malley while losing his humanity. In *Iced,* he sacrifices himself to the Crimson Hag to distract her from killing the *sidhe*-seers, determined to spare Dani from having to choose between saving the abbey or the world. Currently staked to the side of a cliff above a hellish grotto, being killed over and over again.

CIAN MACKELTAR: (*Spell of the Highlander*) Highlander from the twelfth century, traveled through time to present day, married to Jessica St. James. Cian was imprisoned for one thousand years in one of the Silvers by a vengeful sorcerer. Freed, he now lives with the other Keltar in current-day Scotland.

DAGEUS MACKELTAR: (*The Dark Highlander*) Keltar druid from the sixteenth century who traveled through time to present day, married to Chloe Zanders. He is inhabited by the souls of thirteen dead Draghar, ancient druids who used black sorcery. Long black hair nearly to his waist, dark skin, and gold eyes, he is the sexiest and most sexual of the Keltar.

DRUSTAN MACKELTAR: (*Kiss of the Highlander*) Twin brother of Dageus MacKeltar, also traveled through time to present day, married to Gwen Cassidy. Tall, dark, with long brown hair and silver eyes, he is the ultimate chivalrous knight and would sacrifice himself for the greater good if necessary.

HUMANS

JACK AND RAINEY LANE: Mac and Alina's parents. In *Darkfever* Mac discovers they are not her biological parents. She and Alina were adopted and part of the custody agreement was a promise that the girls never be allowed to return to the country of their birth. Jack is a strapping, handsome man, an attorney with a strong sense of ethics. Rainey is a compassionate blond woman who was unable to bear children of her own. She's a steel magnolia, strong yet fragile.

DANCER: Six feet four inches, he has dark, wavy hair with gorgeous aqua eyes. Very mature, intellectually gifted seventeen-year-old who was homeschooled, and graduated from college with a double major in physics and engineering by sixteen. Fascinated by physics, he speaks multiple languages and traveled extensively with wealthy, humanitarian parents. His father is an ambassador, his mother a doctor. He was alone in Dublin, considering Trinity College for grad school, when the walls between realms fell and has survived by his wits. He is an inventor and can often think circles around most people, including Dani. He seems unruffled by Barrons, Ryodan, and his men. Dani met Dancer near the end of *Shadowfever* (when he gave her a bracelet, first gift from a guy she liked) and they've been inseparable since. In *Iced*, Dancer made it clear he has feelings for her. Dancer is the only person Dani feels like she can be herself with: young, a little geeky, a lot brainy. Both he and Dani move around frequently, never staying in one place too long. They have many hideouts around the city, above- and belowground. Dani worries about him because he doesn't have any superpowers.

FIONA ASHETON: Beautiful woman in her early fifties who originally managed Barrons Books & Baubles, and was deeply in love (unrequited) with Jericho Barrons. Fiendishly jealous of Barrons's interest in MacKayla, she tried to kill Mac by letting Shades (lethal Unseelie) into the bookstore while she was sleeping. Barrons exiled her for it, and Fiona then became Derek O'Bannion's lover, began eating Unseelie, and was briefly possessed by the *Sinsar Dubh,* which skinned her from head to toe but left her alive. Due to the amount of Fae flesh Fiona had eaten, she could no longer be killed by human means and was trapped in a mutilated body, in constant agony. Eventually she begged Mac to use her Fae spear and end her suffering. Fiona died in the White Mansion when she flung herself through the ancient Silver used as a doorway between the concubine and the Unseelie King's bedchambers—which kills anyone who enters it except for the king and concubine—but not before trying to kill Mac one last time.

ROARK (ROCKY) O'BANNION: Black Irish Catholic mobster with Saudi ancestry and the compact, powerful body of a heavyweight champion boxer, which he is. Born in a Dublin controlled by two feuding Irish crime families—the Hallorans and O'Kierneys—Roark O'Bannion fought his way to the top in the ring, but it wasn't enough for the ambitious champ; he hungered for more. When Rocky was twenty-eight years old, the Halloran and O'Kierney linchpins were killed along with every son, grandson, and pregnant woman in their families. Twenty-seven people died that night, gunned down, blown up, poisoned, knifed, or strangled. Dublin had never seen anything like it. A group of flawlessly choreographed killers had closed in all over the city, at restaurants, homes, hotels, and clubs, and struck simultaneously. The next day, when a suddenly wealthy Rocky O'Bannion, champion boxer and many a young boy's idol, retired from the ring to take control of various businesses in and around Dublin previously run by the Hallorans and O'Kierneys, he was hailed by the working-class poor as a hero, despite the fresh and obvious blood on his hands and the rough pack of ex-boxers and thugs he brought with him. O'Bannion is devoutly religious and collects sacred artifacts. Mac steals the Spear of Destiny (aka the Spear of Longinus that pierced Christ's side) from him to protect herself as it is one of two weapons that can kill the immortal Fae. Later, in *Darkfever,* Barrons kills O'Bannion to keep Mac safe from him and his henchmen, but it's not the end of the O'Bannions gunning for Mac.

DEREK O'BANNION: Rocky's younger brother, he begins snooping around Mac and the bookstore after Rocky is murdered, as his brother's car was found behind the bookstore. He becomes lovers with Fiona Asheton, is ultimately possessed by the *Sinsar Dubh,* and attacks Mac. He is killed by the *Sinsar Dubh* in *Bloodfever.*

SEAN O'BANNION: Rocky O'Bannion's cousin and Katarina McLaughlin's childhood sweetheart and adult lover. After the Hallorans and the O'Kierneys were killed by Rocky, the O'Bannions controlled the city for nearly a decade until the McLaughlins began usurping their turf. Both Sean and Kat despised the family business and refused to participate. The two crime families sought to unite the business with a marriage between them, but when nearly all the McLaughlins were killed after the walls crashed, Katarina and Sean finally felt free. But chaos reigns in a world where humans struggle to obtain simple necessities, and Sean suddenly finds himself part of the black market, competing with Ryodan and the Fae to fairly distribute the supply of food and valuable resources. Kat is devastated to see him doing the wrong things for all the right reasons and it puts a serious strain on their relationship.

MALLUCÉ: (aka John Johnstone, Jr.) Geeky son of billionaire parents until he kills them for their fortune and reinvents himself as the steampunk vampire Mallucé. In *Darkfever,* he teams up with Darroc, the Lord Master, who teaches him to eat Unseelie flesh for the strength and enormous sexual stamina and appetite it confers. He's wounded in battle by Mac's Spear of Destiny. Because he'd been eating Unseelie, the lethal prick of the Fae blade caused parts of him to die, killing flesh but not his body, trapping him in a half-rotted, agonizing shell of a body. He appears to her as the Grim Reaper in *Bloodfever,* and after psychologically tormenting her, abducts Mac and holds her prisoner in a hellish grotto beneath the Burren in Ireland, where he tortures and nearly kills her. Barrons kills him, and saves Mac by feeding her Unseelie flesh, changing her forever.

THE GUARDIANS: Originally Dublin's police force, the Gardai, under the command of Inspector Jayne, eat Unseelie to obtain heightened strength, speed, and acuity, and hunt all Fae. They've learned to use iron bullets to temporarily wound them and iron bars to contain them. Most Fae can be significantly weakened by iron.

If applied properly, iron can prevent a Fae from being able to sift.

INSPECTOR O'DUFFY: Original Garda on Alina Lane's murder case, brother-in-law to Inspector Jayne. He was killed in *Bloodfever,* his throat slit while holding a scrap of paper with Mac's name and address on it. It is currently unknown who killed him.

INSPECTOR JAYNE: Garda who takes over Alina Lane's murder case after Inspector O'Duffy, Jayne's brother-in-law, is killed. Big, rawboned Irishman who looks like Liam Neeson, he tails Mac and generally complicates her life. Initially, he's more interested in what happened to O'Duffy than solving Alina's case, but Mac treats him to Unseelie-laced tea and opens his eyes to what's going on in their city and world. Jayne joins the fight against the Fae and transforms the Gardai into the New Guardians, a ruthless army of ex-policemen who eat Unseelie, battle Fae, and protect humans. Jayne is a good man in a hard position. Although he and his men can capture the Fae, they can't kill them without either Mac or Dani's weapon. In *Iced,* Jayne earns Dani's eternal wrath by stealing her sword when she's too injured to fight back.

CHARACTERS
OF UNKNOWN GENUS

K'VRUCK: Allegedly the most ancient of the Unseelie caste of Royal Hunters—although it is not substantiated that he is truly Unseelie. He was once the Unseelie King's favored companion and "steed" as he traveled worlds on its great black wings. Enormous as a small skyscraper, vaguely resembling a dragon, it's coal black, leathery, and icy, with eyes like huge orange furnaces. When it flies, it churns black frosty flakes in the air and liquid ice streams in its wake. It has a special affinity for Mac and appears to her at odd moments as it senses the king inside her (via the *Sinsar Dubh*). When K'Vruck kills, it is the ultimate death, extinguishing life so completely it's forever erased from the karmic cycle. To be K'Vrucked is to be removed completely from existence as if you've never been, no trace, no residue. Mac used K'Vruck to free Barrons's son. K'vruck is the only being (known so far) capable of killing the immortal Nine.

SWEEPER: A collector of powerful, broken things, it resembles a giant trash heap of metal cogs and gears. First encountered by the Unseelie King shortly after he lost his concubine and descended into a period of madness and grief. The Sweeper traveled with him for a time, studying him, or perhaps seeing if he, too, could be collected and tinkered with. According to the Unseelie King, it fancies itself a god.

ZEWs: Acronym for Zombie Eating Wraiths, so named by Dani O'Malley. Hulking anorexic vulturelike creatures, they are five to six feet tall, with gaunt, hunched bodies and heavily cowled faces. They appear to be wearing cobwebbed, black robes but it is actually their skin. They have exposed bone at their sleeves and pale smudges inside their cowls. In *Burned*, Mac catches a glimpse of metal where their faces should be but doesn't get a good look.

PLACES

ARLINGTON ABBEY: An ancient stone abbey located nearly two hours from Dublin, situated on a thousand acres of prime farmland. The mystically fortified abbey houses an Order of *Sidhe*-Seers gathered from six bloodlines of Irish women born with the ability to see the Fae and their realms. The abbey was built in the seventh century and is completely self-sustaining with multiple artesian wells, livestock, and gardens. According to historical records, the land occupied by the abbey was previously a church, and before that a sacred circle of stones, and long before that a fairy shian, or mound. *Sidhe*-seer legend suggests the Unseelie King himself spawned their order, mixing his blood with that of six Irish houses, to create protectors for the one thing he should never have made—the *Sinsar Dubh*.

ASHFORD, GEORGIA: MacKayla Lane's small, rural hometown in the Deep South.

BARRONS BOOKS & BAUBLES: Located on the outskirts of Temple Bar in Dublin, Barrons Books & Baubles is an Old World bookstore previously owned by Jericho Barrons, now owned by MacKayla Lane. It shares design characteristics with the Lello Bookstore in Portugal, but is somewhat more elegant and refined. Due to the location of a large Sifting Silver in the study on the first floor, the bookstore's dimensions can shift from as few as four stories to as many as seven, and rooms on the upper levels often reposition themselves. It is where MacKayla Lane calls home.

BARRONS'S GARAGE: Located directly behind Barrons Books & Baubles, it houses a collection of expensive cars. Far beneath it, accessible only through the heavily warded Silver in the bookstore, are Jericho Barrons's living quarters.

THE BRICKYARD: The bar in Ashford, Georgia, where MacKayla Lane bartended before she came to Dublin.

CHESTER'S NIGHTCLUB: An enormous underground club of chrome and glass located at 939 Rêvemal Street. Chester's is owned by one of Barrons's associates, Ryodan. The upper levels are open to the public, the lower levels contain the Nine's residences and their private clubs. Since the walls between man and Fae fell, Chester's has become the hot spot in Dublin for Fae and humans to mingle.

DARK ZONE: An area that has been taken over by the Shades, deadly Unseelie that suck the life from humans, leaving only a husk of skin and indigestible matter such as eyeglasses, wallets, and medical implants. During the day it looks like an everyday abandoned, run-down neighborhood. Once night falls it's a death trap. The largest known Dark Zone in Dublin is adjacent to Barrons Books & Baubles and is nearly twenty by thirteen city blocks.

FAERY: A general term encompassing the many realms of the Fae.

HALL OF ALL DAYS: The "airport terminal" of the Sifting Silvers where one can choose which mirror to enter to travel to other worlds and realms. Fashioned of gold from floor to ceiling, the endless corridor is lined with billions of mirrors that are portals to alternate universes and times, and exudes a chilling spatial-temporal distortion that makes a visitor feel utterly inconsequential. Time isn't linear in the hall, it's malleable and slippery, and a visitor can get permanently lost in memories that never were and dreams of futures that will never be. One moment you feel terrifyingly alone, the next as if an endless chain of paper-doll versions of oneself is unfolding sideways, holding cutout construction-paper hands with thousands of different feet in thousands of different worlds, all at the same time. Compounding the many dangers of the hall, when the Silvers were corrupted by Cruce's curse (intended to bar entry to the Unseelie King), the mirrors were altered and now the image they present is no longer a guarantee of what's on the other side. A lush rain forest may lead to a parched, cracked desert, a tropical oasis to a world of ice, but one can't count on total opposites either.

THE RIVER LIFFEY: The river that divides Dublin into south and north sections, and supplies most of Dublin's water.

TEMPLE BAR DISTRICT: An area in Dublin also known simply as "Temple Bar," in which the Temple Bar Pub is located, along with an endless selection of boisterous drinking establishments including the famed Oliver St. John Gogarty, the Quays Bar, the Foggy Dew, the Brazen Head, Buskers, The Purty Kitchen, The Auld Dubliner, and so on. On the south bank of the River Liffey, Temple Bar (the district) sprawls for blocks, and has two meeting squares that used to be overflowing with tourists and partiers. Countless street musicians, great restaurants and shops, local bands, and raucous Stag and Hen parties made Temple Bar the *craic*-filled center of the city.

TEMPLE BAR PUB: A quaint, famous pub named after Sir William Temple who once lived there. Founded in 1840, it squats bright red and cozy, draped with string lights at the corner of Temple Bar Street and Temple Lane, and rambles from garden to alcove to main room. The famous pub boasts a first-rate whiskey collection, a beer garden for smoking, legendary Dublin Bay oysters, perfectly stacked Guinness, terrific atmosphere, and the finest traditional Irish music in the city.

TRINITY COLLEGE: Founded in 1592, located on College Green, recognized as one of the finest universities in the world, it houses a library that contains over 4.5 million printed volumes including spectacular works such as the *Book of Kells*. It's ranked in the world's top one hundred universities for physics and mathematics, with state-of-the-art laboratories and equipment. Dancer does much of his research on the now abandoned college campus.

UNSEELIE PRISON: Located in the Unseelie King's realm, close to his fortress of black ice, the prison once held all Unseelie captives for over half a million years in a stark, arctic prison of ice. When the walls between Man and Faery were destroyed by Darroc (a banished Seelie Prince with a vendetta against the Seelie Queen) all the Unseelie were freed to invade the human realms.

THE WHITE MANSION: Located inside the Silvers, the house that the Unseelie King built for his beloved concubine. Enormous, ever-changing, the many halls and rooms in the mansion rearrange themselves at will.

THINGS

AMULET: Also called the One True Amulet, see **The Four Unseelie Hallows.**

AMULETS, THE THREE LESSER: Amulets created prior to the One True Amulet, these objects are capable of weaving and sustaining nearly impenetrable illusion when used together. Currently in possession of Cruce.

COMPACT: Agreement negotiated between Queen Aoibheal and the MacKeltar clan (Keltar means hidden barrier or mantle) long ago to keep the realms of mankind and Fae separate. The Seelie Queen taught them to tithe and perform rituals that would reinforce the walls that were compromised when the original queen used a portion of them to create the Unseelie prison.

CRIMSON RUNES: This enormously powerful and complex magic formed the foundation of the walls of the Unseelie prison and is offered by the *Sinsar Dubh* to MacKayla on several occasions to use to protect herself. All Fae fear them. When the walls between Man and Fae began to weaken long ago, the Seelie Queen tapped into the prison walls, siphoning some of their power, which she used to reinforce the boundaries between worlds ... thus dangerously weakening the prison walls. It was at that time the first Unseelie began to escape. The more one struggles against the crimson runes, the stronger they grow, feeding off the energy expended in the victim's effort to escape. MacKayla used them in *Shadowfever* to seal the *Sinsar Dubh* shut until Cruce, posing as V'lane, persuaded her to remove them. The beast form of Jericho Barrons eats these runes, and seems to consider them a delicacy.

CUFF OF CRUCE: A cuff made of silver and gold, set with blood-red stones; an ancient Fae relic that protects the wearer against all Fae and many other creatures. Cruce claims he made it, not the king, and that he gave it to the king as a gift to give his lover. According to Cruce, its powers were dual: it not only protected the concubine from all threats but allowed her to summon him by merely touching it, thinking of the king, and wishing for his presence.

DOLMEN: A single-chamber megalithic tomb constructed of three or more upright stones supporting a large, flat, horizontal capstone. Dolmens are common in Ireland, especially around the Burren and Connemara. The Lord Master used a dolmen in a ritual of dark magic to open a doorway between realms and bring through Unseelie.

THE DREAMING: It's where all hopes, fantasies, illusions, and nightmares of sentient beings come to be or go to rest, whichever you prefer to believe. No one knows where the Dreaming came from or who created it. It is far more ancient even than the Fae. Since Cruce cursed the Silvers and the Hall of All Days was corrupted, the Dreaming can be accessed via the hall, though with enormous difficulty.

ELIXIR OF LIFE: Both the Seelie Queen and Unseelie King have a version of this powerful potion. The Seelie Queen's version can make a human immortal (though not bestow the grace and power of being Fae). It is currently unknown what the king's version does, but reasonable to expect that, as the imperfect Song used to fashion his court, it is also flawed in some way.

THE FOUR STONES: Chiseled from the blue-black walls of the Unseelie prison, these four stones have the ability to contain the *Sinsar Dubh* in place if positioned properly, rendering its power inert, allowing it to be transported safely. The stones contain the Book's magic and immobilize it completely, preventing it from being able to possess the person transporting it. They are capable of immobilizing it in any form, including MacKayla Lane as she has the Book inside her. They are etched with ancient runes and react with many other Fae objects of power. When united, they sing a lesser Song of Making. Not nearly as powerful as the crimson runes, they can contain only the *Sinsar Dubh*.

GLAMOUR: Illusion cast by the Fae to camouflage their true appearance. The more powerful the Fae, the more difficult it is to penetrate its disguise. Average humans see only what the Fae want them to see and are subtly repelled from bumping into or brushing against it by a small perimeter of spatial distortion that is part of the Fae glamour.

THE HALLOWS: Eight ancient artifacts created by the Fae possessing enormous power. There are four Seelie and four Unseelie hallows.

The Four Seelie Hallows

THE SPEAR OF LUISNE: Also known as the Spear of Luin, Spear of Longinus, Spear of Destiny, the Flaming Spear, it is one of two hallows capable of killing Fae. Currently in the possession of MacKayla Lane.

THE SWORD OF LUGH: Also known as the Sword of Light, the second hallow capable of killing Fae. Currently in the possession of Danielle O'Malley.

THE CAULDRON: Also called the Cauldron of Forgetting. The Fae are subject to a type of madness that sets in at advanced years. They drink from the cauldron to erase all memory and begin fresh. None but the Scribe, Cruce, and the Unseelie King, who have never drunk from the cauldron, know the true history of their race. Currently located at the Seelie Court. Cruce stole a cup from the Cauldron of Forgetting and tricked the concubine/Aoibheal into drinking it, thereby erasing all memory of the king and her life before the moment the cup touched her lips.

THE STONE: Little is known of this Seelie hallow.

The Four Unseelie Hallows

THE AMULET: Created by the Unseelie King for his concubine so she could manipulate reality as well as a Fae. Fashioned of gold, silver, sapphires, and onyx, the gilt "cage" of the amulet houses an enormous clear stone of unknown composition. It can be used by a person of epic will to impact and reshape perception. The list of past owners is legendary, including Merlin, Boudicca, Joan of Arc, Charlemagne, and Napoleon. This amulet is capable of weaving illusion that will deceive even the Unseelie King. In *Shadowfever*, MacKayla Lane used it to defeat the *Sinsar Dubh*. Currently stored in Barrons's lair beneath the garage, locked away for safekeeping.

THE SILVERS: An elaborate network of mirrors created by the Unseelie King, once used as the primary method of Fae travel between realms. The central hub for the Silvers is the Hall of All Days, an infinite, gilded corridor where time is not linear, filled with mirrors of assorted shapes and sizes that are portals to other worlds, places, and times. Before Cruce cursed the Silvers, whenever a traveler stepped through a mirror at a perimeter location, he was instantly translated to the hall, where he could then choose a new destination from the images the mirrors displayed. After Cruce cursed the Silvers, the mirrors in the hall were compromised and no longer accurately display their true destinations. It's highly dangerous to travel within the Silvers.

THE BOOK: See also *Sinsar Dubh* (she-suh DOO). A fragment of the Unseelie King himself, a sentient, psychopathic book of enormous, dark magic created when the king tried to expel the corrupt arts with which he'd tampered, trying to re-create the Song of Making. The Book was originally a nonsentient, spelled object but in the way of Fae it evolved and over time became sentient, living, conscious. When it did, like all Unseelie created via an imperfect Song, it was obsessed by a desire to complete itself, to obtain a corporeal body for its consciousness, to become like others of its kind. It usually presents itself in one of three forms: an innocuous hardcover book; a thick, gilded, magnificent ancient tome with runes and locks; or a monstrous amorphous beast. It temporarily achieves corporeality by possessing humans, but the human host rejects it and the body self-destructs quickly. The *Sinsar Dubh* usually toys with its hosts, uses them to vent its sadistic rage, then kills them and jumps to a new body (or jumps to a new body and uses it to kill them). The closest it has ever come to obtaining a body was by imprinting a full copy of itself in Mac as an unformed fetus while it possessed her mother. Since the *Sinsar Dubh*'s presence has been inside Mac from the earliest stages of her life, her body chemistry doesn't sense it as an intruder and reject it. She can survive its possession without it destroying her. Still, the original *Sinsar Dubh* craves a body of its own and for Mac to embrace her copy so that it will finally be flesh and blood and have a mate.

THE BOX: Little is known of this Unseelie Hallow. Legend says the Unseelie King created it for his concubine.

THE HAVEN: High Council and advisors to the Grand Mistress of the abbey, made up of the seven most talented, powerful *sidhe*-seers. Twenty years ago it was led by Mac's mother, Isla O'Connor, but the Haven got wind of Rowena tampering with black arts and suspected she'd been seduced by the *Sinsar Dubh*, which was locked away beneath the abbey in a heavily warded cavern. They discovered she'd been entering the forbidden chamber, talking with it. They formed a second, secret, Haven to monitor Rowena's activities, which included Rowena's own daughter and Isla's best friend, Kayleigh. The Haven was right, Rowena had been corrupted and ultimately freed the *Sinsar Dubh*. It is unknown who carried it from the abbey the night the Book escaped or where it was for the next two decades.

IFP: Interdimensional Fairy Pothole, created when the walls between Man and Faery fell, and chunks of reality fragmented. They exist also within the network of Silvers, the result of Cruce's curse. Translucent, funnel-shaped, with narrow bases and wide tops, they are difficult to see and drift unless tethered. There is no way to determine what type of environment exists inside one until you've stepped through, extreme climate excepted.

IRON: *Fe* on the periodic table, painful to Fae. Iron bars can contain nonsifting Fae. Properly spelled iron can constrain a sifting Fae to a degree. Iron cannot kill a Fae.

MACHALO: Invented by MacKayla Lane, a bike helmet with LED lights affixed to it. Designed to protect the wearer from the vampiric Shades by casting a halo of light all around the body.

NULL: A *sidhe*-seer with the power to freeze a Fae with the touch of his or her hands (MacKayla Lane has this talent). While frozen, a Nulled Fae is completely powerless, but the higher and more powerful the caste of Fae, the shorter the length of time it stays immobilized. It can still see, hear, and think while frozen, making it very dangerous to be in its vicinity when unfrozen.

POSTE HASTE, INC.: A bicycling courier service headquartered in Dublin that is actually the Order of *Sidhe*-Seers. Founded by Rowena, who established an international branch of PHI in countries all over the world to stay apprised of all developments globally.

PRI-YA: A human who is sexually addicted to and enslaved by the Fae. The royal castes of Fae are so sexual and erotic that sex with them is addictive and destructive to the human mind. It creates a painful, debilitating, insatiable need in a human. The royal castes can, if they choose, diminish their impact during sex and make it merely stupendous. But if they don't, it overloads human senses and turns the human into a sex addict, incapable of thought or speech, capable only of serving the sexual pleasures of whomever is their master. Since the walls fell, many humans have been turned Pri-ya and society is trying to deal with these wrecked humans in a way that doesn't involve incarcerating them in padded cells, in mindless misery.

SHAMROCK: This slightly misshapen three-leaf clover is the ancient symbol of the *sidhe*-seers, who are charged with the mission to See, Serve, and Protect mankind from the Fae. In *Bloodfever,* Rowena shares the history of the emblem with Mac: "Before it was the clover of Saint Patrick's trinity, it was ours. It's the emblem of our Order. It's the symbol our ancient sisters used to carve on their doors and dye into banners millennia ago when they moved to a new village. It was our way of letting the inhabitants know who we were and what we were there to do. When people saw our sign, they declared a time of great feasting and celebrated for a fortnight. They welcomed us with gifts of their finest food, wine, and men. They held tournaments to compete to bed us. It is not a clover at all, but a vow. You see how these two leaves make a sideways figure eight, like a horizontal Möbius strip? They are two *S*'s, one right side up, one upside down, ends meeting. The third leaf and stem is an upright *P*. The first *S* is for See, the second for Serve, the *P* for Protect. The shamrock itself is the symbol of Eire, the great Ireland. The Möbius strip is our pledge of guardianship eternal. We are the *sidhe*-seers and we watch over Mankind. We protect them from the Old Ones. We stand between this world and all the others."

SIFTING: Fae method of travel. The higher ranking, most powerful Fae are able to translocate from place to place at the speed of thought. Once they could travel through time as well as place, but Aoibheal stripped that power from them for repeated offenses.

SINSAR DUBH: Originally designed as an ensorcelled tome, it was intended to be the inert repository or dumping ground for all the Unseelie King's arcane knowledge of a flawed, toxic Song of Making. It was with this knowledge he created the Unseelie Court and castes. The book contains an enormous amount of dangerous magic that can create and destroy worlds. Like the king, its power is nearly limitless. Unfortunately, as with all Fae things, the Book, drenched with magic, changed and evolved until it achieved full sentience. No longer a mere book, it is a homicidal, psychopathic, starved, and power-hungry being. Like the rest of the imperfect Unseelie, it wants to finish or perfect itself, to attain that which it perceives it lacks. In this case, the perfect host body. When the king realized the Book had become sentient, he created a prison for it, and made the *sidhe*-seers—some say by tampering with their bloodline, lending a bit of his own—to guard it and keep it from ever escaping. The king realized that rather than eradicating the dangerous magic, he'd only managed to create a copy of it. Much like the king, the *Sinsar Dubh* found a way to create a copy of itself, and planted it inside an unborn fetus, MacKayla Lane. There are currently two *Sinsar Dubh*s: one that Cruce absorbed (or became possessed by) and the copy inside MacKayla Lane that she refuses to open. As long as she never voluntarily seeks or takes a single spell from it, it can't take her over and she won't be possessed. If, however, she uses it for any reason, she will be obliterated by the psychopathic villain trapped inside it, forever silenced. With the long-starved and imprisoned *Sinsar Dubh* free, life for humans will become Hell on Earth. Unfortunately, the Book is highly charismatic, brilliant, and seductive and has observed humanity long enough to exploit human weaknesses like a maestro.

SONG OF MAKING: The greatest power in the universe, this song can create life from nothing. All life stems from it. Originally known by the first Seelie Queen, she rarely used it because, as with all great magic, it demands great price. It was to be passed from queen to queen, to be used only when absolutely necessary to protect and sustain life. To hear this song is to experience Heaven on Earth, to know the how, when, and why of our existence, and simultaneously have no need to know it at all. The melody is allegedly so beautiful, transformative, and pure that if one who harbors evil in his heart hears it, he will be charred to ash where he stands.

UNSEELIE FLESH: Eating Unseelie flesh endows an average human with enormous strength, power, and sensory acuity; heightens sexual pleasure and stamina; and is highly addictive. It also lifts the veil between worlds and permits a human to see past the glamour worn by the Fae, to see their actual forms. Before the walls fell, all Fae concealed themselves with glamour. After the walls fell, they didn't care, but now Fae are beginning to conceal themselves again, as humans have learned that the common element iron is useful in injuring and imprisoning them.

VOICE: A Druid art or skill that compels the person it's being used on to precisely obey the letter of whatever command is issued. Dageus, Drustan, and Cian MacKeltar are fluent in it. Jericho Barrons taught Darroc (for a price) and also trained MacKayla Lane to use and withstand it. Teacher and apprentice become immune to each other and can no longer be compelled.

WARD: A powerful magic known to druids, sorcerers, *sidhe*-seers, and Fae. There are many categories, including but not limited to Earth, Air, Fire, Stone, and Metal wards. Barrons is adept at placing wards, more so than any of the Nine besides Daku.

WECARE: An organization founded after the walls between man and Fae fell, using food, supplies, and safety as a lure to draw followers. Rainey Lane works with them, sees only the good in the organization, possibly because it's the only place she can harness resources to rebuild Dublin and run her Green-Up group. Someone in WeCare authors the *Dublin Daily,* a local newspaper to compete with the *Dani Daily*; whoever does it dislikes Dani a great deal and is always ragging on her. Not much is known about this group yet. They lost some of their power when three major players began raiding them and stockpiling supplies.